SEMPER FI

Book One: The Empire's Corps
Book Two: No Worse Enemy
Book Three: When The Bough Breaks
Book Four: Semper Fi
Book Five: The Outcast
Book Six: To The Shores
Book Seven: Reality Check
Book Eight: Retreat Hell
Book Nine: The Thin Blue Line
Book Ten: Never Surrender
Book Eleven: First To Fight
Book Twelve: They Shall Not Pass
Book Thirteen: Culture Shock

SEMPER FI

CHRISTOPHER G. NUTTALL

The characters and events portrayed in this book are fictitious. Any similarity to real persons, living or dead, is coincidental and not intended by the author.

Text copyright © 2016 Christopher G. Nuttall
All rights reserved.
No part of this book may be reproduced, or stored in a retrieval system, or transmitted in any form or by any means, electronic, mechanical, photocopying, recording, or otherwise, without express written permission of the publisher.

ISBN-13: 9781542340991
ISBN-10: 1542340993

http://www.chrishanger.net
http://chrishanger.wordpress.com/
http://www.facebook.com/ChristopherGNuttall

All Comments Welcome!

DEAR READER

Semper Fi is the fourth book in the universe of *The Empire's Corps*, following the adventures of the Marines on Avalon. In order to gain maximum enjoyment, you should probably read *The Empire's Corps* and *No Worse Enemy* first: both are currently available on eBook. *When The Bough Breaks* is largely stand-alone, telling the story of what happened on Earth in the final days of the Empire.

You can download samples of the first three books – and many others – from my website and then purchase them on Kindle. If you like my books, please review them – it helps boost sales and convinces me to write more in certain universes.

As I am not the best editor in the world, I would be grateful if you email me to point out any spelling mistakes, placing them in context. I can offer cameos, redshirt deals and suchlike in return.

Have fun!

Christopher Nuttall

HISTORIAN'S NOTE

Semper Fi takes place two years after *No Worse Enemy*, with rumours (but no hard data) of what happened on Earth finally filtering through to the worlds on the Rim.

PROLOGUE

System Command, Commodore Rani Singh thought, with a flicker of genuine amusement.

It had been intended as a punishment. Admiral Bainbridge had not appreciated it when she'd turned down his advances and had promoted her sideways, straight into System Command, Trafalgar Naval Base. Everyone knew that System Command was staffed by those in disfavour with their superiors – it involved less paperwork than court martial and dishonourable discharges – and those assigned to Imperial Navy bases lacked even the opportunity for graft that their counterparts assigned to civilian systems enjoyed. Her career had come to a screeching halt.

Or so the old goat had thought.

Rani's family had meddled with their genes for centuries, pushing the limits of genetic engineering as far as they would go without crossing into direct technological enhancement. At forty-two, she looked nineteen – and beautiful. Long dark hair framed a dusky face, with dark eyes that seemed both alluring and forbidding. The white uniform, tailored to hint rather than reveal, drew the male eye. Men had always stared at her, only to discover that Rani rarely shared her favours with anyone, even those who could help her career in exchange. But then, she'd always considered herself to possess some integrity. She had no intention of selling herself merely to gain rank, not when it would have destroyed her career in the long run.

It still galled her, four years after her assignment to Trafalgar, that it had taken her so long to understand the opportunity the Admiral had placed in front of her. She'd spent two months in a funk before resolving to do the best she could with what she had…and then it had hit her. System Command controlled everything, from personnel assignments to orbital docking stations for 15th Fleet; there was hardly anything in the system that didn't require approval from her subordinates. A person with ruthless ambition and a complete lack of scruples – and loyalty to the Empire – could go far. She could even make herself a warlord in her own right.

She settled back in her chair and studied the orbital display. Bainbridge and his cronies couldn't see the truth, but she could; the signs of decay and impending disaster were all around them. Rumour had warned her that the Empire might abandon Trafalgar long before she had received the formal notification, spurring her to make preparations for that day. The Grand Senate thought that she would shut the base down and then follow Bainbridge back into the Empire. Rani had other plans.

15th Fleet wasn't as mighty as it had once been – seven battleships, nineteen cruisers and thirty destroyers – but it represented the largest force in the sector, enough to wreck several worlds. If, of course, it was used properly. Bainbridge just didn't have the imagination to see the possibilities – and besides, he had links to the Grand Senate. Rani had none…and knew that the Grand Senate would be unable to respond to her plans before it was too late. If some of the rumours were to be believed, Earth itself was on the verge of catastrophe.

She keyed her personal console, sending a message to her allies. Putting the force together had been easy, so easy that she'd been convinced that Bainbridge was setting her up…. until she'd realised that even Imperial Security had too much else to keep them distracted. Now, her loyalists were on their way to the battleships, where they would take control, allowing her to secure the naval base without fighting. She already held the four orbital defence stations in her thrall.

Smiling, she listened to the first set of messages from her assault forces. Thankfully, the Grand Senate had ordered the Marines – who would normally have had a platoon or two on the battleships – to head towards the Core Worlds, instead of leaving them in place. Without the Marines, it was almost pathetically easy to overawe the crews and take over the ships. It helped that she'd arranged shore leave for most of the crewmen before launching her operation.

"Admiral Bainbridge has been shot attempting to escape," Colonel Higgs said. He was one of her closest allies, someone who had good reason to resent Bainbridge and his fellow aristocrats. She'd given him specific instructions to make sure that Bainbridge didn't survive the coup. "And the ships are ours."

"Excellent," Rani told him. "Proceed with part two."

Her smile grew wider as she contemplated the possibilities. If Bainbridge and his ilk wouldn't allow her to rise in their Empire, she'd damn well build one of her own. And her Empire would be far stronger than theirs…

After all, who was going to stop her?

Chapter One

When considering authority, it is important to realise that all authority ultimately stems from force – from the barrel of a gun, as the old saying has it. Those who claim authority and yet are unable to back up their orders with force have no authority, even though it can take time for others to realise it. The teacher forbidden to punish his charges, the policeman forbidden to make arrests and the CO forbidden to discipline his men have no authority.

-Professor Leo Caesius, *Authority, Power and the Post-Imperial Era*

"Captain," Lieutenant Andy Reynolds said, "I think we have a bite."

Captain Layla Delacroix leaned forward in her command chair, studying the display. CSS *Harrington* had been flitting from system to system, patrolling the edge of Commonwealth space and looking for pirates to kill. Chasing pirates was largely an exercise in futility, she knew, particularly the pirates who had survived the Admiral's defeat two years ago, but sometimes it was simple enough to lure the bastards in for the kill.

"Good," she said, as the enemy icon solidified. They weren't even *trying* to be stealthy. "Once they enter civilian detection range, send them a standard challenge. Let's see what they say."

"Aye, Captain," Reynolds said.

Layla shook her head as the young man turned back to his console. And he *was* young, barely seventeen…and far too young for a bridge posting, at least according to the Imperial Navy's regulations. But the Imperial Navy was gone, leaving the makeshift Commonwealth Navy to hold the line. Competence mattered more than family connections in the

Commonwealth Navy and Reynolds had shown himself to be competent in the countless exercises she'd run since assuming command. And yet he had never truly been tested.

She ran through the scenario in her mind as the pirate ship closed in. They were definitely hostile, if only because they were aiming to intercept *Harrington* well short of the phase limit – and not even *trying* to communicate. The bureaucratic rules and regulations that had governed interstellar shipping had died along with the Empire, but most spacers were still trying to honour the unwritten protocols for ship-handling, including the very basic rule that one *didn't* come close to another starship without permission. It risked accidents – and misunderstandings. The pirates were making their intentions very clear.

And they didn't know what she was, she told herself, and smirked. *Harrington* was new-build, the first heavy cruiser to come rolling out of the shipyard orbiting Avalon's largest moon. She wasn't *that* dissimilar to a standard Imperial Navy cruiser to the naked eye, but the pirates wouldn't realise that she was a military starship until they got too close – and by then it would be too late. If they'd known, they would never have risked engagement. What sort of pirate would risk his ship and crew for nothing?

"Captain," Reynolds said, "they are entering civilian detection range."

"Challenge them," Layla ordered.

The Empire had forbidden civilian crews from purchasing or installing military-grade sensors and weapons systems on their starships, a regulation that had largely been ignored. Military-grade equipment was so much more capable than civilian models that possessing it was a necessity along the Rim, even before the Empire withdrew from the outermost sectors. The pirates must have assumed that they would be detected as soon as they entered military detection range, but would they know for sure? Not, in the end, that it would matter.

"No response," Reynolds reported, after a long moment.

"Alter course to evade," Layla ordered. A harmless merchantman could neither fight nor run from a warship, but the crewmen would certainly *try*. Very few pirate crews would treat their captives decently. The men would be killed, the women would be raped and *then* killed – unless they had useful skills or could be ransomed back to their friends and families. It was worth doing whatever was in their power to stay alive and free as long as possible. "And scream for help from the inner system."

She imagined the pirates smirking as they heard the radio message and smiled, coldly. It would take hours for the message to crawl its way to the system's sole inhabited planet – and there was little that Selig Salaam could do to help a freighter on the edge of the system. Even if there was a warship near the planet, it would take hours before it was in position to intercept the pirates, by which time the helpless freighter would have been gutted and left to drift throughout interstellar space. It could take years to rediscover the ship, particularly if the pirates left her heading out of the system.

"The pirates are altering course themselves," Reynolds said. "I'm picking up targeting emissions."

Layla nodded. "Send a second message, more panicky than the first," she ordered, calmly. The pirates didn't know it, but they were already well inside her missile envelope. Escape was impossible. "And then…"

"Missile separation," the tactical officer barked.

The pirates had fired to miss, Layla realised, just to prove to the freighter that they actually carried weapons. Some freighter crews were supposed to know nothing about weapons, or to believe that the only armed starships belonged to the Imperial Navy, although Layla suspected that was just rumours spread by the big interstellar shipping corporations. No freighter crewman could afford to be so ignorant, if only because deep space punished ignorance and incompetence with a thoroughness and indiscrimination a Drill Sergeant would have been hard-pressed to match.

"Detonation," the tactical officer said, as the pirate missile vanished from the display. "One standard warhead, Captain. No nukes or laser heads."

"Unsurprising," Layla said. The tactical officer was experienced, thankfully. He was earmarked for a command of his own once the next generation of cruisers rolled out of the yards. "They wouldn't want to waste either on a harmless merchantman."

"Captain, we're picking up a message," Reynolds said. "They're demanding that we cut our drives and prepare to be boarded – or else."

Layla's lips twitched with genuine amusement. "Then we'd better do as we are told," she said, dryly. "Helm; cut drives. Let them come to us."

The pirate ship closed in as *Harrington's* drive field faded away to nothingness, leaving the ship drifting through interstellar space. Layla studied the report from the sensors, noting that the pirate ship was definitely ex-Imperial Navy, although probably not a rogue unit that had decided to turn pirate and go hunting the ships it had formerly protected. The Imperial Navy had been decommissioning ships and laying off crewmen for decades prior to the decision to abandon the Rim, but it had still had thousands of starships in service before losing contact. No one knew what had happened to those ships.

Six months to Earth, she reminded herself. A starship had been dispatched to investigate a rumour, heard fifth-hand, that Earth had been destroyed. So far, the ship and crew had not returned. *Anything could be happening over there and we would never know.*

"Fat and happy," the tactical office commented. "Don't they have any common sense at all?"

"We're just a harmless merchantman," Layla reminded him. "Even if we had weapons bolted onto our hull, we wouldn't be a match for a real warship."

They shared a predatory smile. "Lock weapons on their drive section," she added. "Prepare to fire."

"Weapons targeted, aye," the tactical officer said.

"They're ordering us to unlock our airlocks," Reynolds reported. "And all weapons are to be secured before they dock."

"Too late," Layla said. The pirate ship was practically close enough to touch. It wouldn't be long before they eyeballed *Harrington's* hull – and then they'd *know* that she wasn't a genuine merchantman. "Tactical…you are cleared to open fire."

The tactical officer tapped a switch. At such close range, the only warning the pirates would have would be when the weapons struck their hull. It was hardly a fair fight, but Layla had no intention of giving them a fair chance. The pirates certainly never gave any of their victims a chance to escape or to fight back. Besides, if they'd been more careful, they would have had a chance to escape before coming into point-blank range.

"Two direct hits," the tactical officer reported. "Their drive section has been disabled."

And if their maintenance is up to the standards we have come to expect from pirate crews, Layla thought, *they're going to lose the rest of their power rapidly.*

"Open a channel," she ordered, tapping her console. "Pirate ship, you are under the guns of a warship. If you surrender, you will be taken into custody and transferred to a penal settlement. Resistance will be met with deadly force."

"No response, Captain," Reynolds said. The pirate ship was already drifting. "They might have lost all power."

"Perhaps," Layla said. She keyed her console. "Marines, you are cleared to launch."

"What a mess," Rifleman Blake Coleman muttered.

Lieutenant Jasmine Yamane couldn't disagree as 1st Platoon's shuttle led the way towards the pirate ship. She had once been a standard Imperial Navy destroyer – a boxy starship studded with weapons and sensor blisters – but the brief assault had inflicted terrifying damage on her hull. The drive section looked to have been completely destroyed, rather than disabled, while air was streaming out of at least two breaches in the hull. Emergency systems should have sealed off the damaged parts of the hull by now, preventing the entire ship from venting its atmosphere out into space, but it looked as though they had failed. It wouldn't be the first time a pirate crew's sloppy maintenance came back to haunt them.

She studied the plans they'd downloaded into their suits from *Harrington's* database and came to a quick decision. "1st Platoon will board though this gash in the hull" – she designated a hull breach through the shared communications network – "and advance towards the bridge. 3rd Scouts will board though a different hole and advance towards the engineering compartment. They might not all be dead, so watch your backs as you move."

There was a brief round of acknowledgements. The Marines sounded confident, as well they might; they'd spent the last two years boarding pirate vessels and bringing their crews to heel. 3rd Scouts sounded much less confident; it would be their first deployment on active service, ever since they had passed the makeshift training program for fighting in space. Jasmine was more worried than she cared to admit about having the Scouts along, but she had to admit that there was no choice. There were only a handful of Marines and they couldn't *all* be assigned to pirate-hunting starships.

"Open the airlock," she ordered. "Marines…*go*."

The vastness of space seemed to welcome her as she led the way out of the shuttle, firing her suit's thrusters so that she would head down towards the tear in the enemy hull. Standard procedure was to board a welcoming vessel through the airlocks, but the pirate crew were far from welcoming. The Commonwealth sent captured pirates to penal settlements rather than simply shoving them out of the nearest airlock, yet Jasmine knew better than to assume that the pirates they were facing believed them. After all, the Imperial Navy had often promised to spare surrendered pirates and then broken its promise.

She winced as she pushed down into the pirate ship, dropping into a corridor that had been mangled by the direct hits. The upper half of a pirate corpse drifted through the corridor, spinning helplessly; Jasmine took one look and knew that there was no point in trying to get the pirate to a stasis tube. There was no sign of his legs anywhere.

"Gravity's off," Blake said, softly. "And air's gone completely."

"In this section," Jasmine reminded him, dryly. "Blake, Joe; take point. Advance."

The pirates had *definitely* slacked on their maintenance, she told herself as they made their way towards the bridge. Even the worst Imperial Navy CO, appointed through family connections rather than any competence, would have refused to serve on such a vessel. The hatches that should have sealed automatically were wide open, allowing the atmosphere to vent out through the gashes in the hull and out into space, while all of the emergency systems seemed to have failed completely. A number of pirates had died before realising what had hit them…they weren't even wearing the shipsuits that would have given them basic protection while they struggled to don their masks. Jasmine hated to think about what her superiors would have said if *she'd* made such a mistake. She would certainly never have graduated from the Slaughterhouse.

She glanced into a side compartment and gritted her teeth. The pirates had kept seven captives there, handcuffed to the bulkheads. Now, they were dead, killed by the people who should have rescued them. There was nothing they could have done differently, Jasmine knew, but it didn't make it any easier. She could only hope that it had been quick; it had certainly been cleaner than what the pirates had probably had in mind for them. None of the prisoners looked to have been saved for ransom.

"Got an airlock here, still sealed," Blake reported.

Jasmine checked her HUD, then nodded. They'd reached the outer edge of Officer Country, where the officers had their cabins…somehow, she wasn't surprised to discover that maintenance was better near the bridge. It was sloppy thinking – it wouldn't save their lives if Officer Country were the only place to retain power after a direct hit – but typical of pirates.

"Set up the bubble, then break it down," she ordered.

Her radio buzzed. "Engineering is a total loss," Lieutenant Aniston reported. "The entire compartment has been shattered."

"Understood," Jasmine said. It was a pity - the Commonwealth Navy would have wanted the pirate ship to add to its small fleet – but it couldn't be helped. "Any survivors?"

"None," Aniston said. "We're searching the remains of the compartment now."

"Keep me informed," Jasmine ordered. She switched back to the Marine command network as Blake and Joe finished assembling the bubble. "Ready?"

"Ready," Joe Buckley confirmed. "Demolition charges are in position. Can we jump in?"

Jasmine smiled. "Go."

The airlock shattered inwards as the two charges detonated, revealing a handful of pirates armed to the teeth. They seemed stunned to see the Marines, as if they hadn't really *expected* the Marines to bother coming for them, then lifted their weapons threateningly. Jasmine barked an order and the platoon opened fire with stunners, sending the pirates toppling to the deck. They'd be picked up after the bridge had been secured.

No effective resistance materialised as the Marines advanced towards the bridge, checking each of the compartments as they passed. Several of them held slaves, captives the pirates had pressed into service on their vessel, all of whom looked too battered and broken to realise that they had been liberated. Jasmine knew that it would be years before they recovered, if indeed they recovered at all. Some of them would be scarred for life.

"Poor bitches," Blake remarked, grimly.

"Have the medics ready to take a look at them," Jasmine ordered. The pirates had, naturally, refrained from supplying their slaves with any shipsuits, although she wouldn't have trusted shipsuits the pirates had provided in any case. Once the ship was secured, they could repressurise the hull, allowing the medics to move freely. "Then keep your eyes front."

The airlock to the bridge was gaping open. Jasmine used hand signals to order Blake and Joe forward, both clutching stun grenades as well as their assault rifles as they moved. If the pirate commander was planning a last desperate defence, they'd jump back and throw in the grenades. She braced herself as the two Marines entered the compartment...

"Brilliant," Blake sneered. "Just *brilliant*."

Jasmine followed them into the compartment and saw what he meant. The pirate commander and his senior officers were conspicuously unarmed, their weapons drifting towards the far side of the compartment. They were holding their hands where the Marines could see them, refusing to give her platoon a single excuse for opening fire. They'd sent their men to slow the Marines, then surrendered...

"Take them into custody," she ordered. At least the penal settlement wouldn't be very pleasant, once the pirates had been interrogated to see if they could point the Marines towards any more pirate bases. Most of the pirate crews knew nothing useful, but their commanders could be very informative indeed. "And then secure the rest of the ship."

"Understood," Blake said. He seemed to share her sentiments. "Perhaps they will die under interrogation."

Jasmine shrugged. Most pirates had no illusions about being made to talk by the Imperial Navy, which was quite happy to use everything from truth drugs to old-fashioned torture to get answers out of its captives. The smarter pirates used implants designed to make interrogation impossible, destroying their minds if they sensed that they were being interrogated. Outwitting even the very basic models was almost impossible.

"Perhaps," she said. She looked for the bright side and found it. "If nothing else, we put this ship out of business and recovered some of their captives. Not a bad day's work."

"Secure the captives," Layla ordered, once the brief report had been completed. "We'll stow them in the stasis tubes until they are ready to be interrogated."

She allowed herself a smile. The brief survey had confirmed that the pirate ship would require months in the yards before she could serve again – if she ever did - but her crew would be eligible for a share of the prize money. For the moment, the pirate ship could be left to drift along the edge of the system until a tug could be dispatched to recover her. It might be several months before they saw any of the cash, but they would see it. Morale was going to skyrocket.

"Captain," Reynolds said, suddenly. "Two ships just came over the Phase Limit."

He hesitated, then continued. "And one of them is broadcasting a Marine distress call."

Layla didn't hesitate. "Signal the Marines," she ordered. "And then take us towards them, full military power."

Chapter Two

This, at base, means that all human societies are ruled by the strong, those who are both willing and able to enforce their demands by force. On the micro scale, a father willing to spank his children wields more authority than a condoning parent; on the macro scale, a political leader willing to use force to get his way wields more authority than a leader unwilling to back up his words with action. And actions always speak louder than words.

-Professor Leo Caesius, *Authority, Power and the Post-Imperial Era*

"Report," Layla ordered.

"The lead ship is a freighter, probably a variant on the *Trucker* design," Reynolds said, as he worked his console. "I don't have a clear reading on the second ship, but I think it is probably a light cruiser, judging by the power emissions."

"Unless they have stepped their emissions down," Layla reminded him. If *Harrington* had shown her full power, the pirates would never have dared go within a million kilometres of her. "Can you pick up an IFF transmission?"

"No, Captain," Reynolds said. "There's just the Marine distress call."

Layla nodded, forcing herself to sit back in her chair and project an appearance of calm, even though her thoughts were spinning through her mind. She had failed the Crucible and therefore been denied her Rifleman's Tab, but much of the Marine ethos had been battered into her head anyway. A Marine did *not* leave a fellow Marine in trouble – and a Marine wouldn't call for help unless it was truly necessary. She had to save the freighter, even though she had no idea who was on it – or who was chasing it.

No IFF from the warship…that was worrying. The Empire's regulations had insisted that all starships carry IFF beacons that announced their presence, despite endless protests from civilian shippers, who saw the beacons as painting targets on their hulls. Layla wasn't inclined to disagree with the civilians; if she'd been in an unarmed ship, she wouldn't have wanted to tell the universe that she was unarmed either. But these days IFF transmitters on civilian ships were the exception rather than the rule. The Commonwealth wasn't fool enough to believe that they served any useful purpose – or that they couldn't be faked, if necessary.

But warships still carried IFF transmitters.

"That has to be a regular navy crew over there," the tactical officer commented, interrupting her thoughts. "They followed a ship through phase space."

"And they're not making tactical mistakes either," Layla agreed. The warship crew were definitely well-trained. "Send a standard challenge."

She scowled inwardly as she studied the display. Shadowing a ship through phase space was incredibly difficult, even for the most experienced officers in the Imperial Navy. That the newcomers had managed it so well suggested that they were either lucky or good – even if they'd known the freighter's intended destination, they wouldn't have come out of phase space so close to their target. They wouldn't need more than twenty minutes to get into firing position – and the freighter couldn't hope to escape.

"We're picking up a response," Reynolds said.

"Put it on," Layla ordered.

"…In pursuit of criminals," an unfamiliar voice said. "Do not interfere or you will be fired upon."

"Check the voiceprint against our records," Layla ordered, although she knew that it would probably be futile. The Imperial Navy records they'd inherited hadn't been updated very well even before the Empire had withdrawn from the Rim. "And target them."

"Aye, Captain," the tactical officer said. "Entering missile range in seven minutes."

"No voiceprint match," the intelligence officer injected. "Captain, that could easily be meaningless…"

"Yes," Layla said, dryly. *She* wouldn't show up in the database either, any more than Reynolds or the other officers and crewmen they'd recruited since the Empire had abandoned the sector. If the ship they were facing belonged to a planetary defence force, or a new military force, it was quite likely that the records were worse than useless. "Repeat the challenge, then order them to stand down until their claims can be investigated."

"Aye, Captain," Reynolds said.

Layla gritted her teeth as they closed in on the freighter. In the days when the Empire had ruled the sector, there had been clear protocols for hunting pirates, terrorists and criminals, even if ships had fled from one sector to another. But now, with the Empire gone…no one was quite sure of what protocol to follow. Her instructions from Avalon ordered her to defend the Commonwealth's territorial integrity and enforce the law, but what was she meant to do if the freighter carried *real* criminals? Or, for that matter, if the light cruiser they were facing was part of a far larger force?

"See if you can raise the freighter," she added. "Tell them to identify themselves."

She watched grimly as Reynolds worked his console. It was quite possible that they had brushed up against the edge of space the Empire *still* controlled, although personally Layla doubted it. The last they'd heard from a reliable source had stated that the Trafalgar and Midway fleet bases were being abandoned. Even so…not *knowing* what they were facing was a nightmarish problem. A minor engagement could start a war.

"Picking up a response," Reynolds said. "Laser and text only. I don't think they want to be overheard."

"Show me," Layla ordered. Text only was rare, unless the bandwidth was limited – or if someone was trying to keep unwanted listeners from learning anything from the message. "And switch to laser transmissions for our reply."

She looked down at her console. The words seemed meaningless – HARPER, BROWN, JAMESTOWN – but anyone who'd been through the

Slaughterhouse would have understood them. HARPER meant that the situation was desperate, BROWN told her that Marines were in trouble – as if she hadn't realised it – and JAMESTOWN warned her that rogue Imperial Navy units were involved. Outside of training, Layla had never heard of *anyone* using JAMESTOWN. There were just too many possibilities for disaster.

"Open a channel to the cruiser," she ordered, making up her mind. There was a click as the channel opened. "Unknown vessel, this is *Harrington*. You are ordered to stand down and hold position while your claims can be investigated. Failure to do so will be met by deadly force."

She studied the position, counting down the seconds until the cruiser could reply. If they fired on the freighter, they might well destroy the runaway ship…but they'd have problems escaping *Harrington* afterwards. On the other hand, they could turn and run; they'd almost certainly make it across the phase limit before Layla could do anything to stop them. But what did the cruiser's CO have in mind? *Layla* would have hesitated before abandoning a pursuit, particularly when she knew nothing about the challenging ship.

The cruiser CO might think that we're pirates, she thought, sourly. It was unlikely, but pirates *had* commanded heavy cruisers in the past, including one that was now part of the Commonwealth Navy. *Or he might not recognise the Commonwealth as having any right to exist.*

That *was* a worrying thought, she acknowledged. The Empire had grown out of the wars that had followed humanity's expansion across the stars, driven by a determination to ensure that disunity would not be allowed to threaten humanity's very existence again. No outside power could be recognised as legitimate by the Empire; it would invite disunity and encourage factions to demand greater autonomy or even independence. If the Empire ever returned to the sector, what would it make of the Commonwealth?

"Picking up a response," Reynolds said. He hissed in sudden alarm. "And they just swept us with tactical sensors!"

"Let me hear the response," Layla said. Lighting up a ship with tactical sensors was regarded as an unfriendly act, a warning that the situation was about to turn deadly. "And light them up with our own sensors."

"Unknown vessel, we are in pursuit of dangerous criminals," the speaker said. "You are ordered to stand down and allow us to complete our mission without hindrance."

Layla scowled as she keyed her console, allowing her to reply. "We cannot allow you to operate in our space," she said, flatly. "We will board the freighter and recover the crew ourselves; if they are guilty, we will hand them over to you."

She waited for the response, thinking hard. The light cruiser's CO had to know that he was outgunned; *Harrington* wasn't even *trying* to hide her true nature. And that meant…either he thought he could still intimidate her or he was desperate to complete his mission. And if it was the former, he had to have some heavy support nearby.

"They just lit us up again," Reynolds reported. "They've locked on."

"Deploy ECM," Layla ordered. The enemy cruiser was altering course slightly, as if she was preparing for a run right at *Harrington*. Their tactics seemed to make no sense at all. "And lock our weapons on their hull."

"Weapons locked," the tactical officer reported. "Missiles are armed, ready to fire; point defence grid is armed, ready to fire."

Layla keyed her console. "Unknown vessel, this is your last warning," she said. "You will stand down or be fired upon…"

"Missile separation," the tactical officer said. "One oversized broadside…"

They bolted missile pods to their hull, Layla thought, as the tactical display sparked with newer icons. No light cruiser could fire such a barrage with internal tubes alone. The extra tonnage made the ship somewhat more sluggish, but it gave them an advantage over a heavier ship…

"Return fire," she ordered. At least the enemy had fired on *Harrington*, rather than the freighter. If they'd fired on the freighter, it would almost certainly have blown the fleeing ship into debris. "Target their drives, if possible."

Harrington shuddered as she unleashed a barrage of her own. The enemy ship altered course again, sheering away from *Harrington's* missiles…then twisting back to fire a second much-reduced salvo from her internal tubes. Layla nodded in reluctant admiration; the enemy crew were clearly well drilled, rather than pirates whose firing patterns were irregular at best.

"Point defence will engage in twelve seconds," the tactical officer said. "Decoys away; ECM at full power…"

Layla nodded, feeling oddly helpless as the missiles roared towards her ship. Several fell to point defence fire, others were decoyed away by the drones or suckered into burning out their drives by the ECM… but four made it through the defensive shield to enter their terminal attack run. One slammed into the gravity shield and detonated harmlessly; the remaining three detonated near the ship. *Harrington* rocked violently as a laser head sent a ray of power into her hull, boring deep into the hullmetal.

"Damage to decks seven through nine," the damage control officer reported. "Damage control teams are on their way."

Layla nodded. Thankfully, the remaining laser heads had missed her hull or the damage would have been worse.

"Continue firing," she ordered, as the enemy ship belched yet another wave of missiles. "And deploy a second wave of ECM drones…"

"Our missiles are entering attack range," the tactical officer reported. "Captain, the enemy ship's ECM is at least as good as our own."

"Understood," Layla said, watching the complex interplay of sensor ghosts that shrouded the enemy ship, drawing off her missiles from their targets. Pirates rarely bothered with any kind of ECM, if only because ECM officers took years to train, even with the best computer support. It was just another sign that they were facing someone much more well-organised than a pirate gang. "Adjust our own systems to compensate…"

"Four direct hits," the tactical officer said, a moment later. "Captain, she's streaming air – and plasma."

Layla smiled, coldly. The enemy cruiser was too small to soak up damage like a battleship and keep fighting. One of her laser heads had dug deeply into the enemy hull; her drive might not have been disabled, but the damage would make it harder for her crew to continue the fight anyway. And if they'd lost their phase drive, which was quite possible, they wouldn't be able to escape the system, whatever happened. They'd have no choice, but to surrender.

"Broadcast a surrender demand," Layla ordered. "Tell them that they will be well-treated."

"They're switching fire to the freighter," the tactical officer snapped. "Captain..."

"Continue firing," Layla ordered, although she knew that it was almost certainly too late. "Angle our counter-missiles to try to cover the freighter..."

"Too late," the tactical officer said.

Layla watched it unfold; five missiles slammed into the freighter, smashing through the hull and detonating inside. It was overkill, she knew, but it was effective. The freighter vanished inside a tearing blast of plasma, utterly vaporised. Moments later, her missiles struck the enemy cruiser and crippled it. But it was still too late to save the freighter.

"They've lost their drives, Captain," the tactical officer said, softly. He sounded bitter; they'd done everything right, but they'd failed to save the freighter. "They're drifting helplessly in space."

"Raise them," Layla said. They hadn't responded to her earlier demand for surrender, but now they had no choice. Even if she'd left them alone, they would have drifted helplessly though space until they ran out of air and suffocated. "Tell them that we will treat them well."

She scowled, inwardly. The Imperial Navy's habit of regarding anyone who fought against it as an illegal combatant didn't encourage enemy crewmen to surrender. After all, everyone knew that illegal combatants could be shot out of hand – or tortured, or treated as slaves, or whatever else their captors felt like doing. There had always been rumours about the fate of some enemy crewmen during the Unification Wars or captured insurgents who'd tried to rise up against the Empire. Layla had never actually seen *proof*, but rumours had a power of their own.

"Picking up a low-level transmission," Reynolds said. "They're offering to surrender."

Thank God, Layla thought. On the other hand, it offered a new headache for her crew. She'd had to leave the Marines and half of the Scouts with the captured pirate ship when she'd gone to rescue the destroyed freighter.

"Have the Senior Chief form a boarding party to support the remaining Scouts," she said, cursing the timing. If the freighter had arrived an hour later, she would have had the Marines back on *Harrington*, ready to capture the crippled enemy ship. "And send a signal to the cripple; any resistance will result in the destruction of their vessel. We don't have the manpower to take the ship by force."

She settled back in her command chair and skimmed through the preliminary report from the damage control teams. None of the damage was major, thankfully, and the internal network had already rerouted itself to compensate for the damage. No pirate ship could have matched that performance, she knew; it demanded a crew who actually knew how to maintain their ship. There had only been one injury, a crewman whose arm had been caught in the airlock when the emergency systems sealed the ship. He was in sickbay and expected to make a full recovery, once the doctor cloned him a new arm.

"Captain," Reynolds said, suddenly. "We're picking up a distress beacon!"

Layla looked up. "Where from?"

"The freighter must have launched a lifepod," Reynolds said. "I think they must have deactivated the beacon until we actually emerged as victors."

"How terrible," the tactical officer observed archly. "That's in violation of the regulations."

"I think we can forgive them, just this once," Layla said, relieved. "Order a shuttle to pick them up, but *carefully*. We don't know why they were running…"

She watched the display as a shuttle was rerouted towards the lifepod. At least they might get some answers from the refugees, as well as the remains of the enemy crew. God alone knew what sort of answers the captives would give, if only because they couldn't be interrogated by Layla's crew. Mistreating crewmen from another state, as odd as the whole concept seemed, would only encourage the mistreatment of Commonwealth personnel.

"The Scouts have picked up thirty-seven enemy crewmen," Reynolds reported, breaking into her thoughts. "Seven of them are quite badly injured."

"Have them put into stasis tubes," Layla ordered, wondering if they *had* enough tubes to go round. The pirates might have to be transferred into the hold and the hatch firmly locked. "And order the Marines to return as quickly as possible. We're going to need them."

She turned as a new report came in. "Shuttle Seven has recovered the lifepod," the tactical officer said. "There were nine people crammed inside."

Layla scowled. Nine people…in theory, a freighter could be operated by two or three people, but that never worked in practice. Most freighters really needed at least twenty crewmen to handle any problems that might arise. It was quite possible that the freighter has lost most of her crew.

"They're requesting to speak with you, urgently," the tactical officer added.

"Have them searched, then brought back to the ship," Layla said. "Tell them that I will speak with them as soon as possible."

She shook her head. "Once the enemy ship is empty, have Engineering put together a crew to see what they can pull out of her," she added. Standard procedure was to purge the computers and then destroy them physically before surrendering – and the enemy crew had been alarmingly professional – but it was worth a try. "I want to know as much as possible before we have to abandon her to interstellar space."

"Understood, Captain," the tactical officer said. "Two of the damage control crewmen have SSE experience. With your permission, I will send them to join the team."

Layla nodded. Hopefully, she told herself, they would get some answers soon.

And, she added silently, they should also hope that she hadn't just started a war.

Chapter Three

The threat of force is worthless unless the person (or country) making the threats has both the demonstrated will and ability to actually carry out those threats. Talk is cheap; action rather less so. Indeed, the more threats a person makes that are ignored (and not then backed up) the more credibility they lose. Eventually, they reach a point where carrying out the threats becomes imperative, if only because no one believes that they will.
-Professor Leo Caesius, *Authority, Power and the Post-Imperial Era*

"They certainly don't *look* like pirates," Blake commented.

Jasmine nodded as she surveyed the row of prisoners propped up against one of the shuttlebay's bulkheads. The mystery cruiser's crew looked surprisingly professional, very unlike the pirates they'd captured from time to time; they sat as calmly as they could, only a handful of them looking at the Marines nervously. Being captured was always a disconcerting experience – Jasmine remembered the Conduct after Capture course she'd undergone at the Slaughterhouse – but it was worse for pirates.

"No, they don't," she agreed, finally. "Did we manage to take anyone senior alive?"

"The highest-ranking person the Scouts took off the ship was a Lieutenant," Joe Buckley said. "Of course, someone here could be the Captain and *claiming* to be a lower-ranking officer…"

"It's possible," Jasmine said. The Marines gave the prisoners one last look and then headed out of the shuttlebay, allowing the Scouts on guard to close the internal airlock. If the prisoners gave trouble, they could simply be ejected into space – and they knew it. "And there were Marines on the other ship…"

She mulled it over as she dispatched most of the platoon to Marine Country and headed down towards the brig. Captain Delacroix had installed the refugees in the brig, pointing out that they didn't know who or what they really were; Jasmine found it hard to disagree with her, even if the refugees *were* Marines. Rogue Marines were rare, but they did exist – and it was surprisingly easy to condition someone into a homicidal killer. Marines were supposed to be resistant to such techniques, yet no one dared take that for granted.

"The leader has the right implants, as do two of his men," Joe observed, skimming through the preliminary report. "But we don't have access to our records here."

"We can confirm their identity on Avalon, if the implants are not sufficient," Jasmine pointed out, stepping into the brig. It was a small compartment with only four holding cells, currently holding the refugees – and the senior pirate. "For the moment…"

She stopped in front of one of the cells and straightened up, showing her uniform. "I'm Lieutenant Yamane, Stalker's Stalkers," she said, identifying herself. "And you?"

The men in the cells stood up and saluted. "First Sergeant Conrad Hampton, retired," the leader said. "And believe me when I say that I am *very* pleased to see you."

"You too," Jasmine said, studying him carefully. Hampton definitely had the right build for a Marine – and he certainly *moved* like one. Even the most capable officers and men from the Imperial Army walked differently, while the Civil Guardsmen generally slouched along. "I'm afraid that we need to ask you some questions."

"I understand," Hampton said. He shook his head, tiredly. "Are you from the Empire?"

Jasmine hesitated, then shook her head. "We're from Avalon," she said, softly. "And you?"

"Greenway," Hampton said. "It's something of a long story."

"Escort him to the interview compartment," Jasmine ordered, as she opened the door. Blake and Joe braced for trouble, but Hampton offered none. "I'm sorry about this, but…"

Hampton surprised her with a smile. "I understand," he said, again. "But do you have some coffee?"

The interview compartment was marginally more comfortable than the cells, but at least it had a coffee machine. Jasmine poured Hampton a cup personally and passed it to him, then sat down facing the retired Marine. His hair had grown out in the years since he'd retired, but he seemed to have kept himself in shape otherwise. Greenway wasn't *that* far from the Rim, one of many planets that would be glad to get a retired Marine as a colonist. But it was still several hundred light years from Avalon.

"I retired five years ago," Hampton said, sipping his coffee. "The wife wanted to homestead somewhere away from the Core Worlds; she felt that society was pressurising her into becoming a useless lump of flesh sitting in front of the entertainer all day. Greenway was looking for retired soldiers to serve as marshals and help train the Civil Guard. It seemed like a good idea at the time and for five years it was – and then the ships just stopped coming."

Jasmine nodded, reviewing the data on Greenway through her implant. It wasn't a deliberately low-tech world, but the settlers wanted to farm and hunt without creating a modern civilisation; the report stated that there was only one real city on the planet and almost nothing in the rest of the system, apart from a handful of industrial nodes. There were probably a number of RockRats as well, she decided. The report's writer hadn't seemed to know or care.

"It didn't really bother us," Hampton admitted. "We weren't really dependent on importing anything from the Empire, even HE3. The moon had enough deposits to meet our needs for thousands of years. There was some trouble from a handful of indents who had been told that they could go back to the Core Worlds after they finished their sentences, but we coped with that well enough. Everything seemed perfect until the next ships arrived. They told us that the Empire was gone and that we were now subjects of Admiral Singh, who had assumed power in the wake of the Empire's fall."

Jasmine's eyes narrowed. "Admiral Singh?"

"She was apparently a Commodore assigned to Trafalgar," Hampton explained. "Our last set of records were a little outdated, so we didn't know for sure. What we *did* know was that her ships were in orbit, demanding our immediate surrender. When we balked, they dropped KEWs on Landing City until we rolled over for them."

Jasmine grimaced, remembering how the Admiral had almost taken control of Avalon's high orbitals. If the team she'd lead hadn't managed to capture the enemy ship, Avalon would have had no choice. They would have to surrender and hope that the Admiral's rule wouldn't be *that* bad. Greenway wouldn't have had a chance.

"They landed exploitation teams, conscripted everyone with any technical aptitude…and started to round up anyone with actual military experience," Hampton added, grimly. "I…decided that it would be better not to stick around and be captured, but my escape plan went wrong. Someone had a son taken into custody and betrayed me in exchange for the son being released, or so I was told. Me and most of the others were taken off-planet the same day and held on the freighter. I think we were due to be transferred to Penance."

"That makes sense," Jasmine agreed. Penance was a hellish world, even by the Empire's lax standards; convicts were given a handful of supplies and dropped onto the surface, where they could either work to settle the planet or die. The Empire didn't care what happened after they were down on the surface. "How did you manage to gain control of the freighter?"

Hampton looked down, embarrassed. "Kate – she was a militiawoman – seduced one of the guards," he admitted. "She got the drop on him, forced him to open the rest of the cells and then we took the ship. We hoped we could get across the phase limit without them realising that something was wrong, but they caught on before we could make our escape good. They chased us all the way here…the freighter was so badly damaged that there was nowhere else we could go. And then we ran into you."

"Luckily for you," Jasmine said. They'd been *very* lucky. Converting a freighter into a prison barge was easy and, with minimal precautions, even the toughest soldiers couldn't escape. "What did…Admiral Singh actually *want*?"

"I think she wants the Empire," Hampton admitted. "From the way her forces were acting on Greenway, I'm pretty sure she has a long-term plan to do just that, if she can. What happened to you?"

Jasmine hesitated, then filled Hampton in on everything that had happened since Stalker's Stalkers had been exiled to Avalon. He'd hoped to hear something of Earth and the remains of the Empire, but she had to admit that all they had were rumours, some of them more absurd than shocking. What sort of idiot would believe that there had been a giant bird growing inside Earth, let alone that it's hatching had destroyed the planet?

"So it's just you?" Hampton asked, finally. "What can we do now?"

"We do whatever we have to do," Jasmine said. She scowled inwardly at his expression, although she knew that he had a point. It *was* a vague statement, something that Marines tended to distrust. And not without reason. "For the moment, we will have to arrange for you and your men to get proper quarters."

"Your brig is better than the freighter," Hampton assured her.

Jasmine smiled. "Until then, I need you all to write down a full report for the Colonel," she added. "He's going to want to know everything you know."

"Which isn't enough," Hampton warned her. "Lieutenant, if Singh has control of Trafalgar…she might have most of the sector fleet too."

"I know," Jasmine said. They'd been outgunned when they'd faced *the* Admiral, but the pirates hadn't been very competent and the Marines had managed to take advantage of their flaws. It would be a great deal harder if they were facing a trained Imperial Navy officer. "But we will have to do what we can."

"Trafalgar was the linchpin of the sector fleet," Layla said. "If Admiral Singh captured *all* of the fleet…she'd have us heavily outgunned."

She flicked through the records, cursing – once again – the Imperial Navy's lax approach to updating the files. Even before the withdrawal, the fleet lists had been in a terrible state; she doubted that the records were even fifty percent accurate. Some starships had been secretly decommissioned and sold, the profits flowing to the bureaucrats who were attempting to feather their own nests; others had been redeployed on short notice and no one had bothered to update the records. At worst, Admiral Singh might have two entire battle squadrons under her command...

It was possible, she told herself, that the ships were poorly maintained. God knew just how many ships had had to be put into long-term storage because the money and trained crewmen to maintain them didn't exist...even the starships on active duty suffered heavily from lack of maintenance. Layla had heard of a ship's crew that had been forced to produce their own replacement components, which had caused no end of trouble when the replacements had been given to a crew that didn't know how to deal with them. But that, she thought angrily, was wishful thinking. They had to assume the worst.

"We can leave the pirate ship here," she said, "and then head back to Avalon."

She looked up at the starchart, running through the possible scenarios in her mind. If they assumed that the occupation force on Greenway didn't *know* where their cruiser had gone, they might take weeks or even months to realise that she was missing. On the other hand, if they assumed the worst, it might take only two to three weeks before the occupation force realised that the cruiser might have run into trouble. What did they have to send after her?

"We could interrogate the prisoners gently," Lieutenant Yamane suggested. "Some of them might be willing to talk."

Layla eyed her, feeling a flicker of the old resentment. She'd failed the Crucible at the final hurdle, ensuring that she could never call herself a Marine. And yet...she was the Captain of a heavy cruiser, an opportunity that she would never have had if she'd become a Marine Rifleman. Which one of them was truly better off? The Marine...or the Captain?

"Perhaps," she agreed, finally. It *was* a good suggestion. "We'll assign the officers sealed cabins, allowing you a chance to work on the lower ranks. Some of them might be willing to talk if we ask properly."

She scowled. "No drugs though," she added, a moment later. "We have to *try* to keep them reasonably sweet."

Lieutenant Yamane smiled. "They're prisoners," she said. "They're not going to be sweet at all."

Layla couldn't disagree. "We can try," she said. "Hampton and his men can have the guest cabins – but keep them under guard. We don't *know* just how much of what they're telling us is true."

"They might volunteer to be injected with truth drugs," Lieutenant Yamane pointed out. "I don't think they *all* have counter-interrogation implants."

"Yes, but they might believe what they're telling us, even under the impact of the truth drugs," Layla said. "There might be no Admiral Singh – it isn't actually an uncommon name. For all we know, the fleet that hit Greenway might be all the fleet they have."

"Another pirate trying to set up as a local ruler," Lieutenant Yamane mused. "I would have thought that they were too professional to be pirates."

"Some pirates have managed to surprise us," Layla said. "Besides, we never quite worked out who was backing the Admiral."

She scowled. *Someone* had provided high-tech support to the Admiral, someone who had remained firmly in the shadows. Commonwealth Intelligence had followed up every lead it had found while searching through the pirate bases, but they'd found nothing. Whoever had supported the Admiral remained unknown – and, presumably, planning their next move.

Her wristcom buzzed. "Go ahead," she ordered.

"Captain, the survey team just completed their search of the enemy ship," the tactical officer reported. "The main computers were trashed, but we recovered some secondary systems and a handful of handwritten notes. It was much cleaner than a pirate ship."

Layla nodded. Pirates rarely bothered to even *clean* their ships – every pirate vessel she'd seen had smelled awful – but they also left evidence scattered around for the post-battle SSE teams to find and use. Admiral Singh's ship, on the other hand, seemed to be clean in both senses of the word.

"Prepare to bring everything you found back to the ship," she ordered, "then shut down the remainder of the cruiser. We'll leave her drifting here until we can get a proper recovery tug to take her back home."

"Let's hope that it all seems worthwhile," Lieutenant Yamane commented. "If Sergeant Hampton was right, Admiral Singh is likely to regard us as competition."

Layla nodded. Avalon had been lucky in many ways; the ADC had spent vast sums of money on the cloudscoop, convinced that Avalon would become an industrial nexus and a springboard for future expansion beyond the Rim. The ADC had collapsed, but the Commonwealth had inherited the cloudscoop and, combined with the supplies the Marines had brought from Earth and freedom from the Empire's burdensome regulations, was starting to produce its own starships. Given time, the Commonwealth would even be able to start producing battleships... hell, they'd already started to make improvements on some technology the Empire had thought couldn't be developed further.

But Admiral Singh would have a big head start...

"See that Hampton and his people get cabins and whatever else they need," she ordered. "We'll be heading back to Avalon within the hour."

"Understood," Lieutenant Yamane said.

Layla watched her step through the hatch, which closed behind her with an audible hiss. The Marine might not have the better part of the deal after all, she decided, thoughtfully. How could command of a small unit of Marines compare to command of an entire starship?

Shaking her head, she picked up her datapad and scrolled through the final report from the damage control officer. There was some damage that really needed the attention of a yard, but otherwise *Harrington* had come through her first real combat test with flying colours. The designers were to be credited, she'd concluded, although there were a few issues that needed to be discussed later on, before the next class of starships was produced. Layla tapped her thumb against the scanner, confirming that she had read and approved the report, then read the tactical officer's summery of the brief action. His conclusions were no surprise; Admiral Singh's ships were considerably more dangerous than any pirate vessel.

She keyed her wristcom. "Memo to all senior staff," she said, trusting the network to pick up on her words. "We will be holding additional exercises during our trip back to Avalon. Facing pirates may have made us lazy; in future, we will assume the worst of our enemies."

Closing the wristcom, she stood up and walked to the hatch herself. At maximum speed, it would still be two weeks before they reached Avalon – and by then, who knew *what* would happen? But then, if they were lucky, Admiral Singh wouldn't have the slightest idea that Avalon was becoming an industrial powerhouse. She'd have the same problem that the Marines on Avalon had had when they'd been hunting pirates. The pirate base was *tiny* on a cosmic scale, almost impossible to find.

But that wasn't true of the cloudscoop, she reminded herself as she walked onto the bridge. If Admiral Singh studied the records carefully, she would certainly be able to pinpoint Avalon as the most likely place to develop into an industrial base. And if she combined that with sighting a new-build starship…

We'd better get ready quickly, she thought. *God alone knows how long we will have before the shit hits the fan.*

CHAPTER FOUR

Throughout human history, well-meaning intellectuals have attempted to deny this fundamental truth. Gunboat diplomacy is, in their worldview, as appalling as the parent who resorts to corporal punishment. Indeed, as they say, it is incredibly easy to move from reasoned and nuanced use of force to using force in all circumstances, even if the situation doesn't really call for it. To paraphrase a very old and respected thinker, you should not behead a child for a minor mistake – but, as another thinker put it, when all you have is a hammer, every problem starts to look like a nail.

-Professor Leo Caesius, *Authority, Power and the Post-Imperial Era*

"As you will have noticed," Jasmine said, "we crossed the phase limit and entered phase space an hour ago. Any hopes you might have had of being rescued can no longer be held."

The enemy officer stared back at her defiantly, although she could see a hint of fear underlying his face. Like most of his crew, he was surprisingly young, young enough to make her wonder just what connections he possessed to be advanced so rapidly. She'd never quite overcome that habit, even though the Commonwealth Navy was also advancing competent officers as fast as possible.

She glanced through the brief physical report from the medic. The prisoners were all healthy, in reasonably good shape; there didn't seem to be any implants, apart from a couple of neural links that had been deactivated after discovery. Jasmine suspected that their superiors insisted on proper exercise, something that was mandatory in the Marines – and the

Imperial Army – but somewhat haphazard in the Empire's other services. It was just another indication that they weren't dealing with the Empire. Admiral Singh was clearly more competent than the average Imperial Navy officer.

"So it would seem," the officer said, finally. "What are you going to do to us?"

That was somewhat problematic, Jasmine admitted silently. The Empire didn't recognise anyone fighting against it as legitimate combatants – and the Commonwealth had never come up with protocols for dealing with POWs. She'd had to do some data-mining to look up precedents, most of them dating from the Unification Wars. The records hadn't been very precise, but she had a feeling that the POWs hadn't been treated very well once the wars had finally come to an end.

"We are going to interview you," she said. "I think you can give us your name, rank and ID code without compromising your operational security. After that…if you behave, we will treat you well. There are plenty of places you can be held that are reasonably civilised."

"Instead of a penal world, I presume," the officer said. "Will you return us to our world?"

"I think that would be a matter for negotiation," Jasmine said. There was no point in sending back crewmen until they had a deal with Admiral Singh. She doubted that thirty crewmen would really make a difference if war broke out, but it was well to be careful. "However, I believe that our side would agree to return you once we start talking."

"That's good," the officer said. He hesitated, then looked down at the deck. "I am Lieutenant George Murchison, assigned to *Proud* as Secondary Tactical Officer."

Jasmine nodded, recognising his reluctance to talk at all. There was always the risk of telling the captors something that would prove useful in the coming war – and he dared not assume that there *wouldn't* be war. Name, rank and ID code weren't particularly informative outside POW camps and exchanges; it was, she suspected, why the protocol had been developed in the first place.

"Thank you," she said. "Would you like to tell us more about Admiral Singh?"

Murchison shook his head, still looking at the deck. "No," he said, finally. There was a hint of bitterness in his tone. "Name, rank and ID code is all that you are getting."

Jasmine understood. Without counter-interrogation implants, it wouldn't be hard to make Murchison talk – or condition him into a willing slave. Murchison could be made to betray his leader, to spill everything he knew to the Marines…and he had to know it. His defiance could prove completely meaningless.

"You will be returned to your cabin," she said, instead. "I hope that the ration bars are remotely edible."

Murchison couldn't help a smile. Ration bars might be edible, but they were never *tasty*, even though it would be easy to make them pleasing to the palate. Earth's famed algae farms pumped out millions of the bars every day, trying to keep ahead of Earth's endless demand for food. Maybe *they* didn't have time to improve the flavour, but Avalon should have had the time…

"Edible," he repeated. "I would like to talk to the rest of my people."

"Once we've completed our survey, you can meet and talk with them," Jasmine assured him, honestly. If all of the prisoners decided to keep their mouths shut, it would be one thing, but she was fairly sure that some of them would start to talk after the shock of losing their ship and being taken captive. If Murchison had a chance to stiffen their spines, however…

"Thank you," Murchison said, stiffly.

Jasmine called for Blake and ordered him to escort Murchison back to his cabin. Captain Delacroix had assigned him a cabin intended for a junior officer; a small box, barely larger than the compartments put aside for crewmen. But it would keep him away from the rest of the captives, in the hopes that it would make the rest of the POWs more tractable. She reminded herself, as Blake took Murchison out of the compartment, to remember that might not be accurate. Senior officers had overlooked the value of NCOs more than once in the past.

The next three captives were hardly more informative, although one of them managed to tell Jasmine that she'd been born on Trafalgar itself before being conscripted into Admiral Singh's Navy. That was odd; the

Imperial Navy had never had to use conscription to fill the ranks, even when the budget had been slashed badly by the Grand Senate. There was no shortage of people willing to enlist…or there hadn't been. Jasmine asked a few probing questions and managed to learn that Trafalgar had heard that Earth had been destroyed, before the crewwoman shut up and refused to talk any more.

"Maybe the rumours you heard are more accurate than the ones *we* heard," Jasmine said, and recounted a couple of the more absurd ones. Who would have believed that Sol had gone supernova? Earth's sun wasn't the type of star to go supernova and destroy the inner system. "Can't you tell us what you heard?"

The crewwoman shook her head, despite the fear in her eyes.

Jasmine dispatched her to a different cabin and called for the next captive. Joe escorted him in; a young man, wearing a torn uniform and a fearful expression. Jasmine suspected that he had had some bootleg rejuvenation treatments from a very early age, retarding the aging process; there was something about his face that made it impossible to guess at his age. Young, obviously, but beyond that…Jasmine made a mental note to ask the medics to take a longer look at the prisoner. Bootleg treatments sometimes caused problems that emerged in later life.

"Please, be seated," she said, and introduced herself. "I need to ask you for some details…"

"You're from the *Marines*?" The young man asked. "The Empire hasn't forgotten us?"

Jasmine blinked in surprise. "I'm a Marine, yes," she confirmed, tapping the Rifleman's Tab on her shoulder. "And you are?"

"We had almost given up hope," the young man gushed. "Ever since *she* arrived…"

Jasmine held up a hand. "I think you'd better start from the beginning," she said. "Who are you and what happened when Admiral Singh arrived?"

"I'm Crewman 2nd Class Elliott Canada," the young man admitted. "And she took my homeworld for her own."

"I see," Jasmine said. Had they hit the jackpot? "The Empire has *not* forgotten you."

"We heard so many rumours," Canada admitted. "Earth had been destroyed, Earth had been sacked, Earth had dropped into phase space and vanished…we didn't know what to believe until the Admiral's fleet arrived. She told us that she was in charge of the sector now and crushed us when we tried to protest."

Jasmine lifted an eyebrow. "Us?"

"I was part of the Democratic Underground on Corinthian," Canada said. He hesitated, then gave her a searching look. "Don't you know *anything* about us?"

"Very little," Jasmine said, honestly. Corinthian was the sector capital, a mere ten light years from Trafalgar Naval Base. She'd never looked at the records in great detail, but if it was the capital it would have a large population and a considerable industrial base – a valuable prize for Admiral Singh…or anyone else, for that matter. "The Empire has been very disorganised lately."

Canada, once he had started to talk, seemed unable to stop. "She took over the high orbitals with her troops and started to conscript our population," he said. "We tried to fight and she *crushed* us; the Democratic Underground was scattered and our very own oligarchies turned traitor and signed up with the bitch. And then…they must not have realised that I was part of the Democratic Underground, because they told me to report for duty."

Or they simply didn't care, Jasmine thought, silently.

"It's been over a year since she arrived," Canada added. "The entire planet is held in the grip of fear. You have to do something!"

Jasmine nodded, thinking hard. The Democratic Underground had had links to the Secessionists, but they preferred to agitate for free democracy rather than the violent separatism advocated by the Secessionists. It was, technically, an illegal group of subversives, yet the Empire's attitude to them had been one of amused tolerance, rather than outright repression. Jasmine had heard, before she'd moved to Avalon, that the Empire tolerated them because they were so ineffectual, which didn't prevent the security services from drawing up files on every known member. If Admiral Singh had decided to repress them, she would have had the information she needed to do it at hand.

"We're going to do something," she assured him. "What happened at Greenway?"

"The Admiral has been expanding her little empire, from what I heard," Canada explained. "We have orders to round up experienced personnel, collect industrial equipment and anything else that might be useful. If the planet's leaders agree to accept her as their ruler, they get to stay in power. If not…they get killed and the planet is bombarded into submission. Greenway was just the latest planet on the list."

Jasmine lifted an eyebrow. "And you did *nothing*?"

Canada stared at her. "What could I have done?"

Mandy sabotaged an entire heavy cruiser single-handedly, Jasmine thought. But it wasn't a fair comparison at all. A ship manned by a crew that was actually *competent*, capable of working together without planning to kill their fellows at the earliest opportunity, would be far harder to sabotage. Besides, if Canada had managed to destroy *Proud*, what good would it have done beyond costing Admiral Singh a light cruiser?

"Good point," Jasmine said, finally. "How many ships does Admiral Singh have?"

"I'm not sure," Canada admitted. "I know she has at least three battleships and several dozen smaller ships, but I don't know the precise figures."

"Pity," Jasmine said. "Do you know how the Admiral selects her targets?"

Canada shook his head.

Jasmine wasn't too surprised. Outside the Marine Corps – if there was anything left of the Marine Corps, apart from Stalker's Stalkers – it was uncommon for junior officers and crewmen to be totally briefed by their superiors. Canada had been lucky to learn as much as he had; normally, he wouldn't know more than what his superiors thought he should know. It struck Jasmine as an odd way to run a military organisation, but it *did* make a certain kind of sense. The Admirals wouldn't want junior officers fretting over grand strategy when they were supposed to be doing their jobs.

"I do know that we were meant to be assigned to scout out another potential target," Canada added, softly. "If we hadn't been in position to intercept that freighter…"

"You might never have found us," Jasmine said, quietly. She came to a decision. "Are you prepared to cooperate completely?"

"If it will free my planet," Canada said, "I will do anything."

"I wouldn't say that *too* loudly if I were you," Jasmine said, dryly. She smiled at his puzzled expression. "We're going to transfer you to a separate cabin; our interrogators are going to ask you hundreds of questions…"

"I can tell you everything," Canada protested. He sounded rather indignant, as if he'd expected better treatment. But then, sending someone to face the interrogators suggested that someone wasn't believed to be *innocent*. "I…"

"Sometimes people don't know what they know," Jasmine explained, patiently. It had surprised her, back when she'd undergone the Conduct After Capture course, just how much the interrogators had managed to pull from her mind. And she'd thought she'd managed to mislead them more than once. The only truly safe thing to do, she'd been told afterwards, was not to get captured at all. "The interrogators know more than I do about pulling information from a person's mind."

She smiled at him. "And then we can decide what to do about Admiral Singh."

"Kill her," Canada said. "It's the only way to stop the bitch before she takes the Empire."

Jasmine privately doubted that was possible. Admiral Singh, at worst, had the entire sector fleet…which would be badly outnumbered by the rest of the Imperial Navy. Standard procedure when dealing with such a threat was to assemble an overwhelming force and advance towards the enemy's homeworld, crushing it in a single blow. Admiral Singh would be hunted down and destroyed.

But what if the Empire was truly gone?

The question had tormented her – and everyone else – since they'd discovered how rapidly the Empire had withdrawn from the Rim. Hundreds of planets had simply been abandoned, the lucky ones securing enough firepower to protect themselves against marauding pirates and empire-builders. Jasmine knew just how many faultlines threatened the integrity of the Imperial Navy; if they'd all exploded…she had a vivid impression of battleships firing on their fellows as the more ambitious Admirals moved to secure their bases and set up their own empires. And there was no shortage of competent officers who had been kept down by their well-connected superiors. What would *they* do if the Empire was so gravely weakened?

"We'll see what happens," she said, vaguely. She'd have to explain, at some point, what they *really* were. Canada would be shocked to realise that he wasn't talking to the Empire's representatives. "Until then, you must answer our questions."

She hesitated, then added a warning. "You must stay in your cabin," she added, flatly. He looked rebellious – no doubt he'd been confined to his cabin on his former ship, if he'd had a cabin to himself – so she explained the reasoning behind the order. "Your former shipmates won't hesitate to kill you if they get a chance."

Canada swallowed hard, but nodded in understanding.

Jasmine watched Blake lead him out of the interrogation compartment, then tapped the small console and replayed the entire conversation. If Canada was telling the truth – and that could be verified, even without drugs or less elegant forms of interrogation – they knew more about the coming threat. There would be war. Admiral Singh was hardly likely to tolerate a threat developing to her rear as she probed towards the Core Worlds. It was far more likely that she would attempt to deal with Avalon and the rest of the Commonwealth as quickly as possible.

But what, Jasmine asked herself, *does she know about us?*

It was impossible to say, she knew; even if the other prisoners were just as cooperative. For all they knew, Admiral Singh had captured traders from the Commonwealth – or sent spies to Avalon, checking up on the cloudscoop. Avalon didn't have the vast detection arrays orbiting Earth; it was quite possible that someone had sneaked into the system, carried out a brief tactical survey and then retreated, without being detected at all. And then...?

The Commonwealth had built up its navy over the past two years, but Admiral Singh still had a big head start. Could she take out Avalon's defence forces and secure the high orbitals? If she had the sector fleet's battleships, she probably could; Jasmine would have been surprised if she *couldn't*. But then, she *was* capturing industrial nodes and transporting them to her base of operations, rather than using them in place. It suggested a certain insecurity...

The Colonel will have to decide what to do, she thought, and forwarded the recordings to Delacroix. The former Auxiliary had her own views on how the universe worked – and besides, she'd actually commanded starships. She might be able to deduce the logic behind Admiral Singh's actions – or suggest questions for Canada and any other cooperative prisoners. The more minds working on a problem, in Jasmine's experience, the greater the chance of finding a proper solution.

The hatch opened, revealing the next prisoner. Jasmine blanked the display and turned to face the middle-aged woman, who seemed oddly relieved to see her. Or perhaps it wasn't so odd after all. Everyone knew what pirates did to their captives. The Marines had explained that the POWS would be well treated, but pirates made promises too.

"Please, be seated," Jasmine said, as the hatch hissed closed. The woman eyed her nervously, but did as she was told. "I am Lieutenant Jasmine Yamane, Terran Marine Corps..."

Chapter Five

> The rule of the strong causes hundreds of problems for humanity, some simple and some complex. If everything I own is mine only as long as I can keep hold of it, I am doomed the moment I show weakness. There are no such things as property rights in a state ruled by the strong – and the strong will rule only as long as they stay strong. When they grow old, their enemies will come for them with daggers drawn – and take all they can get.
>
> -Professor Leo Caesius, *Authority, Power and the Post-Imperial Era*

"Imagine," Professor Leo Caesius said dramatically, "a single human marching towards a cliff."

He smiled at his audience and continued. "That human will see the cliff in front of him and come to a stop – unless, of course, he wants to commit suicide. He may stop and turn to the right, walking alongside the cliff, or he might turn back and walk away from the cliff. But he has successfully avoided death by walking *off* the cliff."

He paused. "Now," he added, "imagine a massive army of humans advancing towards the cliff.

"The people in the lead may see the cliff coming, but can they stop? Even if they do, they will be pushed forward by the people behind them – and, no matter how much they kick and scream, they will be pushed over the cliff. So too will the people just behind them; they may not even realise that the cliff is there until it is too late. How many people will fall to their deaths before the remainder manage to stop?"

The question hung in the air for a long chilling moment. "A single human can turn right or left or even go backwards," Leo said. "But how easy is it to change the direction of a colossal mass of humans? How many of you have learned to march as part of the Knights? Can an entire army change its route before it is too late?

"It is incredibly difficult to alter course when there are so many humans involved," he said, softly. "And that sums up the problem with the Empire."

He smiled inwardly at their reactions. History and Moral Philosophy wasn't an elective in Avalon University – and contributed nothing towards a student's grades - but it was a surprisingly popular class. The youth of Avalon needed to understand what had killed the Empire and what might kill the Commonwealth, if they let it. In the end, the future was in their hands.

"There were countless people, myself included, who saw the disaster looming over Earth," he continued, "but they were ignored. The actions of hundreds of thousands of people could not save an empire that consisted of *trillions* of humans, or even warn them of their impending doom. Instead, the population of the Empire kept marching in step towards the cliff, largely unaware that it even existed."

The remainder of the lecture passed quickly, as he detailed just why the Empire's population had been so unaware of the dangers. Several students stood up to ask questions – intelligent ones, unlike the timewasters he recalled from Earth – and he answered them as best as he could. The feeling of encouraging a student to actually *think* had been rare on Earth, but on Avalon he felt it nearly every day. It was hard, now, to remember how much it had bothered him when he had been exiled from Earth.

"The core of the problem," he concluded, "was that the vast majority of the population took their eyes off the politicians. This gave them free reign to build their political empires, enhance the civil service, take control of the media and gain a stranglehold on power. In the name of decency, they placed restrictions on all communications, making it far harder for dissident views to spread throughout Earth, let alone the remainder of the Empire. We shall discuss the results of such interference tomorrow."

He stepped off the podium, gathered up his notes and watched as the students filed out of the hall. It was smaller than the lecture halls on Earth – Avalon University's entire population of faculty and students would have vanished without trace in Imperial University – but somehow that made it easier to use. Besides, the students here were almost scary in their determination to actually *learn*. The students in Imperial University, apart from a handful of rare exceptions, had always given him the impression that they were just marking time.

But then, Avalon University was a *practical* university and placed a great deal of focus on discipline. There were no extensions for students who didn't finish their coursework on time, no tolerance of students who acted badly in class…and a complete absence of worthless courses that gave the students an impressive-sounding degree and absolutely no job prospects after they graduated. Indeed, now that the technical colleges were up and running too, Avalon University was tending towards pure research, opening up new fields of study that the Empire had believed closed.

Leo didn't know what would happen in the future, but he hoped that, in some small way, he had played a role in reopening the human mind. There were times when he felt slow and stupid compared to his students, the ones who questioned everything with a determination he could hardly match. Earth's attitudes had sunk into his mind more than he had known, he'd realised, when he'd finally put his finger on what was bothering him. Everyone on Earth *knew* that a gravity shield could only protect the prow of a starship, but on Avalon the students were asking *why*…

He heard a cough and looked up to see Colonel Stalker leaning against the wall, waiting for him. Leo felt a sudden shiver running through his body; the last time the Colonel had come to see him unannounced, it had been to tell him that his eldest daughter was missing, presumed dead. Now…Mandy was in the Commonwealth Navy and Mindy was a Knight…

The Colonel must have read his face because he shook his head. "Your family is fine, as far as I know," he said. "*Harrington* just came over the phase limit – Captain Delacroix sent a message here as soon as she arrived."

Leo frowned. "A message?"

"Code Theta," Colonel Stalker said. "We may have some trouble on our hands."

Leo winced. He'd attempted to model the collapse of the Empire, but there were so many variables that all of his models ended up completely chaotic within hours. How could *anyone* hope to predict which worlds would remain loyal, which worlds would fall to warlords…and which worlds would destroy themselves in civil war, once the Empire's iron grip had been removed? The Commonwealth had discovered three worlds that had almost destroyed themselves through infighting… God alone knew how much worse it was going to be towards the Inner Worlds. There were planets where bitter hatreds had only been held in check by the Empire's superior force. But those hatreds had never been exorcised.

Code Theta, however, referred to another contingency. Leo had predicted that the fall of the Empire would eventually lead to successor states; hell, Avalon and the Commonwealth was effectively one such state. Now, if Code Theta had been sent, the Commonwealth had encountered a second successor state…

"I see," he said. "I take it that contact wasn't entirely friendly?"

Colonel Stalker smiled, but it didn't touch his eyes. "You could say that," he said. "I've called a meeting of the Commonwealth Council. *Harrington* has already sent a full copy of the records to Avalon. I would appreciate it if you attended the meeting."

Leo nodded. He wasn't a member of the Council, but he *had* served as an advisor – as well as one of the writers of the Commonwealth Constitution. It had been an interesting – and humbling – experience, one he'd enjoyed more than he'd expected. In the end, they'd ended up with ten pages and a government that – he felt – should work reasonably well.

"I'll come," he said, wondering briefly why the Colonel hadn't simply called him. He knew the answer a moment later. His wristcom was always turned off during lectures. "This isn't going to be good, is it?"

"It never is," Colonel Stalker told him. "Ever."

President Gabriella Cracker looked around the Council Chamber as the Councillors, each one representing a single star system in the Commonwealth, took their seats. It still surprised her that the Council managed to work as well as it did, but they *had* learned a hard lesson about practicalities after the Empire had abandoned the Rim. The survivors of the war that had threatened to tear Avalon apart, or the Admiral's reign of terror, knew better than to waste time with political games.

No one was entirely happy with the Commonwealth's system – which, she'd been assured, was the mark of a good compromise. Some star systems had wanted their entire populations taken into account, while other star systems were politically divided, each faction wanting the right to send their own representatives to Avalon. If the Admiral hadn't concentrated a few minds, Gaby suspected that there would have been no agreement – and no Commonwealth. As it was, the Council would never have the authority the Grand Senate had wielded at the height of its power. There was simply too much scope for misuse.

She allowed herself a quick smile as Colonel Stalker entered the chamber, with Professor Caesius in tow. Their affair was common knowledge; surprisingly, it hadn't reflected badly on either of them. The media had been quick to portray it as two sides in a war coming together to build a better future...which, in Gaby's eyes, proved that the media was either tightly controlled or very silly. There didn't seem to be any middle-ground, although the torrent of new media organisations formed after the end of the Cracker Insurgency had finally given way to a handful that maintained reasonably good standards and a wide readership.

"Ladies and gentlemen, be seated," she said, as the door closed with an audible click. "This meeting is now in session."

She nodded to Colonel Stalker. "Edward, if you will begin...?"

Colonel Stalker stood up and walked over to the display. "Two weeks ago," he said, "there was an encounter in the François System between CSS *Harrington* and a light cruiser formerly under the control of the Imperial Navy – and now in service to a rogue warlord..."

Gaby listened as he outlined everything that had happened, then showed them the sensor logs from *Harrington*. They'd assumed that they would run into multi-system successor states sooner or later, but no one had predicted a violent clash between the two navies. It would make it difficult to negotiate, she realised sourly. Once blood had been shed it was harder to convince both sides to sit down and talk.

"I do not believe that Captain Delacroix could have acted in any other way," Colonel Stalker said. "We could not allow them to just capture the freighter and take the prisoners back to their system…"

"Because the prisoners included one of your Marines," Julian Waterford said, sharply. "Would your Captain have acted any differently if the freighter *hadn't* carried a Marine?"

Gaby winced, inwardly. Julian had long carried a torch for her, even during the darkest days of the war on Avalon…and he'd taken her relationship with Colonel Stalker badly. He was twenty-five and yet he acted more like a teenage brat when the Colonel was involved. Gaby would have sent him out of Camelot if he hadn't been a war hero and an elected representative in his own right. Besides, when the Colonel *wasn't* involved, Julian was more mature than he looked.

"We had no way of knowing what was really going on," Colonel Stalker said, quietly. "Even if there hadn't been a Marine involved, we would have had to know the truth before we allowed them to recapture their prisoners. For all we knew, they could have been pirates. It wouldn't be the first time an Imperial Navy ship turned rogue."

"But this is worse," Gaby said, dragging the conversation back on topic. "A hostile state, controlling the Trafalgar Naval Base…"

"And much of the industry in the sector," Colonel Stalker admitted. "We could be badly outgunned."

"Right," Councillor Yvette Quinn said. She represented Sangria, one of the worlds that had been occupied by the Admiral's forces before the Marines had liberated them. Her homeworld was currently one of the Commonwealth's strongest supporters. "Do we know *anything* about this Admiral Singh?"

"I've conducted a search through the records," Colonel Stalker said. "The closest match we have is Commodore Rani Singh, who was appointed to Trafalgar Naval Base two years before we lost contact with the Empire. Unfortunately, *Singh* isn't exactly an uncommon name and our records haven't been updated." He shrugged. "We think she's the most likely suspect, but there is no way to know for sure."

He tapped the control and an image of a brown-skinned woman appeared on the display, staring down at the councillors. "Her file suggests a slow, but steady rise in the Imperial Navy until she was shuffled sideways into System Command at Trafalgar. *Something* must have happened to her career…"

Julian scowled. "What?"

"It could be anything," Colonel Stalker said. "The files are not precise, but at a guess I'd say she made a powerful enemy. Her files don't suggest the kind of powerful connections most senior officers need to rise above Commodore, so she might just have been pushed aside by her superior. As to why…there are too many possibilities. All we really know is that she didn't screw up too badly."

He smiled at their puzzlement. "Without powerful political connections, she would have been put in front of a court martial for her mistake – if she *did* screw up," he said. "But there is no suggestion in the files that she ever faced a court. Whatever she did wasn't something that could be made public."

Gaby looked up at the woman's face and suspected she knew the answer. Admiral Singh was beautiful. Someone like her would attract the attention of her superiors – and not in a good way. If Avalon's old Councillors had been happy to abuse their position to satisfy their lusts, how would Imperial Navy officers act?

"The situation is as follows," Colonel Stalker said. "We do not know how long it will be before Admiral Singh realises that she's lost a starship. However, given the interrogation reports, we have to assume the worst. She will come looking for us."

"Really," Julian said. "And how do you know that she will *find* us?"

"The cloudscoop isn't exactly a secret," Colonel Stalker pointed out. "If Admiral Singh looks through her records for Rim-ward worlds that could support a fleet, and she will, Avalon will be the most likely suspect. The records won't mention any of the *other* cloudscoops."

Gaby nodded. HE3 was the lifeblood of the interstellar economy, fuelling everything from planet-side fusion reactors to starships making their way between the stars. If the cloudscoop hadn't been built, they would have had to reduce power consumption or fall back on older methods to generate power – which might have been impossible in the time they had left before the HE3 ran out. She'd heard of several worlds that had fallen all the way back to barbarism when their stockpiles finally expired.

The Commonwealth had made a breakthrough when the newly-trained engineering students had started working on new cloudscoops. There were ways to construct them that reduced time, even if they were less efficient than the original cloudscoop. They wouldn't last, Gaby had been told, and required even more maintenance, but they allowed the Commonwealth to diversify its supplies and build up a reserve. And, just incidentally, to boost the fledgling economy.

"Losing the original cloudscoop wouldn't be a complete disaster now," she said, slowly.

"No, but losing everything we've built in this system *would* be," Colonel Stalker pointed out, grimly. "None of the other industrial systems in the Commonwealth have the same level of development – and they won't for years to come. We just have to build too much up from scratch. Losing Avalon would be…disastrous."

"We could talk to her," Councillor Rittman suggested. He represented the industrialists and traders, both of whom depended upon the shipyards being constructed in the Avalon System. "This…incident aside, I'm sure that there is no logical reason for us to fight."

"She's clearly expanding outwards," Colonel Stalker pointed out. "If she was prepared to overwhelm Greenway, she won't hesitate to keep heading Rim-ward until she encounters us. Talking to her could merely draw her attention here too soon."

"And tell her that there's something here worth taking," Gaby added. She'd seen that mindset before, first in the old Council and then in the Admiral's pirates. "We don't dare attract her here until we have some way to deal with her."

"Which raises the obvious question," Julian said. He wasn't *quite* sneering, but Gaby knew him well enough to hear it in his voice. "*Do* we have some way to deal with her?"

Colonel Stalker smiled. "I'm working on it," he said. At least he *sounded* confident. "*Harrington* is due to arrive in orbit in five hours. Once she docks at Orbit Station, we will debrief the crew and defectors – and transfer the other prisoners to a safe holding facility. And then we will decide what to do next.

"Until then, I'm declaring an alert in the system," he added. "We hold regular exercises, but this one will be different. An attack could come at any moment."

Gaby nodded, although she knew that it would probably take several weeks before Admiral Singh's fleet could arrive. "The situation is grim," she said warningly, "but there is no need to panic. We have time to think and act."

And she hoped to God that she was right.

Chapter Six

Furthermore, the strong may act in arbitrary ways. One day, taxes (extorted at what is effectively gunpoint) may be low; the next, they may be high. Those close to the strong will use their influence to gain concessions that may not be open to those without influence. While there is a certain tendency to regard an outright dictatorship as stable, this is only true as long as the dictator remains strong. A state ruled by the strong tends to face civil war when the dictator finally dies.
-Professor Leo Caesius, *Authority, Power and the Post-Imperial Era*

"Home again, home again," Blake said, as the platoon walked into the red light district of Camelot. "I swear…the city just keeps expanding."

Jasmine nodded. Camelot held the university, several of the technical colleges – and, of course, the Commonwealth Council. The city's population had almost quadrupled within the first year of the Commonwealth's existence, even though many of the original settlers had been moved out to the countryside and granted lands of their own. Unsurprisingly, the red light district had *also* expanded, although it was nowhere near as bad as it had been the first time she'd visited the city. The students and other visitors preferred a gentler atmosphere.

She looked up as the larger of Avalon's two moons slowly rose into the sky, casting an eerie light over the city. Other specks of light moved around the planet, each one a large orbital station in its own right; that too had expanded since *Harrington* had departed Avalon to patrol the outer edge of Commonwealth space. It was an odd reminder that even without the Empire, life went on. She caught sight of a group of students making their way into one of the tamer bars and smiled to herself. The young seemed to like the idea of getting along without the Empire much more than any of the Marines. Without it...what were they?

Protectors, she told herself firmly. *And warriors.*

"Here we are," Blake said, as they reached the bar. It had largely been taken over by the Knights when they made their weekly trips into the city; the owner, never one to miss out on a chance to make money, had promptly renamed it the Hard Dazed Knights. "Joe – you're buying the beer."

"It's my bloody stag night," Joe protested, without heat. "I thought *you* were buying the beer!"

Jasmine rolled her eyes as they walked into the bar and found an isolated table in one corner of the large room. The Hard Dazed Knights was tamer than she'd expected, the first time she'd visited, although there were a handful of women dancing on a stage at the other end of the room. Most of the young recruits for the Knights came on their first leave and blew through their wages in a few hours – some things, it seemed, were universal. The same thing had happened on the Imperial Army's training worlds. Jasmine had heard that the Knights had actually considered copying the Imperial Navy and adding courses in money management for the young recruits. She had never been able to decide if such courses were practical or condescending.

"We should hire a couple of the girls," Blake told Joe, as he waved for the waitress. "They could show you a *really* good time."

"I'm getting married," Joe reminded him. "I don't think that Lila would approve."

"Pussy," Blake said. "You're not married *yet*!"

He shook his head. "I don't understand how you managed to convince a girl to marry you," he added. "Doesn't she *know* what you do for a living?"

The waitress came over before Joe could reply.

"Beer for us all," Jasmine said, quickly. "And some snacks."

"*Special* ones," Blake said. "My friend here is getting married soon."

"We offer recreational drugs," the waitress said.

"That's useless," Joe pointed out, crossly. "We can't be drugged…"

"Just normal snacks," Jasmine said, feeling an odd twinge of sympathy for Blake. He and Joe had been friends for years and seeing him married off had to hurt. Jasmine had felt the same when she'd been promoted, even though she'd finally settled down into her new role. "And keep the beers coming."

"It's the thought that counts," Blake said. "Let the world know that we blew half of the platoon's funds on our mate's stag party!"

"I'll let *you* explain the discrepancy in our funds to the Colonel," Jasmine said, dryly. "Or to Sergeant Patterson."

Blake nodded, reluctantly. "Perhaps we should just have a good time," he said. "Plenty of beer will help with that."

The waitress returned with a large tray of beers, which she put down in the centre of the table. Jasmine took one of the glasses, waited until the others had taken their own and then lifted it for silence.

"We are gathered here today," she said, as dramatically as she could, "to say our farewells to a brave soldier, a man who has saved my life on five occasions…"

"Seven," Joe put in, quickly.

"*Seven* occasions," Jasmine corrected herself, "and whose life I have had the pleasure of saving on four occasions in return. I think it is safe to say that 1st Platoon would not be the unit it is without Joe Buckley's constant presence…if only because he sucks up all the bad luck that would otherwise blight our lives."

There were some chuckles. Joe Buckley's record for getting into scrapes and then getting out of them by the skin of his teeth was unmatched throughout the company.

"But now he is taken from us, cut down, removed from the line of battle…"

"Jesus, Lieutenant," Joe protested. "You make it sound like I'm *dead*! I'm only getting married."

"Married?" Blake said. "You might as well be dead!"

"Yes," Sergeant Chester Harris said. "It is the thought of my wife being thousands of kilometres away that warms my heart."

"See?" Blake asked. "A *life* sentence."

Jasmine snorted into her beer. "My friends…I give you Joe Buckley and Lila," she concluded. "May they have a long and happy life together."

"Joe and Lila," the Marines echoed back.

The beer tasted slightly different from the last beer she'd had, although *that* wasn't uncommon on Avalon. There was no shortage of brewers intent on capturing as much of the market as they could, rather than the handful of highly-regulated breweries on Earth, and much of their reputation was made by word of mouth. The better ones could expect to rake in thousands of credits, particularly by selling to the bars near the military bases.

"I can't believe that you're leaving us," Blake said, after several more beers had been ordered and drunk. "We're a *team*!"

"I'm only going to the training grounds," Joe said. "I'll be back in a few months, count on it."

"After several weeks of reconditioning," Harris said, warningly. "It's easy to grow lax on the training grounds."

Jasmine nodded. She'd done a few weeks there herself, serving as a drill instructor, before being promoted to Lieutenant. Harris was right; it was easy to grow lax with one's personal exercise, even though it was important to set a good example. Nothing motivated young recruits more than watching their superiors going through the same exercises – and regularly outpointing them. If the Imperial Army or the Civil Guard had done the same, it might have made both forces far more capable.

"Or you'll stay there, captivated by the sweet Lila," Blake said.

"Go find someone nice yourself," Joe suggested. "You shouldn't keep chasing the whores…"

"You should be backing me up here," Blake objected. "We're comrades! Buddies! We're like…like Caesar and Brutus."

"Brutus *killed* Caesar," Harris pointed out.

"Well…Macbeth and McDonald," Blake said, after a moment's thought.

"That's Duncan," Jasmine corrected. "And *Macbeth* killed Duncan."

Blake scowled into his beer. "Well, Romeo and…"

Joe lifted his fist threateningly.

"I was going to say Mercutio," Blake said, quickly.

Harris snorted. "Wasn't he killed by a member of Romeo's family?"

"You know what I mean," Blake said. He scowled down at his beer. "Can't we order something that actually gets us drunk?"

"There isn't anything that really makes us drunk," Harris said. "But I think you've drunk too much anyway. Flush it out of your system."

Blake gave him a cross look. "If there isn't anything that can get us drunk," he said carefully, "what is the harm in drinking more beer?"

Jasmine made a show of considering it carefully. It was true; Marines couldn't really get drunk – and, if necessary, they could flush it out of their system. But alcohol did cause a buzz if the Marine let it happen.

"Just drink water for a while," she said, finally. "And I'll drink water too."

"Yes, mother," Blake said.

Harris leaned forward, capturing their attention. "I was chatting to Sergeant Hampton," he said, changing the subject. "From what he was saying, we may end up going underground and fighting an insurgency against Admiral Singh."

"That would be…bad," Joe said. "Can she blow through the defences here?"

"Possibly," Harris said. "But then, she's also been moving industrial nodes back to her base on Corinthian. That should limit her ability to expand for a while."

Jasmine scowled. The Empire – and the Commonwealth, to some extent – had worked hard to decentralise their production nodes. Losing Earth would be painful, but the Empire's economy would survive; hell, if they lost the bureaucrats who insisted on painstakingly going through every regulation before granting approval to businessmen, the economy might improve rapidly. But if Admiral Singh was concentrating her industry on Corinthian…

She'd been right. It *did* imply weakness.

But it might not matter, she reminded herself firmly. One Marine might be outnumbered by a platoon from the Civil Guard, but the Marine should still be able to win a fist fight.

"But she'll see us as a threat," Jasmine reminded them, again. "I think we might have to assume the very worst."

"Yeah," Harris agreed. "I just hope the Colonel has something good up his sleeve."

"There's nothing we can do about it now," Blake said, dryly. "It's time to give Joe a good send-off."

Jasmine watched Blake heading over to several of the waitresses, then turned her attention back to the beer. She'd grown used to being the senior officer, even if there was an uneasy balance between the comrade she'd been and the senior officer she'd become. Normally, a newly-promoted Lieutenant would have been transferred to another platoon, maybe even out of the company completely. *That* wasn't an option on Avalon.

Hampton's words had bothered her more than she wanted to admit. Somehow, she'd always assumed that the Slaughterhouse would be safe and that the Marine Corps would have regrouped there if *something* had happened to Earth. But who knew what had happened thousands of light years away? Even the more muted rumours they'd heard from traders – and the handful of enemy crewmen willing to talk – had suggested that a firestorm had swept through the Core Worlds. The thought of what modern weapons could do when unleashed on a heavily-populated planet was terrifying.

She'd felt alone ever since she'd realised – truly realised – what command actually *meant*. Now, she wondered if they were alone in the universe…

It seemed impossible that the remainder of the Marine Corps had been wiped out, but it had also seemed impossible that the Empire could ever abandon worlds it had settled and protected for so long. Marines would do their duty as long as they could, yet if chaos swept across the Core Worlds the Slaughterhouse might be destroyed in the crossfire. And the Corps had enemies…one of them might take advantage of the opportunity to attack the Slaughterhouse directly. For all she knew, the Slaughterhouse might be radioactive ruins by now…and the remainder of the Corps had been destroyed.

"That's the price of command," Harris said. "*Worrying*."

Jasmine gave him a sharp look, wondering how he'd read her mind.

"Long experience," he said, answering her unspoken question. "It is a Sergeant's job to keep the Lieutenants aware of their own shortcomings."

Jasmine shrugged. "I can discuss my shortcomings later," she said, watching as Blake clambered onto the stage to dance with two of the girls. "Should I start worrying about *Blake*?"

Harris gave her a sharp look. "You've never had someone in your platoon marry before?"

"No," Jasmine said, flatly.

"It always causes problems," Harris warned her. "You know how a platoon is meant to work – all of the members must trust one another perfectly, forsaking all others." He gave her a droll grin. "Someone getting married and having children messes up the balance. All of a sudden, they can no longer afford to put the platoon first. It's natural for the married man's teammates to feel that they've been abandoned by someone who was very close to them."

Jasmine nodded. Marine Corps regulations banned sexual relationships within the Corps, but Marines were very close to one another, close enough to fuel all sorts of jokes by soldiers from the Imperial Army. Joe's departure would hurt Blake; they'd been partners for nearly four years. Blake had even turned down an offer of a stint at the training grounds himself, just to stay with the platoon.

Maybe they thought I was a traitor, she thought, sourly. Promotion was an expected part of a Marine's career, particularly if one had the talent to do well at higher levels. But promoted officers were not normally left in command of their former comrades…she shook her head, dismissing the thought. She would just have to do the best she could.

"We shall hope for Joe's safe return," she said, stiffly. Reaching into her belt, she produced her terminal and opened it up. "Keep an eye on Blake for a while."

"That might be difficult," Harris observed. "Blake's found a new friend."

Jasmine looked up in time to see one of the dancers leading Blake into a hidden stairwell. The upper levels of the building were separated into tiny bedrooms – without, she'd been informed, any sound-proofing. Not that she'd been up there herself; it was easy for a male Marine to find companionship from the opposite sex, but far harder for a female. They tended to intimidate the men.

"Let's hope that he doesn't get kidnapped again," she said, looking back at her terminal. As always, the device had picked up hundreds of messages for her as soon as she'd logged into the system-wide network, mostly junk. On Earth, there had been all kinds of regulations covering the use of the planetary datanet to advertise products, most of which had been completely ineffective. It hadn't been until much later that she'd realised that the regulations were really intended to keep the datanet from being used by dissidents. "We might not be so lucky this time."

Harris snorted. "There isn't a war on yet," he said. "I'll keep an eye on all of them."

Jasmine nodded, skimming through the important messages. There was a brief note that several new prototype weapons were available for testing and asking if 1st Platoon would be interested, then a handful of messages from Mandy, including one that asked if she wanted to meet up when she was next on Avalon. Jasmine checked the Marine network and discovered that 1st Platoon was still officially on leave, then sent a message back asking Mandy to let her know when she would be planet-side.

She smiled, remembering how Mandy had grown up – and how she'd beaten the Admiral almost single-handedly. It was hard to maintain a friendship outside the Marine Corps, but there were times when Jasmine thought that Mandy was all that kept her sane. She couldn't really *talk* to the rest of the platoon and most of the officers seemed far in advance of her.

The evening wore on, with the remainder of the Marines finding their own companionship – and trying to drag Joe into joining them. Joe seemed rather more defiant than any of them appeared to expect, even when three waitresses removed their tops and tried to cuddle up to him. Jasmine had to laugh at their expressions when he pushed them away, scowling towards Blake. His friend's sense of humour was sometimes thoroughly weird.

"Hey, I could take *you* upstairs," one of the waitresses said, looking directly at Jasmine. "I don't bite."

"No, thank you," Jasmine said, silently promising Blake the most unpleasant punishment duty she could imagine. It *had* to be his idea of a joke. "I *do* bite."

She looked over at Harris and smiled. "Make sure they get back to barracks in time for roll call," she ordered, as she stood up. "And try not to break *too* much furniture."

"Yes, Lieutenant," Harris said.

Jasmine walked over to Joe and stuck out a hand. "I wish you the very best with your marriage," she said, as he took it. "And I will do my best to ensure that we can come to the wedding."

"I've got Blake lined up to be my best man," Joe said. "He'd better come to the wedding or I'll have to pull someone random off the street."

Jasmine chuckled. "Good luck," she said. "And don't let Blake get you down."

She walked out of the bar and headed down the street, back towards the spaceport. The cool night air washed away what remained of the alcoholic daze, leaving her feeling merely tired. It was normal to feel tired easily when on leave, she'd been told, but she didn't understand it at all. Maybe everyone was just too tense during operations.

Her terminal bleeped. Mandy was in orbit; according to her, she'd be planet-side in two days. Jasmine replied, promising to meet if she could, then returned the terminal to her belt and kept walking. Once she was back at the barracks, she could sleep. God alone knew how long it would be before 1st Platoon was thrust back into action.

Not long enough, she thought. *Or maybe it won't be soon enough.*

CHAPTER SEVEN

Managing the transition from ruler to ruler is vitally important for stability – and where, as I noted above, so many dictatorships have failed. Monarchy, the evolution of rule by the strong, works by guaranteeing an understandable succession, one backed up by society itself. In theory, civil unrest and instability can be avoided – and, by granting vast power to the monarch, society will be ruled by someone strong enough to keep the rest of the strong in check. In practice, this often depended upon the character of the monarch himself. Weak monarchs lost power to their nobility…and, eventually, the countries they ruled started to fragment.

-Professor Leo Caesius, *Authority, Power and the Post-Imperial Era*

Dawn broke over the Mystic Mountains, sending rays of sunlight beaming over the city and down into the Council Hall. Edward opened his eyes as the light shone through the window, feeling, as always, slightly out of place. The Presidential Residence was very definitely not his bunk on Castle Rock. Shaking his head, he swung his legs over the side of the bed and stood upright, then walked over to the window and gazed out over the city. Camelot was slowly coming to life.

The debate over where and how the Commonwealth President should live had taken almost as long as the debate over the Constitution, with one side arguing that the President should live frugally and the other side claiming that the President should have a residence appropriate to the dignity of the office. Eventually, Gaby had ruled that she would have the uppermost floor of a mansion that had belonged to one of the old councillors – and turn the rest of the building into offices. It wasn't a perfect compromise, but it was probably the best they could do. Besides, by law, the President was restricted to one term in office.

He smiled to himself as Gaby stirred, awakening slowly. She'd once led the Crackers...which had forced her to stay on her toes, ready to run in the event that their hiding place was discovered. Now, she slept deeply and *relaxed*, something she could never have allowed herself while the war was still being fought. Edward allowed himself a moment to admire her as she sat upright, the blanket falling away to reveal her breasts, then he turned and walked towards the shower. There was no time to lie in bed.

His terminal bleeped as he switched it from sleeping mode to active, allowing the messages that had acuminated overnight to drop through the buffer and into his inbox. Edward surveyed them quickly, attaching his electronic signature to a handful that needed his approval, then put the terminal down as he entered the shower. Compared to a Marine barracks, the bathroom was staggeringly luxurious.

But the Grand Senators would turn their noses up at it, he thought, dryly. He'd seen enough of the luxury the Empire's upper classes surrounded themselves with to know why they'd become so corrupt. Power corrupted...but so did luxury – and getting what one wanted as soon as one wanted it. He'd done what he could to ensure that the Commonwealth's leadership didn't go the same way, yet there was no way to guarantee that it would never happen. The next few generations would just have to keep a closer eye on their leaders.

He stepped into the flow of running water and washed the sweat from his body, closing his eyes as he ran the water over his face. A moment later, he heard the door and opened his eyes, just in time to see Gaby entering the compartment and joining him under the water, her hands clutching his back. As always, she seemed drawn to the scars that no amount of regeneration treatments could erase. Edward felt his body react as her fingers touched him and sternly pushed the feeling down. They didn't have time.

A soldier who won't fuck won't fight, the naughty part of his mind pointed out. The saying dated all the way back to Major General Kratman.

But then, he'd also commented that a soldier who fucked when he should be fighting wouldn't be fucking or fighting in future.

"I have to go," he said, after a brief exchange of kisses. "I'll see you in the chamber?"

"If you know what you want to do," Gaby said. "Do you have any clear plan yet?"

Edward scowled. It had been two days since *Harrington* had returned to Avalon, two days during which he'd supervised the interrogations of the defectors and studied the files, grimly aware that inaccurate information could get people killed. On the face of it, the Commonwealth Navy was outgunned four to one – at least. If Admiral Singh had captured other ships, including units from several planetary defence forces, the odds were probably stacked even more against the Commonwealth. And her crews were actually competent...

He wasn't an expert in ship-to-ship combat, but he'd studied both the raw records from *Harrington* and the reports from the analysts. They'd concluded that Admiral Singh's crews were far more disciplined than the pirates – no surprise there – and that they were probably kept firmly under supervision too. If there were other unhappy conscripts on the ships, they were unlikely to be able to damage the ships or defect. They'd probably be kept in near-complete ignorance of the universe around them.

"I have half a plan," he said. It had been gelling in his mind ever since he'd read the debrief records. "It's just incredibly dangerous."

How much did Admiral Singh *know*? The question had been bothering Edward ever since *Harrington* had returned home, even though it was impossible to answer it. If she knew about the Commonwealth, she might send her ships to Avalon sooner rather than later – too soon for Edward's planned operation to take effect. But if she didn't know...he shook his head. He should know better than to bother himself with unanswerable questions.

"Let me know when you have a workable concept," Gaby said. "The Council will want to approve it."

Edward nodded, ruefully. He'd worked hard to ensure that the Commonwealth Council didn't have the ability to interfere in military decisions, beyond setting the overall objectives of any operations, but it had ensured that the Council took a careful look at any planned missions. Not that that was a bad thing, he was prepared to admit; the Grand Senate had either meddled or insisted that too much be done with too little. But it also meant that maintaining security was almost impossible.

And it will grow harder if the planetary forces have to be called in, he thought. Each Commonwealth planet was responsible for its own groundside defence, ensuring that there was no need for a single Commonwealth Army. The system had its advantages – the Council claimed that there was no force to bully planets into falling in line – but it also had its weaknesses. It wouldn't be long, Edward suspected, before some worlds started refusing to exercise their armies against other armies. But how else could they learn?

He walked back into the main room and picked up his uniform, his hands pulling it on without any real thought. Unlike the Scouts, the Knights or the Commonwealth Navy, the Marines had kept their old uniforms, even though they had belonged to the Empire. Gaby had expressed her concern over that, pointing out that it might upset factions that were glad the Empire was gone, but Edward had insisted. The uniform belonged to a tradition that dated back to the days before the Unification Wars. Besides, there were barely eighty full-fledged Marines in the Commonwealth. There was little hope of training up new Marines.

Gaby stepped back into the main room, wrapping a dressing gown around her body. Edward felt an odd twinge running through his heart, wondering just where their relationship was going. On Earth, everyone would expect it to last as long as it lasted, with no recriminations when it ended, but Rim worlds tended to take a more serious view. They should be considering marriage…and yet she was the *President*. There was no way that marriage wouldn't cause problems for her career.

"I've got a meeting at Castle Rock," he said awkwardly, giving her a brief hug. "I'll call you once I know what I'm doing."

Gaby smiled, kissing him on the lips. "Be seeing you," she said. Her smile grew wider. "Try not to be seen as you slip out of the back door."

Edward was still chuckling at the thought as he walked down the stairs and out of the main entrance. The President's security was provided by a team of Knights – for patriotic reasons, Gaby had insisted that Avalon's home-grown military guarded her and the rest of the Council – but it was still miniscule compared to the layers of security that surrounded the Grand Senators on Earth. He nodded to the guards as they checked his ID, then waved him towards the gates, even though he had his doubts over the security. It would be alarmingly easy for a handful of trained soldiers to put the President's life in serious jeopardy.

But we can't risk having the President lose touch with the ordinary man, he thought, sourly. There were times when he felt that they carried the whole concept too far. *And yet it only takes one nutcase with a gun to change history.*

He pushed the thought to one side as he walked over to the aircar and pressed his fingertip against the sensor, allowing it to confirm his identity and open the door. There were only a handful of aircars on Avalon; there was little point, Edward had been told, in constructing more when the planet was nowhere near as congested as Earth. The only people who were allowed to use them were government and military officials. Climbing inside, he engaged the autopilot and ordered it to take him directly to Castle Rock, then unhooked his terminal from his belt. There were no shortage of messages that weren't considered urgent, but needed a glance anyway.

I spend too much time doing paperwork, Edward thought, as the aircar headed out over the ocean. In hindsight, accepting the position of Supreme Commander of the Commonwealth Military might not have been the cleverest move if he'd wanted to avoid paperwork. But he'd wanted to ensure that it was kept as low as possible. *Damn it!*

He smiled ruefully as Castle Rock came into view, illuminated by the rising sun. The island had been barren when the Marines had arrived, but three years of development had turned it into a formidable military base, complete with training grounds, barracks and office buildings. Edward gritted his teeth when he saw the latter; he'd given strict orders that no officer was to spend longer than six months at a desk, rotating them in and out of combat or training assignments. It helped to avoid the problems paper-pushers in the Imperial Army had caused for the fighting men, but it also created its own problems. Every solution seemed to cause new problems.

The aircar dropped to the ground near the main building and Edward climbed out, keeping his hands in view. Unlike Camelot, Castle Rock's facilities were guarded by armed Marines – and, even though his aircar had been allowed to pass through the defence screen, they wouldn't take chances. He'd done what he could to spread their facilities out, but an attack on Castle Rock could still prove disastrous. The Marines recognised him as they strode towards the aircar, yet they checked his ID implant anyway. Edward would have reprimanded them if they'd done any less.

Command Sergeant Gwendolyn Patterson met him as he stepped into his office, looking – as always – briskly efficient. She'd refused to be rotated out to the training grounds, choosing to move between serving as an NCO when Edward took command of a platoon and serving as his assistant when they were in the office. Edward suspected that there would come a time when he would have to give up command completely; it was unlikely that Stalker's Stalkers would ever deploy again as a single unit. Even now, forty of his Marines were scattered over the Commonwealth, providing the training and discipline that the local forces needed desperately.

"Colonel," she said, saluting. "The latest intelligence reports are on your desk."

Edward returned the salute, then groaned. "Anything useful from the prisoners?"

"Nothing much, beyond basic details," Gwendolyn said. "The intelligence staff were suggesting that we could move to more…*rigorous* methods of interrogation."

Edward shook his head. "They're not pirates," he said. "We can't brutalise them."

"The defectors don't know enough," Gwendolyn said, playing devil's advocate. "If we use truth drugs…we might be able to interrogate them without them ever realising that they *had* been interrogated."

"We accepted their surrender on honourable terms," Edward reminded her. "We can't force them to talk if they don't want to talk."

He could understand her point – and why the intelligence officers were so frustrated. They were almost blind; the defectors simply didn't know everything Edward needed to know. But at the same time...mistreating the prisoners would be bad policy. It would almost certainly come back to haunt them. And it would be grossly dishonourable.

Besides, he reminded himself, the techniques for erasing a person's memory were simply unreliable – and they left markers in the brain. The first thing Admiral Singh's medics would do when they were returned would be to check for conditioning, which might well reveal that *something* had been done to their minds. And then the medics would keep hammering away at the memory blocks until they broke.

"No," he said, as he sat down behind his desk. "We won't interrogate them any more rigorously than we have."

Gwendolyn nodded, looking neither pleased nor displeased.

Edward flipped open the file and read it quickly. Five enemy crewmen had chosen to defect; three of them conscripts from Corinthian. They'd all told the same basic story; Admiral Singh had arrived in their system, established her authority and taken control. And then she'd started conscripting everyone who had the training and experience she needed to help build her empire. Having faced his own manpower problems, Edward could understand exactly what drove her to drag in as many people as she could.

One of the other defectors had been a crewman on a freighter before being conscripted into Admiral Singh's forces. *His* story was a little different from the others; he'd noted that freighter crews had been granted exemption from conscription, as long as they paid their taxes. But his father, the CO of an independent freighter, had tried to cheat...Edward winced. Taxes on interstellar shipping *always* dampened the economy.

The fifth defector had been a crewman on Trafalgar before Admiral Singh had taken control. He'd confirmed that Admiral Singh had once been Commodore Singh, but he hadn't been able to add anything else to their growing stockpile of knowledge. Reading the transcript, Edward realised that the defector had been a loser, someone who had little ability or inclination to try to climb to higher positions. He was mildly surprised that Admiral Singh's forces had even *tolerated* the man.

He turned back to the transcript from Elliot Canada and read through it again carefully, considering the different possibilities. It wasn't a surprise that Corinthian had had a faction of the Democratic Underground on the planet, or that Admiral Singh had managed to eliminate most of its members within weeks of her arrival. But there would be remnants, surely. It was something that could probably be exploited, given time...

"Contact Captain Caesius and ask her to come to Castle Rock as soon as possible," he ordered. "Once she confirms, invite Lieutenant Yamane and Sergeant Hampton to join us."

"Yes, sir," Gwendolyn said. "Do you have a plan?"

"I very much hope so," Edward said.

It wasn't going to be easy – and it wasn't going to be something *he* could direct. In fact, he would have preferred a team of Pathfinders – or some of the even *more* secretive units – to handle the mission, one he could disavow if necessary. There was no way that *he* could take command; it would be far too revealing. Even allowing the junior lieutenant to take command was risky.

But the risk is already present, he thought, and scowled. Every interrogation suggested that Admiral Singh was determined to snatch up as much territory as possible. There was no reason to believe that she would leave Avalon alone, particularly once she realised just how rapidly the Commonwealth was advancing. Edward had read her file carefully and realised that she was likely to be very dangerous. Anyone who had advanced so far in the Imperial Navy without powerful connections would be extremely competent indeed.

"Captain Caesius says that she can be here in an hour," Gwendolyn reported, tapping her wristcom. "Do you want to move the meeting to the secure room?"

Edward nodded. "Post an armed guard outside," he said, flatly. "We don't want *anyone* to hear of this until it's too late."

Gwendolyn smiled. "Does that include the President?"

Edward hesitated. If the entire operation exploded in their face, which was a very strong possibility, Gaby would want to be able to swear blind that she hadn't known anything about it. On the other hand, she had insisted on knowing what was going on – and *someone* outside Castle Rock would have to know.

"I'll brief her personally," he said, shaking his head. "After we have a working concept, that is. We may discover that the whole plan is unworkable."

He looked down at the transcript, scowling. How much time did they have before the shit hit the fan?

Not enough, he thought, remembering the days when they'd moved from system to system, hunting the Admiral's forces. A single mistake could have cost them everything. *We never have enough time.*

CHAPTER EIGHT

> Worse, all of the dangers inherent in having a tyrant (with the possible exception of solving the succession crisis) also applied to having a monarch. A monarch could be influenced by his cronies, a monarch could change the rules at a whim – the stability often came with a high price tag. In effect, one problem had been solved, but the others remained in being.
> -Professor Leo Caesius, *Authority, Power and the Post-Imperial Era*

"Jasmine!"

Jasmine looked up in surprise and saw Mandy Caesius running towards her, wearing the blue uniform of the Commonwealth Navy. The girl still seemed surprisingly young, even though she'd been through hell when she'd been a pirate captive – and slave. But then, she'd thrown herself into her new career in the navy, using it to overcome the scars on her soul.

"Mandy," she said, in honest delight. "I thought you weren't coming down until the evening!"

"Colonel Stalker called me down," Mandy said, as she wrapped her arms around Jasmine and hugged her tightly. "He didn't say *why*."

"He wouldn't have done," Jasmine said, looking up at the main building. "Shall we go inside?"

Mandy nodded, allowing Jasmine to lead the way into the building. The Marines on guard duty vetted them both – Jasmine couldn't help noticing that male eyes followed Mandy everywhere, despite the uniform – and pointed them towards the secure room. There were two more Marines on guard duty outside the room, both wearing light combat armour and carrying heavy rifles. *Someone* was taking security very seriously. Jasmine surrendered her terminal and wristcom to the guards – Mandy seemed more reluctant to surrender either – and stepped through the heavy door. Inside, the silence was almost deafening.

"It's quiet," Mandy said, softly. Her voice sounded odd under the suppressor field. "Why are we here?"

"You can't operate any surveillance equipment in a secure room," Jasmine said. "If we happened to be carrying a bug, it wouldn't work in here."

The heavy door – almost an airlock – opened again, revealing Colonel Stalker, Sergeant Hampton and Command Sergeant Patterson. Jasmine stood to attention and saluted; Mandy followed, a little more hesitatingly. Powerful men who demanded respect reminded her far too much of the pirates – and how they'd treated her. Colonel Stalker, thankfully, understood – or at least didn't make an issue of it.

"At ease," Colonel Stalker ordered. "Please take a seat. We don't have much time."

Jasmine obeyed, unable to avoid noticing how Mandy took the seat furthest away from the Colonel. She saw a flicker of sympathy on the Command Sergeant's face before it was veiled behind a usual unreadable mask. Technically, Jasmine outranked the Command Sergeant, but she'd always looked up to the older woman. She'd forgotten more than Jasmine had ever learned as a Marine.

"The situation is as follows," Colonel Stalker said. He ran quickly through the full story, from the encounter with the refugees to the interviews with the prisoners – and defectors. "We must assume that Admiral Singh will attack as soon as she realises we exist – and because of the encounter with *Proud*, she is likely to realise sooner rather than later."

Jasmine nodded. Making sure that everyone was on the same page was tiresome – she'd attended too many briefings where the officers would say the same thing over and over again, just to make sure that it had been memorised. The Imperial Army had been particularly bad at briefing its troops. There were times when Jasmine had wondered how they all managed to go in the same direction once the operation was launched.

"If it comes down to a straight fight, we will lose," the Colonel continued. "The sheer disparity in firepower will see to that."

There was a faint gasp from Mandy. She'd spent the two years since her escape from the pirates helping to build the Commonwealth Navy. They'd done an amazing job, Jasmine knew, but they hadn't even begun to match a standard sector fleet's tonnage. In hindsight, concentrating on light units might have been a mistake, even if they *had* needed to protect their shipping and purge the pirates from Commonwealth space.

"But we have improved on many Imperial Navy systems," Mandy protested. "Won't they give us an advantage?"

"Not enough of one," Colonel Stalker said, quietly. "Admiral Singh will take more casualties than she expects, if she comes here, but she *will* win. Given a couple more years, we could prevent her from getting into range of the planet itself..."

He scowled. "We won't have that time," he warned them. "Right now, the clock is ticking. We have to act fast."

Jasmine nodded, although she honestly couldn't see what they could do.

"Admiral Singh's position seems to be basically insecure," Colonel Stalker said. "There is good reason to believe that she faces opposition on Corinthian. The Democratic Underground might have been scattered, but there were other groups on the planet – and new ones, now that she is holding the planet in an iron grip. We can use them to our advantage. Lieutenant" – Jasmine straightened to attention – "I want you to lead a team to Corinthian."

Jasmine blinked in surprise. "You want to *help* rebels?"

"There is a certain irony, I admit," Colonel Stalker said. "We fought to suppress a revolution on Avalon and now we're attempting to encourage one, but I don't see any other choice. If we can give Admiral Singh enough problems on her base of operations, she won't be able to come after us."

"Buying enough time to build up our defences," Mandy said.

Jasmine frowned at her tone. There was a...*ruthlessness* in Mandy, one that had developed after her time with the pirates. It bothered Jasmine, even though she knew that *she* would probably be accused of ruthlessness too. The girl who'd been a spoilt brat before coming to Avalon might well go over the line the Marines had been trained to avoid at all costs.

"Quite," Colonel Stalker said.

"A little hard on the inhabitants," Sergeant Hampton pointed out. His gruff voice seemed to capture their attention effortlessly. "She was quite willing to bombard Greenway into submission. What makes you think that she won't do the same to Corinthian?"

"It's her centre of operations," Colonel Stalker said. "If she uses planetary bombardment, she'll be hurting herself as much as she hurts the rebels."

"It's not going to be pleasant for anyone," Hampton said. "Even if she *doesn't* use planetary bombardment, and I don't think we can count on it, there are still hundreds of other ways to control a population, particularly one trapped on the planet. The rebels will be massively outgunned."

"I know," Colonel Stalker said. "I just don't see any other choice."

Jasmine considered the plan. If it worked, they would buy time for Avalon. But even if it succeeded, the damage to Corinthian's population could be devastating. The Empire had plenty of experience in holding entire populations in bondage. Even slipping down to the planet could be incredibly difficult. If Admiral Singh was as competent as her file suggested, she would have purged all of the incompetent officers from her crews. That alone would boost efficiently and morale by an order of magnitude.

It *would* be devastating. But she couldn't think of anything else.

"They have a cloudscoop," Mandy pointed out. "Why don't we destroy it?"

Colonel Stalker gave the younger girl an oddly respectful look. "Not a bad idea," he said, "but they'd have their cloudscoop as heavily guarded as our own. Slipping close enough to destroy it might be difficult."

"Besides, they have other cloudscoops," Sergeant Hampton added. "And probably vast stockpiles of HE3."

Jasmine nodded. The Rim might not be able to produce much HE3, but the systems closer to the Core Worlds were each supposed to have a cloudscoop of their own. Given how easy it was to operate the scoops once they'd been built, it was simple to build up a stockpile in case of emergency. Earth, according to rumour, had built up *billions* of tons of HE3, hiding the supplies on the edge of the system. Admiral Singh might be hurt if they took out the cloudscoop, but it wouldn't prove fatal.

"It's worth bearing in mind," she mused, out loud.

"Mandy will take command of one of the light freighters," Colonel Stalker said, "with a crew made up of disguised naval personnel. Officially, the ship will be registered to Williamson's Freehold, which will disguise her origins neatly. The cover story will say that the crew was stranded for several months in an isolated system, then obtained some fuel and headed to Corinthian in hopes of buying more."

Mandy coughed. "We might want to suggest that the freighter is buying HE3 for the system," she said. "That would give us a good reason to visit Corinthian."

"You can work out the cover story," Colonel Stalker said. "Just make sure that it holds enough water to avoid attracting suspicion."

Jasmine smiled at Mandy's expression. The Marine Corps delegated as much as possible to the officers on the spot; having Mandy, who would have to carry out the mission, construct her own cover story made a certain kind of sense. Jasmine would check the story, of course, but it would be Mandy's responsibility.

"You need to get the team down to the planet," Colonel Stalker continued. He looked over at Jasmine. "I can't tell you what to expect when you get down to the surface. The defectors don't know the current state of affairs. We also might not be able to get any messages or supplies to you once you're down."

"And if you're captured," Hampton added, "Admiral Singh's people will likely shoot you out of hand."

"It is a known risk," Jasmine said. "We won't be in uniform."

She scowled. There *were* ways to slip through a planet's orbital defence network, but they were risky as hell. A single mistake could draw attention from the planet's defenders and then they would be dead.

"We're going to need to spend some time lurking in the outer edge of the system, gathering intelligence, before committing ourselves," she added. "We might also want to cause a diversion to distract them when we enter the planet's atmosphere."

"It's in your hands," Colonel Stalker assured her. "You may call upon anything you require from the stores."

"We might need a second freighter," Jasmine said, slowly. She would have to call the platoon back to barracks and then go over the basic concept with them. Blake and Joe – she winced as she remembered that Joe wouldn't be coming with them – had more experience than herself. They might well have a few ideas for making the whole idea work properly. "Can we draw some missile pods too?"

"Just older missiles," Colonel Stalker said. He held up a hand. "I don't think I need to remind you that this is *not* to be discussed outside your platoon."

Jasmine nodded. "Can we take Mr. Canada with us?"

"I've already agreed to escort him," Sergeant Hampton said. "If he causes trouble…"

He drew a finger across his throat. Jasmine rolled her eyes.

"Sergeant Hampton has been reactivated for the duration of the crisis," Colonel Stalker said. "He and two of the other escapees have volunteered to accompany you – the others will be routed into the defence force here."

"Seniority won't be a problem," Hampton assured her. "I can happily go back to being a Rifleman if you wish."

"Sergeant will do for now," Jasmine said, concealing her amusement. Retired Marines often didn't *stay* retired. "You can be responsible for looking after the rest of your people until we check you out on the equipment."

She scowled. Taking Marine combat armour to Corinthian would be far too revealing if Admiral Singh's forces discovered them. There were some ex-Imperial Army battlesuits they'd captured from the pirates, but they weren't in very good condition, although they did have the advantage that they didn't have to be personalised. But then, if they showed up with a large amount of weapons and equipment, hard questions would be asked in any case. Admiral Singh probably didn't like the thought of people carrying weapons on her world.

"You can set the mission up," Colonel Stalker said. "Just keep me informed of your decisions."

"Yes, sir," Jasmine said. She felt a strange mixture of excitement and fear; it *was* exciting, something she'd never done before…but at the same time, it was terrifying. There would be no support to help her or her Marines escape the consequences of her own mistakes. "When do you want us to depart?"

"Within the week," Colonel Stalker told her. "I don't want to give Admiral Singh any more time to realise that she's lost a ship than we can avoid."

"Understood," Jasmine said. She scowled as another thought struck her. "The platoon will miss Joe Buckley's wedding, unless we can bring it forward..."

"I can perform the ceremony at any time," Colonel Stalker said, wryly. "Tell him...tell him that the platoon has to leave within the week and ask if he wants to move the ceremony forward. If he agrees, we can alter the other schedules to accommodate the guests he wanted to invite."

Jasmine nodded. The plan had been to hold a private, Marines-only ceremony on Castle Rock and then hold a more public ceremony in Camelot. Joe Buckley might have to go weeks between the two ceremonies, but...she smiled, ruefully. If he didn't want to change either, she would support his decision.

Colonel Stalker looked over at Mandy. "Do you understand what you have to do?"

"I'll coordinate with Jasmine," Mandy said. She sounded a little nervous, now that she'd finally realised just what they were trying to do. "Two freighters...they're both going to have to be old build. We might want to bring a stealthed destroyer along as well."

"Send me the list of requirements and I will approve it," Colonel Stalker said. He stood up, formally ending the meeting. "Don't fuck up."

Jasmine nodded. "No, sir," she said. "We won't."

She looked over at Sergeant Hampton. "I'll be holding a full muster of the platoon this evening," she added. "You and your friends – and Mr. Canada - are welcome to come, but we'll be going into lockdown immediately afterwards until we depart. Make sure they understand that, all right?"

"I'll make them understand," Sergeant Hampton said. "After what we went through on Greenway, I'm sure we can endure a few days of lockdown."

Jasmine stepped through the hatch and recovered her terminal and wristcom from the guards. The terminal bleeped, informing her that Sergeant Harris had taken most of the platoon out for a punishing run around Castle Rock, leaving her feeling oddly guilty that she hadn't joined them. But then, she had been summoned to face the Colonel instead…

"Jasmine," Mandy said, catching up with her. "Do you want to join me for a drink?"

"Sure," Jasmine said, after a moment of hesitation. She would have to download the files on Corinthian, then read through the interview transcripts again…there was just too much that they would have to do. And if they failed to find a way to slip down to the planet, the entire operation would have to be aborted. "Just remember…no shop talk."

Mandy nodded as they stepped out of the main building and walked towards the coffee shop. Alcohol was strictly prohibited on base, with threats of dire punishment handed out to recruits on their first orientation talk, even though it couldn't affect the Marines. Not, Jasmine considered, that it really mattered. The coffee was very good.

"It's been too long," she said, as they sat down with a mug of coffee each. "How have you been?"

"Shipping backwards and forwards," Mandy said. "And yourself?"

"Shipping backwards and forwards," Jasmine said. They shared a laugh. "I think you've probably been doing more interesting missions than me."

"I don't know," Mandy said, thoughtfully. "I handed *Sword* over to her new Captain four months ago, then spent two more months commanding one of the new-build cruisers. It was quite exciting."

Jasmine smiled. "I bet you never thought that you would command a starship while you were on Earth," she teased. "Aren't you glad you came?"

Mandy nodded. "I still wonder what happened to my friends at times," she admitted. "And then I'm glad to realise that I'm out here, well away from Earth."

"It took you long enough to realise it," Jasmine said.

Mandy flushed. "I was a stupid brat," she said. She shook her head, firmly. "Michael found someone else. It shouldn't bother me, but it does. Why?"

"Poor emotional control," Jasmine said, deadpan. She smiled at the girl's shocked expression. "It's been two years since you dumped him. Do you want him back?"

"Yes…no…I don't know," Mandy admitted. "There are times when looking at him reminds me of everything and times when I just want to crawl into his arms and hide. Does that make sense?"

"I think you were promoted too far while too young," Jasmine said. Marines went through hell before receiving their tabs, but the ones who couldn't take it were weeded out before they reached the Slaughterhouse. Mandy hadn't volunteered to be enslaved by the pirates for several months. All things considered, she'd done extremely well. "How are you coping with command?"

"Fairly well," Mandy said, softly. "There are just times when…when I feel unsteady."

"Make sure that you have a steady XO," Jasmine said, wondering if she should take her concerns to Colonel Stalker. The last thing they needed was a starship commander having a breakdown while the ship was in combat. "And watch yourself carefully."

"I hope we'll have more chances to spar while we're in transit," Mandy said, grimly. "I need to *learn*."

"I'll do my best," Jasmine promised. Mandy had taken to unarmed combat like a duck to water, although she would probably never match Jasmine or Captain Delacroix. It wasn't an uncommon reaction among liberated pirate captives. "And I'll keep an eye on you."

It bothered her, more than she wanted to admit, that Mandy showed almost no reaction to her words.

CHAPTER NINE

The eventual shift to parliamentary democracy moved the source of power from the monarch's person (and lineage) to the people. Power was vested in a representative body that could overawe the strong and, at least in theory, provide both stability and an ability to overcome the succession issues that had plagued earlier states. When there was a clear idea of how the next leader was to be selected (and eventually replaced) it was possible to plan ahead, far more so than in any other state. Furthermore, as the parliament (however named) was elected by the population at large, it was difficult to question its legitimacy.

-Professor Leo Caesius, *Authority, Power and the Post-Imperial Era*

Jasmine scowled as she straightened her dress uniform, silently grateful that she didn't have to wear the gaudy designs favoured by the Imperial Army or the Civil Guard. Marine dress blacks were formal without being too spectacular or uncomfortable, but she didn't know any Marines who actually *liked* wearing them. But there was no choice.

Besides, she thought, *four days in lockdown was quite bad enough.*

A trumpet blew and she straightened to attention, followed rapidly by the rest of the Marines. "Company…present…arch," Command Sergeant Patterson bellowed. "Mate and match!"

Jasmine unslung her rifle from her shoulder and held it upwards, forming one half of an arch. The other half was formed by Sergeant Barr, who had taken two hours off the training field to attend the wedding. Jasmine kept her expression blank as Joe Buckley, flanked by

Blake, appeared at one end of the line of Marines and marched down the middle of the arches. At least they'd been able to come out of lockdown early enough to rehearse the ceremony before it actually began. Forming the marital arch didn't look difficult, but it was harder than it seemed.

Joe Buckley stopped in front of Colonel Stalker and saluted. After a long moment, Colonel Stalker returned the salute, then motioned for Joe Buckley to step backwards.

"Dearly beloved," Colonel Stalker said, in a soft voice that seemed to carry to the edge of the field, "we are gathered here today to witness the marriage of Rifleman Joseph Buckley to Lila Namath, a woman who has shown her willingness to enter our family. We welcome her to the fold."

Jasmine turned to look as Sergeant Howell, standing in for Lila's father, escorted her through the rifle-formed arches. The girl wore a white dress and a veil that hid her face, although her dress was tight around her breasts and hips. She certainly *looked* to have a good figure, Jasmine decided, wondering why Joe hadn't seen fit to introduce Lila to the platoon beforehand. But then, Blake would probably have scared her off, wrecking the platoon's unity in the process.

Lila stopped in front of Colonel Stalker and bobbed a curtsey to him. The Colonel saluted her in return, then looked past her towards the rest of the Marines.

"Form ranks," Command Sergeant Patterson ordered.

The first time Jasmine had heard that order, back in Boot Camp, it had been a disaster; the Drill Instructors had not been impressed as the recruits crashed into one another. Now, the platoon moved smoothly into lines behind the happy couple, showing their support – and, Jasmine realised in a moment of irrelevance, blocking their line of escape. She couldn't help wondering, as Colonel Stalker cleared his throat, if that had been deliberate. Both parties could have backed out well before the ceremony got underway.

"Marriage is a commitment," Colonel Stalker said. "Those who marry into the Marine Corps join something far greater than the sum of their parts. Their partners are as much as a part of the Corps as those who have suffered through the Crucible to win their Rifleman's Tab. They are there to support their partners – and through them, the Corps. It is no small commitment – and it is no shame to admit that it is beyond one's ability to handle."

He was right, Jasmine knew, although a civilian would have difficulty in understanding it. A military position was far more than just a common *job*; a military partner suffered stresses and strains that had torn thousands of marriages apart. It wasn't uncommon for a wife to be separated from her husband for months, if not years…and then only to see her husband for a few weeks before he was called away again. She would raise their children alone, without enough help or support…and, if the husband was badly wounded, she might even end up taking care of him as well.

The Marine Corps tolerated marriages and did its best to support them, but it often wasn't enough. Jasmine had worked her way through Boot Camp and then the Slaughterhouse; Lila hadn't…and couldn't really understand what was going to happen until she experienced it. Jasmine could only hope that what she and Joe had formed was strong enough to last the decades, because Joe couldn't stay at the training grounds indefinitely. Sooner or later, he would go back on active duty and leave Avalon for weeks or months at a time.

She smiled ruefully at Joe's back. At least a male Marine *could* get married. Marriage was often the end of a female Marine's career.

"Lila Namath," Colonel Stalker said, quietly. "Will you take this man as your lawfully wedded husband, forsaking all others, in sickness or in health, to be with him until death do you part?"

"I do," Lila said, softly.

"Through him, you are marrying the entire Marine Corps," Colonel Stalker added. "His duties will impose upon you – and you will owe duties to the Corps yourself. Will you accept this burden?"

Jasmine felt a tear prickling at the corner of her eye. Military wives *had* to work together; they were the only ones who understood what their fellows were going through. A Marine's wife was an Auxiliary even though she'd never been within a thousand light years of the Slaughterhouse, one who was vitally important to the morale of her husband's platoon – and, for that matter, for the other wives. At least Lila wouldn't have to deal with wives from the Imperial Army. The senior ones often believed that they shared their husband's rank.

"I will," Lila said.

"Joseph Buckley," Colonel Stalker said. "Do you take this woman to be your legally wedded wife, forsaking all others, in sickness and health, until death do you part?"

"I do," Joe said.

Command Sergeant Patterson raised her voice. "Where is the ring?"

Blake made a show of searching through his pockets, then produced a tiny box from his sleeve. Colonel Stalker took the box and opened it gently, revealing a simple gold and silver ring. Normally, wedding rings for Marines were produced on the Slaughterhouse – in their own way, they were as unique as Rifleman's Tabs – but this one had been produced by a jeweller in Camelot. It would be replaced if contact was ever re-established with the Slaughterhouse, Jasmine knew, but it just didn't seem likely.

Maybe we need to start producing our own Rifleman's Tabs, she thought. It was against tradition, but so much tradition had already been dented when the Empire withdrew from the sector – and much further towards the Core Worlds, if the defectors were to be believed. Admiral Singh would not have dared move against the Empire so openly if she believed it still posed a threat. After all, previous rebellions by military officers had drawn a sharp response.

Colonel Stalker held the box in front of Joe Buckley. "Take the ring," he ordered, quietly, "and place it on her finger."

Joe obeyed.

"With this ring," Colonel Stalker said, "I pronounce you man and wife. You may now kiss the bride."

Joe gently pulled the veil aside and kissed Lila on the lips. Jasmine smiled when she saw the girl; she looked fragile, but there was an inner strength and determination that might just keep her going when times grew hard. And she clearly loved Joe…she joined in the cheers and whistles as the kiss grew longer and longer, before they finally separated, still holding hands. Blake wolf-whistled cheerfully and Joe tossed him a look that promised bloody revenge in the future.

"We shall now proceed to the mess," Command Sergeant Patterson ordered. "Form ranks behind the couple and advance!"

―――

Edward allowed himself a smile as the Marines followed Joe and his new wife into the mess hall, which had been specially decorated for the occasion. The cooks *had* joked about feeding the happy couple on standard rations, but after they'd pushed the joke as far as they could they'd consented to produce a proper wedding cake and a decent meal. One advantage of serving on Avalon was that it was easy to obtain proper food. There was no need to tolerate the algae bars of Earth when planet-side.

It was a pity that Gaby couldn't join them for the ceremony, he thought, let alone the handful of other Marine wives who had either followed the company from Earth or married Marines after they had arrived on Avalon. Tradition was tradition, however; the wives would meet Lila officially later, although Gwendolyn had ensured that she'd had a chance to meet them before the wedding. The stories they'd told obviously hadn't put the poor girl off. But then, Joe Buckley was a good Marine, even if he was also a trouble magnet. Perhaps a stint on the training grounds would be good for him.

There was no rank in the mess, at least not when there were no visitors from the Imperial Army or the Civil Guard. Edward had attended enough post-conference dinners hosted by Imperial Army officers to understand why they kept running into trouble; the vast majority of the officers had simply lost touch with their men. The worst ones issued orders from a safe distance, never noticing or caring that the orders were unmatched to the situation. It worried Edward, the more time he spent behind his desk, that he might lose touch too. Micromanaging was a deadly temptation.

He watched with some private amusement as the cooks put a large dish of roast meat in front of the happy couple, then started to serve the rest of the Marines. Gwendolyn growled a command that they'd damn well better not get used to being served, but she was smiling as she said it. Edward took his own plate and started to eat, realising that the cooks had spent *hours* preparing the dinner. It would be wrong not to eat as much as he could.

Lieutenant Yamane didn't seem to be having problems with the platoon, but that was going to change. Edward had had enough experience to know that taking someone out of the unit *always* caused problems, particularly when there was no time to retrain properly. In some ways, that wasn't a bad thing; 1st Platoon couldn't take its standard weapons and armour to Corinthian. But it prevented the newcomers from being properly integrated into the unit. Even the most experienced Marines had their quirks that had to be accounted – and then compensated – for.

And then Blake Coleman was likely to turn into a problem, if he didn't find a new partner soon.

Edward surveyed 1st Platoon thoughtfully, making a mental note to have a brief talk with Sergeant Harris before the platoon departed on its mission. Rifleman Carl Watson had transferred over from 4th Platoon; unlike most of the other Marines, he had experience in fitting into a completely new unit. Sergeant Howell had noted that Watson was a joker, but when the chips were down he performed very well. He would have to overcome the stigma of replacing a beloved member of the platoon, yet he'd done that before. Harris would ensure that the right steps were taken.

And beyond that, it isn't your problem, Edward told himself, sternly. *You cannot micromanage an operation several hundred light years from Avalon.*

Once the meal was finished, Blake Coleman stood up to give the traditional speech.

"I had a lot of stories to tell you about Joe – a freaking great mass of stories to tell you – but he threatened to reveal certain incidents on our first shore leave if I talked about them in public," Blake said. He leered cheerfully around the room, ducking the handful of vegetables thrown at him by various Marines. "I ran through hundreds of them and he vetoed them all, even the one about..."

He whistled tunelessly for a long moment. The Marines chuckled.

"But the memory that sticks in my mind was the day we were ambushed on Han," Blake said, more soberly. "Everything was chaotic back then; half of the units on the planet didn't know what the other half were doing... it was a freaking nightmare. There we were, patrolling through a small complex of houses, when some bastard flips a switch and we're suddenly being fired on from all angles. We later discover that the Imperial Navy officers who were watching from orbit were tricked; the insurgents had hacked their systems and edited the waiting ambush out of the records. After that, we learned a few lessons…

"We were pinned down," he continued, returning to the original story. "The situation is grim; the bullets are crawling towards us and we don't have anywhere to go. Joe pulls out a grenade launcher and starts laying down fire, hurling grenades in all directions. He must have hit *something* because the fire started to slack off, just long enough to let us run towards the nearest house. We throw grenades through the murder holes some ingenious insurgent has cut in the walls, then crash in through the door. There's no one inside.

"We think – *hey, this is a good place to hole up* – and start using the building as cover. A moment later, the floor shatters and we fall down… right into the shitter. It turns out that the villagers used it as a communal shithole; no luxury toilets in that nameless hellhole, no sir! All seven of us fell right in…all I'm saying is thank God for nasal implants, know what I'm saying?"

There were some chuckles from the Marines who hadn't been there at the time.

"And then – and *then* – Joe starts babbling about fart gas and what would happen if some idiot strikes a match," Blake said, when the chuckles had died down. "We can't help it; we're swimming in the shit and we're laughing our asses off. We're still laughing when four Raptors bring two additional platoons as reinforcements. And Joe even asked them if they wanted to join us!"

His face darkened. "Word got around and everyone outside the platoon took to holding their noses every time we walked past," he added. "Good thing we were in the middle of a war, you know. We would have put inter-unit relations back a few months.

"Joe is very good at getting into trouble," he concluded. "But he's also very good at getting out of trouble. I think that Lila and Joe will have a very long and happy married life together."

He raised his glass. "Lila and Joe!"

Edward concealed his surprise. Either Blake had had an epiphany or Sergeant Harris had had a few words with him. But then, remembering Han might have concentrated his mind on the more important matters in life. The planet had been utterly nightmarish, not least because Imperial Intelligence had been so badly misled in the early weeks of the war.

Gwendolyn nudged him after four other speakers had feted the happy couple – and told stories about Joe that were reasonably clean.

"Your turn, sir," she said.

Edward stood up. Maybe there was no rank in the mess, but he still got silence quicker than the other speakers.

"When I went to the recruiting booth," he said, "the Sergeant manning the desk told me that there were three certainties in life; death, taxes and the Terran Marine Corps. Whatever happened, the Marines would stay true to the legacy of honour and service left behind by their predecessors, a legacy that was founded in the days before humanity's explosion across the galaxy. The Empire would be eternal – and so would we.

"It seemed so simple back then. What could shatter the Empire? Humanity's domains scattered across hundreds of thousands of light years. There were millions of settlements, playing host to a population so vast as to be literally unimaginable. We might lose battles, we might see systems fall to rebellion or even outside attack, but we never doubted that we would win the war.

"But the Empire has fallen, destroyed by its own weight."

He took a breath. "In its wake, we are left with a series of unprecedented questions," he continued. "What is the proper state of affairs? Which government do we support – do we fight for? Can the Marine Corps even survive without the Empire?

"There are those who will say that even to *ask* such questions is treasonous. We are sworn to the Empire, but it has abandoned us – and far more than just us. What is the value of our legacy when the Empire is gone?

"We are a brotherhood, forged in war, that exists to defend our society," he said. "*That* is the true value of the Marine legacy, an unbroken record of protection and service. *That* is what we will keep with us and pass on to the next generation. Here, on Avalon and throughout the Commonwealth, we have built a society worth protecting with our lives.

"There is a new threat on the horizon, the latest in a series that may never end," he concluded. "But we will meet it, and defeat it, because we are Marines. The few, the proud, the faithful."

He looked over at 1st Platoon, feeling a wave of pride as they stood straighter. "Enjoy yourselves tonight," he said, quietly. "Tomorrow…you will go to war."

CHAPTER TEN

However, this tended to cause problems of its own. When the elected politicians lost touch with their people, they started inching towards supreme power – little caring that they were doing irreparable damage to the political system. It didn't matter if they were convinced that they were doing what was in the best interests of their people or if they were motivated by personal ambition; either way, they were damaging the system. In effect, the arbitrary power that had blighted dictatorships and monarchies could also rise to threaten the democratic system.

-Professor Leo Caesius, *Authority, Power and the Post-Imperial Era*

"This is going to be a hell of a mission."

Layla looked down at the operational plan, then up at Lieutenant Yamane. The Marine had come onboard and requested a private conference in Layla's stateroom. "I'm surprised the Colonel allowed you to request *Harrington*," she added. "She isn't actually a stealth boat."

"Stealthy enough to sneak around a heavily-defended star system," Lieutenant Yamane assured her. "This system isn't guarded by a handful of half-assed pirates."

Layla nodded. *Harrington* hadn't been specifically designed for covert operations, but it was relatively easy to remain undetected as long as one avoided making any betraying emissions or moving too close to enemy sensors. Space was incomprehensibly vast and a starship, even one of the massive colonist-carriers, was nothing more than a speck of dust on such a scale.

On the other hand, they needed accurate readings from Corinthian – and they could only get those by slipping close to the planet…

"We should be able to get the data you want," she said, finally. "And then we'll be there to support you if necessary."

"If necessary," Lieutenant Yamane agreed.

She didn't *sound* doubtful, Layla noticed, but Marines were trained not to show doubt or hesitation, even when a rational mind would have quailed. Even if Admiral Singh *hadn't* improved Corinthian's defences after she'd taken the world for herself, it would still be tricky to get down to the surface without being intercepted and destroyed. If the sensor networks were even half as capable as the networks surrounding Earth, it would be impossible.

Shaking her head, Layla looked down at the operational plan. At flank speed, it would still take nearly a month to reach Corinthian, a month when too many things could go wrong. By now, Admiral Singh would know that she'd lost a starship – and might even have a rough idea what had happened to it. The possible scenarios kept running through Layla's head; if Admiral Singh dispatched a squadron to retrace the destroyed cruiser's flight path, they would encounter the Commonwealth. And then…?

"We'll leave in an hour," Lieutenant Yamane said. "Did your crew get some shore leave?"

"They spent most of it in the Black Hole," Layla said, referring to the RockRat-produced and operated entertainment facility in orbit around Avalon. It seemed an unnecessary expense, but it was cheaper than sending spacers and orbital yard dogs down to the surface at the end of their shifts. "I think they were happy when they came straggling back."

Lieutenant Yamane grinned. "I'm glad to hear it," she said, as she stood up. "There are just a few final preparations to make and then we can depart."

Layla watched her walk through the hatch, then looked back down at the datapad. The coolly rational part of her mind told her that *Harrington* wouldn't make a difference if she stayed with the Commonwealth Navy, not if Admiral Singh came knocking with her entire fleet. They'd be outgunned…probably quite badly. But the rest of her felt bad about leaving her comrades behind, knowing that they might fight and die without *Harrington*. Maybe she should have urged Lieutenant Yamane to pick a different vessel as her escort.

But we already know what we're facing, she told herself, as she stood up. There were no shortage of tasks *she* had to attend to before they departed, if only because she didn't have a proper XO. The shortage of trained and experienced personnel forced her to act as her own XO, or pass certain responsibilities down to the lower ranks. If they'd had the manpower pool the Imperial Navy had been able to call upon...

She shook her head. If they'd had the manpower pool *Admiral Singh* could call upon, they'd be controlling half of the former Empire by now.

No one would have considered *Lightfoot* beautiful. The freighter was a blocky shape built for functionality rather than elegance, studded with a handful of sensor nodes and a couple of visible weapons. *They* were technically forbidden by Imperial Law, but before the Empire had withdrawn from the Avalon Sector the freighter crew would have simply bribed any inspecting officials to ignore them. Even popguns could deter pirates if the freighter *looked* willing to fight.

Jasmine watched through the porthole as the shuttle headed down towards the docking port on the underside of *Lightfoot's* hull. Up close, *Lightfoot* looked old; her hull was pitted and scarred by hundreds of years in space, passed down from owner to owner. The design itself dated back thousands of years, one that had never really gone out of service. But then, unlike military starships, there was no real need to continually improve freighter designs. Or so the Empire had believed.

The three starships – *Lightfoot*, *Billy Butcher* and *Harrington* – were holding position on the edge of the Avalon System, just outside the Phase Limit. They were far from prying eyes, but Jasmine had taken the precaution of disseminating a cover story, just in case the pirates still had eyes and ears in the system. Anyone who asked would see two freighters carrying newly-constructed farming equipment, escorted by a heavy cruiser that just happened to be going in the same direction. It was unlikely that any pirates would risk their ships – and their lives – just to steal farming equipment, particularly equipment specifically designed for a low-tech planet.

There was a dull thump as the shuttle's airlock mated to the freighter's, then a hiss as the pressure equalised, allowing Jasmine to leave her seat and step into the freighter. As always, the new ship smelt different, although nowhere near as bad as a pirate ship. But then, freighter crews tended to actually take *care* of their ships. They had the discipline that pirate crews often lacked, even when commanded by a truly fearsome officer.

Sergeant Harris met her as she stepped through the second hatch. "Welcome onboard," he said, one hand saluting her. "We've moved most of our makeshift gear to *Butcher*, then set up on *Lightfoot*."

He didn't sound happy about the makeshift gear. Jasmine didn't blame him. *She* wasn't happy either, even though it had been her idea. If they had to pose as mercenaries, something they'd done before, they couldn't use Marine equipment or uncomfortable questions would be asked. It was possible that pirates wouldn't notice the difference, but Admiral Singh certainly would if she saw the gear. They'd just have to suck it up and deal with the makeshift equipment. At least they'd managed to maintain it better than the pirates they'd taken it from.

"Good," Jasmine said, allowing him to lead her down the metal corridor. The freighter seemed oddly barren compared to some of the others she'd seen. They'd have to do something about that or it might alert an experienced observer. "What about our other cover story?"

"Everything is set up," Harris assured her. "If we have to make open contact, we can pose as a freighter crew or a group of mercenaries."

Jasmine nodded. Ideally, she would have preferred to avoid all contact with Admiral Singh's forces – they dared not assume that Admiral Singh would be as incompetent as the pirate leaders – but there might be no choice. If they had to make contact, they'd just have to hope that the cover story held up under scrutiny. At least it would be fiendishly difficult to disprove without sending a starship on a two-month round trip.

On the other hand, if they captured a copy of Marine records, they might be able to ID us, she thought, sourly. Marine records were meant to be classified, eyes-only to senior Marines, but there had been a copy at Trafalgar Naval Base. Admiral Singh could have captured the files, or simply subverted the Marines serving on the base. Jasmine had wondered why they hadn't done anything to stop Admiral Singh from taking power. Could it be that they'd *joined* her?

It was unthinkable. But so much else that should have been unthinkable had already happened.

She pushed the thought to one side as they stepped into the compartment that had been put aside for the Marines. It was surprisingly comfortable, certainly when compared to a more standard transport vessel, although there were no bunk beds for the Marines. Instead, mattresses had been laid on the deck and covered with homespun blankets produced on a low-tech world. They should pass for products from Gordon's Hope. According to the files, Gordon's Hope exported almost nothing outside its own system.

"These mattresses are very comfortable," Blake assured her, from where he was lying on the deck. "The freighter crew must be slipping."

Jasmine snorted. "We shall have to suffer in luxury, just this once," she said, dryly. The platoon – she noticed, with a pang, the absence of Joe Buckley – came to attention, allowing her to inspect them briefly. "And we will have to rehearse our cover story until we have it word-perfect."

It would be easy to pose as mercenaries; mercenary companies were famous for taking anyone with experience and not asking too many questions. Jasmine had heard that it had been common for a soldier to serve out his first five-year term in the Imperial Army and then move to join a mercenary company, where pay was better and there were fewer officers who hadn't earned their commissions on merit. The last report had suggested that entire regiments were making the shift from army units to mercenaries, although it hadn't been very clear. By now…

If things had been a little different for us, she asked herself, *would we have become mercenaries too?*

She had a sudden vision of Imperial Army units becoming mercenaries, moving from world to world and fighting on behalf of their paymasters, even fighting their former comrades. Mercenaries had been big business before the Empire's withdrawal from the sector; now, without even the thin veneer of law the Empire had enforced on the companies, it would only get worse. In some ways, it would be preferable if they just seized power for themselves.

"As long as they don't look too closely," Hampton pointed out. "We don't all *look* as if we'd come from Gordon's Hope."

Jasmine nodded. Gordon's Hope had been founded, like so many other low-tech colonies, by a single ethnic group, a religious sect that disdained contact with the outside universe. They would all have the same skin tone…and her platoon did not. It was quite possible that other refugees would have been stranded there, but it might be hard to convince suspicious customs officials that was what had actually happened. Gordon's Hope would be very much a last resort for spacers. The world had nothing that outsiders would actually *want*.

Apart from food and women, she thought, sourly. Quite a few low-tech worlds had been brought into line by the Admiral and forced to pay tribute – protection money – to his forces. The Marines had liberated several dozen girls from various pirate bases, only to discover that they were no longer welcome on their homeworlds. Most of them had eventually wound up settled on Avalon.

"We can tint our skin, if necessary," Jasmine said, finally. She cleared her throat. "We will also be running exercises every day, as best as we can, starting tomorrow. Get plenty of sleep."

She smiled at their expressions. It was difficult to carry out proper exercises without the right equipment, but Marine-grade systems would be far too revealing. She'd had a heavily-modified VR entertainment system installed on the ship – she hadn't been surprised to discover that half of the pre-installed entertainments were pornographic – yet it had its limits. But they'd just have to make do with what they had.

"And we'll also have to work through the files," she added. The more eyes reading through the files, the less likely it was that they'd miss something important. "They're on the ship's datanet and will be accessible from tomorrow."

She dismissed the platoon and looked over at Sergeant Hampton. "Are your people settling in all right?"

"Kate and Steve seem to be doing fine," Hampton said. "The Captain was kind enough to assign them small cabins; they're not used to bedding down with other people. Even in the militia they never shared sleeping compartments with the opposite sex. I've also done my best to prep them for exercises, but..."

He allowed his voice to tail off suggestively. Jasmine understood; the militiamen wouldn't have had the years of experience enjoyed by even the rawest Marine. It wouldn't stop them being capable – she'd seen some semi-legal planetary militias that looked better than the Civil Guard – but it would take them time to blend in, if they ever did. On the other hand, if they were posing as mercenaries, they shouldn't show the polish of a Marine unit. It might raise too many questions.

"We'll see how they do," Jasmine said. In her experience, militiamen didn't do so well away from their own homeworlds. "And Mr. Canada?"

"Has a cabin of his own," Hampton said. "He *was* interrogated pretty thoroughly. I think we can trust him, at least to some extent."

Jasmine scowled. *Trustworthy* was not a word she had been taught to apply to defectors, no matter how useful they were. She knew that the interrogators had gone through Canada's brain with a fine-toothed comb, checking for everything from dishonesty to conditioning and memory modification, and they'd found nothing. And she couldn't blame Canada for wanting to see Admiral Singh defeated. But trusting him completely still went against the grain.

"We'll add him into the exercises too," she said, reluctantly. They'd need him when the time came to make contact with the underground on Corinthian, assuming it still existed. Admiral Singh's forces might have clamped down so hard that resistance was futile. "And you can keep an eye on him."

"It will be my pleasure," Hampton said. "Babysitting is always fun."

Jasmine recalled a handful of reporters who had been attached to the Marines on Han and smiled. None of them had been prepared for the war...and very few of their dispatches had ever been distributed around the Empire. It hadn't been until much later that she'd learned that the reporters had no control over what was actually broadcast as *news*. Articles, footage and suchlike that didn't fit the official story was simply discarded, no matter how much effort the reporters had put into filing it.

But the reporters had had to be babysat at all times. They hadn't known the simplest things about being on a battlefield; she'd heard that one of them had even tried to pick up an unexploded mortar shell the insurgents had fired into a military base. God alone knew how many of them had been seriously injured through simple ignorance; Jasmine had even heard that one particularly stupid reporter had tried to get an interview with an insurgent and had been raped, tortured and murdered for his pains.

"Matter of opinion," she said. She looked over at Harris. "I'll be on the bridge."

The freighter bridge looked far less orderly than a military starship's bridge, she couldn't help noticing. There had originally been an order to it, but years of refits and equipment updates had changed it beyond recognition. Consoles were scattered everywhere, attached to systems that had been added to the hull or simply placed inside the bridge. The freighter's small crew, wearing an assortment of uniforms and shipsuits, looked just as disorderly.

Mandy was standing in front of a console, studying it thoughtfully. "We can replace that system while we're in phase space," she said, as she saw Jasmine. "Everything ready?"

"Yes," Jasmine said. "We can depart now."

Mandy smiled. "Making the ship *look* like it has been poorly maintained without actually damaging anything isn't easy," she said. "But we wouldn't have access to proper supplies on Gordon's Hope."

Jasmine nodded and stepped backwards as the younger girl began to bark orders. Her crew might have looked unprofessional, but they clearly knew what they were doing. But then, freighter crews that *didn't* know what they were doing ended up dead. They just didn't have the manpower to cushion the impact of incompetent officers and crewmen, unlike the Imperial Navy.

She felt a dull throbbing echoing through the deck as the phase drive came online, powering up for the jump into phase space. Mandy spoke briefly to the other two Captains, then issued the order. Jasmine felt space twisting around them – a more uncomfortable sensation than it would have been on a military starship – a moment before they lurched into phase space. Two of the other crewmen looked a little green; an uncomfortable transition could make less experienced crewmen sick, or worse. There were people who literally could not endure travelling in phase space and had to remain in stasis for the entire trip.

"We're on our way," Mandy said, softly. "One month to Corinthian."

"Plenty of time to think and plan," Jasmine agreed. The journey would be boring, but she had a feeling that they'd wish they were still in transit when they finally arrived. They would be completely on their own. "Let me know when you're ready to spar."

With that, she walked back down to the Marine compartment. Like the rest of the platoon, she needed her sleep. Tomorrow they would start exercising in earnest.

Chapter Eleven

> On the face of it, this seems absurd. How could politicians act against the interests of those who put them in power?
> -Professor Leo Caesius, *Authority, Power and the Post-Imperial Era*

Corinthian was *hers*.

Admiral Rani Singh stood in front of the massive window and stared out over Landing City, admiring the shining towers that surrounded the former Governor's mansion. Corinthian had been settled for over seven hundred years and had been the sector capital for five hundred, giving its inhabitants an excellent series of opportunities to milk the sector for all it was worth. The governorship had been a prize for the Empire's most well-connected officials; even in times of economic hardship, they'd still managed to make vast amounts of money through bribes and corruption.

She smiled coldly as she remembered the previous Governor, a short fat man who had amassed a colossal fortune. He had never really realised the doom overshadowing the Empire – and his comfortable post – until it was far too late. Rani's ships had arrived in orbit, seized the high orbitals after a brief battle and forced him to surrender, promising safe conduct back to the Empire. She hadn't had any intention of keeping that promise; as soon as the governor and his family had boarded one of her ships, she'd had them transported to Penance. The thought of the Governor, an aristocrat in all but name, struggling to survive on the hellish world never failed to keep her warm at night. And his family would be lucky if they were only forced into slavery by the convicts who had made themselves the rulers of the penal world.

Once she'd imprisoned and exiled most of the senior civil servants – and the most deeply corrupt officials – she'd installed her own people in the system, ensuring that she held power firmly in her grasp. It hadn't been easy to do it without destroying the system, but her demonstrated willingness to use force had helped smooth the way. Most civil servants were little more than cowardly bullies; quite willing to pressure those without the ability to strike back, but folding as soon as they faced someone with real power. Splitting up the civil service into two competing entities had probably helped too. Both entities struggled mightily to embarrass the other, competing for her favour.

And, as long as they were competing, they weren't joining forces to oppose her.

Trafalgar had had the fleet base, a small population of camp followers…and little else. Her *new* base of operations had a vast population, a sizable industrial base even before she'd started raiding nearby star systems for their industrial facilities…and no shortage of useful resources like HE3. It might not be able to match the massive industrial nodes built up in orbit around Earth, but given time it would provide the resources to conquer a small empire for herself. And her heirs, once she'd had them. She certainly didn't want her empire to break up after her death.

She looked down towards the streets, watching as they slowly came to life. They looked like ants from the mansion, scurrying around…every single one of them working, directly or indirectly, for her. It had been easy to win them over at first, to convince them that she had their best interests in mind…and when she'd shown the iron fist under the velvet glove, it had been far too late for them to resist. Not that it would have mattered, in any case. As long as she held the high orbitals, her position was invulnerable.

Her wristcom buzzed. "Admiral, Director Horn and Vice Admiral Sampson are here to see you," Carolyn said. Her aide was one of the most faithful people she had – and well she might be, when anyone who overthrew Rani would kill her as their first step towards consolidating power. Carolyn had more power than her formal title suggested and Rani had allowed her to abuse it, just enough to make enemies. It kept her firmly under Rani's control. "Should I send them in?"

Rani turned, surveying the former Governor's office. It was larger than the stateroom Admiral Bainbridge had enjoyed on his flagship, large enough to serve as a tennis court, and strikingly luxurious. Rani had considered herself thoroughly cosmopolitan and yet she'd been astonished when she'd seen the sheer luxury the Governor had surrounded himself with, no doubt funded by bribes. Even so, she was surprised that he'd had *any* fortune left by the time she'd overthrown him.

"Yes, please," she ordered. "I'm ready for them."

She strode back towards the Governor's chair and stood in front of it, hands clasped behind her back at parade rest. A moment later, the door opened, revealing two very different men. Vice Admiral Sampson was tall and almost inhumanly handsome – like Rani, his family had spliced genetic improvements into their DNA for centuries – while Director Horn was short, mousy and looked like just another civil servant. Rani wrinkled her nose as the little man came to some semblance of attention. He was *necessary*, but that didn't mean that she had to *like* him. Besides, the air always seemed to smell unpleasant when he was around. Who would have thought that such a little man could be so depraved?

"Be seated," she ordered, and sat down on the Governor's chair. It was almost an exact copy of the Emperor's Throne from the Imperial Palace on Earth, an artefact that might no longer exist if the rumours were true. The Governor had clearly wanted to impress his visitors, suggesting that he had been overcompensating for something. Maybe he'd known, deep inside, just how fragile his position truly was. Or maybe it had been more basic.

She met Sampson's eyes. Genetic modification wasn't the only thing he had in common with her; he'd had his own career destroyed by a superior officer with more clout than common sense. He would have spent the rest of his career languishing on a cloudscoop mining facility if Rani hadn't discovered him, read his record and decided to offer him a vitally important role in her new empire. Sampson hadn't taken more than a few seconds to decide to throw his lot in with her, despite the oaths he'd sworn to the Empire. But then, the Empire hadn't bothered to keep its side of the bargain.

"Report," she ordered.

"*Proud* is definitely missing," Sampson said, flatly. "She chased the refugee freighter to François, a new colony world seven light years from Greenway...and vanished. Commodore O'Hara conducted a brief survey, but found nothing."

Rani kept her face expressionless as she considered the possibilities. Any serving officer with a lick of sense knew that accidents happened – and that some starships vanished in phase space, never to be seen again. But *Proud* had been in hot pursuit of a freighter; her disappearance while engaged in such a mission might not be a coincidence.

"If the ship vanished in phase space, there might be nothing to find," she mused, out loud. "But we know there's another power forming Rim-ward, don't we?"

"Oh yes, Admiral," Horn said. "Our intelligence assures us that it is there."

It was harder to keep her face expressionless when Horn spoke. Rani knew more than she wanted to know about his disgusting habits, even if those habits *did* make him very useful – and loyal, because anyone outside her circle who discovered the truth would execute him on the spot. And Horn had been opposed to her planned intelligence-gathering efforts, including allowing independent traders to operate in exchange for sharing what they saw with her intelligence officers. He'd seen it as giving rogue elements too much independence.

She needed no display to visualise her empire – and the unexplored reaches of space surrounding the worlds under her control. What was happening core-wards? She'd heard rumours, picked up refugees...but there was little hard data. And yet, if *she'd* taken power, why not other Admirals? There could be other empires forming out of the ruins of *the* Empire, each one a potential threat to her. Her fleet was powerful enough to overawe the sector, but it was tiny compared to the rest of the Imperial Navy. How much of it was still intact? There was no way to know.

It was unlikely that any power forming rim-ward could actually threaten her position, she knew; they would be forced to build up an industrial base and a navy from the ground up. Depending on what they had available, it could take them decades – or more – before they posed a genuine threat. By then, she would have overrun them – assuming, of course, that stronger powers hadn't overrun her. It was quite possible that the rumours that spoke of outright civil war burning through the Core Worlds were accurate.

"So it does," she said, thoughtfully.

"Commodore O'Hara reports that his squadron is ready for an immediate attack in retaliation," Sampson added. "I believe that he intends to hit François."

"Denied," Rani said, sharply. It would take nearly ten days to get the order to Commodore O'Hara; she'd given him specific orders not to press any further rim-ward, but he might well act on his own authority. She knew better than to try to direct his every move from seventy light years away. "Besides, if there *was* another ship, it wouldn't have come from François."

Sampson nodded. They'd both looked at the files; François was a newly-settled world, barely seventy years old. Indeed, lacking a gas giant, it had lagged behind most of the other worlds in the sector; it hadn't even been *settled* until a group of outcasts had been shipped there and told to make the best of it. Development corporations wouldn't waste their time with a world that could never become an industrial powerhouse. No, François didn't have *anything* more than a handful of in-system spacecraft. It couldn't have taken out a light cruiser on its own.

"There is an alternate possibility," Horn suggested. "The ship might have been sabotaged."

Rani had already considered that possibility, before dismissing it. Sabotaging a ship wasn't easy – and the fleet's security precautions were extensive enough to make it impossible for a conspiracy to form without being detected. It would have taken a disloyal senior officer to destroy the cruiser single-handedly – and she had taken steps to verify their loyalty before promoting them.

"We should enhance our security precautions on the starships," Horn continued. "We need to ensure that the crews are loyal..."

"They won't *stay* loyal if we push the precautions too far," Sampson snapped. It was an old argument; like most bureaucrats, Horn wanted to expand his domain, while Sampson wanted to keep meddlers out of his own kingdom. "Even routine security checks can encourage disloyalty."

Rani smiled inwardly, although she was careful not to show any hint of approval or disapproval. Sampson was quite right; she'd been selected for random security checks and interrogations when she'd been a junior officer and they'd certainly helped convince her that rebellion was a good idea. On the other hand, she knew first-hand how easy it was for senior officers to lose track of what was going on. Random security checks might help break up a conspiracy before it became dangerous.

"But the disloyalty is already there," Horn protested. "We intercept countless messages on the datanet encouraging rebellion; the underground is *still* out there, no matter how many cells we bust. What if they manage to take control of some of our ships?"

"That would be bad," Rani said, "but do you have any proof that the underground is planning anything dangerous?"

"No," Horn admitted, "but that's only because we're riding them so hard."

"You think," Sampson said. "But we isolate the fleet crewmen from the planet's population. One won't spread to the other."

Horn scowled at him. "Are you sure?"

Rani held up a hand. "As always, we have to strike a balance," she said. It was *fun* watching them compete for her attention and approval – and, like so much else, it kept them from uniting against her. "Director Horn; you and your department will review the files on all of the conscripts and flag up any that might demand more focused attention. I suggest" – she allowed some ice to slip into her voice – "that you don't just concentrate on the young and nubile. This is too important to allow you to waste time."

Sampson gave Horn an icy look. Rani had put an end to powerful officers abusing the junior officers and crew, but security officers, upon being given an inch, took a mile. The thought of facing one of Horn's 'customised' interrogations would definitely provoke a mutiny. It was bad enough that she had to indulge him with the wives and daughters of suspected underground activists.

And to think that the man had a lovely wife, Rani reminded herself. The universe was truly strange at times.

"Of course, Admiral," Horn said. He didn't sound pleased, but he would do as he was told – or else. "I shall have my staff see to it at once."

Rani nodded, then looked over at Sampson. "Once Director Horn produces a list, have your staff review it," she ordered. "If anyone is suspicious to both sets of reviewers, we may as well start interrogating them."

Sampson didn't look any happier, but he nodded reluctantly.

"In the meantime, have scoutships prepared to survey the stars rimward of here," Rani added. "We can try and see who owns what, then prepare to move as we see fit. Tell the scouts that we want them to remain undetected; we may as well try to maintain the advantage of surprise."

"Assuming that we haven't already lost it," Sampson pointed out. "We still don't know what happened to *Proud*."

"That reminds me," Rani said. "General Davis is to be relieved of command and recalled back to Corinthian. Losing a freighter to prisoners who should have been shackled to the walls was thoroughly incompetent and I expect a full accounting. We don't have ships to waste."

"No, Admiral," Sampson agreed. "However, the General did do a fine job of subduing the planet's inhabitants."

Rani scowled. Corinthian's shipyards could produce freighters, but most of them were being retooled to produce new warships. It said something about the general condition of the shipyards that the ones built from scratch were nearly ready – and it would be months before the retooled ones were active once again. If the Governor had spent his fortune actually maintaining the source of his wealth…

"That's true," Horn said, surprisingly. "The General put a vigorous security network into place as soon as he took control. Losing a freighter is a minor problem compared to gaining an entire planet with thousands of trained inhabitants."

"Maybe," Rani said. Horn was right; they desperately needed more trained manpower. She'd started new training courses for vocational students, but staffing them forced her to take trained officers from their posts. It was yet another balance that had to be maintained. "But he did lose the freighter."

She relaxed, slightly. "Tell the General that I want a full accounting – and new precautions put in place to prevent it from happening again," she said. "Once I've read his report, I'll make my decision about his future."

"Thank you, Admiral," Sampson said.

Rani smiled. She'd made one thing very clear to her senior officers – and the civil servants, although that had been harder. There would be absolutely no tolerance for bullshit; if someone screwed up and tried to hide it under a mass of weasel words, she would ensure that their deaths were thoroughly awful. On the other hand, if someone honestly admitted to a mistake she would be more lenient. Half of the Imperial Navy's problems had sprouted from bullshit scattered around by officers trying to avoid the blame. Most of the rest had come from aristocratic officers and their clients – and she was already rid of *them*.

"You are dismissed," she said, standing up. "Report to me as soon as you have completed the security check."

She watched them leave, then turned to look back out of the window. Landing City was buzzing with life, all hers. She controlled the fate of every man, woman and child in thirty star systems. It was a heady feeling; she could do anything and there was nothing they could do to stop them. No *wonder* the Grand Senate had become so corrupt, so indifferent to the needs of the Empire, she realised. The power they'd commanded had been utterly intoxicating.

In orbit, she knew, repair crews were struggling to rebuild the planet's orbital defences and convert a handful of asteroids into additional weapons platforms. It was slow going, but when the project was completed it would require a full Imperial Navy fleet to break into the high orbitals… and she doubted that one would be sent against her any time soon. Indeed, if the more extreme rumours were true, there was literally nothing left in the Core Worlds. They had been scorched clean by nuclear fire.

Rani privately doubted that was true, although she'd ensured that the rumour leaked onto the datanet to convince the population that there would be no help coming from the Empire. Corinthian was hardly the first world to fall to a rebel faction, but they'd all been recovered – until now. Even if the Empire was still intact in some form, the withdrawal from the outermost sectors suggested that the Grand Senate no longer had any interest in trying to maintain the status quo. By the time they changed their minds, if they did, her position would be impregnable. They would have to negotiate with her on equal terms. They'd *hate* that, but they would have no choice. She'd ensure that they knew it too.

And if the Empire was truly gone…?

The future seemed bright, full of promise…and all hers.

Chapter Twelve

The answer, unfortunately, is simple – and rooted in human nature. An average person can be very smart, capable of understanding that the world is not black and white. A group of people, on the other hand, is nowhere near as smart as the stupidest person in the group. They tend to look for simple answers and reward political leaders who offer them, even though there are rarely any real simple answers to be found.
   -Professor Leo Caesius, *Authority, Power and the Post-Imperial Era*

"You've gotten better," Jasmine said, as Mandy threw a kick at her. "Much better."

"Not as good as you," Mandy said. She sounded frustrated. "I should have gone to the Slaughterhouse too."

"You wouldn't have made it through Boot Camp," Jasmine said automatically, and then stopped herself. The spoilt brat Mandy had been *wouldn't* have survived Hell Week in Boot Camp, but the woman she'd become might have managed to pass through the Slaughterhouse and receive a Rifleman's Tab. Or maybe not; quitting was easy in Boot Camp. The recruits just had to walk up to the Sergeants and admit they couldn't take it. Mandy hadn't been able to simply quit the pirate ship.

"Probably," Mandy said, unaware of Jasmine's thoughts. "I'm sure you were much better than me when you started too."

Jasmine shrugged. She'd grown up on a far less developed world than Earth, where outdoor activities were keenly encouraged, rather than being pushed to one side in Earth's towering cityblocks. But then, outdoor sports had always encouraged independence of mind and that was the one thing Earth's rulers were desperately keen to suppress. The last time Jasmine had been on Earth, the system had seemed so fragile that one false move could start an apocalypse.

"Not as good as you are now," she assured the younger girl. "But you keep trying to close with me. That's a mistake. You can't fight me at close quarters or I'll kick your ass."

"Maybe I should spar with one of your subordinates," Mandy said. She grinned, suddenly. "Am I allowed to ask them?"

Jasmine blinked in surprise, wondering if Mandy was trying to distract her. "There's no regulation against it," she said, recalling a handful of Imperial Navy officers who had sparred with the Marines on a regular basis. Some of them had been pretty good too. "Or do you have something else in mind?"

Mandy flushed. "Maybe," she said, trying to be coy. "Does it matter?"

"It might to whoever you ask to spar with you," Jasmine said. She dodged another kick, then lunged forward, knocking Mandy to the deck. "And it can get dangerous."

"Life is dangerous," Mandy said, ruefully. Jasmine was holding her down too firmly for her to escape. "I wish I'd known that three years ago. I might have been able to do something about it."

Jasmine stood up and held out a hand, helping Mandy to her feet. "It isn't that easy," she admitted. "But you've come a long way."

She looked down at her friend, remembering how Mandy had looked when they'd first met. Beautiful, with long red hair spilling down over a shirt two sizes too small…but also weak, unprepared to face the untamed universe. Now, after several months of captivity and two years of hard work and training, she looked…healthy, as strong and confident as she could be. And yet there was still the vague hint of brittleness surrounding Mandy, warning Jasmine to keep an eye on her friend.

Jasmine's wristcom bleeped. "We'd better shower and leave the compartment," she said, letting go of Mandy's hand. "Others want to use it too."

She stripped off the exercise suit as she stepped into the shower compartment, allowing warm water to wash over her body. Mandy joined her a moment later, the hesitation she had first shown when sharing a shower long gone. Jasmine looked away from her, granting her friend what privacy she could, as the water flow terminated. Hot air blew down over them, drying the water off their bodies. Jasmine smiled, remembering how some civilians had reacted to showers on military starships. Water was strictly rationed by the crew.

Outside, she pulled on her shipsuit and checked the telltales quickly. It was far too easy to imagine a disaster in phase space, one that might damage a starship as ill-maintained as *Lightfoot* seemed to be. Wearing a shipsuit might make the difference between life and death, although Jasmine knew better than to make more of the garment than it was. Her instructors had always staged decompression exercises near compartments where emergency life support equipment could be found.

"Let's face it," the Drill Instructor had said, when the recruits had asked. "If you're not near emergency gear, you're dead. Bend over and kiss your ass goodbye."

And if you suffer an accident in phase space, you're dead anyway, Jasmine thought, as she waited for Mandy to join her. There were stories of starships limping out of phase space after suffering a serious accident, but as far as she knew they were just stories. It was far more likely that a starship would be able to travel from star to star at sublight speeds, which would take years, than survive an accident in phase space.

"I need to go back to the bridge," Mandy said, as she checked her wristcom. "We're due to arrive in three hours."

Jasmine nodded. It had been a tedious trip – normally, Marines travelled in stasis if the journey time was longer than a couple of weeks – but it was finally coming to an end. She felt the old shiver in her chest as it finally sank in that they were about to test themselves, once again, against a powerful foe. Admiral Singh might be far more capable than any of their other enemies. She certainly had a great deal more firepower.

The Admiral just had a single heavy cruiser, she thought. *Admiral Singh may have nine battleships.*

She winked at her friend, then headed out of the compartment and down towards the refitted hold. Sergeant Hampton had taken it over and turned it into a small exercise room for the non-Marines, forcing his fellow refugees – and Mr. Canada – to work hard in hopes of preparing themselves for the oncoming mission. Jasmine opened the hatch and glanced inside, seeing the three non-Marines working through their routine. Kate looked horribly sweaty, sweaty enough to make her shirt cling to her chest, revealing the swell of her breasts. Tired, worn…she still looked attractive enough to catch a man's eye. No wonder she'd managed to break the refugees out of their prison and help them to get control of the freighter.

"Lieutenant," Blake said, as he came down the corridor. He'd been reluctant to work with his new partner at first, but the certainty that they would be going into action soon had concentrated his mind. Besides, Watson was definitely a joker; he'd reluctantly admitted that his former comrades had called him Winker, although he had no idea why. "We just completed our set of personal exercises."

"And coming here to tell me about it?" Jasmine asked, as she closed the hatch to ensure that the non-Marines weren't disturbed. "I wonder why."

Blake pasted his best shit-eating grin on his face. "We were trying to prove our dedication by reporting to you in person?"

Jasmine rolled her eyes. "That sounds plausible," she said, sardonically. "And how did your exercises go?"

"We die only one quarter of the time now," Watson assured her. "And we scored a new record in the shooting gallery."

"For what it's worth," Blake admitted. He hadn't been the only Marine to be unhappy with the makeshift facilities. "The system crashes every so often; the hack isn't really perfect at all."

"We'll just have to make do," Jasmine said, although he understood his point. "It's civilian gear and can't be pushed too far."

She scowled. The shooting galleries the Marines used to test their skills included holographic representations of civilians; men, women and children, all caught up in the combat zone. Shooting one in the midst of combat cost the Marine points – and hundreds of press-ups if the Marine actually went into negative points. Her class of recruits had wondered if the Drill Instructors actually rigged the galleries to ensure that they were *always* doing press-ups. Even *Han* hadn't had so many civilians caught up in the line of fire.

But civilian VR systems weren't supposed to include civilians at all. Jasmine had never been a gamer – VR games had been rare on her homeworld – yet she'd heard enough to know that they'd had as much of the violence as possible stripped out of them. Indeed, some of the more violent games had been banned...which hadn't stopped bootleg copies of the games being smuggled from world to world. It said something about the Empire's skewed priorities that there was almost no effort being made to prevent pornography vile enough to suit the most depraved tastes, or entertainment videos that were even more depraved, being shipped from world to world.

I suppose that if they're masturbating, they're not plotting, she thought. But how much of the Empire's population wasted their lives away in front of the entertainment screen?

"We'll probably lose the next championship match," Blake predicted, glumly. "3rd Platoon will laugh at us."

"If we get back safely, we can spend a few weeks breaking ourselves of the bad habits," Jasmine said. She keyed her wristcom, flipping to the Marine channel. "General muster; right now."

She led the way down into the compartment where the remaining Marines were rapidly mustering, forming up in neat rows. Sergeant Harris inspected them, then looked over at Jasmine and reported that the Marines were all present and correct – apart from Sergeant Hampton. Jasmine hadn't expected him to attend; his task was to whip the non-Marines into shape, rather than serve as part of the platoon. He didn't want to admit it, but it had been years since he'd served in the Corps.

"We will be arriving at the edge of the Corinthian System in three hours," she said, making a show of glancing at her wristcom. The Marines followed suit; the wristcoms were linked to the freighter's main computer, allowing them to watch the countdown to arrival. "Once we're there, we may not have much time to plan our approach."

There was no disagreement. They'd gone over all of the possibilities, from brazenly flying into the system disguised as mercenaries to posing as a freighter crew...to sneaking through the defences in armoured combat suits. One of the scenarios, proposed by Sergeant Hampton, had even included a missile attack on the planet as a diversion, purportedly in the name of the Greenway Liberation Front. Jasmine wasn't sure she liked *that* idea- one of the missiles striking the planet's surface would be disastrous - but they might not have a choice.

"We should not be detected as we drop out of phase space," Jasmine continued, "but you have to be aware that Admiral Singh might have patrolling craft on the edge of the system. In that case, we will slip back into phase space before they can eyeballs us – hopefully, they will take us for pirates who thought better of sticking around. Luckily, we can catch up on our sleep while waiting for *Harrington* to complete her survey of the system."

"More sleep," Blake said. "I'm rested here, Lieutenant."

"Hurry up and wait, again," Jasmine said. She grinned. "Sorry."

She could understand Blake's irritation. It seemed to be true of all military organisations in history; they bust a gut getting into position, then they had to wait for the order to carry out the next stage of the offensive. At least they weren't working with the Civil Guard on *this* operation. The officers held back the start time so their men could get ready, but the men knew it so they kept lagging, forcing the start time back still further…if the Core World Civil Guard had ever managed to surprise the enemy, no doubt the guardsmen had been equally surprised. Jasmine knew that *she* would have been.

"Don't worry," she added. "Once we know what we're doing, everything will go very quickly indeed."

"And then we will wish we were back in our comfy beds," Sergeant Harris said, stiffly.

Jasmine smiled, then glanced around the compartment, moving from face to face. "This is going to be the trickiest mission we have undertaken – ever," she said. "We won't be fighting pirates or insurgents – we will *be* the insurgents. And we're blind. We have very limited intelligence and what we have is completely out of date. I cannot warn you enough that we must not take anything for granted."

She allowed her smile to widen. "Which is pretty much what we always get from Imperial Intelligence," she added. "We have to get back in that mindset."

There were nods from the Marines. Commonwealth Intelligence worked better than Imperial Intelligence had ever dreamed of working, if only because there were fewer layers of bureaucracy for the information to work its way through. Imperial Intelligence would probably have worked better if there hadn't been so many different analysts competing to see how much they could remove because it didn't suit their worldview.

"You've read the debriefing notes," she concluded. "Admiral Singh is operating a reign of terror – and it is our job to do something about it, as well as keeping her too busy to think about raiding the Commonwealth. We must not fail. We *will not* fail.

"We are Terran Marines; the most capable military force in history. If it can be done, we can do it. We *will* do it."

She watched their faces, knowing that they too felt the butterflies she felt before the mission actually began and there was no longer any time to worry about what they were doing.

"Dismissed," she said, quietly. "Relax, eat some of the foodstuffs we took onboard at Avalon, catch some sleep…because soon we will be moving."

The Marines relaxed and scattered, some heading for the gaming rooms while others walked towards the dining compartment. Jasmine watched them go, feeling oddly conflicted. It hadn't been a very good speech, she was sure. Colonel Stalker would have made a much better one while rallying the troops to attack the enemy. But what else could she have said?

She turned and strode out of the compartment, back towards where Sergeant Hampton was drilling the non-Marines. He looked up as she opened the hatch, then listened gravely as she told him to ensure that his people relaxed too. None of them had seemed very happy with even the mildest proposal for reaching the planet. If they had to do it the hard way, Jasmine had privately determined that the non-Marines would be sedated. The experience bothered Marines and experienced spacers alike. It would be nightmarish for groundhogs.

"I'll make sure they get some rest," he assured her, when she finished. "And you too, Lieutenant."

Jasmine nodded, although in truth she didn't feel like resting. Part of her was as keyed up as the rest of the Marine Riflemen. Shaking her head, she walked to the mess and found one of the ship's crew preparing fried chicken for the Marines. She hesitated – the tradition of senior officers serving their men before an operation was normally only applied to Captains and other higher ranks – then took the ladle and started to serve the food herself, without comment. The cook looked surprised, but other Marines understood.

Their faces reminded her of the first time she'd been served by a senior officer, back on Han. It had felt weird, she remembered, but at the same time it had been a link to the traditions they'd learned about at the Slaughterhouse, traditions none of them had really grasped until they'd entered the field as qualified Marines. Marine officers were taught to serve first, then lead; Imperial Army officers never had the experience of being grunts down in the trenches.

Once the platoon was fed – traditionally, the Marines had to help with the washing up, but the cook chased them out before they could break more than a couple of plates – they went back to their compartment and tried to sleep. Jasmine felt too keyed up to sleep still, but she concentrated on her mental disciplines and eventually felt sleep reaching for her. She must have slept, but it still felt as if she hadn't slept at all when she felt the starship returning to normal space. They had arrived in the enemy star system.

She stood up, left Sergeant Harris in command and hurried to the bridge. The main display, far smaller than it would have been on a warship, was showing a star and little else. At this distance, it was impossible to see Corinthian itself, although it would show up on gravimetric sensors. Starships, on the other hand, would not.

"Transit completed, Captain," the helmsman whispered. There was no need for anyone to *whisper*, but few escaped it when they were sneaking around a hostile system, as if the slightest sound might jinx the entire mission. "We are holding position, two AUs short of the phase limit."

Mandy nodded. "Run passive sensor sweep," she ordered. "Are we alone?"

There was a long chilling pause. "No active starships detected," the sensor officer reported. Several crewmen breathed signs of relief. "Some limited chatter from in-system."

Jasmine felt a shiver running down her spine. Someone could be lying doggo, hiding in seemingly-empty space…and watching for intruders with passive sensors alone. They'd be almost impossible to detect until it was far too late. The odds were vastly against it, but it was still a worry. She'd be worrying until they made it down to the surface.

"Take us into stealth," Mandy ordered, "then contact Captain Delacroix. Inform her that she is cleared to proceed."

And good luck to her, Jasmine thought.

CHAPTER THIRTEEN

> On Old Earth, the development of atomic power prompted a level of hysteria in the ill-educated mind that unscrupulous politicians used to their own advantage. No one would deny that nuclear power had dangers, particularly when the power plants were built by states that cared little for simple safety precautions. However, such dangers could be averted – but the 'nuclear is evil' mindset was too deeply embedded to be easily removed. The simple fact that every development throughout history offered its own dangers was overlooked – or ignored.
> -Professor Leo Caesius, *Authority, Power and the Post-Imperial Era*

Layla felt the tension rising on her bridge as *Harrington* slipped into the Corinthian System. The crew knew that detection was unlikely, particularly as long as they stayed well away from any of the settled worlds, but a single mistake might reveal their presence. She watched the display, schooling her features to remain calm, as the sensor crews built up an outline of the system's defences. It was starting to look truly intimidating.

Avalon hadn't had any settlements off-world, apart from the cloud-scoop and a handful of RockRat habitats. Corinthian, on the other hand, had settlements on all fourteen planets and countless asteroid mining facilities. It was impossible to tell *just* how heavily industrialised the system had become at such a distance, but the worst-case estimate suggested that Corinthian would have over ten times the industrial power of Avalon, probably a great deal more. The system had been settled for much longer, for one thing, and had benefited from investment on a scale Avalon had never been able to match.

The passive sensors revealed hundreds of sublight ships moving from world to world, carrying raw materials to the industrial nodes orbiting Corinthian and transporting manufactured goods to the other worlds. There were dozens of interstellar freighters milling around, mostly heading out of the system on least-time courses to the phase limit. It was impossible to determine if they were independents or if Admiral Singh had conscripted them as easily as she had conscripted starship crews, but it didn't matter. Instead, it suggested that Admiral Singh ruled an empire of considerable size and power.

"Launch probes," she ordered, softly.

Taking *Harrington* too close to the planet was risky; a single betraying emission could give them away. Pirates might ignore the odd flicker that suggested the presence of a stealthed starship, but they dared not assume that Admiral Singh's sensor crews would do the same. She had enough starships to play cat and mouse with the intruder, trying to force it into an ambush…and if they managed to get a close look at *Harrington*, it would be far too revealing. Instead, the Imperial Navy-issue probes would advance towards the planet – and if they were detected, they wouldn't raise any additional alarm bells.

Hours passed before the probes started sending back sensor imagines through the undetectable laser links binding them to their mothership. Layla watched, feeling cold ice congealing around her heart, as she saw seven battleships in orbit around Corinthian, each one two kilometres of death and destruction. They were the most formidable starships in the universe, even if they did cost several times as much as a battlecruiser and required over three thousand crewmen to run properly. Admiral Singh had a hard core of force to support her empire.

"They look to be in good working order," Specialist Montez said. He'd been assigned to *Harrington* for the duration of the mission, a young man who had demonstrated a remarkable talent with sensor systems. "I don't think that they're poorly maintained."

He scowled. "Their sensors are stepped down," he added, "but that's standard for military starships. I don't dare assume that they're damaged."

Layla nodded, sourly. Military-grade sensors tended to wear down rapidly when operating at full power, a problem that the Imperial Navy's beancounters had never seemed to understand. Most starships kept their sensors stepped down until they were ready to go into battle, conserving the equipment as much as possible. After all, if it was worked too hard, it might fail in the midst of battle – and the entire ship would be lost before it could withdraw. A blind ship would be almost completely defenceless.

She scowled as she recalled the training exercises she'd gone through when she'd transferred to the Commonwealth Navy. One particular scenario, designed so that everything that could go wrong *did* go wrong, had ended up with her starships completely blind…and trashed by enemy fire. It had been a humiliating lesson, but one she'd had to learn. The Imperial Navy training programs had their limits…yet they were surprisingly informative if approached with a willingness to learn.

The figures kept scrolling up in her display. Seven battleships, nineteen heavy cruisers, thirty-seven destroyers…enough firepower to take the Commonwealth Navy on in open combat and utterly trash it. At some point, the imbalance would be great enough that training and discipline couldn't even the odds; *Sword's* headlong attack on Avalon illustrated that nicely, for those who cared to learn. If the pirate ship hadn't been sabotaged, the results would have been disastrous. The Commonwealth would have been snuffed out before it even came into existence.

"There are only a couple of orbital fortresses," Montez said, out loud. "The files said that there were five."

Layla frowned, studying the images. Corinthian, according to the files, had had five fortresses in orbit around the planet, enough firepower and sensor arrays to make approach difficult, at least without being detected. But instead, three of the fortresses were missing and the battleships had taken their places. That suggested…what? Had they been towed to one of the other settled planets to add to their defences, or had they been destroyed when Admiral Singh arrived to take control?

A question for Mr. Canada, she thought. Several asteroids were also in orbit; the images from the probes suggested that they were being converted into makeshift fortresses to replace the missing units. The originals had probably been destroyed then, she decided; asteroid-based fortresses were tough, but they had their limits. And they could turn into disasters if the enemy hit them hard enough to knock them out of orbit. If there had been any other choice, Admiral Singh would not have risked using them at all.

Piece by piece, the sensor crew built up an image of the planet's sensor network. It was formidable, although nowhere near as tough as Earth's network; sneaking into orbit without being detected would be almost impossible. The active sensors would be bad enough, but if Admiral Singh had followed standard doctrine she would have scattered passive sensor nodes around the planet, each one listening carefully for hints of a stealthed starship – and utterly undetectable, at least when restricted to passive sensors. An active sensor sweep would have given the game away in any case.

Layla watched as the probes tracked a freighter that docked at one of the orbiting stations, attempting to determine how freighter crews were treated. There were brief transmissions between the station and the freighter, but none of them were more than orders and acknowledgements. The probes couldn't see inside the ships, which meant that there was no way to know how the customs officers were handling the newcomers. There were just too many possibilities. If the ship was just being unloaded, it would be safe enough to bring *Lightfoot* into orbit – but if the ship was being searched and the crews questioned, it would raise too many dangerous possibilities. Somehow, Layla doubted that the Admiral would just accept a sealed package. The Commonwealth was gentle, but questions were asked of all freighter crews who came in from outside explored space.

Or should that be re-explored space? She wondered, absently. The star charts they used to navigate would be good for hundreds of thousands of years – stars moved, but so slowly that countless human generations could go by before the charts needed to be updated – but the political situation could change overnight. Instead of the comforting certainty of the Empire, there was no way to know what lay outside their sector…or what threats might be lurking core-wards, waiting to pounce.

She shivered as she realised that she might have discovered why so many people had been reluctant to believe that the Empire could fall.

Everything about it had seemed solid, unchangeable, from the heavily-settled Core Worlds to the lightly-populated worlds along the Rim. The thought of the ties that bound the Empire together shattering was not only terrifying, it was inconceivable – or, rather, it had *been* inconceivable. If more people had taken precautions before the Empire had finally shattered...

Like what? She asked herself. *What could they have done?*

"The freighter crew doesn't seem to be getting any shore leave," Montez said, as the orbital crews started to unload the freighter. There was no way to determine what it had actually been carrying. "Or maybe they'll be allowed to move to a holding orbit once they've unloaded their hold."

"Maybe," Layla agreed. It wasn't her decision, but in her view it would be too dangerous to risk trying to smuggle the Marines down onto the planet. *Lightfoot* could dock openly, as an independent freighter trying to find a new source of HE3; the Marines would have to find a different method. They dared not risk being trapped on an orbital station. "Assign a probe to monitor them, then swing the others over to get some good images of the planet."

She watched as hours ticked by, an endless tide of data flowing into her ship's datanet. The planet's surface didn't seem to have changed *that* much, apart from the impact zone of a dozen KEW strikes, presumably dropped by Admiral Singh to convince the inhabitants that she meant business. Compared to Han, where KEW strikes had been called down every ten minutes during the height of the fighting, it was remarkably peaceful. Too peaceful.

Montez put his finger on it. "There's almost no civilian chatter at all," he said, studying the live feed. "Just a handful of military-grade transmitters."

Layla frowned. Outside a low-tech world, there should have been a considerable amount of radio chatter – and no one would accuse Corinthian of being a low-tech world. Even during the early days of Avalon's settlement, there would have been no shortage of radio transmissions; it was far easier to use radio than set up landlines the Crackers could have cut at leisure. The absence of radio transmissions from Corinthian was...worrying.

"They may have moved everything onto the datanet," Montez suggested, thoughtfully. "The planet has been settled long enough for the net to be just about everywhere."

"Or it could be another way to control the population," Layla mused. The datanets the Empire produced – apart from the ancient systems used by Earth and the Core Worlds – were orderly, simple to use.... and easy for the administrators to control. There would be no shortage of pornography, or mind-numbing entertainment, but if anyone dared show too much interest in politics it would attract attention.

"It could be," Montez agreed. He tapped a switch, altering the image. "There's a lot of new construction here, near Landing City. That wasn't there four years ago."

"Looks prefabricated," Layla said, after a moment. "You think that's housing all of the immigrant workers?"

"It's probable," Montez said. He ran a series of analysis algorithms. "The computers think that there's no shopping malls there, or anything other than residential apartments."

Layla heard the warning in his tone and nodded. Computer analysis had its limits – and had been known to make terrible mistakes, even when reasoning from impeccable logic. If they misidentified something during the first sensor sweep, the mistake would throw off the rest of their analysis. On the other hand, it did seem reasonable. Layla had seen the soulless accommodation thrown up for immigrants on other worlds and they tended to lack shops and other facilities that the immigrants might need – or want. The Civil Guard had often ended up fighting in them after the immigrants, sick of mistreatment, had started to riot.

She looked over at him. "What's your population estimate for the entire planet?"

"Roughly two to three billion," Montez said. "There's plenty of sprawl outside the cities to house people, but..."

He shrugged, expressively. Layla understood. Once again, there was no way to be certain.

But if the population is truly that large, we are definitely in trouble, she thought. The Commonwealth's entire population, counting children, was roughly two billion, scattered over thirty worlds and countless tiny settlements. It was impossible to be sure because the Commonwealth's founders had deliberately shied away from the intrusive population surveys the Empire had conducted regularly, leaving such matters in the hands of local governments. But if Admiral Singh had a larger population on a single planet, she'd have a much larger pool of potential crewmen and soldiers to draw on. It would take a few years to set up training facilities, but once they were underway her power would rise rapidly.

She scowled. "Can you tell if there are military deployments in the midst of civilian formations?"

"It's difficult to be sure," Montez admitted. "There are no shortage of military transmissions, but they seem to be concentrated in some places and scattered in others. It may require further analysis."

"Understood," Layla said. Overall, she doubted that they could pull much more intelligence out of the planet at this distance. It was frustrating – they still knew almost nothing about the situation on the ground – but there was no point in complaining about it. "Pull back the probes; position them so they can continue to monitor the planet from a distance."

"Aye, Captain," Montez said. He tapped his console, issuing orders. Once emplaced, the probes would record everything that happened near the planet – everything *visible*, she reminded herself. It was highly unlikely that they would be discovered unless Admiral Singh's forces had a major stroke of luck. "They're on their way."

Layla looked over towards the helm. "Take us towards the cloud-scoop," she ordered. "I want to take a look at their system before we leave."

She settled back in her command chair, fighting the tiredness that threatened to overcome her, as *Harrington* inched its way out of the system. There were officers who had been able to sleep, even when their starships were sneaking through enemy-controlled star systems; she honestly didn't know how they'd done it. Even if she'd gone into her stateroom for a brief nap, she would have found it hard to sleep without drugs – and taking a sleeping pill while her ship was in danger would have been unforgivable. At least her crew could take breaks, once they were relieved by their seconds.

Slowly, the system's largest gas giant came into view. The Empire had been mining it for HE3 for over seven hundred years, but it would be millennia before the gas giant was depleted. Layla had once heard of a pressure group on Earth having hysterics about humanity accidentally sucking Jupiter dry, such an absurd concept that it could only have originated on one of the Core Worlds, where a loss of touch with reality seemed to be a requirement for political office. She had no idea what had happened to the pressure group, but given how important HE3 was to the Empire, she suspected that it hadn't been pleasant. Maybe they'd just been rounded up and exiled to a low-tech world.

"I'm picking up a small network of defence stations and nine cloudscoops," Montez said. "They're running sweeps at random, Captain. I don't think we should risk going any closer."

Layla nodded. "Hold us here," she said, as the main display started to fill up with data, "and see what you can tell me about their system.

She shook her head in disbelief. Admiral Singh must have dismantled the cloudscoops in the three nearest systems and transported them to Corinthian, she decided, ensuring that the Admiral had a near-monopoly on HE3. It would give her a stranglehold over the other planets, keeping them from rebelling against her too openly – or they'd simply be cut off from their supply. She'd need an entire fleet of transports to move the fuel, but that wouldn't be a problem for Corinthian's industrial base. It only took a few months to construct a basic freighter.

The Admiral was also paranoid about something happening to her system, she decided, as the sensors picked up a small defence fleet orbiting the gas giant. Two more battleships floated near the cloudscoops, where thirty smaller ships buzzed around, running random patrol orbits that would make it hard for any stealthed ship to get too close. Unlike the defence forces orbiting Corinthian, the force guarding the cloudscoops were running their sensor systems at full power. *Nothing* could be allowed to threaten the cloudscoops.

But Avalon does the same, Layla thought. The cloudscoops were the linchpin of the interstellar economy. Losing even one of them would hurt; losing all of them would be disastrous. She considered a handful of possible attack scenarios before realising that it would require most of the

Commonwealth Navy to break through the defences, exposing them to Admiral Singh's fleet. Colonel Stalker was unlikely to authorise such a gamble.

"Pull us back," she ordered finally, "and take us back to the rendezvous point."

She fought down a yawn as the helmsman obeyed. Once they were away from the gas giant, they'd transmit everything they'd picked up to the other two ships – and then there would be time for a nap before they started the next phase of the mission. And then…

Layla tapped the console, bringing up the images of the cloudscoops. Admiral Singh's industrial base was truly formidable. If it could be captured…the Commonwealth would become a great deal more powerful very quickly. If…

She shook her head. The first priority was preventing her from taking action against the Commonwealth. Everything else could wait.

CHAPTER FOURTEEN

> The issues facing any state, therefore, required a balancing act. A state must have enough power to overawe the strong; conversely, it must also have limits on that power to prevent the politicians from becoming the strong. At the same time, it must reward hard work without accidentally suppressing it – or ruining its own economy. It must also be capable of heeding the will of the people while, at the same time, ignoring the ignorant. Sadly, this balancing act is very difficult to maintain. For one thing, how does one actually define 'ignorant?'
>
> -Professor Leo Caesius, *Authority, Power and the Post-Imperial Era*

"She isn't as secure as she would like to be," Jasmine said.

She tapped the display showing the locations of military transmitters on the ground. "She's got small units deployed near the farms and isolated factories," she added. "Not unlike what we did, back when we were fighting the Crackers. They're there to either guard the food production facilities or keep the population under control."

"Or both," Sergeant Harris commented. "If she holds the food supply in her grip, she can keep the cities without having to spread her forces too thin."

Jasmine nodded. Keeping a full-sized city under control required thousands of soldiers; she couldn't fault Admiral Singh for wanting to find an easier way to keep control. Given a population in the millions, the civilians would eat through their food stocks in a matter of days if the food supply happened to be cut off – and then they'd riot, before they died. But if they knew that Admiral Singh could cut them off at any time, they'd obey. How could they be blamed for doing otherwise?

She looked at the display again, silently tracing the location of the small garrisons. It was quite possible that there was an insurgency going on outside the cities, although with so much firepower in orbit the insurgency was unlikely to get beyond the harassing stage. The Crackers had come alarmingly close to taking over Avalon before the Imperial Navy had dispatched a single destroyer to smash their army from orbit. Admiral Singh had enough firepower to make that look like a love tap.

But then, she won't want to smash the farms herself, she thought, contemplating the possibilities. *She's just as dependent upon them as the locals*.

"We cannot guarantee remaining undiscovered if we dock at their orbital stations," Mandy said, softly. She'd studied the records of the visiting freighters carefully. "We could go in naked and see what happens…"

"Too risky, at least at first," Jasmine said.

She shook her head firmly. There was no way to know how Admiral Singh's men would react to their arrival – and to their cover story. They might just sell Mandy some HE3, hire her to work for them…or seize the ship on some pretext. The latter had been common during the waning days of the Empire. It had somehow never occurred to the bureaucrats that if they came up with excuses to punish independent shippers who annoyed them, the independent shippers would simply avoid their worlds.

"That leaves the other operational plan," Sergeant Hampton said. "Using a missile pod to cause a distraction while we slip in from the other side."

Jasmine nodded. She'd considered leaving the missile pod out of the plan, but the readings they had on the enemy sensor network suggested that they were going to *need* a diversion. If Admiral Singh's forces had something else to worry about, they might miss the Marines trying to slip through the defences. They'd also steer their course so they moved well away from the orbital installations. It was unlikely that a sensor contact near the stations would be ignored.

She tapped the display. "*Harrington* will drop us into space here," she said, pointing to a specific location near the planet. "We'll drift in towards the planet while *Harrington* dog-legs around the edge of their sensor network and emplaces the missile pod here. Once we start slipping into detection range, the missile pod will be triggered – and start screaming its message to the Admiral."

Hampton nodded. "It should alarm her," he said. His comrades had recorded the message, just to ensure that they got the accent right. If they were *very* lucky, Admiral Singh might even assume that the freighter that had emplaced the missile pod was the freighter Hampton had captured and used in his escape. "It has its risks…"

"Yes," Jasmine said. "*Risks.*"

Using a false-flag operation galled her at the best of times, but it was worse when there was a helpless planetary population who were likely to bear the brunt of any punishment from the Admiral. Greenway's population might be made to suffer for something that had nothing to do with them. There was no choice; they were, to all intents and purposes, at war, but it still didn't sit well with her.

She looked over at Hampton's comrades. "You will be sedated for the drop," she said, recalling her very first training drop. She'd thought that she was ready for it – and she'd still wet herself when they'd been launched out of the spacecraft and sent falling towards the planet below. She hadn't been the only one to lose control of her bladder either. It was funny how *that* had never been mentioned in the recruitment leaflets. "You'll wake up on the planet."

Or dead, she added, in the privacy of her own mind. But there was no choice. There were people who couldn't wear a combat suit without feeling claustrophobic. Marines drilled endlessly so they could endure hours of boredom without panicking, but the militiamen had never had any training in using the suits. Besides, if they *were* detected, they'd die without ever knowing what had hit them.

"We will aim to land here," she added, altering the map so it showed a specific location two hundred kilometres from Landing City. It might take them several days to walk to the city, if they couldn't find any other transport, but landing too close to the capital might be noticed. "If we can, we will make contact with the locals and see what they can tell us."

She scowled. There was no way to know what sort of reception they'd get. Some people might help them, some might turn them away…and some might call for the Admiral's forces. Perhaps they would be outright collaborators, perhaps they would justify it to themselves by claiming it would spare their friends and families punishment when Admiral Singh found out, but in the end it would hardly matter. All that mattered was that their presence would be exposed.

They'd practiced hiding from hunting teams on the Slaughterhouse, but it was always difficult to hide when the enemy could flood the area with thousands of troops.

She looked around the compartment, then smiled at her platoon. "We will transfer to *Harrington* within the hour, so make damn sure you're not carrying anything that might identify us," she added. "And then we will head in-system."

Kate and Steve gulped. Clearly, the reality of what they were going to do hadn't struck them until now. Jasmine concealed a smile and motioned for Sergeant Hampton to escort them back to their quarters, where they would both be strip-searched, just in case. Everything from their outfits to the weapons they carried had been carefully inspected to ensure that they offered no clues to their origin, but the slightest thing could give them away. They weren't even allowed to carry photographs of their families.

She watched them go, followed rapidly by the rest of the landing party. At least she could trust her Marines not to carry anything too revealing, although she knew that an intrusive body-scan would reveal far too much. Marine Riflemen didn't receive the intensive implants used by Pathfinders and other highly-classified units, but what they did have was unique to the Marine corps. The medics had camouflaged the implants as best as they could, stepping them down so they seemed civilian-grade if someone made a brief scan, yet an intrusive investigation would discover their true nature. And then the mission would be blown.

There's no choice, she told herself, grimly. It didn't make her feel any better.

"Good luck," Mandy said, once everyone else had left the compartment. "In a week or so, we will try to make contact with them."

Jasmine scowled. Once the Marines were gone, *Lightfoot* could be stripped of everything that might be too revealing, but it was still dangerous. At least no one would be too surprised by the freighter crew using counter-interrogation implants. They were very common along the Rim. If Admiral Singh simply confiscated the ship…

"Watch yourself," she growled, finally. If she could have forbidden it, she would have – but Mandy was right. They needed to slip more people into Corinthian and establishing a 'legitimate' freighter identity would be a step towards opening a hidden channel…assuming, of course, that the security officers on the planet weren't incredibly paranoid. "And make damn sure you strip the ship first."

Mandy bowed her head. "You make damn sure you survive," she said, as she gave Jasmine a hug. "And you still owe me a drink."

Jasmine laughed. "I always owe you drinks," she said. "There's something wrong with your accounting."

She left the compartment and walked down to Sergeant Hampton's compartment, where the three militiamen and Elliot Canada were dressing quickly. "Nothing to report," Sergeant Hampton said. "We're all clean."

"Good," Jasmine said. None of the volunteers looked happy – and Jasmine found it hard to blame them – but they'd just have to suck it up and deal with it. Whatever mementos they'd brought along of their families would have to be left on *Butcher* until they returned from Corinthian. "Mr. Canada, I need a word with you."

The defector looked up at her nervously as she escorted him into the next compartment. "We are going to rely on you once we're down on the ground," she said, "so tell me now; are you up for it?"

Canada swallowed, but nodded.

"This isn't going to be easy," Jasmine warned him. How many times had she said that over the past month? "If we are detected, we will likely die. You might make a mistake that gets us caught. If you do, I will kill you personally. Do you understand me?"

"Yes," Canada said. He hesitated, then confessed. "Everything I know about the Democratic Underground is out of date."

Jasmine concealed her amusement. She already knew that; the analysts had pointed it out, in enough detail to thoroughly get on her nerves. The Democratic Underground could have been wiped out, or subverted, or simply left to rot…there was no way to know, at least until they reached the planet's surface and made contact. And that would be risky as hell.

"It's good that you know that," Jasmine said, patiently. "Still, don't take *anything* for granted."

She stepped backwards and looked at him appraisingly. Not a Marine – and not someone with the ambition to drive him onwards and upwards in the Commonwealth Navy. But he'd been brave to come forward and braver still to volunteer for the mission to Corinthian, despite the colossal risks. And he was clearly terrified at the thought of spending hours in a suit, drifting helplessly through space. Jasmine knew exactly how he felt.

"Get your kit together," she ordered. "It's time to go."

Jasmine felt her own apprehension rising as the platoon transferred to *Harrington*. Captain Delacroix didn't hesitate; as soon as the platoon were onboard, she took her starship back towards Corinthian, taking every precaution to remain undetected. Jasmine watched through the vessel's sensors as they dropped down from above the system's plane, a tactic that ensured that they remained well clear of any in-system spacecraft. Most of the freighters heading out of the system did so on different courses. Once they crossed the phase limit, they vanished into phase space and were gone.

She scowled as the full immensity of Admiral Singh's little empire finally struck home. This wasn't a world controlled by pirates – or tyrants who had seized power in the wake of the Empire's fall. Corinthian was a heavily-developed world, ruled by a competent dictator who commanded a formidable fleet. And fifteen people, only twelve of them Marines, were going to set themselves against such an edifice? All of a sudden, the half-drawn plan seemed thoroughly insane.

One step at a time, she reminded herself. It was the classic solution; a large problem could be solved by breaking it down into a series of smaller problems. Right now, they had to get down to the planet's surface. After that, they could worry about the rest of the operation.

"Don your suits," she ordered, quietly.

The makeshift suit she'd worn since they'd departed Avalon still didn't feel right. It was older than Jasmine herself; it just didn't have the fluid reaction of the combat suit she'd left behind on Avalon. The HUD was practically *civilian*, the embedded weapons felt puny and there was almost no camouflage system. They'd modified some of the suit's systems and replaced the antigravity generator, but the rest of it had been left alone. Jasmine found it difficult to understand why the suits had once been considered state of the art.

Because it was all they had, she thought, as the suit's servomotors hummed to life. She checked the telltales, one by one, and relaxed slightly as she realised that everything seemed to be in working order. The Sergeants moved from Marine to Marine, checking their suits with handheld diagnostic tools, then moved on to the non-Marines. Their suits would have to handle the descent on their own, without human input. They'd have to be checked far more carefully.

"We're approaching the drop point," Captain Delacroix's voice said. She sounded funny through the suit's speakers, as if her voice was oddly accented. "Are you ready to be deployed?"

Jasmine looked over at the non-Marines. Sergeant Hampton pressed an injector tab against Kate's neck; a moment later, her head slumped inside the suit. She was lucky, Jasmine realised, that she wasn't using a standard Marine combat suit; the battlesuit, responsive to its owner's moves, would have crumpled to the deck. Steve and Elliot Canada were already out of it. They'd wake up on Corinthian – or in Heaven.

"All present and correct," she said, as she pulled her helmet down over her head. The suit's internal air tanks had been replaced, thankfully. According to the techs, the first time they'd opened the suits the air had tasted like old socks. It was a great improvement over the average pirate vessel, but it wouldn't have endeared anyone to the suits. "We're ready, Captain."

"Good luck," Captain Delacroix said. It was hard to make out any genuine emotion in her warped voice. "I'll keep a light in the window – and see you all again soon."

Jasmine smiled, ruefully. Did Delacroix still wish that she'd passed the Crucible now?

She felt the tension rise as the hatch hissed open, revealing the inky blackness of space, broken only by the constant glow of thousands of stars. It was easy to forget just how large the stars were when they were hundreds of light years away; they looked tiny, impossibly small. Even

Corinthian itself was only a tiny orb in the distance, illuminated by the light of its parent star.

The gravity field let go of her as she stepped out into space, allowing the thrusters to start pushing them towards Corinthian. It would take hours to reach the planet's orbit, whatever else happened. She shivered again as she concentrated on her mental disciplines. Being alone among the stars, unable to talk to her fellows, could lead to madness. Instead, she would have to concentrate on something else.

Time seemed to slow to a crawl as they drifted forward. The suit's sensors were pathetic compared to a modern battlesuit, let alone a starship; almost nothing sounded an alert until they were almost at the planet itself. Jasmine watched with growing concern as the suit picked up a prowling destroyer, before the enemy ship vanished into the distance without – apparently – having seen a thing. It shouldn't have been a surprise – the suits were tiny, as well as stealthy – but she was still nervous. Detection would mean capture – or death. The suits couldn't hope to avoid engagement if they were picked up.

Corinthian grew larger and larger as they approached, a blue-green orb surrounded by sparkling lights, each one a colossal orbital station or starship. From such a distance, there was no sign of settlement on the planet's surface, but very few worlds had *anything* that showed up to the naked eye from orbit. Earth, of course, was covered in megacities and a few of the Core Worlds were just as bad...Corinthian, however, hadn't been settled anything like as long as humanity's homeworld. There would be parts of it, she suspected, that were still as empty as most of Avalon. It might make an excellent breeding ground for an insurgency.

The files had stated that Corinthian's natural wildlife hadn't really put up a fight when plants and animals from Earth's ecosystem had been introduced to their new home. It wasn't surprising; few ecosystems were anything like as aggressive as Earth's – or, at least, what Earth had been before humanity had polluted the planet beyond repair. Right now, someone who knew basic field craft could survive for years on Corinthian without being detected, just by eating the plants and capturing small animals. If Avalon was any guide, there might be an entire subculture living in the forests, hidden from the rest of the world.

Or simply refugees from Admiral Singh's rule, she thought, wryly. *Why not? It happened on every other world too.*

She almost jumped as the timer buzzed. It was time to begin their final approach.

CHAPTER FIFTEEN

That is a dangerous question to ask. Any group tends to band together against the outside universe – and determine itself as the font of all wisdom. Ask anyone and they will come up with a list of deserving people who should get a say in affairs – and people who should not, simply because they are believed to be ignorant. Few doctors, for example, would cheerfully accept non-doctors telling them what to do if they had the power to prevent it.
-Professor Leo Caesius, *Authority, Power and the Post-Imperial Era*

"That's odd," Specialist Cassie Lang mused. "What's that?"

Her supervisor walked over from his console and peered over her shoulder. He was old, old enough to have spent nearly fifty years in the Imperial Navy before retiring, but he was a good teacher. Cassie had heard horror stories about what supervisors did with young trainees under their command, yet nothing had actually *happened*. The worst he'd done was chew her out for making the same mistake twice.

"Someone seems to have forgotten how to stealth themselves," the supervisor said, with grim humour. "They're broadcasting a signal that will draw our eyes towards them…"

Cassie sucked in a breath as the signal suddenly strengthened. "The Greenway Liberation Front demands that you withdraw from our planet at once," it said. "If you do not…"

The display sparkled with angry red icons, each one blazing towards the planet. "Missile separation," Cassie said, remembering her training. "We have thirty-one missiles incoming!"

"Fucking amateurs," her supervisor said, as alarms started to howl. Cassie shot him an inquiring glance. "Those missiles will burn themselves out before they reach engagement range."

He tapped a switch. "Planetary defence grid armed and ready to fire," he said. "Missile tracking systems online; uploading targeting data now. Fire as soon as they enter range."

Cassie nodded, calming down. The missiles would burn out their drives and go ballistic, flying along a perfectly predictable course. They'd be picked off before they had any hope of actually hitting anything, even the nearest target.

Her console bleeped another alarm. "Sir, the missiles are activating ECM," she said, puzzled. All of a sudden, there were hundreds of missiles racing towards the station…she knew that most of them were sensor ghosts, but it was hard to separate them from the real missiles. "I…"

"Don't panic," her supervisor said, although he sounded more tense himself. "They're still going to burn themselves out before they reach engagement range."

More and more sensor systems came online, burning through the missile ECM through sheer power. Many of the sensor ghosts simply vanished, allowing her to see the real missiles as their drives started to burn out. One by one, they went ballistic…just as they entered engagement range. The point defence network picked them off with ease.

Her supervisor's wristcom buzzed, once. "The Admiral is sending a squadron of ships out to see if they can find the missile carrier," her supervisor said. "They won't have gone too far away…concentrate all of our sensors on the approximate location and see if we can pick anything up. This is your best chance to impress the Admiral."

Cassie smiled. She'd heard that junior officers and crew – even trainees – who impressed the Admiral were promoted upstairs as a reward. It would mean more money for her family, even though they hadn't been keen on her volunteering to work for Admiral Singh. But the alternative was being conscripted – and conscripts had little control over where they were posted. Some of the rumours she'd heard made lecherous superiors sound like nothing.

"I'll do my best, sir," she assured him.

"See that you do," her supervisor said. "The world is watching."

"Captain, they're launching sensor drones," Montez said. "I think we alarmed them."

Layla nodded. The brief attack had been harmless; as she'd expected, all of the missiles were destroyed before they reached engagement range. But Admiral Singh would have to assume that the Greenway Liberation Front really existed and that it was capable of mounting attacks on Corinthian. She would have to do everything she could to hunt them down before the next attack slipped through the defences.

"Take us back," she ordered, as several enemy starships broke orbit. They'd reacted with commendable speed, she noticed, although keeping their drives and sensors stepped down had slowed their reaction time. The next attack would find a far more prepared enemy. "We don't want them to get anything from us, even a brief sensor contact."

Admiral Singh's forces swarmed around the planet like a mass of angry bees, pinging every *hint* of a suspicious contact with their sensors. Layla watched with grim amusement as they stumbled over one of the probes, only to have it explode in their faces before they could recover it. The other probes seemed to be intact and undiscovered, even though they were beaming data out of the system, back towards the two hidden freighters. By the time the day was over, she told herself, they should have a rough order of battle for Admiral Singh's fleet.

Not that it really matters, she thought, sourly. *We don't need precise figures to tell us that we're outgunned.*

She shook her head, then mentally said a prayer. The Marines were on their way in now.

Corinthian changed rapidly as they approached, moving from a distant orb hanging against the darkness of space to something that was truly massive. Jasmine's perspective shifted as the suit's thrusters hummed silently, just before they started to drift into the planet's atmosphere. There was no sense of motion as they drifted through interstellar space, but her suit seemed to bump and creak the moment they touched the upper edge of the atmosphere. Seconds later, the antigravity systems took hold and they started to drop towards the planet below.

It was rare for a stealthy combat drop to be even attempted, at least outside training. Normally, if they *had* to hit a well-defended planet, the Marines would be escorted by missiles, KEWS and sensor jammers designed to make it difficult for the planet's defenders to target individual Marines. This time, they dared not attract attention. Even leaving a trail of fire as they fell out of the sky would be dangerous.

The suit rocked again as it fell further, the ground coming up towards them at terrifying speed. It was strange to feel so vulnerable, even though she knew they were sitting ducks if they were spotted. Slowly, bit by bit, the signs of civilisation came into view. Her suit's sensors were hardly the best, but they had no trouble picking up towns, villages and roadways connecting the settlements together. Corinthian's population had invested heavily in their infrastructure and it showed. Now, Admiral Singh was collecting on their investment.

Jasmine had assumed that they would be blown off course and so she was pleasantly surprised to discover that they were heading towards their target. She turned slightly, twisting the suit, until she could see Landing City in the distance. The city's lights broke through the darkness, an ever-present glow that was unmatched on Avalon, even in Camelot. It would ruin their night vision, Jasmine told herself, before shaking her head in amusement. People who wanted to see the night sky rarely lived in cities.

A dull chime ran through the suit as the fall slowed still further. The ground was coming up now, covered in trees; Jasmine had a moment to brace herself before she crashed through the canopy and fell through the trees, right into a bog. Her suit started to sink into the mire before she started to reverse the antigravity flow, levitating herself up and out of the mess. Moments later, the remainder of the platoon crashed down beside her.

"What a mess," Blake commented.

"It could be worse," Sergeant Harris said. "We could be back on Han."

Jasmine nodded in agreement as they staggered towards the edge of the bog. *That* hadn't been included in the maps they'd studied before picking their landing spot. But then, detailed maps of every planet in the Empire weren't considered vital information, at least unless one happened to be living there. It wouldn't be the first time that the maps of a world they'd deployed on hadn't matched the reality. Han had been particularly bad for that.

"It could be," she grunted. The suit's night vision wasn't perfect in the trees; it was difficult to see just where she was putting her feet. An enemy ambush would probably have killed them all. "Or it could be better."

They reached the edge of the bog and sat down, using the trees as cover. If someone had picked up a hint of their descent, orbital sensors would be focused on the region, looking for someone – anyone – who was remotely suspicious. Her suit's passive sensors weren't picking up anything, but she knew better than to assume that meant that they were safe. The suits themselves would be far too revealing if they were seen from orbit.

"Wake up the sleeping beauties," she ordered, once the Marines had recovered from their ordeal. "We need to dig a pit."

None of the non-Marines looked happy at being awoken, although they were all stunned to realise that they'd made it down to the planet. Jasmine ordered the Sergeants to help them out of their suits while the rest of the Marines dug a deep pit, then sealed the suits and dropped them into the Earth, finally covering them with a jammer mesh. The enemy would actually have to dig down to recover the suits, if they stumbled across the pit. By the time the Marines had finished, it was difficult to tell that there had ever been a pit at all.

Jasmine glanced at her terminal, then started to lead the way towards the nearest road. The trees seemed to close in on them as they walked, leaving the Marines glancing around nervously, watching for possible enemies. Owls hooted in the distance as they moved, nearly drawing fire; Jasmine shook her head in disbelief, then moved onwards. It was nearly an hour before they reached the road and found a vantage point they could use to spy on traffic.

"Lights," Blake muttered, nodding towards a small building in the distance. "You want to go take a look at it?"

"Yep," Jasmine muttered. If it was a farmhouse – or an enemy guardpost – she wanted to know about it before dawn broke. "Sergeant Harris, stay here and watch the road; Blake, Carl, you're with me."

They followed the road, careful to remain hidden in the undergrowth, until the building came into view. It was a small checkpoint guarding a crossroads, forcing anyone who wanted to use a vehicle to stop for inspection. Jasmine doubted that they could prevent people on foot from simply evading them, but anyone who wanted to use a vehicle would probably have to be checked – more than once, she suspected. The Knights had used a similar system on Avalon.

Not that it prevented Blake's kidnappers from smuggling him out of the city, she thought, ruefully. But then, it hadn't been the Marines who were responsible for providing security at the time.

Up close, she could see three buildings; a small office and a pair of makeshift barracks. It seemed excessive to her; as far as she could tell, there were no actual advantages from having three separate buildings. She motioned for Blake and Carl to remain in reserve and slipped closer, trying to get into a position where she could stare into the windows, then sucked in her breath sharply when she spied four girls inside the closest barracks. They didn't look happy at all.

The second barracks held at least five men, she decided, after listening carefully. Their Imperial Standard held a faint accent that reminded her of Canada's, suggesting that they were collaborators; their chat about the latest football game held very little useful information. If there was a sixth man in the office, he was being very quiet; Jasmine started to slip back into the shadows, cursing mentally as one of the men strode out of the barracks. If he'd carried a light and shone it around, he might well have seen her…

Instead, he strode into the second barracks and barked a command, ordering one of the girls to come to the other barracks. Jasmine gritted her teeth as she realised what was happening; the girls had been kidnapped and pressed into services as drudges, perhaps even sex slaves. The Civil Guardsmen had been fond of the tactic, little caring that it provoked intense hatred among the girls and their relatives. They were paid too little to care. Jasmine was surprised that Admiral Singh tolerated it, but she had a feeling that the farmers simply weren't that important to her. Keeping the collaborators sweet might be more important to her than the farmers and their feelings.

She gritted her teeth as the guard re-emerged, dragging one of the girls with him. It was easy to see the signs of mistreatment, from starvation to outright beatings; Jasmine wanted to lunge forward and break the man's neck. But then they would have to kill all of the guards and that would attract attention from the rest of Admiral Singh's forces. Unless they'd forgotten all common sense, the guards would probably be expected to check in every so often…and when they didn't, reinforcements would immediately be dispatched to investigate.

They didn't dare attract attention, she knew. It didn't make the decision not to intervene any easier.

Jasmine crawled backwards, watching helplessly as the girl was pulled into the barracks and the door was firmly shut. It was easy to hear her protests as the guards molested her…Jasmine cursed silently again, then blinked in surprise as she saw one of the other girls slipping out of the building and heading for a trench behind the barracks. They didn't even have a toilet!

She motioned for Blake and Carl to watch the guardsmen, then slipped after the girl. As soon as she had finished her business, Jasmine came up behind her and covered the girl's mouth with one hand, preventing her from making a sound. She had to hold the girl tightly; her captive no doubt believed that one of her captors had decided to have some fun. Under other circumstances, she would probably have been right.

"I'm from the Empire," she whispered, as she girl struggled helplessly in her arms. "*Look* at me."

The girl turned. Jasmine had her hair cropped close to her skull, but she was unmistakably feminine, *not* someone working for the guards.

"We're working to free your planet," Jasmine said, as the girl relaxed. "Can you get away from them?"

"They know who we are," the girl said, her voice just above a whisper. She had the same accent as the guards. "If we flee, our parents will be punished."

Jasmine nodded. "Then we will have to make them think that you're dead," she said. "What do they make you do for them?"

"Cook, clean and..."

The girl's voice broke off. "Other things," she added, after a moment. Tears started to trickle down her face. "They're *horrible*."

"I know," Jasmine said, giving the girl a hug. "Listen, I'm going to be back here tomorrow night with friends. What do you have inside your barracks?"

"Beds and a food processor," the girl said, puzzled. "Why..."

Jasmine grinned. It was easy to make a food processor explode.

"I'll take care of it," she promised. "Don't tell your friends. If the guards find out, it will not be easy to get you out."

She watched the girl walk back to her barracks, then slipped back to join Blake and Carl. It was easy to hear the girl who had been dragged into the male barracks, but Jasmine felt a little better. They'd be back tomorrow night and, hopefully, they could bury all traces of their presence.

"Hellishly risky, Lieutenant," Carl muttered, as the three Marines walked back into the darkness. "You could have been caught."

"The risk was worth taking," Blake muttered, before Jasmine could say a word. "Besides, we need intelligence."

Jasmine mulled it over as they reached the rest of the group, then headed into the forest. It hadn't been *that* long since they'd been exercising in the Badlands of Avalon, ordered to build shelters and forage for food and drink. From what she'd seen, hiding in the forest here during daytime would be much easier.

"Start building the shelters," she ordered, once they'd reached a place she was confident they could defend, if necessary. A makeshift shelter wouldn't last for long, but it would give them a place to rest up before they headed towards Landing City. "Elliot, I need to talk to you."

Canada looked over at her, puzzled. "Lieutenant?"

"There's a guard post down there," Jasmine said, and explained quickly. "Do you know anything about what sort of guards they put out here?"

"No," Canada admitted. He sounded rueful, as if he believed that he hadn't been very useful. "I lived in the city."

Jasmine wasn't too surprised. "We'll gather more intelligence tomorrow," she said. She'd had to ask. If Canada *had* heard something that might be useful, it could have given her an additional advantage. But she would just have to make do. "And then we can start making our way towards the city."

The shelters were primitive, rough…and far better than some of the places she'd slept in the past. She assigned Sergeant Harris and Blake to take the first watch, then bedded down under the mesh of sticks and leaves they'd used to camouflage their presence. For a long moment, she considered the best way to get the girls out – and use the food processor to cover their tracks – and then closed her eyes and went to sleep.

They'd landed on the planet's surface. Tomorrow, the *real* fun would begin.

CHAPTER SIXTEEN

Worse, few humans are capable of tamely accepting, of their own free will, that they are among the ignorant. They may come up with lists of deserving candidates for the vote, but they will rarely exclude themselves, even when it is clear that they have no actual need to have a say in events. In short, almost everyone will be vain enough to believe that their say in events will never be taken from them.
-Professor Leo Caesius, *Authority, Power and the Post-Imperial Era*

"So," Rani said, very coldly. "What happened?"

There was no point in penalising her subordinates for matters that were outside their control, she knew. They'd just hide matters from her if they thought that they were going to get the blame, a common problem in the Imperial Navy. On the other hand, if someone *had* screwed up, she wanted to make damn sure that person was not in a position to screw up again.

"Someone emplaced a missile pod outside the defence grid and fired a number of missiles towards the planet," Vice Admiral Jubal Birder said. He was the CO of the planet's fixed defences, which made him Sampson's rival. They kept an eye on each other for her. "The missiles had no hope at all of actually *hitting* anything; they burned out before they could reach their targets. We picked them all off and then swept local space in hopes of discovering the enemy ship. We found nothing, apart from a single recon drone. It self-destructed, of course."

Rani nodded. She would have liked to have someone to blame for the brief crisis – if nothing else, it had exposed a number of weaknesses in the defence grid – or for the failure to engage the enemy starship, but she knew that would have been difficult, if not impossible. One ship, even a civilian freighter, could have slipped into the depths of the system long before the missile pod went active and started launching missiles towards the planet. The crew had probably watched the whole affair, including her starships swarming around like angry ants, from a safe distance.

"The drone suggests that we are dealing with more than just terrorists," Sampson said, into the silence. "Pirates don't often dare to confront an armed destroyer, let alone an entire planetary system."

"Or someone could have bought the drone off the pirates and used it against us," Horn countered. A possible outside threat would automatically increase Sampson's power base, Rani knew, weakening Horn's relative position. "You can buy anything on a pirate base. They could have hired a crew of mercenaries there."

"True, but their broadcast claimed that they were fighting on behalf of Greenway," Sampson said, dryly. "I don't think that they would want to compromise themselves *so* badly."

Rani scowled, inwardly. It had been easy to occupy Greenway's high orbitals, but it had been harder to take the ground and secure it. The locals were tough fighters, genuinely devoted to their homeworld; they were staunchly patriotic in a manner that few in the Core Worlds would have recognised, let alone emulated. And some of them *had* managed to capture one of her freighters…could it be that the freighter had doubled back and attacked Corinthian? No, that was absurd. Where would they have found the missile pod?

And, she thought, *what happened to Proud?*

"So we clamp down harder on Greenway, to make the point that resistance is futile," Horn said. "And then we redouble our efforts to bring all of the mercenaries into the fold – or eliminate them."

"Good thought," Rani agreed. She looked over at Sampson. "Send a message to Greenway ordering a couple of punitive strikes."

Sampson looked doubtful, but he didn't object openly.

Rani smiled to herself. "In the meantime, we will run additional patrols of the system and see what we stumble over," she added. It wasn't in her nature to sit where she was and wait for the enemy to show himself again, but there was little choice. "And once we get the reports of the scoutships, we can plan our operations towards the Rim."

She met Horn's eyes, wondering – again – how such a harmless looking man could be so unpleasant. "How much leaked to the planet below?"

"Rumours that the Imperial Navy attacked in force," Horn reported. "We swept most of them out of the datanet, of course, but it is harder to do anything about word of mouth. Quite a few chatterboxes have been identified and we're watching them now, trying to see if they're part of a wider network before moving in…"

"Good," Rani said. "Do you know how word leaked down to the surface?"

"The broadcast was picked up by civilian receivers too," Horn admitted. "And I think there was probably some chatter between installations in orbit and the ground…it might be impossible to identify a specific person to blame."

His eyes glittered. "We could pick a handful of people and publically punish them for being unable to keep their mouths shut," he added. "Their example would encourage the others…"

"To rebel," Sampson said. "We never told them that they should keep their mouths shut about possible threats from outside."

"I would have thought that went without saying," Horn said, smoothly. "We do not encourage people to talk outside of work."

"But people *do* talk," Sampson countered. "We can punish deliberately bad behaviour, but not…not just *talking*."

Horn scowled at him, seeing his advantage slipping away. "But what about spreading rumours?" He demanded. "If the population comes to believe that the Imperial Navy is coming to the rescue, what are they going to do?"

"And if we clamp down on it," Sampson said, "we will lend *credence* to the rumours. People will come to believe them."

Rani listened, thinking hard. Horn was right; if the population started to *believe* the rumours, they might start getting rebellious. It was hard to say why anyone outside the Core Worlds would feel any loyalty to the Empire – Corinthian had been ruled by an Imperial Governor and exploited by interstellar corporations, like so many other worlds – but they had had Rani's forces telling them what to do for the last two years. By now, they would probably be feeling nostalgic for the Empire.

But on the other hand, Sampson was also right; if they clamped down on the rumours, people would think that they were *scared*.

And well we might be, she thought darkly, *if the Imperial Navy actually was coming back.*

"There's no point in random punishment," she said, before the bickering could get any worse. "If we can find someone originating these rumours, we will deal with him. Everyone else…we will just ignore them. Completely. Let our silence show our contempt."

She looked around the table, wondering how many of her chief subordinates would be stupid enough to see it as a sign of weakness. No one doubted that she was more competent than Admiral Bainbridge – a comatose squirrel would be more competent than Admiral Bainbridge – but he'd had legitimacy conferred on him by a system that had existed for over three thousand years. Rani had balanced the different departments as best as she could, preventing any or all of them from gaining an advantage, yet she was still vulnerable if one of them decided he could make a grab for supreme power. Admiral Bainbridge hadn't had to worry about one of his subordinates stabbing him in the back.

The thought made her smile. Perhaps, if the Admiral *had* worried about such an unthinkable event, he would still be alive today.

"Tobias, stay behind," she added. "Everyone else…dismissed."

She watched as the room emptied, noticing how her subordinates kept their distance from one another – particularly from Horn. The man was *diseased*. Very useful, but also very dangerous; one day, she might have to sacrifice him to keep her position. She wondered, absently, if Horn knew that *he* was vulnerable, or did he mistake the appearance of power for true power?

"Admiral," Sampson said, as soon as they were alone. "You don't think that they were terrorists, do you?"

"They would have had to be pretty incompetent terrorists," Rani said. In truth, she wasn't sure of *what* the mysterious attackers had hoped to achieve. Firing missiles from a position well outside their engagement range had caused panic, but little else. "Or maybe they were pirates attempting to distract us."

"Maybe," Sampson said, "or maybe another power is intervening in our territory."

Rani considered it, stroking her chin as she thought. "They'd have given away their existence," she said, "the moment they opened fire. Why not bring in a full battle fleet and launch an attack at point-blank range? They might well have won."

"Assuming that they *have* such a fleet," Sampson pointed out. "You know how many ships we lost, Admiral."

Rani nodded. They'd managed to secure the heavier ships, but several of the smaller ships had been gutted by internal fighting. The commanding officers of destroyers – even light cruisers – tended to be closer to their men than the commanders of battleships…and not all of them had been inclined to swear loyalty to Rani. Some of them had had to be chased down and destroyed, but a handful had escaped. Two years later, Rani still had no idea what had happened to them.

"You think that the escapees could be finally showing their hand," she said. It was difficult to keep a starship going for two years without visiting a shipyard at least once. They'd have to cannibalise non-essential systems to keep the rest going…maybe they'd linked up with pirates or black colonies. They'd be happy to trade spare parts for future services. "But they'd know better than to waste a missile pod."

"Perhaps," Sampson said. "Or perhaps there's something we're not seeing."

"True," Rani agreed. "But all we can do is watch and wait."

She tapped a switch, activating the holographic display. Her scouts had already identified several other worlds that would make good conquests, including two with small industrial bases of their own. A third had factories on the planet's surface, which was inconvenient; they couldn't be moved to Corinthian without considerably more effort than she was willing to spend on the matter. Instead, they'd just be given a list of components to produce and supply to her growing empire – or else.

Expansion was necessary, as was increasing her own industrial base, but it brought its own dangers. The more space she controlled, the more space she had to patrol…and the more authority she had to delegate to lesser commanders. If she didn't give them enough ships, they couldn't carry out their mission; if she gave them too many ships, they might consider rebelling and setting themselves up as independent states. Why not? It was exactly what she'd done. Part of the reason she'd uprooted every industrial node she could and had it transported to Corinthian was to make it impossible for anyone else to create an industrial nexus of their own. But were *all* of her subordinates capable of realising that they couldn't last long if they declared themselves independent?

And dragging everything to Corinthian caused other problems. If someone took the system, her empire was doomed; there simply wasn't enough material to rebuild outside Corinthian itself. She dared not leave the planet for long…and she'd divided up command authority, despite the risks, knowing that it would make it harder for one of her people to stage a coup. But if the planet was attacked, a divided command was asking for trouble…

"Yes, Admiral," Sampson said. he gave her a half-bow. "With your permission…?"

"Dismissed," Rani said.

She sat down on the Governor's throne and scowled. Admiral Bainbridge had spent most of his time enjoying himself, leaving his subordinates to do the work. The former Governor of Corinthian had been even worse. Rani's forces had discovered a harem of genetically-modified sex slaves in his quarters, trained in all the arts of pleasure – or so their supervisor had been quick to assure his captor while he'd been bargaining for his life. Many of his subordinates had had their own sources of pleasure.

Rani picked up the datapad with all the documents she had to read and shook her head. She honestly couldn't *think* where they'd found the time.

On the other hand, she told herself, power was very definitely its own reward.

There were enemies everywhere.

Grytpype Horn had been told to always keep that in mind when he'd first been recruited for Imperial Intelligence, after he'd been caught spying on people who lived in the neighbourhood. Imperial Intelligence had told him that he had a natural talent for intelligence work; they'd been particularly impressed by how he'd sneaked microscopic cameras into the mall's changing room. If he'd had better equipment, they'd added, he would never have been caught at all.

Horn had taken to intelligence work like a duck to water. It was spying on people, it was learning information that others wished to conceal…and it was perfectly legal. He could – and often had – insist on full searches of crewmen he considered suspicious…and there was nothing they could do about it. Even their commanding officers could do little more than issue protests to Horn's superiors, who often commended him for being thoroughly pro-active in his pursuit of spies, subversives and sabotages.

He still wasn't quite sure when he'd made the decision to join Admiral Singh, rather than have her arrested for plotting a mutiny against Admiral Bainbridge and the Imperial Navy. There had been rumours, whispers passed from intelligence officer to intelligence officer, that the Empire was in deep trouble…or, on a more personal level, that his over-zealousness had finally gone too far. If the Empire was to fall, it would be replaced… and Horn had no illusions about his popularity. He was the most hated person on Trafalgar Fleet Base, bar none. Everyone hated and feared his all-seeing eyes.

Except Admiral Singh, who had found him useful. And being *useful* meant that someone would have to keep him alive.

Watching an entire planet – to say nothing of the orbital stations, asteroid habitats and settlements on the other worlds – was far harder than monitoring Trafalgar. There had been very few places on Trafalgar that hadn't been under one kind of surveillance or another, even – and the thought always made him smile – the changing rooms and sleeping compartments. Even the privacy tubes were bugged…he kept a database of some of the more interesting footage he'd recorded over the years and looked at it when he was bored.

But a planet was far harder to monitor. The datanet was massive, there were vast sections of Landing City that were utterly unmonitored by the security network…and the rest of the planet was even harder to keep under surveillance. Horn had built up networks of informants very quickly – it never failed to amuse him just how easy it was to convince someone to betray their fellows, if the right motivation was applied – but it still worried him. *Anything* could be being planned in the shadows, anything at all. And he had no illusions about what would happen to him if there was a coup either.

He looked up as one of his bodyguards lumbered into the office. The man was big, brawny…and had been carefully conditioned to be loyal to Horn, even unto death. He would obey orders without question, no matter what they were, and never thought for himself. The conditioning prevented it. Horn knew that others in the Admiral's inner circle preferred to have bodyguards that could actually think, but he disdained them. A bodyguard who could think was a bodyguard who could turn disloyal.

"A message has arrived from the interrogation chambers," the bodyguard said. Even his voice was flat, utterly unemotional. There was no light behind his eyes at all. "They are ready to begin the session."

Horn smiled. Constant vigilance had led them to yet another cell of plotters – and his forces had swooped down on them in the dead of night. Their families had also been rounded up; he couldn't help licking his lips at the thought of the treat in store for him and his more enthusiastic assistants. It was amazing how talkative parents became when they realised just what fate was in store for their children if they didn't start talking fast.

"Excellent," he said, standing up. "Let us go see what we can learn."

The bodyguard led the way as they walked out of the office and down towards the interrogation chambers, passing dozens of assistants who worked on monitoring the bureaucrats who made the planet actually *work*. Not everyone had the stomach for *real* intelligence gathering, but they could still be useful. Horn still kept a close eye on them, just in case.

He stepped past the two guards outside the interrogation chambers and into the first room. Inside, there were a set of computer monitors showing the chambers…and the first suspect's daughter, being strapped to a table by a pair of leering men. Behind her, a man – her father, Horn assumed – was struggling against a set of iron shackles, desperately pleading with his captors. Horn allowed himself a moment of disappointment. Judging by the man's expression, he was going to break before the real fun could begin.

The next monitor showed a teenage boy lying face-down on a table, being systematically whipped until the blood flowed freely. He'd been caught stealing food, according to the files, and dragged into the interrogation chambers. The food might have been sold on the black market, or to criminal gangs…or to people intent on remaining unregistered. He was loudly protesting his innocence, but no one was listening.

Horn smiled and licked his lips. *This* wasn't going to be disappointing. This was true entertainment – and intelligence gathering. And he honestly didn't understand why others disagreed. Did they gain no pleasure from watching the forbidden?

CHAPTER SEVENTEEN

> However, this runs into a major problem with the democratic system. The more voters there are in the system, the less value each single vote has. Cases where a politician has lost an election by precisely one vote are vanishingly rare – and, of course, it is completely impossible to predict in advance when that will be. The net result is that democratic elections often become about the lowest common denominator.
> -Professor Leo Caesius, *Authority, Power and the Post-Imperial Era*

"They check in every hour on the hour," Sergeant Harris reported, as Jasmine crawled up to where he'd been watching the guardpost. "I guess they don't have the imagination to do anything else."

Jasmine nodded. Sergeant Harris had slipped back towards the guardpost at first light and watched it from hiding all day. Apparently, the crossroads they'd discovered wasn't very busy; the other Marines had only reported seeing seven large vehicles driving down the road, all apparently belonging to farmers. Oddly, they had been powered by gasoline, rather than anything cleaner – or related to HE3. Jasmine couldn't help wondering if Admiral Singh was restricting its distribution on a colossal scale.

"Three of them search; two stay back and watch from a safe distance," Harris added. "The girls generally stay in or near their barracks until they're called upon; they don't seem to have any real freedom at all."

"I guessed that," Jasmine said, tartly. The girls were hostages to their relatives good behaviour. If they ran off, their families would suffer. It was a more effective way of keeping them prisoner than chaining them down every night or guarding them constantly. "Tonight, that is going to change."

They'd talked through the plan twice, until they all knew what was going to happen. Once darkness fell completely – and the guards had made their call to their superiors – the Marines would creep closer and carry out the plan. If they were lucky, Jasmine knew, the guards would never even realise that the Marines had been there. But if they weren't lucky, they would just have to kill the guards and make it look like an accident.

The sun dipped down over the horizon and darkness fell across the land. Jasmine had a sudden sense of *Déjà Vu*, remembering midnight walks on her homeworld many years ago, before looking towards the faint glow in the distance. Landing City never slept, any more than Camelot did…and it was a much larger habitation. In contrast, the farmhouses they'd observed had been hidden in the darkness.

She looked back towards the guardpost and smiled. Someone was playing music, a thumping tune she vaguely recognised from her time on Earth. Unlike Avalon, it seemed that Corinthian hadn't developed its own musical tradition after being separated from the Empire, although maybe it was just a matter of time. Corinthian had a more integrated population than Avalon ever had.

And the music would make it harder for the guards to hear them as they crept towards the cabin.

Jasmine used hand signals to issue commands, then started to crawl down towards the guardpost, followed by Blake and Carl. Up close, she could hear the lyrics as the singer attempted to deafen everyone in the vicinity, an endless stream of obscenities that was somehow considered high art. Jasmine's father would have clouted her for listening to such songs, she thought, before deciding that it was probably a good thing she hadn't heard it while she was a child. She couldn't think of any more pointless ways to rebel as a teenager.

She motioned Blake and Carl to watch the guardroom while she tapped on the door of the female barracks. It opened, revealing the girl she'd seen the previous day – and a trio of shocked faces. One of the girls was missing. Jasmine put one finger on her lips and tried to ask, using her hands, where the fifth girl was. The girl she'd met pointed to the guardroom. Jasmine sucked in her breath sharply, then beckoned for the girls to come out of the building and walk away from the guardpost. They'd have to get the fifth out by force.

Carl shaped a message with his hands. *Stun grenade?*

Yes, Jasmine signalled back. *Now.*

She braced herself as Carl removed the grenade from his belt and tossed it through the opened window. There was a burst of male swearing, followed by sudden silence as the gas blew through the small building. Stun gas worked surprisingly quickly, assuming that the targets hadn't been immunised to the gas; Jasmine clutched her pistol tightly as she opened the door, scanning for potential targets. All five of the men – and a girl, wearing nothing more than her panties – had slumped to the floor. None of them had been immunised.

"Get the girl out of here," Jasmine ordered, as she swept the room for useful intelligence. A map of the surrounding area lay on a table, displaying a handful of guardposts and a small military garrison, only seven kilometres away. She snapped a photo of it with her camera, then searched the rest of the room. One drawer proved to contain a surprising amount of paper money, marked in a language she didn't recognise. Jasmine took the money and stuffed it in her bag.

"Thief," Blake commented.

"Rig up the food processor," Jasmine ordered, ignoring his dig at her. There were regulations about what to do when discovering enemy funds, although they tended to be largely ignored by both the Army and the Civil Guard. Jasmine would have handed them over to Colonel Stalker if he'd been on the same planet. Instead, she'd have to use them to fund their mission. "Hurry."

She looked down at the stunned men, then gently pressed a neural disrupter to the first man's skull. His body twitched, then died. Jasmine felt an odd pang of guilt – no matter how much the men deserved it, this was cold-blooded slaughter, not honest battle – before moving on to the next one. It was hard to prove that a neural disrupter had been involved even without additional damage to the victim's body. If they worked at long ranges, they would have been the most feared assassination weapon in the universe. But they could only operate at point-blank range.

Sergeant Hampton slipped down to join them as they stepped out of the guardpost. "Here," he said, holding out a set of injector tubes. Blake took them and headed back into the guardpost. They'd taken some blood from each of the girls, enough – Jasmine hoped – to convince a forensic team that they'd died in the fire. "They're a little upset, but happy."

"Glad to hear it," Jasmine said. The girls wouldn't be waiting; they were already being taken back to the hidden shelters. Once Blake had completed his jury-rigging, they'd have to move fast. There was no way to know how much time they had before the nearby garrison responded to the fire. "Blake?"

Blake re-emerged from the guardhouse. "She's ready to blow, Lieutenant," he said. "When do you want it to blow?"

"Five minutes," Jasmine said, as she led the way back up to the OP. She could still hear that damned music ringing in her ears. What sort of idiots maintained a guardpost while deliberately deafening themselves? No doubt their superiors would have punished them, if they cared. Jasmine still remembered the lecture she'd received from a Drill Instructor after falling asleep on watch. "Ready?"

Blake nodded, producing the detonator from his pocket. "Ready," he said, as his thumb hovered over the switch. "Now?"

Jasmine smiled. "Now," she said.

The guardpost exploded in a sheet of fire. Food processors could be rigged to blow with a little effort, particularly cheap designs; Jasmine had a private suspicion that the one Blake had rigged to explode wouldn't be the first one that *had* exploded, even if it was unusually violent. But with ten people in the same room, it might just have been knocked to the floor and exploded…any investigator would be hard pressed to explain exactly *what* had happened. At the very least, there would be some reasonable doubt.

She kept one eye on the sky as the Marines slipped further into the forest, but it was nearly ten minutes before they heard the first helicopters clattering their way through the sky. One of them passed high overhead, suggesting that it had come from a different direction to the garrison they knew about. Another one, on the other side of the mountains? There was no way to know.

If Jasmine had been in command of the recovery party, the first thing she would have done – once it became obvious that there was no one left to save – would have been to sweep the area, looking for possible insurgents or terrorists. With that in mind, she kept the Marines moving until they were well away from the fire, hoping that Sergeant Hampton had ordered the girls carried if they hadn't been able to keep up. There was no sign of pursuit, which both pleased and worried her. The enemy could have been tracking them through a drone or orbital surveillance and was just waiting to see where they would go.

Finally, they reached the RV point and linked up with the rest of the Marines. The girls looked uncomfortable – none of the Marines had realised that they didn't have clothes suitable for the night, only skimpy nightdresses – but relieved to be well away from their tormentors. Jasmine saw one of them staring towards the glow in the distance, where the fire was still blazing merrily, her eyes shining with tears. After so long as a captive, it was possible that someone might have stopped caring about those at risk if she fled.

They'll have to be watched, she thought, remembering how some of the pirate captives had eventually fallen in love with their captors. The human mind was good at adapting to new situations, even if the methods made little sense to an external mind. Falling in love with a rapist? Mistaking rape for affection? It was absurd, but very human.

"Get some sleep," she ordered, once the girls had drunk some nutrient glop from a pre-packaged meal. It included a sedative that would help them to rest – and avoid nightmares that might draw attention to where they were hiding. "We'll keep you safe."

She ordered most of the Marines to sleep as well in the makeshift shelters, while she and Sergeant Harris kept watch. No enemy forces seemed to come close to them, apart from a second helicopter that buzzed past a kilometre from where they were hiding. It didn't seem to be running a search pattern, although it was impossible to be sure. *She* might have ordered the helicopter to buzz randomly in the hope of sparking a noticeable reaction.

The sun was rising high in the sky when the girls finally began to stir. Jasmine had Kate keep an eye on them, suspecting that they would prefer to see a female face than more men, no matter how trustworthy. Rape victims tended to shy away from all men, the innocent along with the guilty. None of them, thankfully, cried out upon discovering themselves in the forest, but they all looked astonished. Jasmine smiled as the girl she'd met started to explain.

"I'm Lori," the girl said, afterwards. "And you're from the Empire."

"That's right," Jasmine said, feeling a flicker of guilt at lying to the girl. It wasn't exactly a lie – the Empire had funded her training – but it wasn't the Empire that was going to go to war with Admiral Singh. "How did you end up in that hellhole?"

It was confusing to hear three of the girls try to answer – the other two just stared at the Marines, as if they couldn't believe their eyes – but Jasmine put it together eventually. Their parents had been farmers, holding large tracts of land in their own name – and Admiral Singh's new authority had ordered them to produce vast quantities of food at a controlled price. When they'd balked, their daughters had been taken from them to ensure their cooperation – and the girls themselves had been told that if they rebelled or escaped, their families would bear the brunt of their punishment.

"I think the first priority is getting in touch with your parents," Jasmine said, once they'd finished explaining. If Admiral Singh's people believed the girls to be dead, they probably wouldn't tell the parents. It would be much easier just to let them continue to believe that the girls were hostages. "Where are your farms?"

Sergeant Harris crept back towards the guardpost as the girls helped to identify farms and other places on the maps, eventually returning to report that the guardpost had been completely destroyed and that the enemy soldiers were starting to rebuild it. They didn't seem very suspicious, suggesting that they'd been convinced by the deception; Harris had slipped in and out without being caught. Still, they were inspecting every vehicle far more closely than before, just in case the fire suggested weakness. The Marines would have to give them a wide berth.

"We'll have to stick with the forest until we reach here," Jasmine said, once they'd hidden all traces of their presence. "Let's go."

Unsurprisingly, most of the girls proved to be capable of keeping up with the Marines as they marched through the forest. Rifleman Roger Severus, who'd studied combat medicine at the Slaughterhouse, had briefly examined the girls and reported that while there were no major injuries, there had been a lot of minor bruises, suggesting that they had been regularly hit and kicked to get them working properly. He'd added that there was a very real possibility that there might be internal damage, but he didn't have the tools to examine them – even if they'd allowed it. They'd been uncomfortable enough allowing him to examine their bodies.

"We used to hunt here," Lori said, as they reached the edge of her father's land. "Rabbits, foxes, deer…we hunted them all, before the Admiral came."

She hesitated. "You might want to wait here," she added. "I can find my father and tell him that you're here."

Jasmine frowned, looking towards the farm. It was larger than she'd realised from the map – and surprisingly populated. Several gangs of workers were busy in the fields, supervised by other men; a shiver ran down her spine as she realised that it was exactly like the penal farms on Avalon. Were the workers prisoners?

"I don't know," Lori admitted. "They weren't there before I was taken away."

Jasmine exchanged a long glance with Sergeant Harris. Sending the girl to contact her father risked her being seen – and one of the workers, if they were really prisoners, might betray her in hopes of having his sentence reduced. But there didn't seem to be any alternative. If one of the Marines went, a clear stranger, it would also be noticed. And the locals wouldn't try to lie for a stranger if the Admiral's security forces threatened them.

"Go, then," she ordered. Wearing what she was, she would definitely attract attention. "And try to stay out of sight."

Lori gave her a brilliant grin. "I know the farm like the back of my hand," she assured her. "I won't be seen."

She slipped off through the trees, walking down towards a ditch that would provide some cover as she slipped towards the farmhouse. Jasmine smiled, remembering a senior recruit from the Slaughterhouse who had also claimed to know a particular area like the back of his hand. The Drill Instructor had been particularly scathing, claiming that he must have been wearing gloves; it hadn't been until later that Jasmine had realised that the recruits had been meant to realise that they were being deliberately mislead. Their leader had played his role to perfection.

Time passed; Jasmine watched, feeling a deeper sense of unease. A whistle blew in the distance and the workers started to head towards a large barn, where young women were already laying out some food for them. It didn't look very appetising, even from their distance, but Jasmine suspected that the workers would be glad to have it. They were probably worked from dawn to dusk.

Her eyes narrowed as she saw a tall man striding towards them, followed by Lori. She'd changed her clothes and put on a headscarf that concealed her hair, Jasmine realised, wondering if she'd just delayed matters so she could change. Her father – or so Jasmine assumed – strode into the woodlands and stopped, looking around.

Jasmine stepped out of the bushes, revealing herself. "The gods be praised," Lori's father said, when he'd stopped gaping at her. He hadn't seen the other Marines from where they were hidden, ready to intervene if things went bad. "You're *real*."

"Real enough," Jasmine assured him. She looked past him, towards his fields. "Who are the workers down there?"

"People who lost the conscription lottery," Lori's father admitted. There was a bitter tone to his voice, a hint of frustration. Jasmine understood; she wouldn't have wanted unwilling workers either. "I don't want them, but I wasn't given a choice."

He scowled. "Do you bring hope?"

"We're the first recon party," Jasmine said, carefully. She didn't want to say too much; if he happened to be captured, he'd be shot full of truth drugs and then be interrogated until he made a full confession. "We need to collect intelligence – and we have to get into the city. Can you help with that?"

Lori's father smiled. "You know," he said, "you saved my daughter. I do believe I can."

He turned and headed back towards the farmhouse. "You can come in," he added. "Bring the other girls. We can talk there."

Jasmine briefly detailed Blake and Carl to accompany her, leaving the other Marines in the woods, and then followed him down towards the building.

CHAPTER EIGHTEEN

> Thus, we see elections being won and lost by struggles over issues that have little practical importance. As a very old sage put it, there are subjects about which everyone has an opinion, no matter how nonsensical they seem. Sexual conduct, for example, is of little importance as long as compulsion (or immature human beings) are not involved – and yet politicians have won office over promising to make such matters of public importance.
> -Professor Leo Caesius, *Authority, Power and the Post-Imperial Era*

"My name is Robert Marhanka," Lori's father said, once they were inside the house and his wife had taken the girls off for a proper wash. "How… how did you get Lori away from her captors?"

"Stealth," Jasmine said, shortly. "I don't know if they will come looking for the girls or not, but you will have to hide them…"

"There's quite a community in the hills," Marhanka said, shortly. "They *will* be hidden."

He leaned forward. "You want information? I can give you information."

Jasmine listened carefully as he spoke, outlining everything that had happened since Admiral Singh had taken control of the planets. There had been a mass registration of farmers, then they'd been given quotas to meet – and woe betide them if they failed to provide enough food on time. Some of the farmers had planned resistance, before their daughters had been taken away to serve as hostages. Since then, they'd had to work – and put up with the presence of unwanted extra hands on the farm. Most of the city-folk hadn't had the first idea of what they were doing and the near-constant presence of their overseers made it harder for the farmers to help them.

"That's the new money they've produced to replace the Imperial Credit," Marhanka explained, when Jasmine showed him the money she'd taken from the guardpost. "I think they were talking about moving to a purely electronic system, but it never got off the ground."

"It might, given enough time," Jasmine said. Avalon's original Council had used a similar system to maintain their grip on power. It had worked – but it had also strangled the economy. "How do you plan to get us down to the city?"

Marhanka hesitated, then nodded slowly. "There's an…underground market," he explained, reluctantly. "They smuggle people into the city as well as food – quite a few conscripts just want to go home after they've been sent out here."

Jasmine frowned. "And that will get us through their security?"

"The people running it have identified a number of security officials who take bribes," Marhanka explained. "They've never been caught."

There's always a first time, Jasmine thought, coldly. She wasn't surprised to discover that corruption was already seeping into Admiral Singh's administration. A ruthless government and a complete lack of regard for rules would encourage others to take what they could get out of the system. Besides, the planet's criminal underground would be very capable of identifying people who might be amiable to a few bribes – or have tastes that needed criminal connections to fulfil. Even the Grand Senate was denied a few pleasures, which was probably why their jaded palates had wanted them.

"I need to get some of us into the city," she said. She didn't want to leave anyone outside the city, but she suspected that she had no choice. Fifteen people travelling as a group might attract attention. "How long will it take you to set it up?"

Marhanka considered. "A day or two," he said. "I've made the preparations before, so tell me: how many people do you want to send in the first batch?"

"Five," Jasmine said, making up her mind. Sergeant Hampton could bring another five in the following day, while Sergeant Harris could remain outside the city with four others. If the shit hit the fan and they were caught, at least he and his men would remain at liberty. "If that isn't too many…"

"We'll just have to get you some forged papers," Marhanka said. He grinned, savagely. "I'm going to enjoy this."

Jasmine frowned. "How did you send the others into the city?"

"There's quite a flow of people going into the city looking for work," Marhanka said. "The bastards pay quite good wages, particularly if you happen to have technical skills and be facing the draft if you turn twenty-one without a job. We'll get you some papers and money, find you a place to stay…you should be fine, as long as you don't do something stupid."

"Understood," Jasmine said. Trying to overthrow the government wasn't something stupid, was it? Not, in the end, that it mattered. She'd known the job was dangerous when she took it. "We won't stay here with you, but lurk in the forest. You can send your daughter to look for us when the time comes to go."

It was two days before Lori came stumbling back into the forest, wearing a wig that made her look like her elder sister. Jasmine intercepted her before she could start shouting or do something else that might attract attention and took her deeper into the forest, but not too close to the hidden camp. It was dangerous dealing with civilians; it was quite possible that Marhanka would sell them out, fearing for his family's life.

"Dad's set up transport," Lori said, once she caught her breath. She unslung her knapsack and produced a cardboard folder. "There are five sets of documents for you and your men; you have to keep them with you at all times. They'll tell you that you have to get a proper ID card in the city, but you can't do that. The papers won't stand up to close scrutiny. You'll need to find another source in the city that won't ask too many questions…"

Jasmine studied the papers quickly. They weren't too detailed, thankfully; there was little that could be used to trap them. The Marines would look like farmer boys from one of the smaller farms nearer the hills, the ones that were having problems meeting their quotas and paying their taxes. It would make perfect sense for them to be looking for jobs in the big city; their papers even claimed that they had limited mechanical skills. It was surprising how such skills – or, rather, the right mindset – translated into space-capable workers.

Once the other Marines were briefed, she allowed Lori to lead them down to where a small open-topped truck was parked, half-hidden in the trees. Lori's father had provided them with some more suitable clothing – Jasmine's shirt was loose, concealing her breasts – but hiding the weapons had been a bit more problematic. If they were stopped by a roving patrol that wanted to look inside the bags, they'd have to fight.

"The driver knows to get you into the city, where a room has been arranged for you," Lori said, as the Marines started to climb into the back of the truck. "After that…"

She looked up at Jasmine, then stepped closer. "Good luck," she whispered, softly. "And bring help."

The truck roared into life, lurching almost as badly as one of the Mammoth tanks the Imperial Army deployed whenever they wanted to *really* impress and intimidate the locals. Jasmine caught hold of the railing and hung on tightly as the truck roared down the dirt pathway and out onto the road. She silently compared their journey against the maps she'd memorised and relaxed when she realised that they were definitely heading towards the city.

There were more signs of civilisation as they kept driving onwards. Countless fields, some tilled by machines and some tilled by people, each one seemingly large enough to provide enough food for an entire town. Dozens of small towns and villages, some charmingly rural and hidden within the trees, others hastily put together from prefabricated components. It was a surprise to see them – normally, such buildings were only seen on newly-settled colony worlds – but it made a certain kind of sense. If Admiral Singh was trying to encourage people to work on the farms, she'd have to provide accommodation for them.

They passed a handful of other vehicles on the road before they finally encountered a checkpoint. Jasmine braced herself, ready to fight, but the guardsmen merely checked their papers, glanced into the rear of the truck and waved them onwards. Bribed…or just incompetent? There was no way to know.

"Maybe we should have fought," Blake muttered. "Did you see the way they were holding their weapons?"

"Or we could have just shouted BOO very loudly," Carl added. "They would probably have shot themselves."

Jasmine nodded. The guardsmen hadn't been very careful with their weapons at all. Clearly, *their* instructors hadn't taken a dim view of accidentally firing a shot…even if no one was hurt. Marine recruits who accidentally pulled the triggers of their rifles were sentenced to extremely inventive punishment duties, or sent back a class. Fire discipline was extremely important.

But the problem with battle was that it tended to separate the incompetent from the competent. On Han, after the first surprise had faded, the Imperial Army and Marines had exterminated large numbers of insurgents. Those who had survived the punishing experience, however, were tougher and more determined – and smarter – than those who had died. The rest of the fighting had been against a smaller enemy force and yet it had been much harder.

She settled back as the truck picked up speed again, passing a dozen large buildings that reminded Jasmine of the mansions Avalon's former Council had built for itself. They appeared to be guarded by private guards, although they looked more competent than the guardsmen they'd seen at the checkpoint. Perhaps whoever owned the mansions had offered to pay more than Admiral Singh…it was possible. Or perhaps the mansions simply belonged to some of her cronies. She'd have to reward them somehow.

"They belong to the oligarchs," Canada said, shortly. "They used to kiss the Governor's ass and in exchange they controlled much of the planet. Now…I suppose they're working for Admiral Singh instead."

"Probably," Jasmine said. They'd have to parse out how Admiral Singh's administration actually worked before they started trying to jam sticks in the wheels. The Empire's formal power structure often bore little relationship to reality. "But we will soon show them the error of their ways."

Landing City's towers were slowly coming into view. It was clear that the planet had been settled for much longer than Avalon; normally, skyscrapers took a couple of hundred years before they started to emerge on a newly-settled world. Small flotillas of aircars buzzed through the air, barely visible even to her enhanced eyesight, suggesting a far more developed infrastructure. Or maybe Admiral Singh allowed the pilots to fly their own aircars…no, that didn't seem likely. Everything she'd done seemed to be about controlling her captive population.

"Another checkpoint," Carl hissed. "Here we go again."

Jasmine scowled, but held herself at the ready again as the guardsmen examined their papers, before passing them back to the driver and allowing them to go onwards. None of them seemed very competent either, even though they were driving into the city itself. The outer edge of Landing City was composed of more prefabricated buildings, but it was still clearly part of the city. Or maybe the Admiral didn't care if there was trouble in the outskirts. It was the core of the city that was truly important.

The district sent chills down her spine, although it took her a moment to realise why. It reminded her of Han; the same utterly characterless buildings, the same air of hopelessness…and the same lack of anything to do, apart from work. There were children kicking balls through the streets – all boys, she couldn't help noticing – and a handful of young teenagers, but most of the people were old. And quite a few of them were clearly as alien to the planet as Jasmine herself.

"This wasn't here when I was conscripted," Canada said. "I don't know who these people are."

Jasmine could guess. Camelot had had to build living quarters for immigrants quickly, once the economic boom had taken off; Corinthian would probably have had to do the same. Except Admiral Singh hadn't tried to produce *nice* apartments; she'd simply deployed prefabricated buildings and told the immigrants to put up and shut up. There were no gardens, no parks, no swimming pools…nothing for the children to do, apart from schooling. And when they grew up, they'd be conscripted into the Admiral's growing military machine.

Bitch, she thought, coldly. *God damn you to hell.*

The truck rumbled to a halt in front of an apartment block, as anonymous as the rest. "Your rent has been paid for a week," the driver said, once he'd jumped out of the cab and motioned for the Marines to join him. "After that, you're on your own. Good luck finding some employment around here."

Jasmine suspected that he had a point. Given how Admiral Singh had deployed her security network, it was quite likely that they would be detected if they stayed in the building – or if they didn't have any clear source of food or money. They would have to figure out what they were doing very quickly, starting with finding a place to hide that wasn't known to anyone else. She suspected that she could trust Lori's father, but how far could she trust his associates?

Blake led the way into the apartment block, wrinkling his nose at the smell. Inside, it was as barren and unprepossessing as its exterior, without even children's paintings to brighten up the walls. It didn't smell as bad as a pirate ship, but judging by the stains on the walls the only real difference was someone attempting to wash the hallway out from time to time. The dull metal that had been used to build the block was waterproof, allowing someone to use a hose to cleanse it. It still left unpleasant traces of human activity.

They walked up a flight of metal stairs and into the apartment. It was almost completely empty; the toilet seemed broken, while the bedding they'd been promised was nothing more than a pile of mouldy blankets. Jasmine had a sudden vision of what life must be like for the average person in Admiral Singh's world, even though she had to admit that it was a hell of an incentive to find a job. Anyone who was content to live in such a shithole probably wouldn't be able to handle a job in any case.

"Could be worse," Carl said, unconvincingly.

"Yeah, we could have fallen into the shit again," Blake said. He didn't sound any happier. They'd been in worse, but that didn't mean they had to like it. He held up his hands to signal a question. "Eyes and ears?"

The Marines searched the apartment quickly and carefully, finding nothing. If there was one advantage to the empty set of rooms, it was difficult to hide bugs, even ones so tiny that they couldn't be seen with the naked eye. Jasmine would have been surprised if the security forces had bothered to bug such apartments, but she swept anyway, just in case. If there had been bugs, they would have to be very careful what they said out loud.

"Clear," she said, finally. The Marines relaxed, then started pulling at the blankets. "We'll start exploring the city tomorrow."

She scowled down at her hand as she walked over to the plastic window and peered down onto the street below. It wasn't going to be easy to locate the underground, let alone make contact without being observed by the security forces – assuming, of course, that they *were* monitoring the underground. But they had to be, unless there was no underground… she dismissed that line of thought as unprofitable and joined Blake in his search for cleaning utensils. There was nothing, apart from a bucket with a hole in the bottom.

"I'm surprised they're not coming down with the galloping shits, all the time," Blake said, as he reconnected the toilet. "This place stinks worse than the field toilets we…"

"Thank you," Jasmine said, hastily. "I don't want to know."

He was right; field sanitation was important, but no one seemed to have mentioned it to the apartment's previous inhabitants. Her imagination formed a picture of them dropping dead before she decided that it was unlikely. Maybe they'd just been pushed to make something of themselves and go up in the world. Maybe.

There was a harsh knock on the door. Jasmine tensed; the plastic window was too small to allow any of them, even her, to climb out. She motioned the other four into the kitchen, then strode over to the apartment door and pulled it open. A dark-skinned young man was standing on the other side, looking at her as if she was something he'd scraped off his shoe, with three others standing behind him. His gaze flickered across her chest before he stepped forwards, into the apartment.

"I'm…calling on behalf of the neighbourhood welcoming committee," he said, as soon as the door was closed. "There are tithes to pay as long as you live here."

Jasmine sized him up. A thug, someone who thought using the word *tithe* instead of *protection money* made him sound smart. Probably nowhere near as important as he thought he was. And too used to bullying people to realise when he'd caught a tiger by the tail.

She gave him a completely sweet, completely fake smile. "And dare I assume that if we don't pay you…*tithes*, we will regret it?"

The thug blinked at her. "Yeah…right?"

"My associates and I will be happy to discuss it with you," Jasmine said. "If you'll look at this for one second…"

CHAPTER NINETEEN

> This also tends to lead to a focus on matters of immediate importance. If, for example, it will cost the taxpayers a considerable sum of money to modify the mass-transit system – and the work does not need to be done immediately – the political leadership will do its best to avoid having to pay for the work, passing it on to their successors. The fact that the cost often increases doesn't deter them – why not, when they don't have to pay?
> -Professor Leo Caesius, *Authority, Power and the Post-Imperial Era*

The fight lasted barely seven seconds. Jasmine slammed a punch into the leader's chest, sending him doubling over in agony, while Blake and Carl dealt with his two friends. None of them were ready for true violence, she noted, as she put her foot on the leader's throat to keep him quiet. They certainly hadn't realised who they were facing.

Although maybe that shouldn't have been a surprise, she thought, once the gangbangers had been knocked down. *They're so used to picking on people who don't dare attract attention that they don't realise that some people might fight back.*

"Knock them both out," Jasmine ordered, as she studied the gang leader. The other two looked like dumb muscle, living proof of the theory of evolution. In some ways, their appearance reminded her of the hints from Earth's undercity that incest was becoming socially acceptable down there. "This one can be made to talk."

The gangster stared up at her in absolute horror, mixed with pain. Jasmine felt a flicker of wry amusement – and horror. Was this what

Admiral Singh considered acceptable? The gangsters living in the shadows, preying on those who could not defend themselves…were they a symptom of how corrupt her society was becoming or were they part of her plan to motivate people to work for her? Probably the former, Jasmine decided; given how regimented society had become, there was plenty of room for criminal organisations to flourish.

"Done," Blake said, banging one gangster's head on the floor until he went limp. "You want us to kill them, boss?"

The gangster looked even more horrified. Somehow, Jasmine doubted that Admiral Singh's security forces would pay much attention to a handful of dead bodies, particularly if they were part of the grey or black economy instead of working for the Admiral. It would be easy to slit their throats and drop them some distance from the apartment, even though some prying eyes might see them and alert the authorities. But that was unlikely. Corinthian's poorest districts, like all of the others Jasmine had seen, probably wouldn't want to do anything to attract the authorities. Besides, they might be grateful that someone had killed the gangsters.

But they will be replaced, Jasmine thought, remembering how hard it had been to eradicate the criminal gangs operating in Camelot, a far smaller city. *Scum like them always are.*

She picked up the gangster by the throat and held him up in front of her. He started to shake, terrified out of his mind. Jasmine sighed, produced a knife from her belt and held it just in front of his right eye. There was a sudden unpleasant smell as the gangster wet himself with fear.

"This is how it's going to be," Jasmine said, keeping her voice deadly calm. "You're going to answer our questions. Once you're done, you will be released."

She smiled at him, feeling his entire body shudder, then dropped him on the floor and pressed her fingers against his neck. "There's a nerve here that twitches if you lie," she lied, smoothly. The gangbanger was too shaken up to question her words. "For every lie you tell us, you will lose one of your fingers. Do you understand me?"

The gangster nodded, desperately. "Good," Jasmine said. "Tell me; what do you actually *do* here?"

It took nearly thirty minutes to get a series of straight answers out of the gangster. They took turns shouting questions at the young man; he seemed to find Blake more intimidating, something that made Jasmine roll her eyes. A very typical attitude for a very typical male thug. The gangster ran what was effectively a protection racket; those who paid his *tithes* were allowed to operate freely, but those who didn't were harassed and eventually beaten bloody until they surrendered. Their writ ran over a single housing estate; they didn't seem to have any authority outside the estate at all. They didn't think they had any connections to the government, but they did have links with larger criminal organisations.

They didn't seem to do much else *beyond* the protection racket, Jasmine realised, which surprised her. If they were in command of the illicit part of the economy, at least in one small set of apartment blocks, why didn't they trade in drugs or prostitution? Or theft? No, that made sense; the people living here simply didn't have very much worth stealing, apart from small amounts of money and food. The gangster, when pressed, admitted that they were kept out of *those* criminal networks; they were handled by senior gangsters, who barely had anything to do with the street thugs.

Jasmine scowled as the scope of the criminal network became clear. The gangbangers might consider themselves semi-autonomous, but they effectively worked for someone more powerful – someone who might notice if Jasmine and her team killed the thugs. Maybe it would have been better to pay up, rather than risk attracting attention; she scowled inwardly, then looked down at the prostrate gangster. On the other hand, a contact within the more powerful criminal organisations might be very useful indeed.

"So tell me," she purred, "where can we find your superior?"

Two hours later – having tied up the gangsters and injected them with some of their own drugs, before abandoning them in the apartment – they found themselves outside a large house, studying the guards with professional interest. The house was built out of brick, rather than the prefabricated components, suggesting that the owner was wealthy or well-connected; the guards looked reasonably capable, although they didn't seem to realise that they were being watched. Jasmine was surprised that

Admiral Singh's security forces allowed the criminal masterminds to operate at all; they didn't seem to be trying to *hide*. On the other hand, they probably paid out a vast sum of money every year in bribes. What good did it do to have a security network if the people operating it took money to look the other way? It had been an old problem on Han.

"They don't seem to be paying much attention to the rear," Blake muttered, after they'd walked around the building. Either the guards were asleep or they were plotting an ambush. "We could get up there easy."

Jasmine nodded. There were no doors at the rear of the building and the windows were all barred, but the bricks were so roughly placed that scrambling up the wall would be easy...and the upper windows were unprotected. It was a curious oversight, something that bothered her, even though she knew that the most powerful crime lords generated so much fear that few would dare to beard them in their den. Few of the crime lords on Earth had operated in total secrecy, after all. Intimidation had kept them alive.

Intimidation and the reluctance of the authorities to actually confront them, she thought, coldly. *And if this goes wrong*.

"Elliot, remain outside," she ordered. Marines were trained to scale walls, even if the handholds were so tenuous as to be barely there, but Canada didn't have that sort of training, a terrible oversight on Admiral Singh's part. "The rest of us will go up the wall."

It had been months since she'd had to scramble up a wall, but her body remembered how to do it; it was merely a matter of finding the right hand and footholds to bear her weight for a few seconds while she found the next one. She scrambled up to the window and glanced inside, ready to draw her pistol if she came face to face with another guard. Instead, she saw a small bedroom that seemed to be completely empty. It was simple enough to scramble inside quietly and drop down beside the bed.

"Seems like a room for a young girl," Blake signalled, when he joined her. "Too many dolls to be anything else."

Jasmine nodded and tested the door. It was locked, but it was simple enough to pick with her multitool. Outside, the air was cooler and she could hear the faint sounds of someone chatting in the distance. Holding up one hand to warn the other three to keep their distance, she crept down the carpeted corridor and stopped outside the next room. Someone was talking in a language she didn't recognise; carefully, she peered around the door and saw two men, seated in front of a large table. One of them looked up and saw her. His eyes went wide with horror.

She stepped into the room, weapon in hand. "Good afternoon," she said, in Imperial Standard. "Please remain still and make no sudden movements. It would be fatal if you did."

Judging from the description they had pulled from the gangbanger, one of them was the crime lord – one of the major crime lords in Landing City. He was a short little man, seemingly harmless; he reminded Jasmine of the bureaucrats she'd had to deal with before they'd been exiled from Earth. But the bureaucrats had been capable of doing great damage, as well as always finding an excuse in the regulations to justify their actions. No doubt this man had sent gangsters around to break legs if the money wasn't forthcoming - always to his eternal regret, of course.

The other man seemed more of an accountant. He certainly didn't offer any resistance as the Marines tied him up, then pushed him against the wall while they dealt with the crime lord.

"Let's start with the basics," Jasmine said, as she pushed an injector tab against the crime lord's forehead. He winced as she shot something into his skull. "You have just been implanted with a long-range death-bringer implant. What that means, assuming you don't know, is that I or one of my comrades can push the button and your head will explode."

The crime lord stared at her in dawning horror. "If you wish to escape the detonation, you will have to hide in a shielded room for the rest of your life," Jasmine continued, lying smoothly. "The implant actually checks routinely to make sure that the destruct signal hasn't been sent. Should it *have* been sent…well, better late than never. Oh, and should you try to remove it, the implant will detonate anyway. The explosive charge isn't very powerful, but it doesn't have to be to destroy your brain.

"What *that* means," she concluded, "is that you have the choice between working for us or being terminated. Do you understand me?"

The crime lord nodded frantically. Jasmine smiled, careful to hide her relief. She'd actually shot him with a drug that would make him more suggestive for a short period of time, although it would take greater nerve than she suspected the crime lord possessed to actually *check* what Jasmine had told him. Digging around in his skull for the implant might trigger it, after all…or do damage on its own.

She'd considered trying to buddy up to the criminal underground, but they might well have betrayed the Marines once they realised just what they actually were. Posing as deserters from Admiral Singh's forces might have won them employment, or might have had the crime lords selling them out…which would have caused no end of problems. Instead…she'd been forced to intimidate the crime lord into helping them. She'd just have to be careful not to push him so far that he rebelled – and discovered that she was bluffing him.

"On the other hand," she added, "if you work with us, there will be considerable rewards for those who remain faithful. I will release you; you can widen your control until you hold the entire city in your hands. Think about what we just did to you – and what we could do to your rivals. Wouldn't that make working with us worthwhile?"

She smiled down at the crime lord. "So tell me," she said finally, "what is your name?"

"Wolf," the crime lord admitted.

Jasmine kept her expression under control. No doubt the crime lord thought that the nickname was intimidating in its own right, although she suspected that anyone with true intelligence would find *sheepdog* to be a great deal more worrying. Wolves preyed on the sheep, but they didn't have the intellect to think long-term…

"Right," Jasmine said, dryly. She smiled as he flinched at her tone. "Now, we are going to talk about your organisation – and how it can be improved."

"I'll have to talk to the guards first," Wolf said. "They may not know who you are."

"Good idea," Jasmine agreed. "Tell them…tell them that we're your special bodyguards and that we have permission to visit you at any time. And *don't* try anything clever. The results will not be pleasant."

She motioned for Blake to escort Wolf out of the room, shaking her head in wry amusement. The crime lord would probably not remain under control, even though his life was at stake – and if he called her bluff, they were in deep trouble. They would have to find something else to use against him before they pushed him too far. If the bedroom they'd seen belonged to his daughter, maybe they could smuggle her away and use her as a hostage.

Damn it, Jasmine thought, in horror. *What are we becoming?*

Pathfinders, according to the whispers she'd heard, destabilised governments all the time. A rebel world might be too strongly held to be recovered without massive casualties; the Pathfinders would go in, sow dissent…and then the Marine Corps would come in and clean up the mess once the enemy forces had ripped themselves apart. Pathfinders were trained to be completely ruthless, to do whatever they had to do, all in the service of the greater good. Jasmine had never truly realised what that meant until she'd found herself carrying out the same kind of mission. What did it say about her that she was prepared to hold a young girl hostage to force her father to comply with her demands?

Nothing good, she told herself.

She looked over at the accountant, still tied and facing the wall. "You are going to tell me everything," she said, as she stepped over to him. He'd soiled himself in fear, probably believing that he would be eliminated as an inconvenient witness. Wolf might well kill him, if only because he'd seen the crime lord exposed as a fearful man. "How much money does Wolf pull in every month?"

The accountant talked rapidly, often too quickly for Jasmine to follow easily, but she soon had a working idea of how Wolf's organisation worked. It was similar to the gangs she'd seen on Han, the ones that had helped make a bad situation much worse; Wolf provided funds and heavy support to the protection rackets and drug dealers, should they need it, in exchange for a cut of their profits. There were agreements between the other senior crime lords, carving up the city between them…all of which were enforced ruthlessly. Not all of their foot soldiers seemed aware of their existence.

They're probably only vaguely aware of the universe outside their apartment blocks, Jasmine thought, as the accountant chatted on, telling them about the officials they had bribed to turn a blind eye to drug dealing and prostitution. The authorities only seemed to care about gun-running, he added; the criminal gangs knew not to try to distribute guns to the population. *That* was no surprise; governments regularly tried to disarm their people, offering an entire series of justifications for their actions. Admiral Singh probably feared revolt.

Wolf came back, followed by Blake. "No problems, boss," he said, shortly. "They seemed to accept us."

"Good," Jasmine said. They could abandon the apartment now, leaving the gangbangers to starve to death…or would that be too revealing? She found it hard to care about the little thugs, even though she knew that they would be replaced within the day. "The first order of business is finding a place to sleep, then we can plan our next step."

"There are rooms here," Wolf assured her. "You can sleep here as long as you want."

Jasmine considered it, briefly. The criminal headquarters would probably be fairly secure – but she didn't trust Wolf very far at all. On the other hand, if they set up a base outside the headquarters, he would probably be able to track them. It would take several weeks before they knew the city well enough to operate without his support.

"We'll have to let the others know," she said, thoughtfully. It was aimed at Wolf; she didn't want him thinking that he could eliminate them all and remain alive. She didn't trust him any further than she could pick up and throw the entire building. "But for this night…yes, we'll stay here."

She smiled at the crime lord. "And we're going to need papers," she added. They'd seen guardsmen randomly stopping people and asking for their papers, although none of the guardsmen had tried confronting the Marines. "We don't want to be arrested when we start walking around, do we?"

Wolf stared at her. "Who *are* you people?"

"Friends," Jasmine said. Someone who had ruled a segment of the city's organised crime might well be smart enough to put it all together, but the story of the implant should keep him in line. She hoped. "That's all you need to know."

CHAPTER TWENTY

> Worse, they will redirect money towards popular, vote-grabbing areas – and away from where it is truly necessary. Providing free health care – free in the sense that there is no direct cost on the recipient – wins more votes than funding the military. But this is a problem with no end. Funding essential healthcare gives way to funding all healthcare – and, once again, who defines 'essential'?
> -Professor Leo Caesius, *Authority, Power and the Post-Imperial Era*

They were watching her.

Danielle Chambers could feel their presence all around her, no matter where she went or what she did. They watched her when she was at school, teaching the children mathematics; they watched her when she was at home, cooking dinner for her husband. She saw their van following her whenever she went to shop; even when she couldn't see them, she knew that they were there. The only thing she didn't know was why they hadn't simply moved ahead and taken her into custody.

She'd heard the whispers; the knocks on the door at midnight, the house abandoned after everyone had been taken away in black vans. The houses even remained untouched for days afterwards, the fear of the security forces so strong that it even deterred the criminal gangs who lurked in the shadows. Everyone had heard stories of what happened to those who were taken into custody – and they'd all seen the executions, broadcast live on all channels. The leaders of the Democratic Underground had died broken men, blubbering for mercy as they were put in front of a wall and shot. She just didn't understand why they'd left her alone.

It couldn't be her teaching, could it? There was no shortage of mathematics teachers – and she knew that she wasn't the best teacher in her school, let alone in Landing City. Maybe they hoped that she would meet up with her old contacts, from the days when it seemed the Empire would weaken and allow them some say in their own affairs, just so they could scoop the remains of the Democratic Underground in one fell swoop. She'd been careful not to go anywhere near her old friends and, as far as she knew, none of them had dared go anywhere near her. Or so she hoped. The alternative was that she was the *last* of the Democratic Underground.

She told herself that wasn't possible. There had been *thousands* of them, carefully laying the framework for a better life in the post-Empire universe. They'd planned to reshape the sector, to elect their leaders instead of dealing with greedy governors appointed by Earth, to rid the system of corruption and filth…there had been so many young men and women, all ready to demand change. They couldn't all be gone…could they?

But it seemed hopeless.

Her home, she suspected, was bugged. Everything they said or did inside, from undressing to chatting about their days at work, was heard by unsympathetic ears. Danielle worried about the day when one of her children would say something that could be taken for disloyalty, knowing that she would be blamed for encouraging it. And she couldn't even give her children any privacy. If she'd found the bugs and removed them, it would also be taken as evidence of disloyalty. She couldn't even discuss the problem with her husband; he'd go mad if he realised that his wife's past might be threatening their children's future. All she could do was endure and pray that something happened before too long.

She passed her kids their lunches and watched, feeling tears prickling at her eyes, as they headed down towards their school. Amber, her eldest, was barely nine years old; it didn't seem fair that her life could be blighted by her mother's past. But if something happened to Danielle – and, by some dark miracle – it didn't include her children, she would be shunned by everyone else. No one wanted to attract doom towards their own children.

And if Amber fell into their hands, if the rumours were true…

She wiped her tears away, picked up her own lunch, and strode out of the door, locking it firmly behind her. Her husband had never wondered why she'd insisted on installing extra locks, although they didn't seem to be much use, not when she was sure that her home was entered on a regular basis and certain items moved around by unfriendly hands. It was hard to be sure…there were times when she thought that she was going mad, before she remembered how many people had just vanished in the months after Admiral Singh arrived, people who made the mistake of speaking out. Paranoia wasn't really paranoia if they *were* out to get you.

The streets, as always, were crowded, providing perfect concealment for someone shadowing her. Trying to look unobtrusive, Danielle glanced around, looking for familiar faces. There was a woman wearing a dress so skimpy that Danielle could see the underside of her ass – was she an agent, shadowing her? And there was a man in a dark suit, a sober expression painted on his face, who seemed to be walking in the same general direction…was *he* shadowing her? Danielle felt the first hints of panic as she walked faster, feeling unseen eyes boring into the back of her neck. She'd be a nervous wreck before too long.

She jumped as a pair of teenage children on bicycles raced past her, heading for the technical colleges that offered their only hope of avoiding conscription when they turned eighteen. Danielle didn't want to *think* about Amber and Rochelle being forced to work for the Admiral, but there was little other choice. They either worked hard to gain technical skills they could use to get good postings, or they were conscripted and ended up in work gangs – or the army. There were rumours about where young pretty conscripts were sent…the thought of her children serving as comfort girls was terrifying. She would sooner poison them both herself.

There was a dark van parked on the side of the road as she turned down towards the school, she noted, and gave it a wide berth. Gas was heavily rationed on Corinthian, officially to preserve the environment – but, she suspected, the real objective was to cut down the population's mobility. Only those with *real* clout could get fuel for their cars, let alone leave the city; God knew that if she could, Danielle would have left without a second thought. It couldn't be so bad out of the city, away from the security forces...could it?

A hand grabbed her arm and yanked her backwards; a cloth was pushed in front of her face. Danielle took a breath to scream, even though she knew it would be useless, but only succeeded in inhaling some more of the drug. It crossed her mind, as her legs buckled, that Admiral Singh's security forces didn't normally drug people...yet it didn't matter. In some ways, it was a relief to finally be arrested.

Darkness fell and she knew no more.

Jasmine watched as Blake and Carl manhandled the woman into the van and slammed the doors closed behind them. She'd been worried about the scheme to take the woman off the streets, but it had seemed like the best of a set of bad options. No one had said anything as the kidnap went into action; indeed, everyone nearby had looked away, determined to avoid getting involved. But then, they had the papers to prove that they were security officers, if anyone dared to ask.

"She breathed in a small dose," Carl reported, as he checked the woman's pulse. "But once we get her some stimulant, she should be fine."

Jasmine hoped so. It had taken two weeks to gain a feel for the city and another week to locate the senior surviving member of the Democratic Underground. According to the files they'd bribed an official to give them, Danielle Chambers hadn't been taken too seriously – and besides, her husband worked at one of the more important factories in the city. They'd just kept an eye on her from a distance, but seen nothing to indicate that she was still involved with subversive groups.

It wasn't a surprise. The older – and better off – parts of the city looked much more advanced than Camelot, but the aura of fear was almost overpowering. Jasmine had never felt anything like it, even on Han; people were scared even to breathe. How could an entire population have been broken so easily? But then, terror *was* a very easy tool to use – and Admiral Singh seemed to have found a balance between terrorising her population into submission and terrorising them into uselessness. And most of the people who might have resisted had already been rounded up and turned into examples to concentrate a few minds.

She scowled as she remembered the public execution they'd watched, from a safe distance. Executions had been public on Avalon too, for a while, but this was different. The gunmen had lectured the crowd for hours on just what their victims had done to deserve to die before finally opening fire, careful to ensure that it took several hits before the victims died. They'd been profoundly shocked; there were *kids* in the crowd! Sometimes, according to Wolf's contacts, schoolchildren were taken to see executions. Admiral Singh clearly believed in starting her intimidation when the children were very young.

Jasmine had once caught a gladiatorial show on Earth and *that* had been sickening, but this was worse. Much worse.

The van drove into a garage and came to a halt. Wolf had been happy to provide a safe house which, officially, belonged to a known collaborator. Jasmine had been quietly arranging living quarters that weren't connected to Wolf at all, just to ensure that they had some place to hide that he couldn't find them, but they'd used enough of his resources just to find the woman. She opened the door for Blake and Carl, who carried Danielle into the next room and placed her on the sofa. Jasmine picked up an injector tab and pressed it against the woman's neck. A moment later, she screamed so loudly that Jasmine had to cover her ears.

"Relax," Jasmine said, firmly. The woman's hands came up, clawing at Jasmine's face in her panic. "You're among friends. You're going to be fine."

She studied the woman thoughtfully. Danielle was in her early thirties, with short brown hair and a face that was homely, rather than pretty. But there was a hint of strength there, strength that had been sapped away over the last two years. Sooner or later, Jasmine had concluded while they'd been watching the woman from a safe distance, she was just going to snap under the pressure. If Admiral Singh's forces ever changed their mind about her, she would vanish into one of their jailhouses and never be seen again.

Unless as a character in a snuff flick, Jasmine thought, as she held the woman down gently. They'd seen those broadcasts too. It took a great deal to shock a Marine, but Jasmine had been profoundly shocked – and angered – by what she'd seen. *Or worse…*

"Relax," she said, again. Telling Danielle anything she didn't absolutely need to know was a risk, but there was no choice. Right now, it was clear that the woman believed that she had been snatched by the security forces. "We're Terran Marines. And we're here to help."

Danielle stared at the woman – and she *was* a woman, although it was hard to tell – in absolute disbelief. She *couldn't* be from the Empire; the Empire was *gone*. On the other hand, the only real source of information they'd had came from Admiral Singh's people and they had good reason to lie. Maybe the Empire *was* still out there, preparing to return to the sector and remove Admiral Singh from power.

She fought for breath, glancing around the room. It was no jailhouse cell; there was a comfortable sofa, a stone fireplace and a small drinks cabinet set against one wall. Unless it was all a trick…but what did she know that made tricking her worthwhile? Everyone she'd known in the Democratic Underground was gone. There was no *point* in tricking her – besides, all of the rumours said that Admiral Singh's forces preferred torture to trickery.

The woman holding her down was smaller than she'd imagined Marines to be, but she was clearly strong – and there was an icy determination in her face, as well as hints that she'd had to undergo reconstruction therapy in the past, a sign of real damage rather than vanity. Her companions were big tough-looking men, one of them a solid mass of muscle; the other thin, wiry and moving constantly, as if he couldn't stay still. They both wore dark suits, but they didn't really seem like the security officers she'd seen. Maybe it was the absence of the ever-present leer.

"I…I don't know what you mean," Danielle said, caution winning out over hope. "The Democratic Underground has been broken."

"Maybe so," the Marine said. She helped Danielle up into a sitting position, then passed her a bottle of water. "But we do need to restart it."

Danielle hesitated. It had been two years of fear, ever since Admiral Singh had arrived. "My children..."

"We can get your daughters out of the city," the Marine assured her. "Today, if you like. But if we do, will you help us?"

"I don't know," Danielle admitted. "I just don't know."

Years ago, there had been no real *danger* in being part of the Democratic Underground. The Governor seemed unconcerned about their activities and they'd never crossed the line into outright sedition, at least by any *reasonable* definition of the term. They'd had the sensation of rebellion, she saw now, without the actual danger that went with it. But now...now she knew just what Admiral Singh did to rebels. Even if her daughters were out of the line of fire, both she and her husband would be in danger...terrible danger. Could she face the torments that had been meted out to her comrades?

The thought was a bitter one. They'd only ever *played* at rebellion. When the game had become serious, they'd folded faster than a busted flush.

"This situation cannot last indefinitely," the Marine said, very quietly. "Admiral Singh's empire is going to collapse under its own weight. If you help us, we can ensure that it is destroyed *without* inflicting horrendous damage on the planet as well. Your daughters will be safe and well..."

"Get them off-planet," Danielle said, firmly. "Get them off-planet and I'll give you whatever help I can."

"That might be tricky," the Marine admitted. "We don't yet have a secure link to orbit, let alone interstellar space. It would be far safer to send them to a farm..."

"But get them off-world as soon as you can," Danielle said. At least they'd been honest. She had a feeling that Admiral Singh's goons would have promised whatever she wanted and then broken the agreement. "Please."

"We'll do our best," the Marine promised. "Now...what is going to happen at your school."

"There's no one at home to answer their call," Danielle admitted. "If they can't get hold of me, they will assume that I was arrested..."

"Call them now, say that you're helping the security forces and you'll be in later," the Marine said. "Does your husband know anything about your activities?"

Danielle shook her head, miserably. At one point, keeping the secret had just been part of the thrill. Now, it was going to destroy their relationship...

"We'll come and pick you and the children up at five in the evening, before your husband comes home," the Marine said. "After that, we'll burn down the house, ensuring that they think you're all dead. You can make contact with your husband later."

"Oh," Danielle said. It *was* a good plan, but Trevor was going to kill her when he realised what sort of trick they'd played on him. "Is there no way you can warn him in advance?"

"He goes to the pub after work for a drink," the Marine said. She scowled. "Maybe we can pull him out, then tell him...do you trust him? Because if he isn't inclined to join us..."

She left the rest to Danielle's imagination. "Leave him," she said, finally. She *did* love Trevor; he was a good man, in his way. It would be safer to have him believe his family dead rather than force him to choose between rebelling and betraying the rebels. He was going to definitely kill her when he found out the truth. "Maybe you can contact him later."

Jasmine recognised the pain in Danielle's eyes and shuddered, inwardly. The hell of it was that it *wasn't* a fair thing to demand of anyone. Maybe they *could* take the risk...but Trevor's choice couldn't be predicted in advance. And if he said no, they would have to hold him prisoner or kill him themselves.

"We will," she promised, wondering just how much Danielle could summarise about the coming nightmare. Trevor might find someone else, believing his wife and kids to be dead – or he might do something stupid, now that he had no family ties to keep him in line. "And then you can rebuild your lives."

She stood up. "We'll drop you off at the school," she said, hoping that they hadn't misjudged Danielle. "And we'll pick you up tonight."

"Oh," Danielle said. "My home might be bugged."

"We can take care of that," Jasmine assured her. It wasn't the first time they'd had to operate under stealth, with a single word making the difference between success and absolute failure. "Just pack each girl a small overnight bag and nothing else. And don't say anything out loud."

Chapter Twenty-One

> This tends to lead to an endless spiral, an endless demand for money to fulfil their political obligations, rather than an attempt to cut spending. Professional politicians, having no connection with the world outside their offices, therefore tend to raise taxes, accidentally damaging the economy. In the end, the political system simply runs out of money – and has to cope with a backlash when the services the population has grown accustomed to simply fail.
> -Professor Leo Caesius, *Authority, Power and the Post-Imperial Era*

Danielle's superior was pleased – and relieved – to see her again. Most people who were 'helping the security forces with their enquiries' tended to simply vanish afterwards, with nothing to say what had happened to them. Danielle didn't hesitate, however, to request permission to take the afternoon off. It was a measure of how rattled her superior had been that she agreed just as quickly. After all, anyone who happened to be associated with a person the security forces had found interesting would probably be found interesting themselves.

Normally, that would have bothered Danielle; this time, she didn't really care as she went through the motions of teaching her class. Mathematics, thankfully, was completely non-political; Admiral Singh wasn't stupid enough to believe that she could change the hard facts simply by issuing orders. Some of the other teachers were questioned regularly just to ensure that they trod the party line at all times, particularly those who taught the social sciences. There was even a rumour that such classes would be terminated altogether, replaced by loyalty-building exercises to ensure that the children all worshipped their mistress.

It made her sick. Every day, children were taught the glories of Admiral Singh's empire, how important it was that they all worked together to expand her conquests…and what they should do if their parents showed signs of disloyalty. Danielle had heard stories of children who had turned their parents in to the security forces for making critical comments about the government, ensuring that no one could truly trust anyone else. The children themselves had been extensively rewarded; there were times when Danielle had remained awake at night, wondering if her daughters would one day betray their mother. If they ever found out the truth…

She completed the morning's classes, then walked out of the building rather than staying and joining the other teachers for lunch. It was never very decent food – and besides, it wasn't one of the meetings when they were all reminded yet again of their responsibilities to Admiral Singh. Attendance might be voluntary, but no one was fool enough to believe that missing one of *those* luncheon dates was an option.

Back home, she went through the motions of preparing lunch for herself while covertly surveying the house, trying to decide what to bring. Normally, she cleaned up the children's rooms for them, even though *her* parents had insisted that she learned to do it for herself. She didn't dare irritate the girls to the point they went to the security forces…if they looked at Danielle's past, they'd definitely arrest and disappear her. The thought made her shudder; what sort of world was it where you didn't dare trust your own children? Or discipline them, if they did something wrong.

It was strange to realise that her workplace, for all of its faults, was one of the better schools in the city. Others were far worse, with bullying, abuse and even rape on a regular basis – and the teachers powerless to discipline the children. Everyone knew someone who had lost their job, or worse, because the children had reported them to the authorities…it stopped, she'd been told, when the children reached the technical schools, but only because the technical schools were important to

Admiral Singh. The kids who went there were utterly unprepared for harsh discipline.

She went through Amber's wardrobe of clean clothes and packed enough for a week in a bag, then moved on to Rochelle's room and did the same. Both girls were growing like weeds, although she worried about the nutritional value of the food they were receiving. In theory, food was sold at a fixed price; in practice, she knew that the real price was often much higher. Why should traders sell at the price the government told them to sell at when they could get more by smuggling? There had been days when she'd been forced to feed the girls oatmeal, porridge and algae-based ration bars. She hadn't had any other choice.

Once she'd packed the bags, she picked up the teddies both girls had owned since they were children and added them to the pile, then left the bags at the top of the stairs and walked into her former study. Most of the books she'd once owned had been declared forbidden – Admiral Singh's list of forbidden books was even longer than the Governor's – and she'd thrown them out, rather than risk having them discovered. If the girls had seen them…they might have told their teachers. And the teachers, convinced that it was a test orchestrated by the security forces, would have reported their words.

There was a small chest of drawers in the room; she pulled the top drawer halfway out, then reached inside and found the hidden compartment built into the wood. She'd seriously considered throwing out the chest of drawers, but it had belonged to her mother and she couldn't bear to part with it, even though trying to conceal anything was seen as evidence of guilt in Admiral Singh's universe. Inside, there were a small collection of notes and coins, issued by Admiral Singh, and an Imperial Credit Coin. The latter was useless on any world Admiral Singh held sway, but if the Empire still existed it might come in handy.

She closed the drawer and stuffed the money in a third bag, then went into the bedroom she shared with Trevor. They'd shared it ever since they'd married, she recalled, feeling memories pressing in around her as she picked up a handful of pictures. Taking them with her was a risk, but she wasn't going to leave them behind. There was one of their wedding day, one of their parents before Trevor's dad had died in an accident... and one of their children when they were very young. She added them to the bag along with a handful of clothes for herself, then picked up the bag and strode outside. It was nearly four o'clock and the girls would be home soon.

As always, they came home immediately, chatting happily about their time at school. Luckily, no one had mentioned to them – if they knew – that their mother had had a run in with the security forces...but then, they went to a different school. Danielle smiled at them and gave Rochelle a hug – Amber thought that she was too old for hugs – before shooing them both into the kitchen. For once, she'd decided to forget keeping food under tight control and cooked them up a large dinner.

Amber looked up with wide eyes. "Are you and daddy going out tonight, mom?"

Danielle almost flinched. "We could be," she said, as smoothly as she could. Trust Amber to remember how she'd been left with a babysitter when her parents had needed a break. Trevor and her hadn't gone out ever since Admiral Singh had arrived. She hadn't really dared sample the city's new nightlife at all. "But you have to eat up now and get ready."

She hadn't given any thought to getting the children into the vehicle, assuming the Marines turned up on time. And they would, she was sure. Would they object, would they fight...would they scream loudly enough to alert the neighbours? But it wouldn't matter. She was hauntingly aware that screams, no matter how loud, were ignored by everyone else. They'd just be grateful that it wasn't them being tortured, or dragged off into a prison van.

The dinner should have been lovely, but it tasted like ashes in her mouth. She ate what she could anyway, then gave the girls a chocolate biscuit each for dessert. Neither of them questioned their good fortune, although by the look in Amber's eyes it was clear that she was plotting mischief and mayhem for when the babysitter arrived. Danielle finally sent them to the living room to play while she checked the kitchen for anything of sentimental value, then placed the bags by the door. She was just heading back to the kitchen when there was a knock at the door.

She opened it before either of the children could get there. Her heart almost stopped beating when she saw a grim-faced man wearing a security uniform, then she relaxed as she realised that it was one of the Marines she'd seen earlier. He gave her a very brief smile, then scowled at her – and at the girls, when they came to see who was at the door.

"I'm afraid I'm going to have to ask you to come to the station," he said, in a grim voice that sent shivers down Danielle's spine. Both of the girls looked appropriately terrified. "Grab your bags and come with me."

The girls didn't seem to realise, in their panic, that their mother had already packed their bags. Danielle, privately relieved, passed them each a bag and motioned for them to head down the path and out onto the street, where a van was waiting for them. The Marine helped the girls into the back of the van, then pressed something against Amber's arm. She yelped in shock, too late to stop him; Danielle had to hold Rochelle so he could do the same to her.

"Blood sample," he muttered, as he pushed the device against Danielle's arm. There was a brief stabbing pain and then nothing. "Stay here."

The door clanged shut and locked. Danielle, praying silently that she wasn't making a mistake, could only wait and see what happened next.

Jasmine watched Danielle and her two children through the hidden monitor as Blake returned to the house, noting the panic on their faces. She gritted her teeth, trying to fight down the guilt at scaring the children so badly; it might be years before they recovered from the trauma. Jasmine had pulled kidnapped children from bandit hideouts and pirate lairs before and the children had never been in very good shape, even when they hadn't been physically abused. Now, she was putting two young girls through the same kind of nightmare…

Blake closed the house's door and walked back, climbing into the van beside her. Jasmine started the engine as he closed the door, giving him an enquiring glance. "It's all set," he said, shortly. "The house is going to go up like a bomb."

Jasmine scowled. One fire that obscured evidence was one thing; two…might start someone wondering if it had been a coincidence. There might have been nearly two hundred miles between the guardpost and Danielle's house in Landing City, but it was still worrying. And it wasn't their only problem. If the kids had really been taught to worship Admiral Singh, it was quite possible that they couldn't be trusted completely.

The thought made her shudder. No one had realised how deeply the hatred was sinking into Han until the planet had exploded, with millions of insurgents concentrating on wiping out the hated settlers from off-world – and then turning on each other, when the Empire had been forced to pull back and concentrate on guarding a handful of outposts. Men and women had slaughtered each other in vast quantities, but it had been the children who had been truly horrifying. Boys as young as five had picked up weapons almost as big as themselves to aim at their enemies, while girls – equally young – had emplaced landmines and IEDs.

Would Danielle's children be equally poisoned by hatred and blinded by propaganda?

She drove off and headed down towards the building they'd taken over, hoping that they could keep the children under control without having to resort to force. Luckily, it was easier to get people out of the city than into it – and once the children were on the farms, they would have to work or starve. It wasn't a good solution, but it was the best they had.

"Time's up," Blake said. He craned his neck around, trying to see behind them. "I set the food processor to explode…there she blows."

"Let's just hope that there isn't much evidence," Jasmine said, shortly. "Were there any bugs?"

"Only a couple, both quite ancient," Blake said. "I don't know just how much surveillance she was under."

Jasmine nodded. Surveillance and counter-surveillance – hadn't been part of either of her MOS courses at the Slaughterhouse, but she'd taken refresher courses as they travelled to Admiral Singh's empire and she knew just how easy it could be to watch someone if you controlled the infrastructure. Done properly, the target would never even know that they were being watched. There would be no tails following them throughout the day.

But that left her with a worrying question. Was Danielle *really* being watched - or was she being paranoid?

She scowled. They'd just have to take every precaution and hope.

Behind them, she saw a pillar of smoke start to rise above the city.

Horn preferred to sleep alone, no matter what pleasures could be had from a pair of nubile volunteers – of course, it spoilt the fun sometimes if they were *really* volunteers – and he disliked it intensely when someone woke him up. On the other hand, it ensured that his subordinates would only wake him up if it were *truly* urgent. When the buzzer rang, he rolled out of bed and snatched up his wristcom. Maybe the Admiral demanded his immediate presence.

"Yeah," he grunted, as he keyed the wristcom. "What is it?"

"An old surveillance flag was tripped," a staffer said. "There's been a fire and the home was on our watch list."

"Oh," Horn said, silently promising the staffer a very uncomfortable few weeks. "And you saw fit to consider this *urgent*?"

"There's a note in the file that any activity related to that flag was to be reported up the chain as soon as possible," the staffer said. He didn't *quite* point out that it had been *Horn* who'd put that flag there in the first place, but the implication was there. "I had to notify you at once."

Horn muttered a curse under his breath, then staggered over to the chair and picked up his dressing gown. "I shall be there in a moment," he said. "Have the data ready for me on the big screen."

Buckling his gown, he strode out of his chambers and walked into the control room, his bodyguards following him like silent hounds. He noticed a number of backs stiffening as he entered and wondered, absently, just who had been slacking off while he'd been sleeping. They might consider monitoring duty stupid, but Horn had never been able to understand why. Monitoring duty was the key to learning what unwanted elements had in mind before they knew it themselves.

"Danielle Chambers," the staffer said, eyeing his boss nervously. Horn believed in indulging his subordinates, particularly the ones with… *interesting* tastes, but he also punished stupidity, laxness and anything else he chose to dislike. "She was a junior member of the Democratic Underground, a *very* junior member. Her husband was a hard worker, so we just kept an eye on her for a while instead of arresting her."

Horn sneered down at the picture. If it had been up to *him*, the entire family would have been arrested – but it would have demoralised her husband's friends. Pity really, he decided, as he inspected the pictures of the girls. It was amazing how few people could hold out when they realised that their children were about to be tortured in front of them. And then they could have some *real* fun.

"There were traces of their DNA discovered in the remains," the staffer said. "We presume that they are all dead."

"Maybe," Horn said. It was an odd coincidence that the second set of victims from a fire caused by a malfunctioning piece of equipment happened to include a known Democratic Underground activist. His paranoia suggested that something wasn't entirely right. On the other hand, it was difficult to lay his finger on just *what* wasn't right. "Have her husband picked up and sweat him a little – level one only, I think. The poor man is bound to be upset, so don't push matters too far."

"Yes, sir," the staffer said.

Horn flicked through the rest of the file quickly. Danielle Chambers had been a very small fish indeed, but she'd also been the senior surviving member of the Democratic Underground – the senior *known* survivor of the Democratic Underground, he reminded himself. Subversives bred like rabbits, he'd been told; given a few weeks of uninterrupted activity and there would be hundreds of the little bastards, ready to upset the Admiral's plans. They would have to be hunted down quickly.

But as far as anyone knew, Danielle Chambers had never returned to the fold.

"Have the wreckage of the house searched thoroughly," he added. It had been searched, back before the decision had been taken to leave Danielle Chambers alone, and nothing had been found. Maybe she'd been experimenting with a detonator that had exploded accidentally and set fire to the house, or perhaps she had been trying to rig up an IED without knowing what she was doing. It did happen. "And then…all we can do is watch and wait."

He brought up a list of other suspects and made notes of the ones who might be vulnerable. "But we can be proactive about it," he muttered, more to himself than to anyone else. "See who jumps when we call."

CHAPTER TWENTY-TWO

> We have, in short, summed up the problem with developing a political system. The politicians have interests of their own – which may not align with the interests of those who voted for them (let alone the interests of those who didn't vote for them). And yet, anarchy, that glorious state where there are no laws, rules or regulations, rapidly gives way to the rule of the strong. We have walked in a circle.
> -Professor Leo Caesius, *Authority, Power and the Post-Imperial Era*

Mandy Caesius *hated* feeling vulnerable.

She'd never really felt vulnerable – or threatened – until her father had been fired from Imperial University. Earth had seemed a safe environment to her – but that had only been true of the cityblocks that were patrolled constantly by the Civil Guard. When they'd been forced to move into another block on the edge of Imperial City, it had rapidly become clear that they were in grave danger. And then there had been the time that Jasmine had upended her and pulled Mandy over her knee, or when she'd been on the pirate ship knowing that she could be raped or murdered at any moment…

"Two destroyers incoming," Jones said. The sensor officer looked worried himself, even though he was nearly twenty years older than Mandy. "They're ordering us to cut our drives and heave to."

"Comply," Mandy ordered. She hadn't expected the Admiral's forces to allow them to enter orbit without searching them first. They were about to find out just how carefully they'd wiped the evidence that the Marines had been onboard her ship. "And step down the sensors. We don't want to alarm them."

On Earth, she wouldn't have been able to tell the difference between a ship with a competent crew and a ship with a crew that barely knew how to replace something if it broke. Now, she looked at the two approaching destroyers and saw starships handled by trained officers, officers who weren't wasting a single erg of energy. She had no doubt that if they ran into trouble, the crews would respond splendidly – and her freighter couldn't give them any real trouble. Even the most heavily-armed freighter in the Commonwealth would be no match for a warship.

One of the destroyers held back, settling into a watching position just outside missile range. They weren't taking that for granted, Mandy realised, as the other closed in, launching a pair of assault shuttles. Both of them looked more advanced – and dangerous – than the shuttles the Marines used on Avalon, but apparently that wasn't uncommon. Jasmine had grumbled about front-line forces often being *last* to receive new equipment before they'd lost contact with the Empire. It made no logical sense, at least to Mandy, yet it seemed to be commonplace.

"They're demanding that we open our fore and aft airlocks for them," Jones said. "And they want you to meet them at the fore airlock."

"Understood," Mandy said. "I'm on my way."

She resisted the temptation to buckle her pistol onto her belt, despite the butterflies in her stomach. A single pistol – the only weapons they'd kept onboard were a handful of pistols and a couple of rifles – wouldn't be enough to keep the boarders out, even if they didn't have two destroyers close enough to blow *Lightfoot* apart before she could escape. Hell, given how poor *Lightfoot's* acceleration curve actually was, they could give her a two hour head start and still overrun her before she reached the phase limit.

There was a dull clunk as the shuttle locked onto the airlock, followed rapidly by a hiss as the pressure equalised. Mandy knew that all Imperial Navy airlocks were standardised, and the Empire had worked hard to ensure that civilians used the same basic standards, but it wasn't uncommon to encounter a freighter with a different model of airlock. The boarding shuttles were designed to latch on to almost *any* kind of freighter.

A moment later, the hatch hissed open, revealing a trio of men in light combat armour.

They didn't seem to be Marines, Mandy realised, feeling an odd sense of relief. Jasmine had confided her fear that the Marines on Trafalgar were working for Admiral Singh now, after the Empire had abandoned them, but the newcomers seemed to move differently. Their combat suits held rank badges and a handful of medals, blazoned onto the black armour. It was yet another sign that they weren't Marines, Mandy noted. Terran Marines *never* marked their armour, certainly not where someone else could see the markings.

The leader seemed to be studying her from behind his mask, then one hand reached up and undid his helmet, revealing a young male face. He gave Mandy an approving glance that almost made her flush, then looked at the Captain's insignia she wore on her shoulder. His surprise, Mandy considered, was almost understandable. The youngest commanding officer in the Imperial Navy's long history had been twenty-seven, not counting the ones who had succeeded to command after their superiors had been killed. Mandy looked younger than her eighteen years.

"Welcome onboard," Mandy said. "I'm Captain Jayne Richards, Mistress of *Lightfoot*."

The leader remembered himself and stepped forward. "Lieutenant Tam," he said, holding out a hand. Mandy shook it, carefully, recognising Tam's display of skill. Shaking hands with someone wearing combat armour could be very dangerous. The suits magnified pressure to the point where it would crush a hand into powder. "I'm afraid that we need to search your ship and interview your crew before we allow you any closer to our world."

Mandy pasted a reluctant look on her face. "Is that actually necessary?"

"I'm afraid so," Tam said. "We don't know anything about you, you see. Please order your crew to cooperate and we can get it done as quickly as possible."

"Right," Mandy said. No merchant skipper would be *happy* about having outsiders crawling through her ship, but there was no choice. "I'll pass on the orders at once."

Tam's crew were very well trained, she noted, as they went through the ship with a fine-toothed comb. They knew most of the hiding places and inspected them, one by one, making sardonic noises when they discovered the small horde of credit coins any freighter crew would have stashed away for a rainy day. Tam pointed out, a little less gleefully than Mandy would have expected, that the credit coins would be worthless on Corinthian. Admiral Singh, it seemed, had started her own currency.

Mandy wasn't entirely surprised. Her father lectured often on how the Empire's currency had been upheld by faith in the Empire – and without that faith, even the most trusting person would hesitate before accepting Imperial Credits. Luckily, Avalon had established a reasonably solid economy before the Empire's withdrawal had become public knowledge and the shift to a new system had been undertaken with a minimum of pain. Still, for a freighter crew that had been stranded on Gordon's Pride for several months, it would be an unpleasant surprise.

"They may be prepared to extend you a loan," Tam said, when she asked him, "but I don't think that anyone would just *take* the money. It's pretty much valueless on the planet below."

She mulled over his words as the team completed the search, turning up nothing more interesting than a handful of high-tech components that might be saleable, and then started to hold interviews. Mandy was silently grateful that they'd worked out the original story in such detail because Tam was skilled at asking probing questions, starting with how they'd become stuck on such a low-tech world in the first place. Her rather shamefaced confession that they'd believed there was no other choice made him laugh.

"I promised I'd take them some HE3," she said, once he'd finished bouncing questions off her. "Can I buy some here?"

"Only if you have some currency to trade with," Tam said, dryly. "I have no idea what the higher-ups will make of it, but I doubt that Gordon's Pride has anything that they might find interesting."

Mandy couldn't help nodding in agreement. Gordon's Pride had no gas giant, no belt of rocky asteroids…and an inhabited planet settled by religious cultists who had been exiled from the rest of the Empire. The only thing they had to offer outsiders was food, drink and women – and

Admiral Singh wouldn't need any of them from the isolated world. Pirates, on the other hand, would probably have raided Gordon's Pride by now. It wasn't as if they could fight back.

"We'll see," Mandy said. There was a brief pause as the rest of the team checked in with their leader. "What happens now?"

"Well, we found nothing of interest, so you're cleared to dock at Orbit Station Three," Tam said. "We have to remain with you until you dock, then you'll be rid of us – and you can talk to the officers there about opening up a line of credit. Do you really *want* to go back to Gordon's Folly?"

"Gordon's Pride," Mandy corrected, automatically. From what she'd seen in the records, Tam's name was more than apt. "Not particularly, but I did give them my word. Is there a better offer here?"

"There might be," Tam said. He grinned at her, suddenly. "And if you would like to join me for a drink on the station, later…?"

Mandy had to laugh. "Why not," she said. It might be fun – besides, she needed to keep Tam sweet. "Once we get settled, though."

They returned to the bridge and resumed their course towards Orbit Station Three. It was orbiting in high orbit, Mandy noted, which was unusual; Avalon's orbiting stations were in low orbit. Apart from adding a few extra minutes to the flight from the surface to the station, it didn't seem to do much else. Maybe Admiral Singh felt it offered a certain psychological separation between Corinthian and the freighter crews. Mandy honestly couldn't think of any other explanation.

"Picking up a data package," Jones reported. "I think it's the rules and regulations."

"It is," Tam confirmed. "I suggest you follow them carefully. They don't like people who *don't* follow the rules."

Mandy picked up a datapad and downloaded the data package into it, skimming through them quickly. It was shorter than the sample of Earth's rules and regulations that she recalled seeing – for some reason, there was a complete copy loaded into the database the Imperial Navy had left on Avalon – but far longer than the one used on Avalon. But then, Avalon's had been designed by people who weren't actually trying to cover their asses.

She checked the price list first and sucked in a breath when she saw it. Unless Admiral Singh's currency was worth less than she had supposed, it was going to be expensive to hold a berth on the orbiting station – and there didn't seem to be any option for a free orbit around Corinthian for an individual starship. Indeed, she realised as she looked at the display, there didn't seem to be *any* freighters holding their own orbits. A security precaution, she decided, but also a trick to extort more money or work out of the freighter crews. Admiral Singh's people had a captive market, which would encourage the crews to find new contracts and ship out again as quickly as possible.

The price tag for HE3 didn't seem to be as high as she had feared, she noted, and most of the other services an orbital station should provide were reasonably cheap. But there were also dire warnings; anyone who wanted to visit the surface had to apply in advance, while smugglers would be immediately dispatched to a penal colony. And, after that, there was a long list of goods that couldn't be shipped down to the planet. Mandy was somehow unsurprised to realise that they included weapons, encryption software and anything else that might have a military application.

She scowled down at the final part of the document, thinking unpleasant thoughts. If a freighter crew ran out of money, the ship would be seized immediately and the crew pressed into service on other vessels until they had paid back the debt. Mandy remembered how conscripted crewmen had been forced to work on the pirate ships; none of them had been very keen to work, but the pirates had been happy to use neural whips until they complied. Mandy had only been whipped once, yet the pain had been so intense that she would have done *anything* rather than feel it again.

"We're picking up a beacon," Jones reported. "They've opened a berth for us."

"Take us in," Mandy ordered, sitting back in her command chair. "We want to impress them, remember?"

"I'll try not to bump their hull," the helmsman said.

Tam snorted.

Up close, Orbit Station Three was a mass of modules that had been hastily jammed together; in some ways, it was more primitive than Avalon's Orbit Station. Mandy frowned, wondering why a world that had been settled for nearly a thousand years made do with such a monstrosity; the design was serviceable, but hardly efficient. Maybe it was just another security precaution, she wondered, as the freighter drifted closer to the berth. If she happened to be carrying nuclear warheads that had remained undiscovered, the worst she could do was blow the orbiting station to dust. She had a feeling that attempting to enter low orbit without permission would result in immediate destruction.

"Airlocks mating…now," the helmsman said. A shiver ran through the hull as he cancelled the last remnants of the drive field. "We have arrived."

"Welcome to Corinthian," Tam said. He gave Mandy a brilliant smile. "If you will come with me…?"

It wasn't a request, Mandy knew. "Coming," she said. She raised her voice as she looked at her bridge crew. "Stand down all systems, then start compiling a list of components we need to replace. *Then* we can think about shore leave."

She allowed Tam to lead her off her bridge, out through the airlock and onto the station, pretending to look around in wide-eyed wonder. The station was as crude inside as outside, with a handful of armed guards standing outside the airlock. She watched as they exchanged words with Tam, then shouldered their weapons and marched off down the corridor. Mandy sucked in a breath – the air had a faint scent she suspected belonged to Corinthian – and then followed Tam into a small office. Another man was seated at a desk, reading files on a datapad. It took Mandy a moment to realise that they were copies of *Lightfoot's* files, the ones they'd forwarded to System Command when they'd come over the phase limit and entered the system.

"You are not on our records," the man said, without preamble. "How do you explain this discrepancy?"

"The records were never complete," Mandy said, refusing to allow herself to be rattled by his tone. Even before the Empire's withdrawal, it had never been wholly successful in monitoring small trading ships, let alone pirates or mercenaries. "And we have never visited this world before."

"So it would seem," the man agreed. He kept his eyes on the datapad. "You are aware, of course, that you have no serviceable currency – and little to trade?"

Mandy nodded. The handful of goods they'd brought from Avalon – marked as having come from Gordon's Pride – might make them some money in the novelty market, but there was no way to predict what they would earn. And Tam had already told her that Imperial Credits were largely useless on Corinthian.

"You may pass your goods onto agents on the surface, who will attempt to sell them for you," the man informed her. "Until then, we will open up a line of credit for you; there is no shortage of shipping contracts for a freighter crew willing to work honestly. We will also provide you with limited access to the planetary datanet. You will be contacted within the day."

No freighter commander would have been *happy* about turning his goods over to agents, particularly without a proper contract. There would be no reason why the agents couldn't sell the goods, for a minimal sum, to themselves.... perfectly legal, if rather underhand. On the other hand, she knew that she wasn't in a good bargaining position. They didn't have much to offer the planet apart from themselves.

"There are shore leave facilities on this station that you may enjoy," the man concluded. "Or you may apply for permission to visit a pleasure resort on the moon. I should warn you that your line of credit will not extend that far, so be careful what you try to do. Should you overspend your line of credit, your ship will be summarily seized in payment."

Asshole, Mandy thought, coldly. She would almost have preferred him to stare at her tight shipsuit, carefully tailored to show off her breasts. The fair part of her mind pointed out that a freighter crew might just take what they could and then vanish once they crossed the phase limit, but she wasn't feeling fair. This man was a prime demonstration of why the Civil Service had led the Empire to ruin.

"Welcome to Corinthian," the man said, looking up for the first time. His face was bland, utterly inexpressive. He must have given the same speech thousands of times before. "And I trust you will enjoy your work for us."

We're in the system, Mandy told herself, as Tam escorted her back to the airlock and gave her his contact code. *We're closer to where we want to be.*

She scowled as she stepped into the freighter. They'd have to check for bugs and other unpleasant surprises before they risked anything else. Tam and his men had had plenty of opportunity to hide a few bugs on the ship. And then they could work out how to get in touch with Jasmine and her team.

CHAPTER TWENTY-THREE

> Maintaining a political system, therefore, requires an endless tug of war between people and politicians – and an awareness that a person who becomes a politician is not automatically exempted from that rule, for any reason. Power corrupts, after all. Indeed, society itself vacillates between being permissive to being restrictive, often as a result of the actions of previous politicians. The battle is never truly won – the balancing act can only be maintained by maintaining the tug of war.
> -Professor Leo Caesius, *Authority, Power and the Post-Imperial Era*

"Is it safe to use a terminal for this?"

Jasmine smiled at Danielle's question, although she had to admit that it was a reasonable point. Most Imperial-produced computers were carefully designed to allow security officers to slip in through hard-coded backdoors and scan the contents, no matter what layers of security the user put in place. There was no shortage of justifications for such access, but in practical terms it made it extremely difficult to keep something a secret if it was loaded onto even an isolated system.

"This terminal is special," she said, seriously. It *looked* like a common terminal from the outside and even acted like one, unless the right codes were inputted. Once the secret features were activated, a user could access the hidden parts of the system without worrying about it linking to the grid and alerting the planet's security services. "And if someone catches us…I dare say we're thoroughly compromised already."

The principles of overthrowing a government had been outlined in the files she'd studied while in transit – and they'd started with an instruction to ensure that she knew how the enemy government actually *worked* before she made proper long-term plans. It had taken a week of research, with Danielle's help, to put together a chart of just how Admiral Singh's government went together. There were still sections of the system that were hazy; Jasmine had a suspicion that there were other sections that were invisible, just because none of their sources had ever realised that they existed.

At first, Jasmine had wondered if she was making a series of mistakes, for the government table of organisation seemed thoroughly absurd. Instead of straight lines leading from top to bottom, it looked more like a hodgepodge of different departments, some reporting directly to the Admiral and others reporting to other departments. There were no less than *five* different security services, three industrial manpower departments and four different military command authorities, a recipe for absolute chaos. It had been Sergeant Hampton who'd pointed out that it was actually a recipe to keep Admiral Singh in control. As long as her subordinates were bickering with each other, they weren't conspiring to overthrow their supreme commander.

That had started Jasmine puzzling out the rest of it. Each of the subordinate commanders was building a small empire of his own, even though it was slowly becoming more and more inefficient. There was no logical reason for a connection between one of her internal security agencies and part of the planet's industrial base, but the connection existed – and, she realised, it wasn't the only one. She'd thought that Avalon's old councillors were masters of the art of kickbacks, corruption and keeping an entire planet in bondage. Now, she realised that they'd barely been journeymen.

The oligarchs had gone over to Admiral Singh *en masse*, as soon as they'd realised that the old government was gone. It was a worthwhile bargain for both parties; the corporate masters gained absolute control over their workers, allowing them to make even more profits, while Admiral Singh gained an industrial base that could be fine-tuned to support her fleet and her growing empire. The more industrial nodes they transferred to Corinthian, the more power the oligarchs gathered, which meant that the other subordinate commanders had to reach for their own power...it was a confusing nightmare, ruled over by a madwoman. In the long term, Jasmine was sure, it would collapse under its own weight.

In some ways, the Civil Service was even worse. The number of bureaucrats on the planet under the Empire had been bad enough, but they'd skyrocketed under Admiral Singh, for just about everything had to be tracked and monitored. It produced yet another means of control – if everything needed a permit, even *applying* for a permit meant being entered in the files – as well as a subtle way to watch for trouble. Someone who purchased additional foodstuffs might be merely wasting food...or they might be hiding someone illegally in their apartment.

Earth had been a nightmarish hive of civilians kept under firm control too, but it had never felt so...*hopeless*. Jasmine had walked the streets of Landing City, gaining a feel for the planet's inhabitants, and she'd been struck by how many of them kept twitching and glancing over their shoulders, as if they expected to be arrested at any moment. Even in the richest parts of the city, there was still an ever-present sense of fear. Admiral Singh had to be out of her mind.

But she's trying to build up her position as quickly as possible, Jasmine thought, remembering how hard they'd had to work on Avalon to produce the Commonwealth Navy. *She doesn't have time to be patient.*

She looked back at the terminal's outline, thinking hard. The Democratic Underground had been thoroughly penetrated long before Admiral Singh had arrived. Danielle had been shocked to discover that several of her most trusted comrades had actually been spying for the governor's private security force, although no one had been arrested until after the governor had been removed and executed. There was no point in relying on it to build up a new network; the original organisers hadn't really *thought* about the consequences if their network was penetrated. They simply hadn't been very careful at all.

But rioting on the planet wouldn't be enough to unseat Admiral Singh. Jasmine had studied the government's position and she had to admit that it was very strong. The opposition in the city was almost completely disarmed, while it faced a loyalist garrison consisting of over ten thousand soldiers, armed to the teeth. Besides, if worst came to worst, Admiral Singh could fall back to orbit and call in KEW strikes.

Or perhaps she can't, Jasmine thought, grimly. *She needs the people in the city, particularly the trained personnel. If she calls down a bombardment at random, she'll be hurting herself too.*

Jasmine had briefly considered trying to assassinate Admiral Singh, but all of their research had suggested that would be very difficult. The Admiral moved between the Governor's Mansion – it was almost a fortress in its own right – and her orbiting battleship; she never seemed to show herself to her population. It was a wise precaution, Jasmine had to admit; breaking into the Governor's Mansion alone would be almost impossible. All of their research had suggested that the Admiral was guarded by yet another security force, which had no connections to any of the others. She would have to be removed some other way.

Or we just have to give her enough problems to stop her thinking about expanding towards the Commonwealth, she thought, as a plan started to take shape in her mind. Wolf's contacts in the Civil Service *had* confirmed that Admiral Singh knew that she had lost a ship – and that she suspected enemy action. Jasmine had hoped that she would blame everything on the refugees, but that had been somewhat unlikely.

"This needs some research," she said. "How many people do you think are willing to rebel?"

"Everyone," Danielle said, quickly.

Jasmine cocked an eyebrow and she flushed.

"I dare say that most people would *want* to rebel," Danielle said, her face still red. "But they don't have any hope."

"True," Jasmine said. "We have to *give* them that hope – and we have to do it without Admiral Singh realising that we're here."

That was going to be difficult. On Avalon, the Crackers had staged the occasional attack inside Camelot itself, but they'd had to be very careful to avoid civilian casualties – casualties that might serve as a rally cry for the council to produce an effective army. If she staged an attack in Landing City, it was quite possible that she would alienate potential supporters… as well as convincing Admiral Singh to start mass sweeps for unwanted guests.

But if they didn't convince potential allies that they could win, the allies would either sit on the fence or betray them to Admiral Singh.

"We'll send a message to Sergeant Harris," she said, a moment later. "I want him to stay outside the city and start making preparations to harass the security forces. Meanwhile...we start making preparations here."

She stood up, leading Danielle into the next room. "The problem with the Democratic Underground is that just about everyone involved knew just about everyone else," she explained. "Once the security forces had uncovered some of your members, it was relatively easy to uncover the rest, simply by liberal applications of torture and truth drugs. And because you didn't take any precautions with your recruiting, you actually brought some spies into the fold. They used the meetings to gather evidence against you."

Danielle flushed, again. "We didn't know what we were doing," she said, crossly.

"And you thought that the power structure you hated would fold when you made your demands," Jasmine added. Power was addictive... and besides, the Governor had had few illusions about the regard his people held for him. He would have been brutally murdered if he'd ever surrendered power to the Democratic Underground and knew it. Maybe he'd even seen Admiral Singh's arrival as a relief, before she'd executed him to make an example. "You can't afford to make the same mistake twice."

She stepped into the next room, where Sergeant Hampton, Blake and Carl were playing cards, while Canada was watching a bland entertainment program on the datanet. "I have a working concept," Jasmine announced, as the players put down their cards. "And I need you to poke holes in it."

"Ah," Hampton said. "The dreaded self-criticism session."

Jasmine nodded. In her opinion, the more minds that worked on a problem, the better – although it didn't seem to work so well in real life. Egos and personality conflicts got in the way. She waited until they were seated facing her and then began, starting with an outline of the problem as she saw it.

"We are going to have to build up rebel cells within the workforce," she said, flatly. "They're the ones most likely to rebel, particularly the ones who have been torn away from their families and brought to this world. On the other hand, we can expect them to be riddled with spies and informants."

"A cell structure, then," Sergeant Hampton said. "Very few of them will know anyone outside their own cells."

Jasmine nodded. She had no illusions about how far Admiral Singh's security men would go if they caught even a *sniff* of rebel activity, or how long civilians could stand up to a rigorous interrogation.

"We can start work in the apartment blocks used by new arrivals," Carl added. "If we used our new connections to ensure that the rebels were hired…"

"Good thought," Jasmine said. She'd intended to start work among the ones who were already working for Admiral Singh, but Carl's idea had merit. "We can also use them for manpower when the time comes to start the uprising here."

She outlined the next part of her plan carefully, piece by piece. "Admiral Singh cannot use maximum force on the planet without damaging her own future," she continued. "However, eventually she will start moving people to orbit permanently – including, I hope, our rebel cells. That will give us an opportunity to snatch control of the orbital infrastructure – or destroy it, if we don't manage to cripple or capture those battleships. But ideally I'd like to take them intact."

There were nods. It would be several years before Avalon could build battleships of its own, certainly enough ships to match Admiral Singh's firepower – and there was no way to know what else lurked core-wards of Corinthian. If they could take the ships intact, along with their crews, the Commonwealth Navy would be delighted. But if not, they would need to be crippled to prevent them from interfering against the rebels on the planet's surface.

"The real problem will be taking the Admiral herself out," she concluded. "We might have to storm the Governor's Mansion ourselves."

"Even if we had all of our equipment, that would be a bloodbath," Sergeant Hampton warned. "The place is built out of hullmetal; we'd need heavy weapons to even blow through the doors. And it's surrounded by heavily armed guards and automated weapons."

Jasmine nodded. A single KEW would take it out, but it was unlikely that they would be able to take control of an orbital weapons platform without being detected. Briefly, she considered trying to slip a missile into planetary orbit, before deciding that it was unlikely to work. It was clear that the missiles they'd used as a diversion the last time had alarmed Admiral Singh's people. They were determined not to let that happen again.

"Perhaps Danielle's husband could help," Blake suggested, nodding towards the woman. "He *does* work on the industrial platforms."

"It's a possibility," Jasmine said. She'd assigned a pair of Wolf's people to keep an eye on Trevor Chambers; they'd reported that he'd moved into a tiny apartment block and spent a great deal of time drinking. He was apparently due to report back to work in a week, if there was anything left of him by then. "But I want to get the rest of the selection process underway before then."

She looked at their faces, seeing their own grim determination looking back at her. The Empire had had plenty of planets that had poor governments, or worse; Han, for example, had ripped itself apart. But this was somehow worse; the government was steadily sucking the life from the system's population, taming them until they couldn't rebel. Some of the records they'd seen on the entertainment screens would have provoked a revolt on Avalon…hell, after some of the details of how the old council had entertained themselves, they'd had to provide an armed guard before transferring them to a penal island.

"There's another possibility," Hampton suggested. "We could probably assassinate some of her subordinates. If we got lucky, Admiral Singh would start thinking that they were fighting amongst themselves…"

"Or use it to put one of our own people in a more useful position," Carl suggested. He smiled at their disbelieving expressions. "Hey, these politicians are corrupt bastards, right? I bet you anything you care to put forward that some of them will have secrets that will shock even their friends."

"Maybe one of them has been stealing from the others," Hampton mused. "If we could identify him…"

"If," Jasmine said. "Wolf will have to work on it."

She scowled at the thought. The crime lord wasn't quite clear on just who they were and what they were doing, but the more they used his connections, the more likely it was that he would put it together – and then… what? As long as he believed that he had a bomb in his skull, he wouldn't want to anger them…but what if he called their bluff?

"We may have to do other things for him," she mused. Wolf wasn't the *only* crime lord in the city, but with a little help he might be able to scoop up part of a rival's network. On the other hand, she had a feeling that would draw attention from the security forces. "I think we'd be better off using him as little as possible."

Wolf had provided them with papers and ID cards that should pass casual scrutiny, but it bothered her, particularly when she'd realised just how often they were asked for their papers by patrolling guards. If the papers were ever checked thoroughly…Wolf had told her that his people had inserted data into the files to confirm that the papers were real, but Jasmine knew how easy it was to make a mistake. And if he'd decided to sell them out…

She pushed the thought aside for later consideration and stood up. "We will start recruiting as soon as possible," she said. Perhaps it *was* better to work with the newcomers to the city first. It would be easier to get away if the shit hit the fan. "I want to review our precautions before we start, using some of Wolf's contacts to identify probable recruits. And then we check them out as thoroughly as possible."

"Of course," Hampton said. "But vetting will be difficult on this world."

Jasmine couldn't disagree. But they had no choice.

Build up a network, she told herself, *then start planning active operations. In the meantime, work on distracting the Admiral by plotting a series of insurgent attacks in the countryside – and hope that it's enough to keep her busy. And pray.*

She thought, briefly, of Mandy. Had *Lightfoot* managed to sign up with the other freighters or had she been seized, her friend and her crew dispatched to a penal colony? So far, there was no way to know. Wolf had been passing them data on orbital movements, but he claimed to have very few contacts up there.

"We will have to do the best we can," she said. "But as long as we keep everyone nicely anonymous, we should be able to back off if we are discovered."

And she hoped, once again, that she was right.

"Give me a nice honest battle any time," Blake said.

"Oh, I don't know," Carl said. "There is something to be said for tricking the enemy into defeating himself."

Jasmine snorted. "But it would be much simpler with the battle," she said. "Here, far too many things can go wrong."

CHAPTER TWENTY-FOUR

> And yet we have a never-ending series of politicians and political leaders who believe that they can not only make choices for their population, but override the will of the population whenever they see fit. The justifications will vary – guns will be banned on grounds of public safety, for example, while drugs will be banned on grounds of personal health – yet the underlying motive will remain the same.
>
> -Professor Leo Caesius, *Authority, Power and the Post-Imperial Era*

I wonder, Lukas Gath asked himself, *if I'm making a mistake.*

He was seventeen, on the verge of turning eighteen – and become eligible for conscription, even though his elder brother had disappeared after making the mistake of questioning the regime too loudly. It was a record that ensured that *he* would never have a chance to build a life of his own; no, *his* conscription period would be spent digging drains, cleaning out toilets and other disgusting work normally reserved for convicts. The only consolation, he'd been told, was that he hadn't been born female. There were worse duties for women who allowed themselves to slack rather than work to better themselves.

One of his teachers had warned him, more than once, about saying rebellious things too loudly. It was only a matter of time, he'd said, before he was overheard by someone who might report him to the regime. But Lukas had found it hard to care. His mother was a drunkard, his father a mystery…and his brother missing, presumed dead. What could they do to him that was worse than watching his mother slowly drink herself to death?

And then he'd been given an address and told to report there, if he wanted to make a difference. And to tell absolutely no one.

He looked up at the apartment and hesitated. It was a moderate dwelling, no larger than the one he shared with his mother…the one they might lose, if they failed to keep up with the rent. He had no idea what was waiting for him inside, but if the regime wanted proof of disloyalty, they didn't need to engage in an elaborate game of charades. They could just pluck him off the street without bothering to think of an excuse. Lukas had no idea how many people had vanished, but he was sure it was in the high thousands.

Bracing himself, he stepped forward and touched the door. It swung open at his touch, revealing a darkened corridor…and a single light at the end. Lukas hesitated again, then walked forward, allowing the door to swing shut behind him. An instant later, strong arms wrapped themselves around him, holding his body so firmly that he couldn't even move his arms.

"Don't struggle," a harsh voice said. "We mean you no harm."

Lukas held himself still – somehow – as a pair of hands ran over his body, searching him so thoroughly that he blushed. He'd been told to bring nothing, apart from his ID wallet; if he'd been caught without it, he would have had to have bribed the guardsmen who'd arrested him…and he had almost nothing he could offer as a bribe.

"He's clean," a second voice said.

"Good boy," the first voice said. His arms relaxed, allowing Lukas to start rubbing the bruised flesh where he'd been held. There was a click and a light came on, illuminating the barren corridor. "Just start walking into the far room."

Lukas glanced up at his assailants. The one who'd held him was the biggest man he'd ever seen, his features concealed under a black woollen mask that hid everything. He glanced at the other man and saw someone smaller, but no less capable. They both wore working overalls that would have passed unnoticed almost anywhere in Landing City.

"Put this on," the bigger man said, firmly. He passed Lukas a mask. "You don't want to be identified here."

Lukas pulled the woollen mask over his face as he walked into the next room. There were five other people sitting there, their faces concealed too. One of them was a girl – he could make out the swell of her breasts, despite the loose-fitting garment she wore – while the others seemed to be young men, just like him. He took the seat he was pointed to, nodded when he was told to remain quiet, and waited.

It seemed like an hour passed as a handful of other masked figures were brought into the room, before the door was finally closed. He looked up as the smaller man sat down facing them, his half-seen eyes moving from face to face. Lukas felt a strange mixture of excitement and fear as he wondered just what the hell he'd gotten himself into. Were they criminals, intent on recruiting new blood, or…rebels?

"You are here because someone believed that you might be…dissatisfied with the regime and that you would have the courage to take a stand against it," the man said. His voice was clearly masked by an electronic distorter, making it impossible to identify him. "We are determined to overthrow it and replace Admiral Singh with a government that is more representative of the people's needs. All of you have lost someone to the regime. You know just how far the Admiral is prepared to go to get what she wants. We're here to give you the chance to strike back.

"We know that you have lived in fear for the last two years," the man continued. "We would understand if you chose to back out. If so, we will inject you with something that causes short-term memory loss and return you to your homes. You will be unable to betray us and you will never see us again. On the other hand, if you stay here, you will be committed. We need you to understand that, if nothing else. Future betrayal will be severely punished.

"The masks you have been given are for your protection. Should you doubt the effectiveness of our memory wipes, you need only consider how little your fellow prospective recruits actually *know*. We know who you are, of course, but we have taken other precautions to ensure that we cannot be interrogated. I'm afraid that you will have to take that on faith."

There was a long pause. "I won't lie to you," the man added. "This endeavour is not without risks. It is possible that Admiral Singh's security forces will catch you – and, if that happens, you will be brutally interrogated and then dispatched. The lucky ones will be killed quickly. If you happen to be unlucky, you will be sent to a work camp and worked to death. After you become involved, you will no longer be able to plead ignorance. The choice is yours."

His eyes seemed to gleam. "Fight...or withdraw now."

Lukas hesitated, unable to prevent himself from glancing at the other potential recruits. His mouth was dry; if he were caught, whatever fate had befallen his brother might befall him as well. But if he accepted the memory wipe...he'd just wind up being conscripted and then sent to slave for Admiral Singh. Or, if he managed to melt away into the underclass, he'd die young.

And he'd loved his brother. He wanted a little revenge.

"I'll fight," he said.

Most of the others agreed. Two, however, admitted in tearful voices that they didn't dare fight. The door opened, revealing two more masked men, and they were helped out of the room, the door shutting firmly closed behind them. Lukas watched them go, wondering just how effective the memory wipe really was. What if someone had recognised him? What if the wipe didn't work?

"Sit and wait," the leader ordered. "In a moment, you will go, one by one, into the next room and take the oath. Once that's done, you will be committed."

He looked around at the remaining recruits. "This is your last chance to back out," he warned them. "Speak now or forever hold your tongue."

Lukas felt the butterflies in his stomach starting to expand, but he said nothing.

"Very good," the leader said. "One rule, while you're here. No names. Ever. You will be assigned code names, which you will be expected to use at all times. What you don't know about your fellows, you can't betray to the security forces."

"I won't talk," one of the recruits said. "I won't..."

"They will shoot you full of truth drugs and then interrogate you," the leader warned. "You won't want to talk – but believe me, it won't matter. They have ways of making you talk."

Jasmine watched through her mask as the first recruit came into the tiny office, his eyes – half-hidden behind the mask – looking around in surprise. She tapped her lips and pointed to the chair, waiting for him to sit down. The voice analysis software got better results when the subject was calm and unworried, but *that* wasn't likely to happen with the new recruits. She'd had awful nerves on her first day at Boot Camp…and all she'd had to worry about was washing out and being returned home in disgrace. Her father might have been darkly amused, but he wouldn't have tortured her to death. The same could not be said of Admiral Singh's goons.

"This is the oath," she said, through the voder. He started at the sound of her voice, but showed little other visible reaction. "You will answer either yes or no to my statements. No other answers will be considered acceptable. If you can't answer the question at all, raise your hand. Nod if you understand me."

He looked shaken, but obeyed. Good. Nerves would make it harder for him to think of a lie.

"You understand that you are joining an organisation dedicated to overthrowing Admiral Singh," Jasmine said. "Yes or no?"

"Yes," the young man said.

"You will not willingly tell anyone *anything* about this without specific permission from your leaders," Jasmine said. "Yes or no?"

"Yes," the young man said.

Jasmine smiled inwardly. The telltale remained green. He wasn't trying to lie.

Unless he's had proper training, she thought, ruefully. Fooling voice analysis software wasn't *that* difficult. It was a great deal harder to fool drugs, or direct mental linkage, but it was harder to use them without being noticed.

"You will follow orders at all times, unless specifically told to act on your own initiative," Jasmine continued. "Yes or no?"

"Yes," the young man said.

Jasmine sensed his impatience, but pressed onwards. "You will tell whatever you learn from us to the security forces," she said. "Yes or no."

"Yes...no," the young man said, catching himself. The sudden reversal had caught him by surprise. "I won't tell anyone anything."

"Yes or no answers only," Jasmine said, coldly. "You will betray us to the security forces?"

"No," the young man said, angrily.

"You are *working* for the security forces?"

"No," the young man snapped.

"Remain seated," Jasmine ordered. The telltales still agreed that the young man wasn't planning to betray them. "One final question. Are you willing to do whatever is necessary to liberate this world?"

"Yes," the young man said, after a moment's thought.

"Good," Jasmine said. She pointed to a door at the far side of the room. "Go through the door, sit down and wait."

She watched him go, then glanced through the more specific report. The young man had shown some hesitation at times, which was thoroughly understandable, but no outright intentional deceit. It was quite possible that he would be tricked or tortured into telling the security forces whatever they wanted to know, yet he wouldn't do it intentionally.

Or so we hope, Jasmine thought. Duress came in many forms.

She reset the system and then settled back in her chair, waiting for the next recruit.

Lukas couldn't help noticing that one of the recruits seemed to have vanished, rather than joining the rest of them in the next room. He kept that observation to himself as the recruiters passed out chocolate bars and fresh juice, suspecting that someone had refused to take the oath – if it *was* an oath. The oath of allegiance they were required to take every day in school to Admiral Singh was far more dramatic than a series of questions and answers.

"The oath was more than just an oath," the leader said, once they were all settled. "You didn't know it, but you were being monitored closely as you spoke. Each and every one of you who passed the test were completely truthful. You will not willingly betray your fellows."

He paused. "You will have noticed that someone is missing," he added. "That person was a paid informer for the security forces. Luckily, they didn't leave a message before they set out to this meeting. We will see to it that they get their memory wiped before they can do any damage."

The girl leaned forward. "Why don't you kill the bastard?"

"Because it might be far too revealing," the leader explained. "Having him wake up in a flophouse, head heavy with all the drugs and alcohol he took…that should be a little more problematic for them to connect with us."

He smiled, coldly. "This is the first day of training for all of you," he continued. "We will start by discussing basic security precautions; as you have just discovered, eyes and ears are everywhere. You will not risk exposing us through being careless. Once you have mastered security precautions, you will move on to other matters. Eventually, you will be separated out into cells and told to prepare for the next step.

"I told you that you were not to share names," he warned. "You will not share anything else, either. No stories about your life, no shared concerns…you certainly will not share your bodies. You will come to think of your comrades as nothing more than their codenames and whatever specific training they receive. There will be times when you disagree about the best course of action, but you will always remember that your comrades are your comrades. You are not to allow your disagreements to threaten the group.

"That won't make sense to you yet," he admitted. "But it will."

There was a long uncomfortable pause.

"Now," the leader said. "The security forces monitor the city through the following methods…"

It was a long session and Lukas's head was aching at the end of it. He'd known that there were cameras covering parts of the city, but he'd never realised how thoroughly they were integrated into the datanet – or how they could be used to track someone without using people who might be seen. On the other hand, they had been told, it was very difficult for the security forces to actually use all the data they amassed. By the time they put it all together, it would be too late.

"But don't ever assume that they're idiots," the leader had warned them. "They can bring you in without an excuse and sweat you…and you may well show them enough to make them suspicious. So be careful. Don't say a word to *anyone*."

Lukas nodded. They'd had the same warning over and over again.

"You know how we will get in touch, and where," the leader concluded. "Now, you will all leave, one by one. And remember…"

"Don't say a word," Lukas said.

"Indeed," the leader agreed. "Not to *anyone*."

The Marines waited two minutes after the last of the recruits had departed, then searched the apartment to ensure that they hadn't left anything behind. It was too dangerous to risk using the place again, even though it *was* ideal. Jasmine packed up the remainder of the voice analysis gear, then carried it out to the van. Inside, the drugged informer lay on the back seat, twitching unpleasantly.

Little snitch, Jasmine thought, darkly. As far as they could tell, he hadn't been threatened or otherwise forced to work for the security forces. He'd just liked the colour of their money, little else. A loyalist would have been easy to understand. She shook her head. If they hadn't thought to test everyone, they might well have been betrayed that same night.

"The unwilling recruits have already been returned," Hampton reported, as he came up behind her. Using the memory drug was a risk – a doctor might think to check for traces in the blood – but they'd taken some precautions. The two recruits would wake up in one of Wolf's brothels, convinced that they'd taken too many drugs the previous night. Drug use was rife in Landing City's schools. Jasmine wasn't particularly surprised. "What about this one?"

"We kill him and dump him," she said, flatly. Properly arranged, it would look like a robbery gone wrong. "After that, we head back to base and prepare for the next part of the operation."

She scowled. Killing someone in battle was one thing – Marines all knew that the only way to win was to destroy the enemy's military – but cold-blooded murder was something else. On the other hand, they didn't have a choice. An informer might merit more careful attention from the security forces than a pair of anonymous students.

"Understood," Hampton said. He gave her a sharp look, as if he understood what she was going through. It was a mystery why he hadn't tried to gain promotion himself, particularly given how many opportunities there were in the Commonwealth. "Do you want me to do it?"

Jasmine shook her head, untruthfully. "The responsibility is mine," she said. It would have been easy to give the job to the Sergeant, but she had a feeling that would be the first step towards becoming a bad officer. Far too many others had given way to that temptation in the past. "I'll do it personally."

CHAPTER TWENTY-FIVE

It is truly said that the path to hell is paved with good intentions. Human history tells us that there are two possible outcomes for well-intentioned 'nanny' politicians. They will either create a nightmare when the time comes to enforce their will (all in the name of their people) or they will build the tools for others, less well-intentioned, to use to take power. Claiming the right to impose curbs on free speech, whatever the motive, means eventually imposing curbs on political discourse – and opposition.

-Professor Leo Caesius, *Authority, Power and the Post-Imperial Era*

Trevor Chambers scowled as he stumbled down the flophouse corridor, heading for his tiny room. The cheap alcohol had tasted vile and there hadn't been enough of it, not enough to render him comatose for the night. God knew he shouldn't be drinking, not with his post on the orbital stations, but he no longer cared. His wife and children were dead. And his superiors, far from doing anything *useful*, had just ordered him to take a break and report back to work the following Monday.

He muttered curses under his breath as he stopped outside the door and searched through his pockets for the keys. He'd drunk just enough, he realised crossly, to make hand-eye coordination very difficult; it took several tries before he finally managed to pluck the key out of his pocket and then force it into the lock. It was so difficult that he actually wondered if he was trying to enter the wrong room before it finally clicked, allowing him to walk inside…

Someone was lying on the bed. Trevor cursed the landlord under his breath as he stumbled forward, ready to evict the unwelcome guest. He'd *told* the goddamned man that he wasn't interested in company, male or female. The landlord might have offered him a bevy of prostitutes to help take his mind off his dead wife, but Trevor had flatly refused. He missed Danielle too much to betray her with another woman. The light switch felt oddly solid in his hand, as if he were dreaming…and then he clicked the light on, gasping as he realised that the woman in the bed was exactly like Danielle.

"Trevor," she said, in a relieved tone. "Thank God."

Trevor stared, convinced that he was going mad. His wife was dead; he'd seen the pile of ashes that was all that remained of the house they'd shared. There had been nothing left of her body – or those of his daughters – apart from a handful of DNA traces. The fire had been so intense that it had wiped out everything else. And yet…he'd been married for over ten years. Every sense in his body was screaming that he was looking right at the woman he'd loved and married, the woman who was dead.

"I faked my death," Danielle said. The tone was perfect, the half-apologetic tone she'd always affected when she'd done something she knew would upset him, even if it was for the best of motives. "There wasn't a choice."

Trevor's head spun, shock rapidly being replaced by anger. How *could* she do this to him? He'd watched as the tiny coffins, all that remained of his family, were opened and the ashes scattered onto the memorial garden…and it had all been faked? How could *anyone* put someone through so much hell?

"I had no choice," Danielle said, again. "I…"

Trevor slapped her, hard.

He watched his wife fall backwards onto the bed, half-shocked at his own action. He'd never hit her, ever. Even when they'd argued and fought, he'd never hit her, but now…maybe it was the alcohol, maybe it was the shock, but he'd hit her. An ugly red mark appeared on her skin as she stared up at him, her eyes equally shocked. Part of Trevor was horrified by what he'd done; the other part felt a certain kind of grim satisfaction in seeing her pain. Was it anything like as bad as the moment when he'd seen the ruins of his house and *known* – he'd *known* – that his family was dead?

"The girls," he said, as a more important question emerged in his mind. He reached forward and pulled his wife forward by the collar. "Where are the girls?"

A dozen possible answers flooded through his mind. If Danielle had been prepared to put him through the agony of losing her, just to fake her own death, what might she have done to the children? It was hard to think of her as a murderess, yet the DNA traces could have been her own daughters burning to death, just to cover their tracks? If she had, he promised himself, he'd strangle her with his bare hands. He certainly couldn't rely on the government to give him and his family justice.

"They're safe," Danielle said. "I had them sent out of the city."

Trevor sat down, heavily. How *could* he have doubted her?

He caught his breath. "Where did you send them?"

"There's a farm, some distance from the city," Danielle said, softly. There were tears in her eyes. "They should be safe there, for the moment."

"For the moment," Trevor repeated. God, he wanted a drink…and yet he had the feeling that drinking more alcohol would be the worst possible thing he could do. "Danielle…what the fuck is going on?"

Danielle took a breath. "I'm a wanted woman," she said, softly. "And I needed to hide."

Trevor listened as she explained how she'd become involved with the Democratic Underground, keeping it a secret from everyone else, including her husband. And how they'd never actually done anything until Admiral Singh arrived, by which time it had been too late. And how she'd kept her head down, fearing that the security forces would arrest her at any moment. And how she'd eventually linked up with another resistance organisation…

"You should have told me," Trevor said, angrily. But what would he have said? He was no coward – no one who worked on the orbital platforms was a coward – but it wasn't just Danielle and himself who would be in danger. Amber and Rochelle would also be in danger if they were exposed. "Why didn't you?"

He shuddered at the thought. If the girls were lucky, they would be farmed out to Admiral Singh's supporters and brought up as proper little followers of the regime. But there were darker rumours, darker suggestions...whispers shared in the brief moments when they knew that they weren't being observed. The girls were hardly mature, but they could still be sent to a very special brothel and...

Trevor swallowed hard, trying not to be sick. And his wife, their mother, had exposed them to such a fate? How *could* she? He wanted to wrap his hands around her neck and strangle the life out of her for being so irresponsible...and yet he still loved her. Maybe they should both take poison and die.

"The house was bugged," Danielle said. "I dared not say anything to you."

"Oh," Trevor said. He thought of everything they'd done in the house and shuddered at the thought of those private moments being observed. Every so often, he'd brushed up against the security forces – they were fond of random checks – and he knew what they were like, what they might choose to observe. "Maybe that does make sense."

He suddenly felt very tired. "Why did you come here?"

"The resistance needs your help," his wife said. "Will you join us?"

Trevor stared at her. She had faked her death...and then she had the nerve to ask for help?

"I'm sorry about what I did to you," Danielle said, quickly. "And if there had been a chance to take you with us, I would have done so. But I had to act fast to protect the girls. If I hadn't, they might have been taken away."

"I see," Trevor said.

He stared down at her beautiful face, still marred by the ugly red mark. Anything was forgivable if it protected the children; he didn't want to *think* about what could have happened to his daughters if they had been taken away by the security forces. But on the other hand...he'd told himself that he had a wife and family as hostages to fortune. It had prevented him from considering doing anything more dangerous than silently cursing Admiral Singh and her regime under his breath. They couldn't kill him for that, could they?

But if he joined her, if he did something more active, they *could* kill him. Everyone was supposed to watch the public executions, just to remind them of what could happen if they were caught plotting treason. Some of the executions were quite imaginative; he'd watched in horror as one young man, convicted of a crime by the regime's judges, injected with a drug that had made his phobias overwhelm his mind. He'd died screaming in absolute terror.

And yet…it was a chance to strike back at the regime. And to have his wife and daughters back.

"Very well," he said, finally. He didn't want Danielle to risk herself any more – and she would, he knew, if he didn't do it for her. When his wife got the bit between her teeth, she just charged forward and ignored the possible dangers. He was mildly surprised that she had hidden herself away for so long. "I will do as you want."

Danielle reached for him and drew him into a kiss. She felt heavenly in his arms, particularly after he'd thought he'd lost her. How could they have started to lose their connection in the bedroom? It had taken her faked death to remind him of just how important she was to him. He hesitated – the flophouse was hardly the romantic hotel they'd shared on their honeymoon – and then pressed ahead, one hand sneaking under his wife's blouse to find her breast.

And then there was nothing in the world, but her.

Jasmine looked away, granting the couple what privacy she could. It had been simple enough to rent the room next to Trevor's and then bore a couple of peepholes through the wall; the builders had skimped on the materials to the point Jasmine was mildly surprised that the building hadn't already collapsed. Indeed, the drilling might well have brought the wall down if they hadn't been very careful.

She sat down and waited, contemplating Trevor's words. When he'd slapped Danielle, Jasmine had almost moved then, bursting through the wall to rip him away from his wife. And yet, he'd controlled himself…Jasmine had known others who would have allowed their fury to overwhelm them. It would have even been understandable; Trevor had been allowed to believe, truly believe, that his wife and children were dead. Jasmine suspected that *she* would not have handled it so well if her siblings had been reported dead...and then she'd discovered that they'd faked their death.

Just what had happened to her family nagged at her mind from time to time. Her father had never been entirely happy with her choice of career, but he'd accepted it...and now he and his homeworld were lost somewhere in the ruins of the Empire. Jasmine's siblings, married or unmarried, had no way to contact her...did they think that she was dead? Or did their homeworld have too many other problems to worry about a single girl who had largely walked away from their family? There was no way to know. Perhaps, one day, the Commonwealth would eventually reach her homeworld...or perhaps it would never expand much further. If Admiral Singh had her way, it would definitely not exist for much longer.

Poor man, she thought, thinking of Trevor.

The sounds of lovemaking finally died away. It wasn't an uncommon sound in the flophouse; their first survey had revealed that it was often used by prostitutes who were unwilling or unable to work in a brothel. Still, Trevor had been so insistent that he hadn't wanted a woman in his room – according to the landlord, when Jasmine had slipped him a reasonably-sized bribe – that someone might ask questions. By then, Jasmine hoped to be long gone.

Her lips quirked. She'd known someone who had dealt with the loss of his husband by screwing several different others, both male and female, over the next few nights. How could Danielle have blamed Trevor for finding solace in the arms of a prostitute when he'd had good reason to believe that his wife was dead? She might have realised that, intellectually, he hadn't intended to cheat, but emotionally she would have felt betrayed.

It hadn't been uncommon in the Empire for someone to be incorrectly reported missing, or dead. Jasmine had reviewed quite a few cases while on punishment duty; they'd all had a soldier or spacer reported dead, then the man had been discovered alive...*after* all of his property had been divided up and his friends and family gone on to make new relationships of their own. Legally, it was always a mess – and it was demoralising as hell to the person who had returned home.

There was a brief flurry of conversation, then a tap on the wall. Jasmine stood up, stepped out of the room she'd rented and opened the door into Trevor's room. She'd seen it earlier, when they'd been checking for bugs and other unpleasant surprises, but the only unpleasant surprise had been discovering what kind of apartment a mourning man considered acceptable. Jasmine had seen pirate ships that were in better condition – and *that* was saying something.

Trevor looked up in surprise as she entered, then made sure that both he and his wife were decently covered. Jasmine wondered idly what she looked like to him; without her uniform or powered armour, she looked more like a fitness fanatic than anything else. But a more detailed examination would reveal the truth. Corinthian had been too settled to play host to many retired Marines, or Imperial Army Special Forces, but a brief check had revealed that they were all missing, presumed disappeared. Jasmine wasn't surprised. Even a regular soldier from the Imperial Army would know enough to give the occupation forces headaches before he was finally rounded up and killed.

"Good evening," she said, shortly. She felt a flicker of anger as she saw the mark on Danielle's cheek, then pushed it aside. "We need to talk."

Trevor couldn't be introduced to any of the other cells, not when he was simply too valuable to be risked easily. Instead, she ran through a series of basic communications protocols with him, including a number of code phrases that could be used to pass on messages. The datanet was heavily monitored, but like most automated systems it could only work with what it saw; it wouldn't realise that a message talking about used aircars was actually plotting sabotage. Jasmine assumed that a certain percentage of traffic *was* reviewed by humans, but there was so much traffic that she doubted it would find anything useful unless they had prior grounds for suspecting someone.

Perhaps we should mark a few people down for suspicion, she thought, grimly. *Give them false trails to follow.*

"There are others who are…unhappy," Trevor said, finally. "I could contact them for you."

"Not on the orbital platforms," Jasmine said, quickly. "They're just too easy to monitor. Pass us names and we will check them out first, before you risk approaching them. One single informer and your cell will be blown open."

"Don't risk yourself," Danielle added, quickly. "I won't lose you again."

Trevor scowled at his wife, unsurprisingly. It would be a long time, Jasmine suspected, before he ever fully forgave her for faking her death – and convincing him that he'd lost both his wife and daughters to a fire. It would hang over their marriage until they either recovered or it ripped them apart.

"No, don't risk yourself right now," Jasmine agreed. "We need to gather intelligence before we can proceed onwards. Your job is to help us do that."

She smiled inwardly as Trevor nodded. Between him and Wolf's files, they should be able to find others who could be subverted – or convinced to join a revolutionary cell. Once they had enough people, they could launch their coup…if Admiral Singh left them enough time. That was the real problem; if they had years, Jasmine knew they could pull the coup off perfectly. But they didn't have years.

"I understand," Trevor said.

"Every weekend, you will come back here, where you will be contacted," Jasmine said, flatly. "We are currently creating a false identity for your wife. Once that's ready, you can move in with her and everyone will congratulate you on finding a new partner. Instead, when you come home, you will report to her…"

"My house was bugged," Trevor said. "What happens if they bug my new house?"

Jasmine frowned. Danielle's house *hadn't* been wired completely for sound; she had a private suspicion that the security forces had lost interest in Danielle after she'd done nothing of interest for several months. But Danielle's paranoia had kept her fearful…she didn't want to say anything to discourage it, not when it might save their lives in future. A little paranoia could be very useful at times.

"We will ensure that there is a place where you can talk freely," Jasmine assured him. She stood up. "I'm afraid I have to leave now. Danielle can stay for a while, if she wants."

She smiled as Danielle clutched her husband's arm, refusing to leave. There *was* love there, no matter how badly it had been damaged. And they were taking advantage of it…

Feeling dirty, Jasmine left the two lovers in the room and walked out of the flophouse, back towards the van.

CHAPTER TWENTY-SIX

> This may seem absurd – after all, the motives are good. But you may also wish to remember the parable of the cooked frog. When dropped into boiling water, the frog jumped out and fled – scalded, but alive; when dropped into a slowly heating pot, the frog stayed put until it was too late. And the cook had boiled frog for dinner. It is rare for freedoms to be lost overnight. Instead, they are traded away, piece by piece, until it is too late.
> -Professor Leo Caesius, *Authority, Power and the Post-Imperial Era*

"Be careful how you insert the pallets," Mandy ordered, as the station's crew loaded the cargo into *Lightfoot's* hold. "They all have to be secured perfectly."

She smiled inwardly at the glances they tossed her, no doubt thinking that she was yet another starship commander nervous about having her deck scratched. It wasn't an uncommon reaction, even on Avalon, where there were genuine penalties for accidentally damaging an independent freighter or breaking the cargo before it could be shipped to its destination. On the other hand, the station crew seemed well trained. Mandy had heard horror stories from spacers who had visited some of the Empire's worlds and they'd often included station crews bribed to ruin the reputation of independent traders.

It had been simple enough, as Tam had predicted, to win a contract. Indeed, there was no shortage of contracts for freighter crews – and this one was easy money. If she'd been a real freighter commander, with no ulterior motive, she would have jumped at the chance to run an in-system mission, particularly when the pay was so good. The Corinthian System was so heavily patrolled that it was unlikely that any pirates would dare stick their noses into the system, let alone risk intercepting a freighter.

She checked the pallets as they were installed, confirming – as any normal spacer would do – that they were both secured to the deck and the security tags were intact. The cargo was generally verified by the loading agents, who then sealed the pallets to ensure that no one could break into the boxes without making it obvious. Some smugglers had ways of circumventing the system, but Mandy had a suspicion that such smugglers rarely operated anywhere near Admiral Singh. Her system seemed designed to catch smugglers who tried to be clever. Still, it was well to check. It was easier to complain before she'd shipped the cargo, even if it was only going as far as the nearest planet.

"Well done," she said, once the last pallet was firmly secured. "Excellent work."

The station crew headed back to the station, allowing her to run a secondary check of her own. If they'd taken advantage of the opportunity to insert a bug into the ship…she probed carefully, but found nothing. But that might just mean that the bug was shut down, waiting for the activation command before it went online – and became detectable. Mil-spec gear would probably have found even an inactive bug, yet using such gear would have been far too revealing. At the very least, hard questions might have been asked.

She checked that the hold was sealed, then walked back to the bridge. Her crew had taken the opportunity to sample the station's pleasures and come back to report that they were minimal – and overpriced. Plenty of cheap alcohol, a handful of VR booths, a large brothel and little else. Mandy suspected that the real shore leave experience on Corinthian was on the moon, or maybe down on the planet itself. But she'd checked the prices and rolled her eyes when she discovered that going down to the surface would push their line of credit too far. The system discouraged visitors without ever quite making it explicit.

The bridge crew, she was gratified to see, looked refreshed after their brief exposure to shore leave on the station. Mandy smiled, sat down in her command chair and began to flick through the rules and regulations for departing planetary orbit. On Avalon, it was merely a matter of picking a departure trajectory, informing System Command and then leaving on schedule. Here, they were assigned a departure route and fined if they deviated from it by even a tiny fraction. Such precautions might have made sense on Earth, but even Corinthian didn't seem to have enough traffic to warrant them. But then, maybe it was just a precaution against the day when the planet became the centre of a much larger empire.

"Bring up the drives," she ordered, once she'd finished reading the instructions. "And then signal System Command and inform them that we intend to make our scheduled departure window."

She sighed inwardly as the drives came to life. Her drink – and then dinner – with Tam had been informative; she'd played the young girl who had been out of touch for months to the hilt and Tam had responded splendidly. Earth, according to the rumours *he* had heard, had been ripped apart by civil war, a bare year – maybe less – after Mandy had been exiled from the planet, never expecting to return. Somehow, hearing it from Tam had brought it home; her friends, the girls she remembered from Imperial University, were gone. A civil war fought out in Earth's orbit would dump a great deal of debris onto the planet below. Earth, so heavily settled that there were few places that weren't either covered with megacity or polluted beyond hope of recovery, would be rendered utterly uninhabitable.

"They've given us permission to leave," Jones reported. "And they've also reminded us of our assigned trajectory."

"Then take us out," Mandy ordered.

A dull shudder ran through the freighter as the drives came up to full power, followed by a faint shiver as she started to move. A freighter was slow and unwieldy compared to the warships she'd commanded, ever since the Commonwealth Navy had decided that she could be trusted with them, but it had a certain inelegant grace of its own. Perhaps, when the fighting was over and peace returned to the galaxy, she could take command of a freighter and just move from star system to star system, trying to make a living through trading. God knew that the Commonwealth hadn't had any truck with the corporate-spawned regulations that had driven the Empire's independent traders to the Rim – or into bankruptcy.

But that might be a long time, she thought. The Commonwealth was nearly a hundred light years across, but it was tiny compared to the Empire – and even Admiral Singh's empire was larger, although it might be a long time before it matched the Commonwealth's rate of industrial growth. Given a few years, between the starship construction program and some of the new technology, Admiral Singh might find the Commonwealth unbeatable. But it was unlikely that she would give them that time.

It was humbling – and quite beyond human comprehension. On a cosmic scale, *Lightfoot* was so tiny that she wasn't even a speck of dust... and Mandy herself was a nanite, if that. The space the Commonwealth controlled was unimaginably vast – and yet it too was tiny, compared to the Empire. Mandy contemplated it for a long moment, then pushed the thought aside. It never did any good to dwell on the vastness of space.

If I'd wanted to do that, I could have stayed with the RockRats, she thought. A brief check had revealed that there were no RockRats in the Corinthian System – or if they were present they were hiding very well - something that didn't particularly surprise her. RockRats had often been at odds with the Empire; they wouldn't tolerate Admiral Singh's more oppressive regime, not if they could simply leave. Hunting them down was generally considered a waste of time by the Empire; Admiral Singh, Mandy suspected, would see RockRat hunting as more trouble than it was worth.

"That's us past the outer edge of the orbital perimeter," Jones reported. "Captain?"

"Take us on a least-time course to Sturgeon Base," Mandy ordered. "And then alert them as to our projected course. We don't want to alarm them *too* much."

She snorted. They hadn't really had a chance to compare notes with other merchant spacers, but she'd had the definite impression that the planetary authorities were just waiting for opportunities to penalise the independent shippers. Displeasing them in any way could result in fines, having one's ship taken away, or worse. It didn't seem a smart way to run an interstellar economy – her father would definitely agree – but it was more to do with control than anything else. The regime wanted to keep *everything* under control.

And keep the Admiral in power, she added, silently. *What else matters to it?*

"Course set," the helmsman said. "And we're off!"

Mandy smiled. "Keep one eye on the sensors at all times," she added. "We don't want anyone sneaking up on us."

She pulled out a datapad from her chair and keyed in her password, accessing the concealed part of the system. It should have remained undetected even if Tam and his men had taken them apart, but she was silently relieved that hadn't been put to the test. Instead, once she'd entered the second set of passwords, she started to write out a report, outlining everything that had happened since they'd arrived in orbit around the planet, followed by her own observations on the system's politics. If nothing else, the data package she'd been given by System Command included an updated set of star charts, telling just how much space the Admiral actually *controlled*. Greenway was listed as the Admiral's latest acquisition – and there was nothing about the Commonwealth.

But just how long, she asked herself, *is that going to last?*

The Commonwealth had been *encouraging* independent traders – and some of them had started to probe beyond the Commonwealth's borders, in search of new markets. A handful of ships had never even been seen again. If the Admiral had captured them…

She would have known about us sooner, she told herself, tartly. The recording of the brief and violent battle between *Harrington* and *Proud* hadn't suggested any advance knowledge of the Commonwealth's existence. Indeed, it was rather the opposite; the Admiral's crew had seemed to assume that they were dealing with an isolated ship. *That* wasn't uncommon – Mandy's own cover story rested on them being stranded on Gordon's Pride for some months – and the ship's CO might just have jumped to the wrong conclusion. It was unlikely that anyone would ever know the truth.

"We're being lazed," Jones snapped, suddenly. "Communications protocols; A-OK. Access codes check out, Captain."

"Confirm," Mandy ordered. Paranoia was a survival trait, particularly when they were so deeply in the star's gravity well that they would be unable to reach the phase limit before they were run down by the system's defenders. "Make damn sure they're accurate."

"Confirmed," Jones said, patiently. He was a veteran of several covert operations; Mandy had never seen him get flustered, even when their ship was under the guns of two destroyers and enemy soldiers were boarding their vessel. "All codes check out."

Mandy relaxed, slightly.

"Send them a full copy of our sensor readings," she ordered, as she keyed the datapad. The hidden parts of the freighter's network would forward her reports along the laser link, where Captain Delacroix and her analysts would study them with great interest. If something happened to Mandy and her crew, at least they would get *some* information out of the system. "And then purge the secure system."

She sat back in her command chair, wishing that they could just rendezvous with *Harrington* in person and talk face-to-face. But it was impossible; they'd be detected moving off their course and there would be tough questions to answer once they got back to Corinthian. Laser communications were completely impossible to detect, let alone intercept, unless someone got very lucky. In all the files she'd reviewed, Mandy had only noted one incident when someone had intercepted a laser transmission, purely through dumb luck and enemy carelessness.

"Messages away," Jones said. "I'll purge the secure system as soon as we receive an acknowledgement."

Mandy nodded. "Make it so," she ordered.

She shook her head tiredly. There was no point in keeping the files once they were copied to *Harrington*. Once they were gone, even a complete data analysis would have difficulty picking up even a trace of their presence. But then, if there was any suspicion directed at her or her crew, they would have to flee before the shit hit the fan. If there was time to flee…

"They've got them," Jones confirmed. "I'm purging the database… now."

Mandy smiled and leaned back in her chair, feeling the tension drain away. Right now, the stealthed probe would be drifting back into the outer system, where it would relay the contents of its secure data storage node to *Harrington*. In the meantime, *Lightfoot* would proceed along her course, dock with the orbiting station and transfer its cargo to the planetary base. And then they could go back to Corinthian.

Five more hours passed before they docked at the base. Mandy spent them trying to catch up on her sleep, leaving Jones in command of her ship. Her sleeping patterns had never been very good since she'd been kidnapped by the pirates; it had been all too clear that the senior pirates could have barged into her cabin at any moment and done whatever they wanted to do to the young and helpless girl they'd captured. But they hadn't realised, she reminded herself, as she always did when the memories threatened to overwhelm her, that she would turn the tables and cripple their ship. *Sword* had been left drifting helplessly in the Avalon System and the Marines had captured or killed the remaining pirates.

She still felt tired when she walked through the hold with the official from the base, who insisted on inspecting each of the security tags before agreeing to accept the pallets. Mandy couldn't fault his paranoia – he would be blamed for any discrepancies in the manifest, once he'd formally accepted them – but she found it irritating. It was a relief when his crew finally came into the hold to take the pallets, then transfer several more pallets of raw materials onto her ship for transport back to Corinthian. At least they wouldn't be in immediate danger of running out of money.

But we're not trusted to take stuff out of the system, she reminded herself, sardonically. *I wonder why.*

The return journey to Corinthian was almost completely uneventful, until they neared the planet and were ordered to hold position while a pair of light starships entered orbit. Mandy puzzled over the orders – it wasn't as if there was any real danger of a collision – until she realised that the two starships were scouts, rather than proper warships. The database she'd memorised had noted that the Imperial Navy rarely used scoutships any longer – *had* rarely used them, she reminded herself. It was easy to imagine just what worlds Admiral Singh might be scouting out.

"We've got permission to dock," Jones reported, once the scoutships were in orbit. "Same place, Captain."

Mandy nodded, absently. Maybe she could go out with Tam again and try to pump him for information. Or maybe he wouldn't know anything. She had had the impression that Admiral Singh's people never told their subordinates anything more than what they actually needed to know.

"Take us into dock," she ordered.

Once they'd unloaded their new cargo, they could start looking for a new contract – while trying to figure out how much the scoutships had actually been able to tell the Admiral. Mandy had seen how pirates scoped out star systems for possible attack. It was surprisingly easy to pick up a vast amount of information without being detected at all.

The datapad Tam had given her chimed as soon as she linked into the local network. There was a note from him inviting her to dinner again, several responses to enquiries she'd sent to people who might be interested in hiring the freighter…and a number of pieces of junk mail. Back on Earth, there had been laws against spamming the datanet, which hadn't put a stop to the torrent of junk everyone with a working datanet address had received daily. It hadn't been until she'd reached Avalon that she'd realised that the laws were carefully written, allowing anyone willing to pay a small fee the right to send as much spam as they wanted. Somehow, Mandy wasn't surprised that Admiral Singh's regime had done the same thing.

She glanced through it…and froze. One of the messages looked perfectly harmless – it was offering fresh food from the planet below, something that freighter crews wanted if they could afford it – but there were a handful of code phases embedded in the text. It couldn't be a coincidence, she knew; Jasmine had finally managed to get in touch with her! Mandy sucked in a breath and started composing a reply, one that would report on the scoutships…and what they might find out. And who knew what would happen then?

Mandy scowled. If Admiral Singh dispatched her fleet at once, the Commonwealth would be in deep trouble. Hell, she might just decide to trash the systems, rather than try to occupy them. It would be one way to ensure that the Commonwealth never became a rival. She gritted her teeth. That was *not* going to happen.

Once the message was written – it looked like an agreement to buy a small quantity of food – she uploaded it into the datanet and stood up, preparing to head down to the hold. The inspectors would want to do their job before they took the pallets, just like the inspectors on the other planet. It never came to an end.

Maybe I shouldn't go trading after all, she thought, as the ship docked with the station. *I just don't have the patience to deal with the bureaucrats.*

Chapter Twenty-Seven

> The Empire's basic failure lay in its inability to maintain the balancing act. In a sense, it was simply too large and yet too centralised to have any hope of keeping the balance. It was impossible to represent its inhabitants fairly, let alone take account of their needs and wants; indeed, even if the Grand Senate had been controlled by the most capable and altruistic humans in history, it would have been a task well beyond its capabilities.
> -Professor Leo Caesius, *Authority, Power and the Post-Imperial Era*

"Well," Rani said, "what do we have here?"

She studied the star chart with considerable interest. Apart from François, the likely destination of the refugees from Greenway, there were four other worlds highlighted as belonging to a new power. Beyond them, there were a handful of other worlds that might well be other members of the same power. Enough, perhaps, to give her and her fleet a fight.

"We surveyed all of those worlds from a safe distance," Captain Timothy Lombardi reported. He looked nervous at reporting to her directly; she could promote him beyond his wildest dreams, or send him to an asteroid mining station for wasting her time. "There was quite a bit of radio chatter talking about a Commonwealth – several other planetary names were mentioned, headed by Avalon. I think that is the core of their empire."

Rani nodded. Avalon had, for some reason that she doubted had made sense at the time, a working cloudscoop. It had been vastly uneconomical before the Empire's fall, but it seemed that holding a near-complete monopoly on HE3 in its sector had given Avalon the chance to build itself into a new political entity. An impressive feat, all the more so given the lack of any other heavy industry on the planet. Perhaps the RockRats had gotten involved. They tended to shy away from planetary politics – RockRats merely split up if political disputes grew too close to violence, an option that was rarely available on a planet's surface without causing other long-term problems – but some of them might have decided to build a political unit of their own.

Actually, she considered, that would make a great deal of sense. RockRats were natural spacers, capable of turning raw asteroids into habitats, industrial nodes and even shipyards very quickly. The Empire had long worried about the consequences if the RockRats had decided to turn on the Empire, rather than tamely flit away into the darkness when the Empire felt inclined to flex its muscles and banish them from the inhabited systems. No one knew how many RockRats there were, not even themselves. Rani had once read an intelligence report that suggested the RockRats might enjoy a population far larger than the Empire's trillions of human beings.

Still, it was well not to jump to conclusions.

"We ran sensor drones near a number of starships and monitored them," Lombardi continued, carefully. "Most of them were ex-Imperial Navy vessels, but there were a number of new-build ships, built to new designs. Nothing larger than a light cruiser, Admiral, yet it is still an impressive achievement."

Rani nodded in agreement. Even her own industry had yet to produce any new designs for starships, not when there was just too much else to do. It was irritating – like any Imperial Navy officer who didn't owe their position to patronage, she had an entire list of suggested improvements for even the oldest designs – but there was no way to speed the process up. Once she was secure, she could get the designers working on the next generation of battleships and heavy cruisers.

"Good," she said, finally. "Do they know of our presence?"

"I don't know," Lombardi admitted. "The chatter we picked up didn't speak of any new threats…"

"But you didn't go close enough to be certain," Rani concluded. She couldn't fault his caution, or his honesty. If he'd risked going closer, he might have been detected, alerting the Commonwealth to Rani's probes. "Good work, Captain. You will be promoted."

She smiled inwardly as Lombardi relaxed, noticeably. One didn't need to distribute patronage to build up loyalty, not when one could reward good work and punish incompetent officers. She considered him for a long moment, considering her options, then smiled outwardly as well.

"I want you to put together an operation to seize one of their ships," she ordered. "A freighter, for preference; they won't be so worried about losing one of them. Once you take her intact, have the ship and crew brought here for interrogation."

"Yes, Admiral," Lombardi said. He hesitated, then asked the obvious question. "When should we depart?"

Rani made a show of considering it. His crews would need some shore leave – and it wasn't *urgent*. Besides, selecting a suitable target would take time.

"One week from now," she ordered, finally. "Make sure your crews have plenty of rest. Dismissed."

Lombardi saluted, then walked out the door.

"Interesting," Horn said, once the door was firmly closed. "Do you think that this…Commonwealth destroyed *Proud*?"

"It seems the most likely possibility," Rani said, coldly. "But there may be no way to find out for sure without invading their space."

She scowled. If the Commonwealth knew nothing about her, it wouldn't be taking any precautions…which gave her plenty of time to scout out its space, plan her offensives and eventually attack. But if the Commonwealth had *captured* her ship, or found out about her empire from an independent trader, it would be making preparations of its own. Just how capable was its industrial base? If it was producing new designs as well as new starships, it had to be quite formidable. And it might be considering ways to attack her right now.

Sampson leaned forward. "We know very little about them," he warned. "We could easily find out that we have bitten off more than we can chew."

"Nonsense," Horn snapped. "How can a handful of ragtag worlds stand up to us?"

"That is the voice of ignorance talking," Sampson snapped. "Winning a war against a space-capable political entity covering a handful of star systems is considerably harder than bombarding defenceless planets into submission."

He pointed a finger towards the holographic display. "The enemy can fall back, bleeding us all the way, while making it hard for us to secure our supply lines," he said. "Every time the Imperial Navy had to overrun a rebel force that held more than a couple of star systems, it always took months – and really, this is on a far greater scale. There hasn't been anything on this scale since the Unification Wars.

"And there's no rule that prevents them from attacking us," he added. "They might just raid our system here…might I remind you, hey, that we have *all* of our industry concentrated here? A few lucky hits and we will be in serious trouble. We will have to keep this system covered, which means that we won't have much firepower to free up to actually invade *their* star systems. And we know almost nothing about them!"

"We know they destroyed one of our ships," Horn said. "That isn't exactly a *friendly* action."

"We *think* they destroyed one of our ships," Sampson reminded him. "We do not *know* that they have done anything of the sort."

Rani kept her face expressionless as they argued. Sampson was largely right; a war between her empire and the Commonwealth, unless the Commonwealth was far weaker than she dared assume, would take months, perhaps years. On the other hand, she dared not try to sign a treaty with them and agree on a shared border, not when the Commonwealth was clearly expanding rapidly. It might manage to overwhelm her empire economically and fight later at a time of its choosing.

And yet, all of her experience with wars between multi-system powers had been largely theoretical.

Some rebellions had taken entire star systems into revolt, a handful had even consumed several systems. But they'd only had a makeshift force in space to defend themselves…and the Imperial Navy had still had to work hard to overwhelm them, despite possessing vastly superior firepower. The Commonwealth was certain to be a great deal more dangerous.

"We shall continue to survey their space – and, once Captain Lombardi has captured one of their ships, we should have some hard data," Rani said, finally. Not *knowing* was the worst of it. She'd had too many bad experiences with what was laughingly called Imperial Intelligence to feel entirely confident about jumping into the unknown. "In the meantime, we will expand our patrols and attempt to intercept any intelligence probes of their own into our space."

Vice Admiral Jubal Birder cleared his throat. "Admiral, there *was* the missile attack on this world," he said. "That might have been supported by the Commonwealth."

Rani nodded. It *was* possible – supporting insurgent groups would tie up her assets, winning time for the Commonwealth to prepare for war – but it seemed a little *too* blatant. On the other hand, it wouldn't be the first time that insurgent or terrorist groups – there was a fine line between the two – took the weapons and then did something that horrified their patrons. Maybe a little careless on the Commonwealth's part, but much of the Rim was awash with weaponry anyway.

"We shall just have to remain vigilant," she said. She looked over at Horn. "Perhaps some extra checks on any newcomers, just in case."

Horn grinned, unpleasantly. "Of course, Admiral," he said. "Might I suggest that we concentrate on anyone who wants to go down to the planet?"

Rani nodded, then looked at the others. "We knew that we would have to fight on a much larger scale one day," she added. "From this moment onwards, we prepare for all-out war."

Jasmine looked down at the brief message and swore under her breath.

"It's confirmed," she said, savagely. "The Admiral is definitely aware of the Commonwealth."

Blake looked over at her from where he was lying on the bed, trying to relax. "What does she have in mind?"

"The source doesn't say," Jasmine said. "But I don't think it will be anything good."

She put the datapad down and wiped her forehead, tiredly. Two weeks spent nurturing the growth of rebel cells, building up a network that should be far more resilient than the Democratic Underground…and, just incidentally, preparing the farmers for their phase of the operation. It wasn't long enough to launch the operation with any hope of success. Even if they threw caution to the winds and gambled, she couldn't predict anything other than ten to fifteen percent chance of actually winning.

But it was going to be a major headache if the Admiral *did* start mounting raids on the Commonwealth. If nothing else, her fleet was going to be distributed widely, making it harder to capture a number of ships. And if she took her battleships alone and hit Avalon, the war might be lost in a single stroke.

Which means that we really need to distract her, Jasmine thought, grimly. *And that means burning up some of our assets.*

"I'll send a message to Sergeant Harris," she said, reluctantly. "They can start carrying out small attacks on the guardsmen, just enough to make sure that they know they're under attack, but not enough to spur the Admiral into massive retaliation."

"We should be out there," Blake observed. "The locals shouldn't have to carry all of the burden by themselves."

"I know," Jasmine admitted, feeling a flicker of guilt. No doubt a Pathfinder would have happily sacrificed as many of the locals as necessary to accomplish his objectives. "But we may not be able to slip out of the city again."

She scowled. It had been hard enough to get Danielle's children out to an isolated farm – and their minders had reported that both of the children were spoilt brats. God knows what they'd thought; they'd been drugged in the safe house and when they'd woken up, they'd been on the farm, with papers to prove that they'd been adopted by the farmer and his wife. They weren't behaving themselves at all…and if they'd known how to get back to Landing City, they might have had to be restrained.

Jasmine shook her head tiredly. Two kids uprooted from their homes. It was just something else to feel guilty about, really.

Recruitment was going well among the young civilians, the ones who were facing conscription or unemployment in their futures. It wasn't going so well among the unwilling immigrants; unsurprisingly, Admiral Singh's people kept a close eye on them and there had been several close shaves. Jasmine hoped that Trevor Chambers would be able to get closer to the ones on the orbital platforms, but that was just too dangerous. The security forces could monitor the platforms far too comprehensively.

And she'd had an idea. It was, she told herself, born of desperation.

"The surveillance on Johan Patterson has been completed," she said, out loud. "We could use him."

Blake sat upright. "Approaching him is way too dangerous," he objected, bluntly. If *he* felt something was too dangerous, it was probably near suicide. Jasmine had seen him pull crazy stunts in the middle of outright firefights. "He's *loyal*."

"But he has a family," Jasmine said, softly. "And we have people who we can send to kidnap his children."

"Lieutenant," Blake started, and then stopped.

Jasmine understood. Fighting a honest battle was one thing, but actually acting like terrorists was quite another. If they kidnapped a child and threatened him, even without actually intending to carry out the threats, it was another step closer to the line. It was funny how…*insubstantial* the line seemed to be when they *needed* to cross it. Or when they told themselves that they had no choice.

But they didn't, did they? The more cells they built up, the greater the chance of a mistake…something that would expose them to the security forces. Jasmine had no illusions about their ability to fight and win now, if the security forces came hunting. They'd lose; at best, they'd have to go underground and start rebuilding. And at worst, they'd be dead and the Commonwealth would fall soon afterwards.

"Start planning the operation," Jasmine said, in tones that should have ended the conversation right there and then. "Unless you can think of another way to subvert someone high up in the security forces?"

Blake hesitated, then shook his head. "I can't," he admitted. "But this is…this is *obscene*."

"I know," Jasmine said, quietly. "I know."

They'd noticed Johan Patterson when they'd been trying to put together an organisational chart for Admiral Singh's security forces.

Patterson worked under Director Grytpype Horn, who headed Internal Security...and, unlike his superior, he appeared to be a fairly harmless man. Not that Jasmine was too impressed; a man who could sign deportation and execution orders without batting an eyelid wasn't too much of an improvement over a perverted sadist. She couldn't help wondering if the *real* reason Horn kept him around was because he needed someone to do the paperwork, someone who could be trusted *not* to indulge himself at an inconvenient moment.

Wonderful, she thought, as she remembered the surveillance results. *We're going to pick on the one person in Internal Security who is halfway decent.*

She'd seen the others, through the intelligence they'd collected. Horn himself was a grotesque pervert, worse than any of the pirates Mandy had encountered; many of his subordinates were worse, as unbelievable as that seemed. Some of their perversions Jasmine hadn't known were possible until she'd seen the surveillance reports. One day, she promised herself, they would all be executed at her hand.

Admiral Singh had to be insane to tolerate it, she'd thought, but Sergeant Hampton had pointed out that it made a sickening kind of sense. If Horn was hated – and enough had leaked out to ensure that he was both hated and feared – he would have nowhere to go, if something happened to Admiral Singh. Everyone who hated him would be racing to see who got to kill him first.

Jasmine had considered going after Horn, but the man was almost as paranoid as his superior. He rarely set foot outside the government complex; he was always guarded by professional bodyguards...Jasmine had had no difficulty recognising the dull expressions of men who had been conditioned to be loyal. They'd die in his defence, if only because their conditioning wouldn't let them do anything else.

But it suggested that Horn was genuinely insecure. Conditioned men lacked the ability to think for themselves; even lightly-conditioned victims lost most of their IQ under the influence of inflexible commands. *Jasmine* wouldn't have trusted conditioned bodyguards if there was any other choice...but then, Horn probably *didn't* have any other choice. Wasn't it annoying when people thought for themselves?

"We don't have a choice," she said, bitterly. Whatever else happened, they would have to move faster now – and to hell with the dangers. As long as Admiral Singh was on the ground, she was vulnerable. "And whatever happens afterwards, happens."

Colonel Stalker might court martial her for her decision, she knew. It would be hard to blame him, she knew; her actions would damage the Marine ethos beyond easy repair. Rogue Marines were rare, but they did happen – and somehow it was their stories that were remembered longer than the thousands of Marines who had lived and died doing their duty. In hindsight, she wondered if the Grand Senate had pushed that deliberately, even though the days that public opinion had meant anything were long gone. They'd wanted to disgrace the Marine Corps…and now it no longer mattered *what* they did.

But there was no choice, she told herself again and again. There was no choice.

It didn't make her feel any better.

Chapter Twenty-Eight

This should not have been surprising. The interests of maintaining the governing system demanded a decentralised approach, but the underlying ethos of the Empire demanded unity. However, the natural trend of the Empire's governing classes actually worked to split the Empire asunder. The rights of the outer colonies, for example, were sacrificed to the demands of the majority inner worlds.
  -Professor Leo Caesius, *Authority, Power and the Post-Imperial Era*

Kate sucked in a breath as she cycled down towards the checkpoint, tasting the hint of gasoline by-products in the air. It still felt strange to smell them; Greenway had used draft animals rather than gasoline-powered vehicles, even before they'd been cut off from the Empire and supplies of cheap HE3. But then, Corinthian had been settled for much longer than Greenway and was far more developed. No doubt concerns over the environment had faded when the local economy demanded the use of old-style vehicles.

She scowled as she saw the checkpoint, a simple guardhouse and a metal barrier preventing any vehicles from passing without being inspected. It looked alien against the landscape – this far from civilisation, she could almost pretend that she was back on Greenway – a dull brooding presence that cast a long shadow over the district. The building seemed isolated, yet Kate knew that it was not. It was merely a tiny part of a network that held an entire planet in bondage.

Don't fuck up, she told herself, as she pulled on the brakes. *Fuck this up and you will be dead.*

She allowed herself a smile as she saw the young man standing outside the guardhouse, an assault rifle slung over his shoulder. From what she'd been told by the militia officers – and the Marines, later – standing guard was thoroughly boring, no matter what was going on around the guardhouse. The guard would probably not pay the wrong kind of attention to a young girl on a bicycle, she'd been assured. Just to be sure, she'd donned a tight shirt that exposed the tops of her breasts to male eyes. The young man would be too busy staring at her chest, she hoped, to pay attention to what else she was doing.

And if you fuck up, she reminded herself…

They'd heard the stories. The forests were heavily populated with refugees and resistance fighters, all driven into hiding by Admiral Singh and her forces. People had been taken away and never seen again, unless they'd graced one of the warning channels Admiral Singh used to show the planet's population what happened to those who defied her. Others had been beaten, or forced to surrender their farms to higher authority – and yet keep working them for the benefit of their new masters. Kate didn't want to *think* about what could happen if she fell into their hands. But she had to risk herself.

She resisted the temptation to glance behind her as she slowed to a halt in front of the guardhouse. The guard was staring at her, so much so that she was tempted to point out that he wasn't looking at her eyes. Instead, she thrust out her chest a little, giving him a show. It took several moments before he cleared his throat and asked for papers.

"Certainly," Kate said. Her accent wasn't good, but it was doubtful that the young man had noticed. "I have them in my knapsack."

She unslung the bag, smiling at him…and produced the stunner. The guard's eyes went wide before she pushed the trigger and he crumpled to the ground with a thud. Kate felt a hint of pity as she climbed off the bike and allowed it to fall over with a crash. A second guard ran out of the guardhouse, right into the stunner's field of fire. She knocked him out too and then checked inside the guardhouse. The reports, she was relieved to see, had been right. There had only been two guards inside the building.

Back outside, she looked towards the forest and raised her hand in signal. The first part of the operation had been completed successfully. Now, they had to capitalise on their success.

She knew they were coming, but she was still surprised when the two Marines materialised out of the forest alarmingly close to her. "Good work," the leader said, gruffly. The other Marine tended to the two prisoners, searching them and then binding them hand and foot to ensure that they couldn't escape. It was difficult to predict just how long someone would remain stunned after being zapped with a stunner. "You nip off back into the forest now."

Kate scowled at him, but nodded. She'd trained with the militia on Greenway, yet it hadn't taken long for her to realise that they weren't anything close to Marine standards. And the next phase of the operation would require careful timing…

"Understood," she said, briskly. "Good luck."

———

Fritz's mind spun as he fought his way back to consciousness. What was wrong with him? Had he been drinking on duty? He hoped not; the last person who'd drunk on duty had been beaten into a pulp by the sergeants and then sent to spend the rest of his conscription period as a target in live-fire exercises. Or so he had been told, but he found it hard to disbelieve the sergeants. They were utterly ruthless with their young charges.

No, he hadn't been drinking, he assured himself. There had been a girl and…

His memory grew fuzzy. Had they…*done* something? He hoped not; the sergeants would have taken a dim view of them *entertaining* themselves when it was just the two of them on duty. It wasn't as if there was a large detachment up here. They'd been told, in no uncertain terms, that duty came before pleasure…and that there was no shortage of whores in the barracks when they were rotated back into base. There was a twang of pain from his hands and his mind cleared, just long enough for him to realise that there was a wire wrapped around his wrists. He was a prisoner!

"The wire is quite sharp," a strangely-accented voice said, as Fritz opened his eyes. "If you pull too hard you're likely to slice off your own hands."

Fritz stared up at the speaker. He was a big bulky man, wearing dark overalls and a mask that concealed his face.

"There are two ways this can go," the man continued. "You tell us what we want to know and we ensure that you remain safe for the rest of the war. Or you refuse and we force the information out of you. After that, you will be left here to face the tender mercies of the security forces after they find out what happened to you."

Fritz stared at him, the rest of his memories clicking into place. He'd let the girl come too close…and she'd stunned him. Where had she even found a stunner? But it had clearly worked out for her; he looked around, hoping to see his teammate, but there was no sign of him. No doubt their captors would be comparing their answers to make sure that they were telling the truth. It *was* a basic interrogation technique, after all.

He hesitated. They'd been told that if they were captured, they had to keep their mouths shut…but he didn't want to be tortured. He hadn't even *wanted* to join the army. But it had been a choice between the infantry or digging ditches and he hadn't wanted to do that either. And rumour had even suggested that there were worse jobs for those who refused to cooperate.

"I…" He swallowed hard and started again. "What do you want to know?"

"Everything," his captor said. "How often do you contact your superiors and what codes do you use to signify that everything is fine?"

Fritz bowed his head and started to explain.

Private Abdul Donner disliked Corinthian; the world was too green for his tastes, with a population that clearly hated each and every single one of the off-worlders who had landed with Admiral Singh. There had been enough incidents to make him thoroughly paranoid, along with most of the rest of his unit; they'd been told that if they thought they were in danger, they could open fire and leave the Admiral to worry about the resulting mess. He gripped the machine gun as the armoured car rolled along the road, watching for the first sign of trouble. Those damned forests came too close to the roadside.

He gritted his teeth. Convoy duty was unpleasant; no one knew when someone would take a shot at the vehicles, forcing them to disembark and search for the shooter, wasting their time. At least the insurgency had been taught a sharp lesson in the months since the conquest; they'd learned to fall back and not engage heavily-armed convoys. He swung the machine gun around as the lead vehicle approached yet another patch of forest, shaking his head in disbelief. If it had been up to him, as he'd grumbled often enough, he would have cleared fields of fire all around the main roads.

But the Admiral forgot to ask my advice, he thought, with a flicker of wry amusement.

Instead, he glanced at the truck. Each one held thirty soldiers, ready to reinforce the garrison that kept watch over the northern farmlands. It was the most dangerous part of the planet; there were just too many mountains and forests for the occupation force to maintain perfect security. Abdul was privately surprised that the Admiral hadn't ordered a saturation nuclear bombardment; it wasn't as if they actually *needed* the food. They had enough farming worlds – and algae farms, if it came to that – under their control to feed the entire population several times over.

He looked back towards the lead vehicle, just in time to see it blown up by a colossal explosion. For an instant, he gaped, watching in horror as the lead truck ran into the fireball and skidded to a halt. The drivers of the other trucks hit their brakes, but it was too late to stop many of them from slamming into the vehicles in front of them. Abdul cursed as the driver of the armoured car swung wide to avoid a truck that had rammed its fellow and toppled over, then swung the machine gun around as the shooting started. Someone had taken pains to set up a really good ambush and they'd walked right into it.

"Open fire," the convoy commander ordered. Half of the troops in the trucks were raw recruits, straight out of basic training; they'd be shitting themselves as the bullets tore through the metal vehicles and flesh with equal abandon. "Push the bastards back from the roadside!"

Abdul depressed his trigger, firing a long burst towards the source of some of the incoming fire. It slacked off sharply; he felt a moment of gratification, which vanished the moment the first mortar shell landed in the midst of the crashed vehicles. Only a tiny percentage of the troops had managed to jump out of the trucks before HE shells blew them apart. The more skilled ones were doing their best to organise a defence, but the soldiers had been taken completely by surprise. Abdul cursed again and swung the gun around, firing randomly into the forest. It should have disconcerted the enemy soldiers.

This won't have passed unnoticed, he told himself, as the enemy fire began to slack off. They'd done all they could do; now, they would have to break contact and escape before reinforcements arrived. The resistance couldn't win a stand-up battle, no matter how much firepower they'd managed to hide away since Corinthian had been occupied. *There'll be helicopters on their way.*

Something exploded, too close to the armoured car for comfort. Abdul felt the blast pick him up and throw him halfway across the road, right into the ground. There was a long moment of pain, then nothing. Nothing at all.

The enemy soldiers were raw, Sergeant Chester Harris realised, as the insurgents ripped their convoy apart. They hadn't even managed to put up a real defence, apart from a handful who seemed to know what they were doing. Chester had expected to get in, land a few blows and then get out again before the enemy pushed him back, but instead he was being offered an opportunity to hand out a smashing tactical defeat.

He shook his head as the next set of mortar rounds struck the remains of the enemy convoy. A final series of explosions tore through the vehicles; the enemy fire, as pitiful as it was, slacked off, coming to an end. Chester watched as flames spread through the burning vehicles, feeling a moment of pity for his opponents. Most of them would have been unwilling conscripts, men who would have preferred not to fight for their planet's unwanted mistress. They hadn't deserved to die.

No choice, he reminded himself.

"Hold fire," he bellowed. Years of experience had taught him how to throw his voice. Normally, they would have used battlefield microburst communicators, but Admiral Singh had sensor equipment that might have been able to pick up the signals. They might as well have called her up and asked her to drop rocks on their position. "Hold fire!"

Silence fell over the battlefield, broken only by the sound of flames burning through the remains of the convoy. The enemy had definitely stopped shooting; Chester couldn't help wondering if that meant they were all dead, or if some of them were still alive, but too injured to continue the fight. Part of him wanted to slip down to the vehicles and make certain they were all dead; he considered it for a long moment before dismissing it. They weren't pirates, or insurgents from Han. Besides, they were almost certainly out of the fight.

"Fall back," he bellowed, shouldering his rifle. It was too much to hope that the enemy soldiers hadn't transmitted a distress call. The enemy would already have reinforcements on the way, probably including helicopters...and the small stockpile of HVMs the resistance had saved were reserved for later operations. "Get back to base, now!"

He allowed himself a tight smile as they scattered through the forest. If nothing else, they'd given Admiral Singh's forces a bloody nose. And, if all of the planned attacks had been as successful, she'd be convinced that half of the countryside was rising against her.

Yeah, we've done great, he told himself. *Now, what are we going to say to those who get mashed in the gears when she starts her retaliation.*

They saw the plume of smoke from miles away as the four attack helicopters raced towards the source of the distress beacon. Standing in the cabin, staring over the pilot's head, Captain Ivan Shako couldn't help shivering at the sheer size of the smoke cloud. There had been so many emergency calls to the closest garrison that the helicopters had been ordered to go to one location, then another, and another…it had taken nearly twenty minutes for the higher ups to start prioritising the distress calls. A convoy of nearly three hundred soldiers had been top of the list.

It was hard to imagine the insurgents having a go at such a convoy; hell, the reason such convoys always moved in force was to *discourage* such attacks. But it was starting to look like the insurgents *had* dared to strike…and that they'd succeeded beyond their wildest imaginations. He gritted his teeth as the helicopters swooped closer, two of them watching from high overhead while the other two flew low, far too close to the damned forest. *Anything* could be lurking there, under the trees, and they wouldn't know about it until it was too late.

He sucked in his breath as the remains of the convoy came into view. Twenty vehicles, fourteen of them troop trucks, burning away merrily. There were bodies everywhere, all mown down by fire that had to have come pouring out of the trees…and a smoking crater, right where the lead vehicle in the convoy should have been. Someone had planned the ambush with care, he realised, as the helicopter slowed to a hover over the burning vehicles. The soldiers had been caught in a trap that would have made it difficult to escape, or to do anything but die.

The Admiral is not going to be pleased, he thought, grimly. If nothing else, enough conscripts had died to make it impossible to conceal their deaths. It wouldn't be long before more young men – and women – started trying to dodge the draft. They couldn't *all* hide, but it would be nightmarish rounding them all up. *We might even suffer a manpower shortage.*

There was a cough from the pilot. "Do you want to rappel down there, sir?"

Ivan shook his head. He'd clambered down lines into battle before, but he had a feeling that there was no point in trying to inspect what remained of the convoy. Instead, a ground team would have to be sent to strip the vehicles of anything useful before the insurgents returned, whatever the risks. The alternative was simply to fire missiles into the vehicles himself.

"No," he said, finally. Besides, the enemy could be lying in wait, hoping to bag a helicopter. Intelligence was sure that they had few HVMs, if any, but Ivan knew better than to take anything Intelligence said for granted. "Take us back to the garrison. There will be plenty more work for us to do."

We'll find the bastards who did this to you, he silently promised the dead men below as the helicopter rose up into the air. *And when we do, we will make them pay.*

CHAPTER TWENTY-NINE

> Naturally, this led to the democratic triumph of the majority. Democrats honoured this as a victory. But the democracy could and did demand anything. And politicians scrambled to win power by giving the people who elected them what(ever) they wanted. The fact that this did long-term damage to the Empire passed unnoticed.
> -Professor Leo Caesius, *Authority, Power and the Post-Imperial Era*

It hadn't been a good day.

Helen Patterson held her son's hand as she walked home, already rehearsing what she was going to say to her husband as soon as he returned from the office. Their son had discovered just what their father did for a living…and he hadn't hesitated to use it to force his teacher into letting him get away with everything. If the headmaster hadn't been made of sterner stuff, Helen and her husband would have remained blissfully unaware of what the little monster was doing. Instead, there had been an uncomfortable interview with the headmaster, leaving her with the dull awareness that she'd raised a corrupt child.

She scowled at her son, who was rubbing his bottom while glaring tearfully at her. Helen had never smacked him before, but after she'd seen his teacher crying because she'd thought that she was going to be hauled off to prison – or worse – Helen had lost her temper and spanked Sirius right in front of both of them. God knew how the brat would respond to that, she thought, silently promising herself that she would keep a closer eye on him in future. She had no idea where the sadistic streak he'd shown had come from either. Helen wasn't sadistic and her husband, for all of his faults, wasn't sadistic either. He had never raised his voice to her, let alone struck his wife or son.

Helen ran her free hand through her long blonde hair. She'd thought she was a lucky woman – and she was, compared to some of the others she knew who moved in the same social circles. How could she have made such a mess of raising her son?

"I hate you," Sirius said, bitterly. "You're going to be sorry."

"And *you*, young man, had better improve your manners or you will go over my knee again," Helen snapped, tartly. It had been a mistake to allow Sirius to realise how powerful his father actually was, even if he wasn't really aware of the details. Helen knew just enough to keep her from sleeping properly, some nights. "Your father will not be pleased."

She nodded to a pair of patrolling guardsmen as they turned into their street. Sirius had wanted a garden, back when he'd had true friends to play with, and Helen had convinced her husband that it would be a good idea. The house was larger than the one they'd shared on Trafalgar – she was a social queen on Corinthian, when she wanted to be – but it was also isolated. She couldn't help mixed feelings about her husband's position; it made her socially powerful, yet it isolated her. No one trusted her completely – and why should they?

"Dad will not be happy with you," Sirius said. "You *hurt* me."

Helen rounded on him and he flinched away, trying to pull his hand out of hers. She felt a moment of bitter regret, wondering if she had done the right thing. But she'd raised a monster and she had to do whatever it took to heal him before it was too late. Too many of the people she'd met who worked with her husband were complete monsters. And her husband's boss was the worst monster of all.

There was a van parked outside their house, she noticed, as they reached the gate. She gave it an odd look, wondering what it was doing there, then ignored it as she fumbled with the security sensor on the gate. A moment later, the van door opened and four masked men emerged. Helen had no time to scream before they grabbed her and Sirius, pressing cloths to their mouths. Her legs buckled as the universe started to blur… and faded away into darkness.

"They got them," Blake reported, softly. His tone dripped disapproval. "Both wife and son. They don't think they were followed."

Jasmine nodded. She'd been surprised that Helen Patterson wasn't escorted at all times; it had taken several days of surveillance to confirm that there *weren't* any security officers following her. It had puzzled Jasmine until she'd realised that very few people seemed to know what Johan Patterson actually *did*. Most people just considered him a senior civil servant, someone who had effortlessly shifted his allegiance from the Empire to Admiral Singh. Hardly the sort of person who demanded attention from the resistance.

No shortage of civil servants, she thought, ruefully. The Empire could have populated entire planets with the multitude of civil servants on Earth alone, let alone the Core Worlds. *Kill one and a thousand will take his place.*

"Let's hope not," she said, grimly. *This* was far more risky than anything else they'd done. If someone realised that Helen Patterson was missing, along with her son, they were going to start a proper search. And perhaps offer a reward that might tempt others into betraying the underground. Wolf might remain cooperative, but Jasmine knew better than to trust his subordinates. "And Patterson himself?"

"Remains at the office," Blake said. "I think he's working late tonight."

They'd timed the kidnapping so it took place simultaneously with Sergeant Harris's offensive in the countryside. The series of attacks, she hoped, would not only keep Admiral Singh occupied on Corinthian, but distract her from the *true* angle of attack. But if someone happened to notice…Jasmine shook her head, irritated. If she had allowed the possibility of failure to convince her not to try something, she would never have bothered to live.

She settled back to wait, quietly monitoring the planetary datanet for news and information. There was little true news, which would have bothered her if she hadn't known just how heavily censored the datanet actually was. The attacks in the countryside would never be mentioned until Admiral Singh had decided how to present them to the population in the cities. Jasmine had a feeling that the Admiral would call them a deliberate attempt to starve the civilian population, something that might just turn the urban inhabitants against the farmers. Avalon's council had done something similar, back during the Cracker Insurgency.

It was near midnight by the time they received a buzz from the monitoring team, reporting that Patterson was on his way home. Jasmine scowled – being caught after curfew would force them to fight their way out or surrender to the guardsmen in the hope they could break out later, no matter what paperwork they carried – but readied herself as best as she could. They had to convince Patterson to see reason before he contacted the security forces and ordered a search...

She slipped out of the vehicle as Patterson's car arrived outside his house and the man climbed out. Jasmine hadn't been impressed when she'd seen his photograph; he was a grey man, wearing a grey suit. He might not have taken any sadistic pleasure in what he did, but he was so completely detached from the realities of his job that he could order anything with nary a qualm. She would almost have preferred a sadist. At least they could be relied upon to let their vile tastes interfere with their work.

Keeping to the shadows, she slipped up to the wall and scrambled over it as quietly as she could. Patterson was walking up the path to the main door, pushing his hand against the security scanner; Jasmine watched carefully as he entered the house, then ran up to the door herself. The lock was an old one, easy to pick with a simple multitool. She was mildly surprised that he hadn't arranged for his house to have a more modern security system. Unless his boss hadn't wanted him to have one...

"Helen?" Patterson's voice called, from inside the building. "Where are you?"

Jasmine opened the door, pistol in hand. Patterson swung around to face her, staring in disbelief. Jasmine had tried her best to act like a young girl from Corinthian, walking in a slovenly manner that would have earned her punishment duties at the Slaughterhouse, but Patterson might well know enough to see through the pretence. No one knew what he'd been on Trafalgar – he was definitely not a native of Corinthian - and if he'd been Imperial Intelligence he might well have had dealings with Marines.

"Don't move," she said, flicking on the laser sight. She didn't need it, but the beam – half-visible in the darkness – was hellishly intimidating. "Your wife and son are safe, as long as you cooperate."

Patterson's mouth fell open. "Who...who are you?"

Jasmine felt a moment of pity. Patterson genuinely *cared* for his wife and child. The pirates didn't care for anyone, but themselves; Avalon's old councillors had been too busy competing for power to care about their families. And if anyone on Han had loved their families, they had been too wrapped up in hatred and rage to show it. But Patterson cared.

And yet, she knew what he did for a living. How could he look his child in the eye when he came home?

How could I do it, if I had children? She asked herself, sourly. *After everything I've done, it might be for the best that I will never have children.*

"We want your cooperation," Jasmine said, ignoring the question and putting her doubts aside. There was no time for self-pity, particularly when it was effectively whining. "If you work with us, your wife and child will remain unharmed. If you refuse, you will never see them again."

She forced as much cold hatred into her voice as she could, trying to convince him of her sincerity. Even with the Commonwealth at stake, she wasn't going to kill the little boy – but she would send him to a farm, with enough memory-altering drugs to ensure that his previous life became a half-forgotten dream. But was that any better than simply killing him outright?

And what would she do with the wife?

Patterson studied her for a long moment. "You must know that this will get you nowhere," he said, sharply. "Don't you know what I do for a living?"

"Of course," Jasmine said, sardonically. "Why do you think you were targeted?"

She stepped forward, into the light. "We have eyes and ears everywhere," she said, warningly. "If you breathe a word of this, to *anyone*, you will receive your wife's head in the mail. You don't want to know what we'll do to your son. Maybe" – she allowed her voice to darken – "it will be like the torments your people have handed out to your enemies.

"We watch your channels, you know," she added, fighting down the urge to be sick. "I was particularly impressed by the execution when the killers sliced a little girl into tiny pieces, right in front of her parents. Such a sickening sight, wouldn't you agree? Or doesn't it bother you to watch a young girl die?"

She stared into his eyes as threateningly as she could. "We could do that to your son," she concluded. "You *know* just what some people can do."

Patterson swayed on his feet. Like others, he'd probably thought that his work could stay in the office; perhaps he'd bought his house to maintain a healthy separation between the suffering he oversaw and his family. But now he had to realise that what his superiors had meted out to Admiral Singh's enemies could be meted out to his family in turn. The nightmare had finally come home.

Years ago, Jasmine had heard a lecture from a Marine Corps psychologist, who'd talked about how easily the values of human society could be pushed aside, if someone approached the issue in just the right way. Everyone could be manipulated, or broken, if the right levers were pushed. If someone believed – genuinely believed – that the person they were torturing was subhuman, they would happily commit all sorts of atrocities on their victim and then go home and eat a perfectly normal meal with their families.

Or they might want to please their superiors. Or they talked themselves into doing it…claiming that the ends justified the means. But once you crossed that line, no matter how strongly you tried to talk yourself out of it, it was always easier to cross it a second time.

It had grown worse, the psychologist had added. Few people could really form close relationships and connections to large groups of people. It was why the Marine Corps used hundred-man companies as the building blocks of larger units – and even that, he'd claimed, was pushing it. At some point, the numbers became so unimaginably large that even the most empathic human couldn't really grasp that the numbers were real people.

"During the Unity Wars, Bloody Kane the Executioner was responsible for depopulating seventeen worlds through orbital bombardment, with a death toll of over fifty *billion* lives," the psychologist had said. "And yet his subordinates had said he was a kind and gentle man. Perhaps the figures were just too large for him to truly understand."

Patterson broke the silence. "What do you want me to do?"

"For the moment, we want you to make excuses for your child and wife," Jasmine said. He had to compromise himself still further before he could be useful. "You will contact the school tomorrow and tell them that you're moving your son to a different school. Your wife's friends are to be told that she is ill – or that she has had to do something that will take her out of the city. You will, of course, make sure that the surveillance monitors don't pick up anything that might…*worry* someone."

Patterson hesitated, then nodded. "Of course not," he said. His voice turned calculating. "I will, of course, require proof that they are still alive."

"It will be provided," Jasmine assured him. "I'll have them write a few notes to you."

"I have money," Patterson said, quickly. "I can pay…"

"We need you in position to help us," Jasmine said. She made a slip that had been carefully calculated. "We want to move goods in and out of the city and you can help us do that."

Patterson relaxed, so subtly that most people would have missed it. Smuggling was big business – and it made sense that a criminal gang would want to have someone in Internal Security in their pocket. He could cooperate without fearing that he was betraying the Admiral…criminal gangs flourished under her regime. So many people wanted things the Admiral wasn't willing to let them have.

"I will be in touch," Jasmine said, lowering the pistol. She doubted that Patterson would try to jump her, but she kept her attention focused on him anyway. "And I strongly suggest that you don't do anything to alert your superiors. They will not be happy with you."

She smiled as she saw that sink into his face. It had probably never crossed his mind that *he* might find himself in an interrogation chamber, strapped to the table as Horn interrogated him, breaking bones and pulling out teeth whenever he thought that Patterson was holding something back. Jasmine had wondered, at first, why the locals didn't seem to use truth drugs. It had taken her a while to realise that a mind like Horn's *preferred* causing pain and suffering, even when there was an easier way to get answers out of an unwilling donor.

"And sleep well," she added, nastily. "You don't want to go into work tomorrow looking like you have something to hide."

Patterson blanched.

Jasmine nodded politely to him and slipped out of the door, moving through the shadows to the wall and scrambling over it, dropping down onto the street. There was no sign of any foot patrol, thankfully, but she stayed in the shadows until she reached the van and climbed inside. Sleeping in the vehicle would be uncomfortable, yet a moving van would be bound to attract attention. Besides, she'd slept in Raptors with a full platoon of Marines and that had been worse.

Blake nodded to her as she pulled the door closed. "Success?"

"Success," Jasmine said. She wanted a shower, but she knew that no matter how often she showered she would never wipe the stain off her soul. God alone knew what Colonel Stalker would say. "He's going to cooperate."

She let out a breath she hadn't realised she'd been holding. A fanatic – or someone who had been conditioned – wouldn't have hesitated to scream for help, even if it meant their family being brutally tortured to death. Patterson had *known* that there was nothing preventing insurgents or criminals from killing his family; the insurgents might well take a little revenge for everything Admiral Singh had done by killing Patterson's wife and child. It would be pointless, Jasmine knew, but it would also be *human*.

"Good," Blake said, gruffly.

Jasmine lay down on the floor, shifting until she found something reasonably comfortable. Blake definitely didn't sound happy – and how could she blame him? Jasmine was walking the thin line between legal actions and illegal acts of war, actions that every Marine had a duty to stop – with lethal force, if necessary. Offhand, she couldn't remember how many Marines had been shot down by their fellow Marines, even though she'd studied the cases at the Slaughterhouse. Only a handful, if she recalled correctly, but some of them had been truly shocking.

She closed her eyes and meditated until she fell asleep. Tomorrow, she would have to make contact again, with her first series of instructions. And they would have to monitor Patterson to ensure that nothing had gone wrong.

And if it does, she thought, before the darkness descended, *we're dead.*

CHAPTER THIRTY

> Indeed, as I have noted in my earlier works, the distance between the governed and the governors was so great that almost anything could be made legal. If a corporation with the Grand Senate's ear demanded specific mining rights, on a world that was already settled, it was merely a matter of pushing the Grand Senate into passing a specific law – and the colonists would wake up to discover that their world was no longer their own. It was no surprise that the Empire fragmented as soon as the power holding it together could no longer do so.
> -Professor Leo Caesius, *Authority, Power and the Post-Imperial Era*

Horn allowed himself a tight smile as Director Tomas faced the wrath of Admiral Singh. The sour-faced man was responsible for safeguarding the garrisons in the countryside, away from the cities…and he'd dropped the ball quite spectacularly. He looked up at the display, with nearly a hundred red lights glowing to mark where attacks had been launched by the insurgents, and shook his head in grim amusement. The attacks had been mere pinpricks compared to the sheer size of the edifice Admiral Singh had assembled, but they had thoroughly embarrassed his rival.

"We didn't have a *word* of warning," Tomas protested, trying to defend himself. "The first we knew about it was when the convoys came under attack."

Horn shrugged, enjoying his rival's discomfort. The attacks had clearly been carefully planned, showing a mindset that suggested someone with real military experience had done the groundwork before the insurgents had shown themselves. They'd started by overrunning a handful of guardposts, capturing and subverting the guards, then used their radios to lull the convoys into a false sense of security...which had come to an end when the insurgents had thrown in their main attacks. They had shown a degree of professionalism that they hadn't shown since Admiral Singh's forces had overwhelmed the planet's defences, two years ago.

Maybe they found someone living alone and convinced him to help them, Horn thought, wryly. There had always been rumours of great military leaders hiding out in the backcountry, although Horn had always known them for wishful thinking. Quite a few insurgent cells they'd broken back in the early months of occupation had claimed that they were supported by a vast group – and they'd believed it too, because the leader had told them the lie to keep their spirits up. It had taken considerable effort to disprove it.

"But then there was an entire series of attacks," Admiral Singh snapped. "Why did you fail to respond in time? Or to call for assistance from the orbital weapons platforms?"

Tomas hesitated. "I thought we could handle it," he said, finally. "I was wrong."

Horn kept his smirk from growing any wider, but it was an effort. Tomas had probably *also* felt that it would disgrace him if he called for help, suggesting that he couldn't handle everything himself. And he would be right. Horn wouldn't have hesitated to capitalise on his rival's weakness – but now he had a far greater opportunity to expand his own power base.

"So you were," Admiral Singh snapped. "And now we have a problem."

She looked up at the display. "Our intelligence network has either been compromised or was simply kept out of the loop," she snapped. "You failed us."

Horn jumped into the silence. "Internal Security would be happy to offer help, Admiral," he said, quickly. "We have trained interrogators who are very capable of breaking resistance."

"Of course you do," Tomas snapped. "You don't have to worry about leaving the farmers alive afterwards. We cannot kill the experienced farmers without ensuring a major drop in food production."

"Then perhaps we should ramp up our own algae-bar production vats," Horn countered. "Do we really *need* the farmers?"

"Unless we want a mutiny, we do," Admiral Singh said. She scowled at Tomas, who lowered his eyes. "I want you to identify a number of possible insurgent supporters and pass their names to Internal Security. They are to be interrogated to ensure that they don't know anything about the insurgents" – she shot a glance at Horn – "a non-*rigorous* interrogation, if you please. Use drugs and lie detectors."

Horn scowled. Where was the fun in that?

"If you find some of them to be guilty, you may take their families into custody," Admiral Singh added. "*I* will decide what to do with them afterwards."

She looked over at Tomas. "*You* will surge forward additional troops and reinforce the garrisons," she ordered. "Your forces will remain linked to orbital surveillance and weapons platforms; if they need help, they are to call for it. If there are further attacks on such a scale, there will be *consequences.*"

Tomas looked grim, but he didn't dare argue.

Horn smiled to himself. Admiral Singh was tolerant of everything, but failure and incompetence. If there was a second series of such attacks, it would prove Tomas incompetent…and he would be removed from his position. As one of her supporters, it was unlikely that he would be executed or exiled to Penance, but he would never wield true power again. And, given some work, Horn could probably *make* Tomas look incompetent. It was unlikely that the Admiral would look too closely at the methods he used to get answers out of his victims.

There had been a fire, several months ago, that had killed a number of girls. The girls had been hostages, in all but name. Their parents lived near the zone where the largest attacks had taken place. Had the parents *known* what had happened to their daughters? It was quite possible; Tomas was supposed to ensure that the girls sent messages home every week, just to reassure their parents that they were still alive, but those messages wouldn't have been sent from the grave. Even if Tomas hadn't told their parents the truth, they must have suspected it when the messages came to a halt.

Horn allowed his smile to widen. No matter the names Tomas threw at him, he thought he knew where to begin.

He looked over at Tomas, who was sweating under the Admiral's gaze, and considered the man's future. There was no point in trying to dicker with him; the man was just as bloody-minded an empire-builder as Horn himself. But it was unlikely that Horn would simply be ordered to take command of External Security as well as Internal Security. Admiral Singh wouldn't allow him to concentrate *that* much power in his hands. However, he knew the most likely candidates for that role and he was fairly sure that he could dominate them.

And who knew where that would lead?

"Run additional checks in the city as well," Admiral Singh ordered, dragging his attention back to her. "And then instruct your agents to watch out for rumour-mongers."

Horn nodded. "Admiral," he said, "what are we going to tell the public?"

"That we lost a handful of soldiers to treacherous attack," Admiral Singh said, coldly. "And that we killed a number of terrorists in return."

Tomas frowned, yet he said nothing.

Horn understood. One thing all of his agents agreed upon was that few people trusted the official statements on the news. With very good reason, he had to admit. Admiral Singh's newscasters lied more than the Empire's had done. Rumours would already be spreading through the city, no matter the security the Admiral had ordered slammed down on anyone who might talk. And then the underground might take heart.

He ignored that thought as the Admiral dismissed him, allowing him to head back to his office. Once there, he called for the files on the dead farm girls and made careful note of their names. If he was very lucky, Tomas would be too distracted covering his ass to notice that Horn had jumped ahead of him. And once he had the farmers in custody, they'd talk, even if he had to write the script himself.

There was a knock on the door. "Come in," he ordered, looking up. A young man, his features so bland that they were utterly unnoticeable, stepped inside. "What do you want?"

"There have been developments," Zed said.

Horn blinked in surprise. Zed was one of his very special agents, charged with keeping an eye on the rest of Internal Security. Horn had happily backstabbed his last superior to get his rank in Imperial Intelligence and he had no illusions about how many of his subordinates wanted to be in control of his little empire. And, given the kind of people he'd been careful to recruit, it wouldn't be long before one of them allowed desire to overcome prudence. He gave them so much freedom, after all.

"Developments," he repeated. Zed was loyal; he had to be loyal. It wasn't as if he could ever take Horn's place, not when hardly anyone knew him as anything more than a lowly office worker. "What sort of developments?"

"Patterson's son didn't go to school today," Zed said. "His mother apparently had to go out of the city."

Horn felt his eyes narrow. Outside the city, now?

"I see," he said. "What happened?"

"Good question," Zed said. "I made enquiries. The brat was apparently in some trouble yesterday; today, the father called the school and said that the boy was being transferred. There was no sign of either of them at the house when we inspected it…"

Horn felt an odd stab of disappointment. He'd known that Tallow, or Alec, or Melvin would eventually try to stick a knife in his back. They were utter degenerates who craved the power to make their fantasies reality – just like Horn himself, he acknowledged inwardly. Sooner or later, they would grow tired of being at his beck and call and try to take power for themselves. On that day, he would know how good his precautions really were.

But Patterson? The man never seemed to show any ambition, or the depraved tastes that powered most of Internal Security. He was just a civil servant, carrying out his orders – if there was anyone Horn could rely on in the department, it was Patterson. And the man was clearly up to *something*. His wife and son were gone. What, Horn asked himself did that mean?

He tapped a command into the terminal and brought up the internal security system. He'd never really told any of his subordinates how closely they were monitored at work, although he suspected that the smarter ones probably knew. There were no blind spots in the office, no place where someone could hold a covert conversation; no wonder his people always seemed to be busy when he looked at them. They suspected that they were probably always under observation.

Patterson looked...wrong. On the surface, he was the same imperturbable bureaucrat he seemed, someone who could take a dinner order one moment and an instruction to commit genocide the next, but there was something odd about his demeanour. He was...*afraid*. Paterson was never afraid.

"Interesting," he said, slowly. "And what have you deduced?"

"Patterson is either making a play for power or someone else is using his love for his family as a tool to control him," Zed said. "The latter is the most likely option."

Horn nodded. Patterson wasn't stupid. He might know that Horn didn't keep a close eye on what his people did in their homes, but something as revealing as hiding his family would probably be noticed. Besides, if he made a bid for power and failed, his family would be slaughtered when they were found. No, someone else had found his weak point and used it against him.

It was odd, Horn considered. Love was an alien concept to him, no matter how many husbands had been willing to break and confess all when confronted with their wives on a torture rack. Sentiment was certainly not something he wished to encourage among his people; it might start them thinking in unfortunate or unprofitable directions. But there had been something oddly reassuring about Patterson's family. Horn's own wife had as little to do with him as she could.

"So someone is," he said, smoothly. He pressed his fingertips together and smiled. "I think we should find out who, don't you?"

Jasmine scowled as she slipped through the side-streets and alleyways, trying to stay out of sight. The rumours about what had happened in the countryside had been spreading throughout the city – the last rumour she'd heard had suggested that over ten thousand of Admiral Singh's men had been wiped out in a single ambush – and the population was restless. Admiral Singh's forces had responded by moving additional forces onto the streets and imposing a curfew at sunset. Right now, they were trying their hardest to actually enforce it.

There were fewer patrollers in the richer part of town, much to Jasmine's silent relief, yet there was still too much chance of being observed. The other parts of the underground had been warned – using the innocuous codes they'd developed for the datanet – to keep their heads down, but Jasmine *had* to make contact with Patterson. If nothing else, they had to be sure that he hadn't aroused any suspicion.

She heard the sound of gunfire in the distance and winced, inwardly. Many of the poorer parts of the city would be harder to control, at least until the rumours had been discredited – and Jasmine suspected that quite a bit of information on how to produce makeshift weapons had leaked out onto the streets. It was astonishing how easy it was to produce a working IED with a few chemicals and a certain disregard for the dangers…she had ordered her cells to remain underground, but there would be others who wanted to riot. The rumours that suggested that the next class for conscription would be called up early had sparked a terrifying amount of discontent.

Maybe it's something we can use, she thought, coldly. Many of their cells were composed of young men who would be conscripted next year – or earlier, if the losses rumour spoke of were anything like accurate. *Get them in position, get them access to weapons…and then hit the Admiral as hard as we can.*

She slowed as she reached the edge of the street and peered around the corner. There was a small APC at one end of the street, with two guards patrolling around the heavily-armoured vehicle…one of them, she realised with a hint of contempt, smoking a cigarette while on duty. A sniper would have had no difficulty picking him off from long range, then vanishing into the shadows while the idiot's comrades were still wondering what had happened. About the only worse thing would have been to salute one's superior in a combat zone, identifying them for enemy snipers.

Jasmine slipped back into the shadows, then moved down the back alleyway until she reached the back of Patterson's house. If she'd been in command of the APC, she would have made damn sure that someone was using a pair of NVGs at all times. A normal combat suit would have camouflaged her heat signature, even without a proper armoured battlesuit, but it would have been too revealing if someone had caught her. Instead, she clambered up and over the wall, then dropped down into his garden. A faint light from inside the house announced his presence.

The back door was locked, unsurprisingly, but it was easy enough to pick. Inside, Jasmine's enhanced eyes adapted rapidly to the darkness, revealing a corridor decorated with scattered paintings. It reminded her of some of the entertainment programs from Earth – *Lives of the Mega-Rich*, if she recalled the title correctly – that had eventually been banned for causing social unrest. *That* shouldn't have been a surprise. The Grand Senators had all been so wealthy that they could purchase a planet, a freighter of valuable artwork or a small fleet of starships with pocket change. Whatever they wanted, they got.

Unless the rumours are true, she thought, grimly. Some of them claimed that the entire Grand Senate had been ritually tortured to death by the Nihilists. It seemed unlikely, but there was little hard data to go on. *Who knows what might have happened on Earth?*

She heard the sound of someone moving in the next room and stopped, listening carefully. One person, she decided, after a long moment. Patterson, she hoped; unlike some of his fellows, Patterson hadn't seen fit to fill his large house with servants. No doubt, given how easily some of them had been corrupted by Wolf and the other crime lords, it was a very smart decision. The hired help often shared their employer's secrets with anyone willing to meet their price.

Carefully, Jasmine opened the door...and stared. It *wasn't* Patterson, but someone else, a man she didn't recognise. For a moment, she considered demanding answers from him, before it clicked in her mind. Someone had discovered what had happened to Patterson and taken precautions. The entire operation had been blown. No, she told herself; the only part that had been blown was Patterson's conversion. The rest of the operation was still good.

She lifted her pistol, then dismissed the thought and jumped backwards. The mask would keep her face hidden; she could dump it and her outfit once she got some distance from the building. But a second after she stepped back into the corridor, the world seemed to vanish in a blue-white blaze of light. A stun field, part of her mind realised, as she staggered and crashed to the floor. Someone had rigged the corridor to trap an intruder…and she'd walked right into the trap. Her remaining implants triggered, but too late to save her from another blast. Pain flared through her mind…

…As she plunged down into darkness.

CHAPTER
THIRTY-ONE

And yet the Empire possessed a certain legitimacy. As paradoxical as it may seem, given its nature, the Empire represented power to its subjects. This was both lucky and unlucky, as when the Empire started to weaken, it wasn't challenged immediately. Lucky, because the disaster might have come sooner; unlucky, because the Empire might then have been capable of evolving to regenerate itself and meet the new challenges. But it fell.
-Professor Leo Caesius, *Authority, Power and the Post-Imperial Era*

Horn looked down at their captive and rubbed his hands together with glee.

"Excellent," he said to Zed. "A perfect operation."

"Thank you, sir," Zed said. "And Mr. Patterson?"

Horn considered. It had been relatively simple to arrange an excuse to keep Patterson at the office, working late, even though the man had been twitchy and clearly nervous, expecting his next meeting with the blackmailer. Tomorrow, Horn would have to give him some kind of explanation; tonight, Patterson would be allowed to have some fun with the girls Horn kept as rewards for his most loyal servants. It should help him to forget his wife and son, if they couldn't be recovered.

"He can sleep in the office tonight," Horn said, finally. "After that... well, we'll see."

It would be a shame to have to demote – or fire – Patterson. He was competent and sane, terms that could hardly be applied to his most trustworthy subordinates. On the other hand, the man had allowed outside concerns – his wife and child – to interfere with his work. It wasn't the kind of dedication that Horn wanted or needed. Maybe it would be for the best, Horn decided, if Patterson wasn't to recover his family. Their loss would give him new cause to focus on Admiral Singh's enemies.

"Yes, sir," Zed said. "And our new captive?"

"Have her moved to Black Block," Horn ordered. It was unlikely in the extreme that the mysterious agent was working alone, but no one else had been apprehended nearby. Whoever she was working for had probably realised that something was wrong and pulled back before they could be caught…unless it was someone living none too far from Patterson's house. "And then do a full workup. I want to know *everything* about her."

He considered possible suspects as he watched his men move the captive into an armoured prisoner transport van. Patterson was in a good position to aid and abet one or more of Horn's enemies; it was quite possible that whoever had captured his wife and child had intended to bring pressure to bear on *Horn* himself – or, more likely, attempt to embarrass him in front of Admiral Singh. After all, the other senior officers hated and feared Horn; they'd do whatever it took to discredit him.

But they weren't the only suspects. There were plenty of criminal gangs who would sell their own grandmothers for leverage over someone in Internal Security – and Patterson was probably about as high-ranking as they could hope to subvert. Or there was the mysterious new terrorist organisation in the countryside. No doubt they'd predicted that Horn would gain greater leverage over the security forces outside the cities and intended to use Patterson to monitor his activities. It seemed one hell of a gamble, but the terrorists had to be desperate. And desperate men did stupid things.

Mulling over the possibilities, he climbed into his car and told the driver to take him to Black Block. He had a long night ahead of him.

Rifleman Blake Coleman loved fighting and fucking, not always in that order. He didn't see it as a weakness, no matter what some sarcastic senior officers had pointed out more than once; peaceniks and wimps didn't join the Terran Marine Corps. If he hadn't wanted to fight – and fight for a decent cause, at that – he would never have walked into the recruiting office and faced the scarred Sergeant on the desk. His love of fighting had kept him alive, while his love of fucking reminded him that there was something else to live for apart from the fight.

Blake knew that it was unlikely that he would be promoted – or even allowed to switch sideways to become a Sergeant. He didn't mind that as much as some of his comrades thought; he *had* been pretty stupid back on Avalon…and besides, promotion meant extra work rather than fighting. Just look at the Colonel, he'd pointed out, when he'd been asked; Colonel Stalker, who'd once led his unit into battle, had been reduced to a desk-jockey fighting hard to remember what it was like to actually *fight*. Maybe he did have a shiny new insignia and a desk, but he'd lost something important. He couldn't fight with the rest of his men.

Damn it, Blake thought, as the prisoner transport van started to move. *What the hell do I do now?*

He watched from his hiding place as the rest of the security troopers, no doubt convinced that they'd swept every possible hidey-hole, climbed into their own vehicles and drove off, leaving Patterson's house alone. Blake gritted his teeth; the view from where he'd been hiding hadn't been great, but he'd seen enough to know that the Lieutenant had been captured, taken alive by the security forces. He gritted his teeth at the thought; he'd reviewed enough entertainment channels to know just what sort of fate was in store for her, if she lasted long enough. It was possible that the interrogation would push her hard enough for her implants to kill her…if she didn't kill herself first.

Silently, Blake slipped out of his hiding place and started to walk down the street, keeping to the shadows. They had to assume the worst; Lieutenant Yamane would talk, eventually. Blake knew how tough the Lieutenant was – and how capable her implants were of keeping her from talking – but they dared not take anything for granted. But Lieutenant Yamane knew too much; if she talked, just about every rebel cell they'd formed would be blown right open. Admiral Singh would be able to defeat them without ever being in serious danger.

"You," a voice snapped.

Blake looked up, his enhanced eyes seeing through the darkness as if it were the brightest day. Two young men stood there, both carrying makeshift weapons; it was all Blake could do to keep from laughing at their pose. He'd produced more dangerous weapons when he'd been showing the new resistance members how to arm themselves. But these little thugs preyed on the rest of the human population, the sheep who *couldn't* defend themselves.

Just like the Civil Guard, Blake thought, with an odd moment of reflection. He was not normally given to reflecting at all. *They exist to put thugs to use.*

"You," the leader snapped, again. "There's a toll for entering our territory at night and…"

Blake rammed a fist into his throat, feeling the thug's neck break under the impact. He dropped like a sack of potatoes, blood spewing from his mouth, and hit the ground with a dull thud. The other thug was starting to move away, somehow resisting the urge to panic and run, but it was already too late. Blake caught him, broke his neck effortlessly and dropped him on the ground beside his leader. Perhaps the rest of the street thugs would take warning that there were more dangerous predators in the darkness than themselves.

Or perhaps not, he thought, remembering some of the unofficial clean-up missions the Marines had performed on Rocky Mountain, before they'd been thrown into the nightmare on Han. *None of these thugs recognise true danger when they see it.*

He scowled and continued to walk. There was no choice. They had to get the Lieutenant out before it was too late. And if that meant risking the rest of the section's lives…well, the Lieutenant deserved it. She'd saved their lives too.

"She's secure," the doctor reported. "But there are a number of odd things about her body."

Horn smiled as he studied the monitor, showing the girl in the examination chamber. Her clothes had been stripped from her, exposing a body that seemed almost freakishly developed. Horn had seen more than one wealthy woman who had used gene-sequencing or the body-shops to improve herself, but this was different. *This* woman had pushed herself right to the limit. His gaze rested on her small breasts for a long moment, before he looked back at the doctor.

The doctor cringed under his gaze. Whatever the general public might believe, it was almost laughably easy to find doctors who were corrupt and willing to break their oaths, no matter how seriously they'd taken them when they'd started to study medicine. Money worked in most cases, but Horn preferred doctors who shared his tastes – or had no moral objections to experimenting on living subjects. Interrogators needed doctors in any case; who else could patch the victims back together so they could be interrogated again?

"Odd things," Horn repeated. "And just what are they?"

The doctor scowled, then flushed. "First, she is almost unbelievably healthy," he said. "I ran a brief DNA analysis and there's quite a few modified genes spliced into her body. In particular, she is stronger than the average human and will *remain* that way, as long as her body receives sufficient fuel. Her eyesight, hearing and sense of smell are all well above the human average.

"Second, despite all of those improvements, there are definite signs of heavy medical treatment in her past," he continued. "Her bones have been broken and put back together using quick-heal or rejuvenation techniques, her body was pushed right to the edge of starvation at one point… in short, whatever she does for a living is physically punishing, even for someone with such a modified genetic base. There are even hints that her maidenhead was removed surgically, rather than by a man."

Horn frowned. "Is there a medical reason for that?"

"There shouldn't be," the doctor admitted. "It's possible that she came from a world that practiced genetic modification on females, preventing them from engaging in sexual intercourse without surgical intervention, but her DNA doesn't show the signs of inbreeding and hackwork that is normally *visible* for a poor bitch unlucky enough to be born to *that* sort of person. Indeed" – he nodded towards the screen – "her reproductive system has largely been frozen. She doesn't even get cramps."

"I see," Horn said. "Anything else?"

"Yes, sir," the doctor said. "There are a handful of implants inserted into her body."

He picked up a datapad and passed it to Horn. "Four of them are at the base of her spine, almost completely impossible to remove without killing her," he explained. "One of them looks like a standard neural link, except it doesn't seem to have any actual *connection* to anything. The other three don't seem to have any visible purpose, at least based on what I can actually *see*."

Horn eyed him, darkly. "Did it occur to you to go inside her and look?"

"It would kill her," the doctor said, tightly. "The implants, whatever they are, are woven too deeply into her physical form. Trying to examine them would, I suspect, cause mental trauma and kill her outright. I'm not even sure how they got inserted without risking her life."

Horn shrugged. He'd known people in Imperial Intelligence who had volunteered for implantation, even though they'd known that the odds weren't exactly on their side. Some of the survivors made hellishly effective agents, but from what he'd heard the odds of survival were roughly one in five. Horn had never seriously considered gambling with his own life, not at such pathetic odds. His life was just too important to him.

He pushed the thought aside for the moment. "And the other implants?"

"One seems to be a fairly standard contraceptive implant, inserted near the vagina," the doctor said. "The other appears to be a weapon, probably a nerve-burst implant, inserted into her finger. I suggest that you don't try to shake hands with her."

Horn smirked at the weak joke. "Remove it," he ordered. "Now."

"She may lose the hand altogether," the doctor warned. "The weapon, whatever it really is, has been woven into her nerves..."

"Do it," Horn said, sharply. "Is there anything else you can tell me about her?"

"Nothing," the doctor said. "I suspect that one of her implants is designed to prevent her from being interrogated. You may wish to take care."

Horn nodded and called for Zed. "You've had plenty of time," he said, when the man arrived. "Did you pull anything on her out of the files?"

"Some very odd results," Zed said. "We ran her fingerprints, retina patterns and DNA code against the files. They produced a very vague file" – he passed Horn another datapad – "that is almost completely uninformative."

Horn scowled down at the datapad. Admiral Singh had insisted on registering everyone on the planet in her database, threatening arrest and detention for anyone foolish enough to think that the law didn't apply to them. It provided a useful tool for managing manpower and, more importantly, for tracking down the relatives of any would-be rebel. And yet there were people who had managed to slip through the cracks, if only by bribing the registers. Quite a few criminals remained unregistered.

The file was bland to the point of being almost completely useless. Jasmine Yamane, if the name attached to the file was genuine, twenty-four years old, granted exemption from conscription on the grounds she worked for the security forces. The ID card she'd had in her pocket when she'd been captured would probably go unquestioned, at least by any patrolling guardsmen. Questioning a security operative was a good way to ensure that one's next station was out in the countryside, patrolling the most rebellious parts of the globe.

But Jasmine Yamane *wasn't* part of *his* security forces...

He considered it, thinking hard. Was the attempt to subvert Patterson the first shot in a campaign against *him*?

It was certainly possible. She was implanted – and *that* suggested someone with a high position in security...or the navy. Vice Admiral Sampson *hated* the security officers – and Horn in particular. Horn had no illusions about what would happen if Sampson took over the planet, replacing Admiral Singh with his own people. And yet, he wouldn't have thought that Sampson had the nerve to launch a covert war. A straight-up fight would be more his style.

Maybe he has an ambitious underling offering him support, Horn thought, ruefully. *He'd* prospered by being willing to do things that Admiral Singh was reluctant to do for herself. The fact it had allowed him to indulge himself as well as build up a significant power base was just the icing on the cake. There was no reason why Sampson couldn't have his own underlings ready to do the dirty work for him.

He looked back at the girl's body and frowned. An alternate explanation was that she worked for a crime lord, someone intent on expanding his operations…someone who wanted to get into a much stronger position by subverting a security officer. It was possible that she'd been implanted before Admiral Singh had taken over the planet and banned any further unauthorised augmentation. And she'd clearly not had the sources in Internal Security that might have warned her that she was walking into a trap.

And yet that seemed unusually daring for a crime lord.

There had been one crime lord, just one, who had tried to treat Admiral Singh as he had treated the Governor. Admiral Singh had unleashed hell on him, literally. His organisation had been ripped apart, his footsoldiers sent to the labour camps while his senior subordinates had been publically executed – and the population had turned out to cheer. The remaining crime lords had learned to keep their heads down after *that*.

Or…could he be looking at an infiltrator?

Horn had worked in Imperial Intelligence long enough to have heard countless rumours about special forces. The Marine Pathfinders, the Green Lights, the Unspeakable Ones…all organisations that were wrapped in secrecy, more rumour than reality. Or so he had been told by his superiors. But if the rumours had some basis in truth…

He looked at the girl's body. Truth be told, she wasn't *that* impressive, certainly not when compared to the rumours. Men and women so enhanced that they were more machine than man, surviving in space without the benefit of spacesuits, each one an army in their own right… what was a little DNA modification and a handful of implants compared to the stories?

And yet….

What if, he asked himself, *she works for the Commonwealth*?

The thought was a nightmarish one for him personally. *He*, not Sampson, was responsible for security in Landing City. If someone had been operating below the radar in the city, there might well be more than one – and *that* meant that he had made a dreadful series of mistakes.

What if his enemies found out? Admiral Singh might have been willing to allow him to indulge himself, but she would hardly tolerate incompetence…and his enemies would take the opportunity to paint him as an incompetent bumbling fool. It could not be allowed.

"We will break her," he said. Zed, at least, could be trusted to assist him without breathing a word to anyone outside the office. *His* position was entirely dependent on Horn. "And then we will decide what to do next."

He scowled. Admiral Singh would not be pleased if he delayed informing her, but he needed to know the truth first. His power and position were all he had. Without them, he was a dead man walking. Whatever else happened, he needed to know the truth.

And if it was the first shot in a plan to unseat him, he promised himself, whoever was behind it would *suffer*.

CHAPTER THIRTY-TWO

> That left us with a dilemma. We needed to replace the Empire, at least in our sector of the galaxy, and yet we needed to avoid the mistakes of the past. This was not easy. The Empire had been shaped by circumstance as much as human will. Our circumstances could be too close at times to the Empire's early history for comfort.
> -Professor Leo Caesius, *Authority, Power and the Post-Imperial Era*

Jasmine kept her eyes shut as she fought her way back into wakefulness, despite the complete lack of awareness of her surroundings. She'd been *captured*, taken alive by the enemy…wherever she was now, she was in the gravest possible danger. Carefully, trying not to betray the fact that she was awake, she reached out with her senses. Where *was* she?

She was lying on a hard metal surface, cold and unyielding against her back. Metal bracelets – manacles, she guessed – were wrapped around her wrists and ankles, holding her firmly in place. They didn't have to be hullmetal to hold her, she knew with a flicker of grim amusement; the dull throbbing pain from her hand suggested that her captors had scanned her body and discovered the hidden weapon implant. She knew from her Conduct After Capture course that the cranial implants might have been discovered too, but it was unlikely that her captors had tried to remove them. The process would almost certainly kill her.

Did they know, she asked herself, what she was? It was possible; Marine implants were highly-classified, the details largely unknown outside the Corps, but the genetic modifications would be harder to conceal.

There was no shortage of people with genetic improvements, some of them close to Marine standards without ever having been *near* a Marine, yet if someone combined the DNA modifications with her implants…she mentally shook her head, straining her ears to the utmost. One way or another, she was sure that she would find out soon.

Her clothes had been removed, she realised, although nakedness didn't bother her after spending several years in various barracks. The room smelled of piss and shit and blood, suggesting that she was in a torture chamber. She'd watched some of the entertainment channels, enough to tell her what was likely to happen. No doubt the interrogators thought that her anticipation would help weaken her resistance. Jasmine remembered her first CAC course and scowled, inwardly. She'd *known* that it wasn't real and it had still pushed her almost to breaking point.

Of course, they were limited in what they could do, she thought, sourly. *They couldn't cause permanent harm.*

Silently, she started to meditate, drawing on the mental disciplines she'd been taught to help her get through intensive training. Her sense of timing had been completely screwed up, but she had a feeling from the aches and pains that it hadn't been long since her capture. The enhanced healing sequenced into her genes should have taken care of the aches and pains by now, unless it hadn't really been *that* long since she'd been captured. Blake and the others would have realised that she was missing by now, surely. They would already have put the contingency plan into operation.

Back at the Slaughterhouse, she'd been forced to memorise a chunk of seemingly-useless information. It hadn't been until they'd been chased over the landscape, captured and shoved into an interrogation cell that the recruits had realised that the information they'd been given was what the interrogators wanted. All they'd had to do was keep it to themselves… which hadn't been easy when one had been starved, beaten, drugged and threatened with far worse, before the session had finally come to an end. Jasmine recalled one recruit, a young man who had fought his way through Boot Camp and the early stages of the Slaughterhouse, losing his nerve during the interrogation session. The last she'd seen of him had been when he'd boarded the shuttle to go home.

A smarter recruit, who had worked for the local police before volunteering to join the Marine Corps, had asked why they didn't use stronger truth drugs. The Drill Instructors had pointed out that such drugs would trigger their protective implants, killing the captives. They'd followed up by pointing out that any interrogator who *knew* what they were dealing with would work hard to pressure someone while trying to avoid triggering the implant. Psychological tools, they'd said, would work better than violence and drugs.

"Good morning," a voice said. It was strongly accented – and not, she noted, with any accent she recognised. "I know you're awake."

Jasmine kept her eyes closed, refusing to move.

"The monitors recording your brain activity say that you're awake," the voice said, with what sounded like excessive patience. "You may as well open your eyes."

Jasmine sighed, but did as she was told. She was in a surprisingly large room, utterly bare apart from the table she lay on and a glowing light beaming down from high overhead. The speaker, a man so pale that she couldn't help wondering if he ever saw the sunlight, gave her a thin smile as he looked up from the datapad in his hand. Jasmine tried to raise her arm and discovered that she couldn't move it at all. She was solidly bound to the table.

"Good morning," the figure said, again. He sounded almost obscenely amused. "I'm afraid that you're in a great deal of trouble."

He paused, as if he expected her to say something. Jasmine, who had been taught that keeping one's mouth shut was often the strongest counter-interrogation tool in the universe, said nothing. Maybe she *was* in trouble, maybe she was about to be tormented until she broke…but she was damned if she was going to make it *easy* for the bastards. Besides, the longer she held out, the longer the others would have to hide and regroup somewhere unknown to her.

"You were captured in the act of trying to force one of my superiors to serve you," the man said, dryly. "Your only hope now is to throw yourself on my mercy."

His face twisted into a smile. "Cat got your tongue?"

Jasmine kept her mouth firmly closed.

"You will change your mind," the man told her. "You see, you are buried deep underground, in a sealed chamber that no one can even enter without the right permission. Any friends you might have on the outside" – he watched her closely as he said that – "are lost to you. There is no way that they will be able to save your ass from us. If you talk, we can make your life more comfortable. If not…"

His smile grew wider. "We can make your life very uncomfortable indeed."

Jasmine watched as he turned and strode into the darkness, then looked over at the manacles. They looked distressingly solid; she tested them anyway, just in case, and discovered that they were definitely immoveable. One of the easiest mistakes to make when keeping someone prisoner, she knew, was to tie them to something that could be broken, given the right leverage. They hadn't made *that* mistake. The table was solid metal, uncomfortable and unbreakable. Even a Pathfinder couldn't have broken free.

She glanced up as she heard something hitting bare flesh, followed by the sound of a woman crying in pain. The sounds grew worse as she listened, each one suggesting horrible tortures being meted out to victims…she shuddered as she heard male grunting and unpleasant little squeaks, suggesting that someone was being entered against their will. Raped, she realised numbly, before remembering the horrific sounds that had been played to the recruits as they sat in their holding cells. They'd been intended to soften them up before the captors returned to start interrogating them properly.

Jasmine closed her eyes, wishing that she could somehow turn off her ears. On the Slaughterhouse, she'd always assumed that the sounds were made by actors – although, she recalled, they'd never been explicitly *told* that the sounds were faked. Here, they were all too likely to be real. The girl she could hear gasping in pain had been no actor, but someone who had offended Admiral Singh. And she was quite likely to be dead by now…Jasmine kept that in her mind, but it didn't make it any easier to hear.

It seemed hours before she heard someone else entering the room. She opened her eyes and saw a grim-faced woman, bleeding from a dozen slashes across her chest, staggering over to the table and leaning on it desperately. It was the only way she could stand upright, Jasmine realised, as she took in the other places where blood was flowing from the girl's body. Just what had they done to her...?

Or was it just an act?

"They captured me," the girl said. "I used to think that I could defy the Admiral. And then they caught me and..."

Jasmine studied the girl's body. She'd seen wounds – real wounds – and the more she looked at the newcomer, the more convinced she became that the wounds were fake. How could she lose so much blood without fainting? It smelled right, but all that meant was that they'd hired a good chemist – or had drawn blood from another victim.

She looked away, refusing to give them the satisfaction of opening her mouth.

"She wasn't fooled," the doctor observed.

Horn nodded. Most civilians would have taken a look at the actress – she had been a real actress before Horn had hired her – and started to spill their guts. The woman was *good* at looking like someone who had been savagely beaten and then raped by a gang of interrogators, even if the blood was artificial rather than real. But their mystery captive hadn't seemed impressed at all.

"So it would seem," Horn said. He allowed himself a cold smile. Breaking someone stubborn enough to hold out against threats and intimidation, however presented, was one of his pleasures in life. "I think she's had enough softening up by now."

The doctor gave him a sharp look. "I don't think she was impressed by the taped sounds either," he pointed out. "And..."

"I noticed," Horn said, happily. "This is going to be *fun!*"

Human imagination was such a wonderful thing, he knew. Draw a bare-bones image for someone – or, in this case, play them a few pre-recorded sounds – and their imagination would do the rest. Later, perhaps, they would see if the captive had the internal fortitude to withstand watching as children were tortured in front of her. It wouldn't bother *Horn* to watch – he'd enjoy himself – but most people would spill their guts to prevent a cute little child from being hurt. Should it be a girl or a boy? People became *very* talkative when a red-hot poker advanced towards a child's privates.

He pushed that thought aside for the moment. "Send in the first team," he ordered. "And we will see if *that* breaks her."

"Yes, sir," the doctor said, reluctantly.

Horn ignored his concerns. The priority might be getting information out of the captive, but there was no reason why he couldn't enjoy himself at the same time.

———

The door opened again, revealing three burly men carrying leather bags. Jasmine watched as they strode into the room, pushed the crying actress out and then surrounded the table, looking down at Jasmine with leering eyes. One of them reached down and grabbed a breast, squeezing it tightly enough to hurt, then sent his hand trailing down towards her thighs…

"That will do, Sid," one of the other men said. "There is an order to this, you see."

Jasmine scowled inwardly. *Good interrogator, bad interrogator?* One to torture and humiliate her, the other to pretend to be her friend? Or was she reading too much into the situation? It was designed to upset her, to make her lose her balance and eventually to force her to talk. She had to bear that in mind at all times.

But her breast still felt filthy where he'd touched it.

"Good evening, young lady," the speaker said. "How are you feeling right now?"

Good evening? Jasmine wondered. The previous visitor had claimed that it was the morning and she was sure that she hadn't lost *that* much time. Her time sense might have been battered, but it was still intact. They were probably just trying to disorientate her.

She kept her mouth closed and had the satisfaction of seeing a flicker of irritation on the man's face.

"We are going to ask you some questions," the man explained, as he pulled some electrodes out of his bag. "Should you lie to us, we *will* know about it – and then you will be hurt."

"So please lie," Sid said. He reached out towards her other breast, his hand hovering just above the flesh. "It is so much *fun* watching people screaming in pain."

Jasmine gritted her teeth, but said nothing. She'd been through worse, she kept telling herself, remembering the horrors of the Crucible – and the inescapable feeling that she'd failed to complete the test in time. It had only been when she'd been escorted into the hall and presented with her Rifleman's Tab that she'd realised that she'd actually passed – very well, according to the Drill Instructors. *Everyone* had been utterly shattered when they'd completed the final exam, but they'd kept going anyway.

She winced as the speaker pulled away her wig and attached one of the electrodes to the side of her head. They'd found out that she'd been wearing a wig at some point, she realised, although she had no idea why they'd left it in place. Perhaps they'd thought that she would be psychologically broken when it was taken away, just before the interrogation began. It seemed absurd, given that she was already naked, but people did cling to the oddest things when they were captives. The human brain, she'd been told, found its own way of coping with stress.

Mandy was a pirate captive, Jasmine reminded herself. *I can endure this.*

"The interesting part about monitoring a person's brainwaves is that one can tell if they're trying to lie," the speaker said. "Or, for that matter, if they're trying to conceal the truth without directly lying. And it is extremely difficult to fool the monitors – certainly not on any long-term basis. You will have no choice, but to tell us the truth."

Not if I keep my mouth shut, Jasmine thought, defiantly.

"We will start with a simple question," the speaker continued. He held a blue rubber duck in front of her. The sight was so incongruous that Jasmine smiled, despite herself. "What colour is this duck?"

Jasmine stared at him in disbelief. After all the build-up, they were going to ask her *that*? It was pointless! A moment later, just before she could open her mouth, she realised what they were doing. Answering a question – *any* question – would weaken her resistance when the time came to answer the *real* questions. And, for all of her determination to resist, they'd almost found the first chink in her armour.

"There is no point in keeping it a secret," the speaker said, almost paternally. "We already know the answer. Why not tell us and save yourself some pain?"

He shook his head, almost sadly. "Sid?"

Jasmine had barely a moment to prepare herself before Sid jabbed something into her chest. The pain shocked her, despite her training; for a long chilling moment she thought that he'd stabbed her with a knife. A modified neural whip, she realised, as he pulled it back from her flesh, his face twisted into a leer. Something designed to cause pain without actually inflicting physical damage.

"That was just a taste," the speaker said. He held the duck up in front of her face. "Will you now tell me the colour of the duck?"

Jasmine gritted her teeth, but shook her head.

"Ah, a defiant one," the speaker said. "But you *will* break."

Sid leaned forward again. This time, he jabbed the neural whip into her left breast. Jasmine couldn't help herself; she screamed in agony, despite all the blockers her implants should have released into her bloodstream. The pain faded, then renewed itself as Sid allowed the neural whip to walk down her body towards her thighs. Jasmine fought to close her legs as he touched her most private of areas with the whip, sending horrific agonies running through her body. The pain was agonising...

And then it was gone.

"Everyone breaks, eventually," the speaker informed her. He sounded almost as if he *cared* about her – an act, Jasmine realised, as much as the wounded and bleeding girl had been earlier. If she was so badly weakened, no doubt she'd respond well to kindness. "You do realise, don't you, that the damage will eventually become permanent?"

Jasmine knew he was right. Neural whips, if overused, could burn out nerves or inflict mental damage on the victim, no matter how strong they were. The damage might be enough to prevent her from returning to duty, to see to it that she was invalided out of the Marine Corps...she gritted her teeth as terror threatened to overwhelm her. She was *not* going to break.

Sid let out a chilling sound and pushed the neural whip against her foot. Jasmine's body tried to spasm, only to be held down by the manacles. For a long moment, she was convinced that she had broken her own legs before the pain finally faded away. Why hadn't her implants killed her? Couldn't they tell that she was being tortured?

"There is no escape," the speaker said. "Talk now and you may escape permanent damage."

"Go to hell," Jasmine gasped.

The speaker smiled at her words. "You will talk," he assured her. "Now, what colour is the duck?"

And then the pain began again.

CHAPTER
THIRTY-THREE

> Eventually, we settled on a federal decentralised power structure. Each star system would have internal autonomy, with near-complete control over its internal affairs, as long as they honoured the Bill of Rights. This failed to settle every issue – a number of systems had several political entities, not counting the RockRats – but it was a step forward.
> -Professor Leo Caesius, *Authority, Power and the Post-Imperial Era*

Internal Security was taking no chances, Blake realised, as he walked past their headquarters wearing a stolen guardsman's uniform. The building was heavily guarded, protected by a large detachment of troops – and, he couldn't help noticing – had only a handful of entrances. Assaulting the building would not have been particularly difficult with a company of Marines in powered armour, but he had no powered armour or other heavy weapons at his disposal. Instead, he had thirty teenagers who had grown up on the streets, Sergeant Hampton and Carl. It didn't seem like enough, somehow.

He'd wracked his brains looking for a way to sneak into the building, before realising that it was likely futile. They'd blocked off the sewers and everything else that could be used to sneak inside unobserved, while he didn't dare wait for nightfall. Besides, they'd probably scattered security sensors everywhere, just in case someone tried to slip over the wall and into the grounds. They would have to go with the desperate plan.

Blake gritted his teeth as he walked away from the building. He liked fighting, but he disliked sneaking around. And yet, if they failed to sneak around properly, they didn't have any hope of recovering the Lieutenant before she either died or was forced to talk. And if *that* happened, the mission would fail. Blake liked to avoid thinking about the context of what they did, but Sergeant Hampton had put him straight. If the mission was aborted, Admiral Singh would have all the time in the world to finish scouting out the Commonwealth and then attack.

He met up with Sergeant Hampton as he waited with the van. "Plan B," Blake said, feeling oddly tired. "I think you were right."

"I told you so," the older Sergeant said. He picked up his datapad. "Luckily, I have a lead on what we need."

Jasmine *hurt*. Every inch of her body hurt, it felt, apart from her face. Sid had threatened to turn the neural whip on her skull, but his superior had forbidden him from trying – either because he wanted to show Jasmine that there was a way out or, more likely, because he knew that using a neural whip on someone's skull could prove fatal. It was probably, she forced herself to remember, another piece of scripted acting for her benefit.

And when they'd finished with her, they'd dragged her off the table and shoved her into a smaller cell.

She looked around as the pain slowly started to recede. They'd been careful not to feed her, which had worrying implications for her future. The *quid pro quo* her genetic improvements demanded was that she ate more than the average human being, just to provide the fuel for her body. If they didn't feed her soon, Jasmine suspected, her body would start feeding on itself just to keep her going. Marines had been known to starve to death when they couldn't get enough food.

The smaller cell was dimly-lit, but she had no difficulty in seeing the solid metal door and the railing they'd used to hold her firmly in place. If she'd been able to move, Jasmine knew, she might have been able to break free, yet it seemed impossible. Or was it…if she hadn't been desperate, she would never have *considered* what she was considering. The fact that it might be interpreted by her implants as torture and lead directly to her death was a very real concern.

But the longer I stay here, she thought, *the greater the chance I will break.*

She gritted her teeth as she started to pull her left hand through the handcuff. The metal seemed utterly inflexible, unwilling to break on her command. And yet…the pain grew stronger as she pulled, feeling her wrist starting to hurt. It was quite possible that she would dislocate her wrist rather than break the bones in her hand…

There was an awful crunching sensation, a wave of pain that almost made her cry out in agony…and her left arm came free. Jasmine felt a hint of triumph as the other half of the handcuff fell to the ground, freeing her right hand. Like most Marines, Jasmine could use either hand, but she preferred her right to her left. Some aspects of cultural conditioning never quite went away. The pain faded slowly as her body's enhancements worked their magic, while she considered the shackles binding her legs. Thankfully, they hadn't been designed to stop someone removing them… no doubt they'd assumed that the wearer would also have their hands cuffed behind their backs.

Bracing herself, she waited. She didn't dare move too openly; it was almost certain that there was a monitor in the cell somewhere, with someone watching her every move. It was quite possible that person had seen her break the bones in her hand just to get some freedom of movement… and if that had happened, she was thoroughly screwed. They'd chain her down and that would be the end of her freedom. She waited, praying for the first time in a very long time, as the seconds stretched out and no one came. They hadn't noticed!

Either that, or they're getting people in powered armour to come deal with me, she thought, bitterly. Even the best combatant in the Marine Corps would have been hard-pressed to win a fight against someone wearing powered armour, particularly when they were naked, unarmed and with one hand effectively useless. *I guess I will just have to wait and see.*

"She told you nothing?"

"Very little," the interrogator said. "I believe that she is on the verge of breaking, however."

Horn smiled as Sid – one of the most vicious little bastards he'd had the pleasure to meet and recruit – snorted. "You should have let me fuck her," he said, darkly. "I could have broken her just by rubbing her nose in her helplessness."

"It wouldn't have worked," the interrogator said, dryly. "The girl has a strong cast of mind – she certainly isn't someone who can be easily traumatised."

Horn nodded. As entertaining as it was watching someone lose all control over themselves, it was more important to extract information from them. They could be executed later.

"But she held up to your tortures," the doctor said. "How many others do you know who could do that?"

"Not that many," the interrogator admitted. "But such mindsets can be worn down. It is just a matter of keeping up the pressure, then alternating it with periods when she can relax and anticipate the next level of suffering."

The doctor looked over at Horn. "The average person could *not* have stood up to such treatment," he said, flatly. "Whoever you have chained up is not someone who can be broken so easily."

"I know," Horn said.

If the girl had talked at once, he would have concluded that she was a criminal – or working for one of his rivals. Such defiance would have been unusual for either; they both knew that their superiors wouldn't come to their rescue. Their only hope would be to cut a deal with Horn, trading information – and the chance to switch sides – for their own survival. After he'd wasted a great deal of effort in breaking them, he wouldn't be so interested in talking.

But the girl was holding out and that meant.... what?

The cold certainty that she *was* an infiltrator spread through his mind. There could be no other explanation; even the toughest of guardsmen would have broken under the battery of torture and manipulation hurled at them by his people. And that meant that he'd fucked up. And *that* meant that Admiral Singh was going to be furious. He might lose everything he'd worked for...

"Break her," he ordered, angrily. "Whatever it takes, break her."

Sid leered. "I know just the right approach to use," he said. "It breaks everyone."

It had taken some careful research to identify the blind spot in the security cameras covering part of the inner city. Wolf hadn't bothered to research the cameras very closely, an oversight that Blake found puzzling – unless he was lying, of course. A man who employed loan sharks to lure people into debt – often manipulating protection rackets to force them into his clutches – wouldn't hesitate to lie if it suited his purposes.

Still, the blind spot existed – and, given enough time, it could be used to his advantage.

Admiral Singh's people had tightened their grip on the city ever since the first reports had come in from the countryside. Blake had been amused to discover that they'd barred most vehicular traffic from moving, but still allowed people to walk around on foot; someone clearly hadn't been thinking about the consequences of their decision. But then, it also allowed them a chance to extort more money from the drivers. Without transport, feeding the city's population would very rapidly become impossible.

"Here she comes," Sergeant Hampton said. "Now!"

Blake stepped out onto the road as an armoured vehicle barrelled down towards him. If he hadn't been wearing a guardsman's uniform, they might well have knocked him down and kept going. They'd certainly heard reports of Internal Security officers doing just that to innocent civilians. Instead, the driver slammed on the brakes and the van came to a halt.

"What the fuck," the driver demanded as he wound down his window, "do you think that you are doing?"

Sergeant Hampton tossed a gas grenade into the cab. The officers grabbed for their weapons, too late, as the gas sent them into slumbers. Blake motioned for their helpers to pull the men out as he ran to the rear of the van and applied his multitool to the lock. It clicked open, revealing a dozen prisoners chained and shackled to the metal walls.

"This is a rescue mission," Blake snapped, as he undid the chains. "Get out of the vehicle and go straight into the house in front. The rest of your shackles will be removed there."

He waited until the vehicle was empty, then motioned for their helpers to get inside while others stripped the uniforms from the officers. Once the door was closed, he clambered up into the cab, allowing Sergeant Hampton to take the wheel. The entire operation had taken less than seven minutes.

Let's just hope that is not too long, he thought, as the vehicle roared into life. *If those bastards were meant to check in*, we're sunk.

He pulled the captured uniform jacket on and checked the paperwork. Luckily, no one seemed to question Internal Security – at least outside their headquarters. And once they were through the security gate, they should have a chance to rip through the interior and free the prisoners.

And if we screw this up, he though grimly, *we're really screwed.*

"We have some paperwork to prove that we're who we claim to be," Carl observed. "And if it fails...?"

"We fight our way out," Blake said, although he knew it was going to be tough. "And we burn down the place behind us."

The recruits – kids, really – who had been brought along on the operation barely knew one end of their SI-352 assault rifles from the other. Thankfully, Admiral Singh had largely agreed with the Civil Guard's assessment that the vast majority of their recruits were idiots who shouldn't be allowed anywhere near a more complicated weapon – the SI-352 was often considered the simplest weapon in the universe, a design dating all the way back to the Unification Wars – but Guardsmen still got more than a few weeks of training before they were expected to carry out anything more complicated than marching in step.

Sergeant Hampton looked over at him. "How does it feel to be on the other side?"

Blake scowled at the Sergeant. He'd liked to think of himself as a righteous man – a man who fought for a cause, even if it was just as simple as ensuring that as many Marines as possible survived the day. And he'd often avoided prostitutes because he never knew if they had entered the business voluntarily or if they'd been forced to open their legs for strange men.

I thought I could take the moral high ground, he thought, as the Internal Security building came into view. *I was wrong.*

On cue, the first stage of the diversion went off.

Lukas had been puzzled by the instructions he had received from their superiors. He was to drive a vehicle to a certain location – papers had been provided to allow them to drive within the city - park on the pavement and then walk away. The instructions had been very clear. Whatever happened, he was not to be anywhere near the car by 1500.

Shaking his head – perhaps the whole escapade was a test to see how well they could follow orders – Lukas parked the car and locked the door behind him, then walked off as casually as he could. No one, it seemed, took any notice of him as he turned the corner and glanced at his watch. It was 1456.

Four minutes later, a thunderous explosion shook the air. Lukas looked back and saw a colossal plume of smoke arising from the direction of where he'd parked the car, then heard sirens howling in the distance. He'd driven a ruddy bomb! Excitement warred with fear in his mind. If he'd known what he was doing…he would probably have frozen up in terror. Instead, if he'd been seen…

Grimly, he kept walking. It wasn't far until he reached the safe house.

"What was *that*?"

"An explosion," Zed reported. "At least one within the city itself."

Horn cursed. First reports were always inaccurate, he'd noted.

"Sound the general alert," he ordered. There would be absolute confusion, but there was no choice. "And get everyone you can draft attached to crowd control duty. We do *not* want a panic."

It seemed that hours had passed before the cell door opened, revealing Sid. Jasmine stared at him, pasting an expression of absolute horror on her face, then lowered her eyes as if she didn't want to look at him. The torturer advanced towards her, one hand carrying a small bowl of stew, the other holding the neural whip. It took very little acting to flinch when he brandished it in her direction.

Let him get closer, she told herself, as he put the bowl of stew on the concrete floor. The smell was a torture in itself, a reminder that she hadn't eaten for hours, perhaps over a day. How long had it actually been? *Let him get closer and then…*

"This is where you get a chance to tell me something I want to know," Sid told her. He pointed towards the bowl with the neural whip. "Tell me something, something I can take to my superiors…and I will feed you."

He slipped closer to her, waving the neural whip towards her chin. "Or you can refuse to talk and I can hurt you," he added. "I…"

Jasmine brought her right arm out from behind her back and slammed it into his throat as hard as she could. He let out a dull gasp, then collapsed; even weakened as she was, Jasmine was still strong enough to crush his throat. Part of her regretted the fact that she wouldn't have an opportunity to repay him for probing her body by shoving the neural whip up his ass, the rest of her insisted that there was no time to waste. She pulled herself upright, undid the shackles binding her leg with her right hand, then ran towards the cell door.

A man stood outside, clearly bored. The last thing he expected to see, Jasmine realised as she threw herself towards him, was a naked girl carrying a neural whip. His mouth dropped open before she bowled him over, pressing the neural whip against his forehead and sending him into gibbering spasms. It crossed her mind that she might just have permanently crippled him before she pushed the thought aside. Like so many others here, he'd known what he was doing.

She ran into the next room and glanced around, looking for anything useful. Two guards stared at her in shock, before she threw the neural whip at the first one's eye and jumped on the second one. He must have been out of shape, she realised; he barely moved before she broke his neck and sent him tumbling to the ground. The other one hadn't had a chance; even if the neural whip had been turned off, it had gone right into his eye.

Carefully, she searched their bodies and removed several weapons and a couple of data terminals. They had no clothes that would fit her, but that hardly mattered. Perhaps her nakedness would help confuse them before it was too late. Bracing herself, she stepped into the next room and saw another guard, his back to her, inspecting a set of consoles. Jasmine slipped forward, caught the back of his head and held the neural whip in front of his eyes. A moment later, she smelled urine...

"Coward," she hissed. She felt the man flinch, although she couldn't tell if it was because of the insult or because he knew how close he was to death. Her voice sounded harsh and unfamiliar in her ears. "Can you unlock all of the cells from here?"

He nodded, frantically.

"Good," Jasmine said. "Do it."

She allowed herself a smile. "And then point me towards your master," she added. "I want a few words with him."

Chapter Thirty-Four

> In addition, each planet would be expected to raise a certain amount of troops for a united deployment as well as look after its own internal security. When a planet had too many problems to comply with those requirements, the Commonwealth attempts to provide political and military support. However, the politics of the Commonwealth allowed most insurgences to eventually be brought to an end. The Crackers, for example, no longer needed to fight the original planetary council.
> -Professor Leo Caesius, *Authority, Power and the Post-Imperial Era*

"There's been an attack," the guard said, as he checked Blake's papers. "Get those bastards inside and then get out again."

Blake nodded. Everyone was rushing around in a panic – and that was good. Even for the Marines, the first few minutes of any attack were *always* chaotic. It was amazing how many details were overlooked while all hell was breaking loose. He took back the papers and drove the van forward, into the underground parking lot. It was a darkened chamber, normally – he'd learned from the interrogations – heavily secured. Now, the guards were distracted.

He opened the door and jumped out of the van, weapon in hand. The remaining guards turned to see him, saw the half-uniform he wore and stared in disbelief. Blake opened fire with his stunner, sending them toppling to the ground before they could react, then marched around the van and opened the rear door. Their allies, the best of the teenagers they'd tried to train in using weapons, came plummeting out, weapons in hand.

"Let's go," Blake hissed. He pulled his own mask over his head as the teens rushed past him, then followed them. Carl had his back, leaving Sergeant Hampton in charge of the vans. It was probably their only way out of the building once the mission was completed. "Use stunners unless they're wearing armour."

His lips twitched, remembering ancient drills, as he took the lead, one hand absently pulling gas grenades off his belt. Using them was a gamble – he'd always assumed that the Internal Security troopers were immunised to the gas, just as the Marines were – but if nothing else they should provide some cover. Unlike the Marines, the Civil Guard had never gone for tasteless and odourless gas. They much preferred to terrify people who saw the gas clouds coming.

An alarm started to ring, echoing through the corridors as they made their way down to the prison cells. According to their sources, Internal Security had hundreds of cells under the ground, where they held prisoners considered too interesting or too important to be dispatched to the penal camps outside the cities. Carl, reading between the lines, had suggested that those prisoners included people the troopers used for sexual pleasure; Blake had quietly promised himself that he would do his best to liberate everyone, not just Lieutenant Yamane. Admiral Singh's Head of Security's career would be unlikely to survive a massive prison break.

He glanced into a side-room, saw a dining table and some chairs and smiled to himself. The troopers on duty had clearly been eating when the alarm had sounded, forcing them to drop their food and grab their weapons. He'd always hated it when that happened to the Marines; on Han, they'd come to believe that a certain dining hall was jinxed. They'd sat down, the food had been served…and the alarm had gone off. Blake threw a gas grenade into the room, creating an unpleasant surprise for anyone who stumbled in without immunisation, and then led the charge onwards, checking each room as they passed. Most of them appeared to be small, reasonably comfortable bedrooms. The amount of loot in a couple of them was staggering.

The rest of the assault force hung back as Blake and Carl went down the first flight of stairs, eventually reaching the upper level of prisoner blocks. There seemed to be a riot going on; several dozen prisoners had been released and were intent on either escaping or avenging themselves on their tormentors. Blake was no stranger to horror, but the sight of a guard who had literally been *bitten* to death made him shudder. Another had had his balls cut off and stuffed into his mouth – an act of revenge, Blake suspected, for rape. He'd seen it before in the bandit camps, when their slaves had realised that the Marines had destroyed the bandit power base forever.

And a third guard was about to lose his life...

He put both fingers in his mouth and whistled loudly. One of the prisoners holding the guard down seemed to be completely out of his mind – blood was dripping from his mouth, none of it his – but the other two stared at the unexpected newcomers.

"We're here to bust you out of here," Blake said, flatly. "But I need to ask that man some questions."

One of the prisoners eyed him suspiciously. "You opened the cells?"

"Yep," Blake lied. He *hadn't* opened the cells, which raised the question of just who *had*? The Lieutenant was a Slaughterhouse graduate, after all; could she have found a way to bust loose at the exact same moment the Marines had launched an attack to liberate her? They'd have to be very careful not to shoot her by accident. "You start heading up and out of the building. There are plans to get you out and away."

He reached forward and dragged the unresisting guard away from the madman, then stunned the madman and issued orders for him to be carried out of the building.

"Now," he said, to the guard. "We have a few questions that need answering."

"What the hell is going on?"

Horn hadn't been so scared since the day he'd been called on the carpet by his superiors for overindulging himself during an interrogation. How had *he* been meant to know that his captive had a weak heart? He should have run a medical check first, Director Gunning had told him, because the precise nature of an interrogation depended on who was being interrogated. The old bastard had even threatened to put him in an interrogation cell just so he could have the pleasure of someone poking away at him without a medical baseline.

It was one of his conditioned bodyguards who answered. "The building has been compromised," he said, in his dull voice. "We must remain here until the crisis is over and fresh troops have swept the enemy out of the building."

Horn stared at him. "Compromised? By whom?"

"Insufficient data," the bodyguard said. "The internal security network has been taken down."

"By whom?" Horn demanded. "I issued no such orders…"

"The network was subjected to an attempted hack," the guard informed him, consulting his terminal. "Operating under your orders, the security officers took the network down to prevent it from being turned against us."

Was he imagining it, Horn asked himself, or was there a glint of pleasure in Horn's troubles in the man's dull eyes? The conditioned couldn't refuse to obey – the stronger the conditioning, the weaker their ordinary personality became – but there were always rumours of some who maintained the mental agility to subvert the conditioning in some way, even if it was just something as petty as laughing at his boss's misfortunes.

"Then get in touch with the Admiral," he ordered. "She needs to dispatch troops at once."

"The main communications network is down," the bodyguard reminded him. "It is possible that the Admiral will send troops on her own…"

Horn stared down at his hands. It was possible, true, but it was *also* possible that Admiral Singh had orchestrated the whole affair just to get rid of *him*. What if she'd decided that he'd become a liability and sent troops to kill him – and, just incidentally, create a martyr for her cause. The only objection to *that* theory he could think of was that few people would mourn him when he was gone.

"Well, I'm not staying around here," he said, finally. "You will clear the way to my personal helipad."

The bodyguard's immovable face still managed to look puzzled. "You are far safer here," he said, finally. "This part of the complex is secure."

"Not if it's the Admiral behind all this," Horn said. It wasn't paranoia if they were *really* out to get you, was it? "Open the door and start clearing the corridor."

After a long moment, the bodyguards began to obey.

———

The third level held a number of female data-entry clerks, kneeling under their desks in a manner Jasmine decided must have been ordained by security. She honestly couldn't understand, at first, why the girls were there at all; didn't they *know* what happened on the lower levels? And then she remembered what she'd been taught and knew that none of the clerks really considered themselves responsible for what happened to prisoners in the building.

None of them seemed to have seen her, so Jasmine left them and ran up to the fourth level, where the administrators lived. A pair of burly bodyguards gaped at the vision of a naked girl carrying a small arsenal of weapons before Jasmine shot them both down, watching with grim amusement as their expressions melted into shock as they died. The map she'd glanced at was helpful; the first office held someone who was even more sadistic than Horn, which was a terrifyingly impressive feat. Jasmine looked into the antechamber and saw a blonde girl, so thin that her bones were clearly visible, trembling as she pressed herself into a chair two sizes too big for her.

"Stay here," Jasmine said, giving her what was intended as a reassuring smile. The girl didn't seem reassured. "Is your boss inside?"

The girl nodded, too terrified to say a word.

Jasmine opened the next door and rolled her eyes at the sheer luxury. Honestly, she wondered, was he trying to compete with the Grand Senators? The owner was screaming into a communications terminal, trying to get a link to someone outside the building, when he looked up and saw Jasmine. His mouth dropped open with shock.

"I wish I had time to enjoy this," Jasmine growled, as the man stared at her. He was shaking so badly that it was a miracle that he was still on his feet. Like most torturers, he was a bully and a coward when facing the prospect of physical harm himself. "I really wish I did."

She shot him through the head and watched as his body hit the ground. The nasty part of her mind, the part that had been pushed to the fore by the neural whipping she'd endured, suggested that she could mutilate his body. Instead, she turned and walked back out of the office, nodded politely to the girl and then hesitated right on the doorway.

"You might want to get out of the building," she said, wondering briefly how the girl had come to work for Internal Security. "This place isn't safe any longer."

The next few offices were empty, apart from one that held someone Jasmine recognised from the list of names and faces they'd put together. He'd been another sadist – and someone had stuck a knife in him when the chaos began. Jasmine puzzled over it for a few moments, then dismissed the problem. No doubt he'd been *entertaining* one of the prisoners when the alarms had gone off, distracting him for a few moments. It had cost him his life.

She smiled as she made her way out of the office and back into the corridor. The next set of rooms belonged to Horn. He was in for a *very* unpleasant surprise.

"She's escaped, Blake," Carl said, as they searched through the terminal. "I don't know *where* she's gone."

Blake winced. He should have expected the Lieutenant to try to escape – it was, after all, one of their duties – but the timing was inconvenient, to say the least. The isolated datanet used by the prison cells, however, made one thing clear. Jasmine Yamane was nowhere within the area it covered. Where had she gone?

Assume she thought she couldn't get over the walls, he told himself. *Where would she go after that?*

The answer was obvious. She'd go up, into the upper levels and try and inflict as much damage as she could before being taken down.

"Get the rest of the prisoners out into the vehicle hall and then flood the cells," he ordered. Sergeant Hampton would have to supervise the rest of their allies, while Blake and Carl went upwards. Or should he remain with the rebels? If this endless indecision was what command demanded, he definitely didn't want it. "If you don't hear from us in ten minutes, assume we're both dead and start phase III."

"Understood," Sergeant Hampton said.

Horn's bodyguards were surrounding him as he made his escape, Jasmine saw; the conditioned men were clearly ready to take a bullet for their boss. If they hadn't been conditioned, would they have bothered? Horn was such a weedy little man, puny and almost laughable…if it hadn't been for the power he held? Jasmine wondered, as she prepared herself, if he'd been treated badly as a child, before deciding that it didn't matter. Whatever the source of Horn's sick fantasies of control, rape and torture, he was old enough to know better.

She levelled the assault rifle and opened fire, gunning down the first two bodyguards before they even knew that there was a threat. Two others knocked Horn to the ground and lay on top of him, while three more jumped forward, weapons at the ready. Jasmine wished, desperately, for a grenade or even for a higher-powered weapon. The bodyguards had been enhanced as well as conditioned.

"Take her alive," Horn squealed, from under the other two bodyguards. "Make her talk."

"I'm talking," Jasmine said, quickly. "And I'm alive!"

The bodyguards stared at her, just long enough for her to bring up her weapon and shoot the first one in the head. Those unlucky enough to be heavily conditioned often had problems following orders that weren't very clear. Judging by the way he stumbled backwards, someone had inserted armour plating in his skull, although he hit the ground in a manner that suggested the plating hadn't been good enough. The other two, shocked out of their puzzlement, came forward and knocked Jasmine to the ground.

She could have taken them if she'd been at peak, but everything she'd done had taken a deadly toll. One of them pushed down on her chest, holding her helplessly in place, while the other tore away the belt and everything else she'd collected along the way. Jasmine gathered herself and launched a wicked kick into his groin, but he just kept plodding on. The conditioning, it seemed, overpowered even such a nasty dose of pain. Or maybe his nerves had been modified as part of the process. Could he even enjoy *sex*?

Horn stumbled to his feet and walked over to her, although he was careful to stay out of reach. "How...how did you escape?"

Jasmine glared at him, but refused to say a word.

"Her wrist, master," one of the conditioned bodyguards said. "She crushed the bones in her own wrist."

Horn's eyes glittered with amusement. "You crushed your own hand to get out of the cuffs," he said, looking down at the ruined hand. "That's... *impressive*."

His face twisted into a smirk. "But futile," he added. "Next time, you will be paralysed from the neck down, unable to feel anything from the rest of your body. Maybe then you'll stay where I put you."

Jasmine looked at him, then down at his trousers. There was a very visible bulge there; he wasn't even trying to conceal it. Horn didn't just enjoy watching someone suffer, it made him sexually excited too. She felt sick as she contemplated all the young women – or men – in Landing City, the people who were his prey, helpless to resist when he sent his men for them. Compared to Horn, the bandits who'd plagued the outskirts of settled territory on Avalon were little more than a minor irritation, the pirates pains in the ass.

"Roll her over," Horn ordered, as his hands began to unzip his trousers. "I may as well indulge myself before…"

One of the bodyguards staggered and fell to the ground. Jasmine had only a second to realise that he'd been shot before the other bodyguards fell too. Horn stared in horror as two new black-clad figures appeared at the far end of the corridor, then crumbled to the ground in a dead faint. Jasmine allowed herself a snicker as she pulled herself out of the dead bodyguard's grip and stumbled to her feet. Horn clearly didn't have the nerve to work as a torturer for long.

"Lieutenant," a very familiar voice said. "Are you all right?"

Jasmine forced herself to remain upright. "Blake," she said. "Thank you!"

"You're welcome," Blake said. "I'd say you should be debriefed, but it would be a waste of time."

Jasmine stared at him…then sniggered. "That's fucking awful," she said. Debriefed indeed! "Pick that bastard up and bring him with us."

Blake gave her an odd look. "You don't want to kill him, boss? He was going to rape you."

"There are plenty of secrets locked within that man's head," Jasmine said. Revenge *was* tempting – but she had a feeling that the planet's future would go smoother if they had a chance to put Horn on trial, after the Admiral was disposed. "Pick him up and bring him with us."

Blake nodded and obeyed.

"We've been splashing *flambé* around," Carl said, as he gave Jasmine his arm. It was hard for her to walk in a straight line now, although she wasn't sure if it was relief or her endurance finally coming to an end. If they ever saw the Slaughterhouse again, she'd have plenty of advice for how they could make the Crucible even worse. "This building will go up in flames when we trigger the bomb."

"Good," Jasmine said, tiredly. "Let it all burn."

CHAPTER
THIRTY-FIVE

> This, we believed, would limit the ability of the central government to manipulate its member states for its own enrichment – or that of corporate masters. After all, even though most of the interstellar corporations had vanished from the sector, we knew that they would eventually reform. Denying the central government ground-capable military forces – at least in large numbers – would make it harder for the government to become tyrannical.
> -Professor Leo Caesius, *Authority, Power and the Post-Imperial Era*

"I thought I told you to stay still," the doctor said, tartly. "This is hard enough without you moving around like a demented harpy."

Jasmine gritted her teeth as the doctor – the very civilian doctor – worked on her wrist. It felt weird trusting a civilian doctor, certainly not one who had come out of the vocational schools on Avalon; the Empire's doctors had run the gauntlet between extremely competent and infuriatingly stupid. She didn't even want to *think* about how many civilians had died because their doctors hadn't deserved the title, or because of their medicines being contaminated or otherwise useless.

"Do as she says," Sergeant Hampton advised. "You smashed your hand pretty thoroughly – it will take more than an injection of quick-heal to make it better. Indeed, if we had time, I'd suggest a regeneration tank."

"There isn't one available on the planet without connections," the doctor said, bitterly. "When I think of the patients who have died because they couldn't get into a tank…"

She shook her head. "I'm afraid that this is going to hurt a little, despite the nerve-blockers," she added, as she pushed a medical manipulator against Jasmine's hand. "Brace for it."

Jasmine winced as a shock of pain ran through her hand, followed by a blissful numbness. The doctor studied the datapad, allowed herself a quick smile and then injected a dose of quick-heal into the wrist. Jasmine felt oddly dizzy as it interacted with the nerve-blockers, then forced herself to relax. Moving about definitely wouldn't help her heal quickly.

"You should have the hand and wrist in full working order by tomorrow, although I'd honestly recommend that you kept it bandaged for the next few days," the doctor said, as she wrapped a bandage around Jasmine's hand. "If you feel dizzy, stay in bed and relax – find a book or something to keep you from getting bored."

She scowled. "You were in excellent health when you were taken," she said. "Thankfully, the neural whip lashings you received don't seem to have done any permanent damage, although your skin is likely to be shedding more in the next few days. I've checked out your nervous system as best as I can with these crappy tools and I don't think there's even minimal damage, which is a relief. However, you may have to retrain your mind. Just as amputees have phantom limbs, neural whip victims have been known to remain convinced that they actually suffered physical harm."

"Oh," Jasmine said. She didn't recall stumbling around because she was convinced – at the back of her mind, if nowhere else – that she was a cripple, but she'd had too much else to worry about while fighting her way out of Internal Security. "And anything else?"

"There was some minor scarring on your vagina and anus, but your enhanced body seems to be healing nicely," the doctor concluded. "Overall, take a few days of rest and you should be back to normal – physically. Mentally…I don't know."

Jasmine watched the doctor pack up her tools and leave the room, then turned to look at Sergeant Hampton. "Mentally…am I fit for duty?"

"I would certainly advise you to take it easy for a couple of days," Sergeant Hampton said, dryly. "You realise we took the torture records out of the building?"

"Oh," Jasmine said. It was funny how she didn't care if her subordinates saw her naked, but she disliked the thought of them watching as she was tortured. "And how many people have seen them?"

"Just myself and Blake," Sergeant Hampton assured her. "You told them almost nothing – certainly nothing of importance. Blake was very impressed."

"Good," Jasmine said, remembering the moments when she'd come too close to snapping under the pain. If Horn and his goons had held her prisoner for longer, would she have broken? Even now, the pain seemed dreamlike…but it had been very real. "Put the recordings under seal. No one else needs to see them."

She shuddered at some of the memories, then pushed them aside as she swung her legs off the examination table and stood up. Her feet tingled unpleasantly as she tried to walk, reminding her that she'd been lashed on the soles of her feet. She lifted her foot and examined it, somehow feeling surprised to see flesh and blood. Her mind kept insisting that she should be looking at a bloody mess.

"I'll escort you to your room," Sergeant Hampton said, firmly. "What sort of books do you like?"

Jasmine shook her head in disbelief. "I'd prefer a complete outline of what happened when you decided to attack the building to free me," she said. Part of her was infinitely relieved; part of her felt that her life might have come at the price of the mission failing. Who knew how much of their little network of rebel cells had been revealed during the brief, but violent fight? "And then…what about Horn?"

"Chained to a bar in the basement," Sergeant Hampton said. "Bastard pissed his pants when he realised where he was – I had to convince Blake not to snap his neck after he saw some of the videos."

"We'll get some answers out of him later," Jasmine said. She *knew* Horn would break. The mere *threat* of torture would have had him gabbing out answers faster than she could record them. "Did his building go up in flames?"

"Completely," Sergeant Hampton assured her. "We got out around fifty prisoners before the flames were ignited…"

Jasmine nodded. *Flambé* – some long-dead Marine had given the compound the nickname and it had stuck – burned at a terrifyingly high temperature, setting fire to almost everything in its path. By the time the fire department had responded to the crisis, the flames would have wiped out the vast paper files, brought down the computer network and wiped out all evidence of their presence. Internal Security had not only lost its boss – and many of its senior officers – but its power base. If nothing else, the reluctance to store duplicate records away from the headquarters had just come back to bite them in the ass.

Assuming the rumours were true, Jasmine reminded herself. The more copies of a given set of records there were, the greater the chance of a security breach – but also of replacing whatever was lost, or stolen. *We dare not assume that they don't have backups.*

She scowled. "Where are the prisoners now?"

"Scattered over the city until we can get them out," the Sergeant told her. "Most of them" – he shuddered – "*several* of them were so badly injured that the scars will be with them for the rest of their lives. A handful of others were hostages to ensure the good behaviour of their parents – we think. I'm not sure why such hostages were stored in the Internal Security building."

"Convenience, perhaps," Jasmine said. "I'll have to see the records."

"You're going to bed," Sergeant Hampton said, firmly. "Once you've rested, you can see the records and decide what you want to do next."

He half-led, half-pulled her into a small bedroom and pointed towards the bed. "The doctor prescribed you some nutritional supplements," he added. "I'll have them ready for you when you wake up."

"You don't have to play nursemaid," Jasmine said. "I…"

The Sergeant surprised her by laughing. "I *know*," he said. "Every year after I retired, all of the Sergeants on Greenway would get together for the annual NCO ball – and it was always I who won the 'who had the smartest LT competition.' All of *my* Lieutenants had started life as Riflemen and knew what they were doing – they normally avoided the mistakes that other lieutenants made as soon as they got the rank. *I* never had to be a nursemaid."

Jasmine snorted. The Imperial Army's Lieutenants often lacked practical experience before they graduated from training and were placed in command of soldiers. Normally, the NCOs had to somehow help the Lieutenants survive the first few months and learn the ropes without getting either themselves or the men under their command killed. It wasn't a problem for the Marines because Marine officers served as Riflemen first, but it hadn't stopped the jokes about Lieutenants being allowed to issue a number of stupid orders during the first few weeks on the job. Blake and Joe had retold the jokes with great pleasure after Jasmine had been promoted.

And then they'd gone back into action and the jokes had stopped.

"I'm sorry to break your record," she said, as she lay down on the bed. "Wake me the instant – and I mean the instant – something happens."

"Of course," Sergeant Hampton said.

Jasmine was still trying to decide if he was being sincere when she drifted away into sleep.

They'd taken him *prisoner*!

The thought was intolerable. How could *anyone* take him prisoner? And yet they had.

Horn glared around the basement and tested his bonds for the umpteenth time. Someone had handcuffed his hands to a railing, then wrapped duct tape around his wrists, just to make damn sure that he couldn't do what that wretched bitch had done – despite all the torture – and break his own bones to break free. All of his ingenuity, so very capable when it came to finding weak spots to use as weapons against people, was failing him. There seemed to be no way out of the trap.

And that meant…what?

If he was dealing with outside agents, they had to be very well organised indeed to launch an attack on Internal Security. Admiral Singh was going to kill him…if he ever saw her again. He'd failed – and she wouldn't tolerate failure, no matter what else she was prepared to tolerate from her senior officers. And most of his contingency plans for escape rather relied on him having the freedom to put them into operation. He knew how to hide from a security sweep, if one happened to be launched. He didn't know how to break free from a combination of handcuffs and duct tape.

And what did *that* mean?

He was trapped. All he had to offer them was himself. And all he could hope was that he had enough time to convince them that he could be useful before they started meting out torture to get him to talk.

Time seemed to slip by so slowly. It felt like hours, or days, before the door finally cracked open, revealing a man wearing a dark mask. Horn opened his mouth, promising everything from power to wealth, as the man knelt down beside him and started to spoon something that tasted faintly like mashed-up ration bars into his mouth. It was ghastly compared to the roast beef, lamb and duck Horn had been entitled to, as one of Admiral Singh's senior officers, but there seemed to be no choice. He forced himself to swallow as it was pushed into his mouth, followed by a small flask of water. Somehow, he hadn't realised just how hungry he was until he'd been offered food.

There are stories of people who died rather than eat ration bars, he thought, *and other stories about where ration bars actually come from.*

All of a sudden, the stories didn't seem so unbelievable.

The man stood up and headed back towards the door, as silently as he had come.

"Wait," Horn said, desperately. "I'm ready to negotiate."

The man ignored him. Instead, he walked out of the door, which closed behind him with a loud bang. Horn stared at the solid metal, unable to quite grasp what had happened. He had money and power and information, all of which would be very important to either spies or a criminal gang, but he was just being ignored? It had been years since he had felt utterly helpless, ever since he'd been shunned and avoided by the other children – when they hadn't been using him as a punching bag just for existing – and he didn't like it.

"I can talk," he yelled at the stone walls. "I can *help* you! I'm on your side!"

There was no response.

Jasmine glanced at the timepiece someone had left beside the bed as soon as she snapped upright, swearing under her breath as she realised that she'd overslept. It took her confused memory several moments to remember that she wasn't actually on watch – and that she hadn't really overslept at all. She'd been tortured, and broken free, and rescued and...and she was safe. It was funny how important that seemed; no one in their right mind could describe a Marine's job as *safe*.

She climbed out of bed and studied herself in the mirror, as dispassionately as she could. There were no scars on her body, although some of her skin cells seemed to be flaking off – as, she recalled, the doctor had warned her would happen. Neural whips might not inflict any real *physical* damage, but they sure as hell could convince someone that they'd been hurt.

Her mind screamed at her as it remembered – finally – that her feet had been lashed too. Jasmine gritted her teeth, held herself firmly in place and concentrated hard on banishing the half-remembered pain. She had *not* lost her feet; she had *not* been permanently crippled. And she had walked halfway across the room without even realising that she was walking on her own two feet. It had just been something normal for her. And yet it still took all of her determination to walk into the shower and turn on the tap.

Hot water washed down over her body, brushing away the last lingering memory of Sid's touch as he'd sought to hurt and humiliate her. Parts of her body felt weak, but it was probably psychosomatic, rather than real pain. Or so she told herself as she turned off the water and picked up a towel, wiping the water from her body. If the pain was just a ghost, the sooner she stopped paying attention to it, the sooner she could return to duty.

If she *could* return to duty.

The thought was terrifying in a way that little else, even returning to the torturers naked and unarmed, could have been. Marines recovered quickly from anything that wasn't actually fatal, but there was always a period when they were poked and prodded by the medical staff before being returned to their units. What if *she'd* been too badly affected by the phantom pain to continue in her role? What if she should be placed on medical leave?

She scowled. There was no senior officer on Corinthian, no one to tell her that she needed to remain on medical leave…if they were on Avalon, she was sure that Colonel Stalker would order her suspended from duty until she received a clean bill of health. But they weren't on Avalon and she was in command. The mission was so unprecedented that the few grounds that existed for relieving Marine officers probably didn't apply. Besides, if Blake or Sergeant Hampton relieved her of command, where could they put her?

In the basement, right next to Horn, her mind supplied. Part of her, she realised numbly, wouldn't even *mind*. She could make Horn *hurt*…and lose her soul in the process.

Stepping out of the shower, she found a shirt, a pair of panties and a skirt placed on one of the small tables. Underneath, she discovered when she picked them up, was a short blonde wig, replacing the long brown-haired wig she'd worn when she'd been captured. Unless *all* of the files had been destroyed, the bastards would probably have an excellent idea of what she looked like by now. She'd have to change as much as possible to fool automated data-sifting programs. Luckily, it was fairly simple to fool them as long as one didn't attract attention.

"Welcome back to the world," Blake called, when she walked downstairs and entered the kitchen. "We missed you, Lieutenant."

"You can take another shot later," Jasmine said, dryly. There was no sign of Carl in the room. "Where is your partner-in-crime?"

"Teaching the young men a few nastier tricks," Blake said. "Word on the streets is confused, but *no one* liked Internal Security. It seems that there are several different stories about what actually *happened* inside the building; no one seems to know the truth. And the official channels have been keeping their mouths firmly shut."

"Can't decide on a good lie to tell," Canada said, as he turned away from the stove. "By the time they think of something, it will be far too late."

Jasmine smiled as he put a plate of bacon and eggs in front of her. It smelt heavenly.

"The Sergeant said that you were to make sure you took your nutrients as well," Blake said. "And that I was to witness…"

"Fine," Jasmine said, crossly. "How many did we lose?"

Blake's face fell. "Four of the rebels died," he said. "Thankfully, everyone was so confused – or it might well have been worse. They couldn't tell if they were coming or going."

"We can't count on that again," Jasmine said. Even the Civil Guard had learned from experience, although it normally only lasted until the educated officer was transferred elsewhere. "Next time it's going to be a great deal harder."

"Well, if it was easy, it wouldn't need us," Blake said. He held up a datapad. "The Sergeant thought that you should work on the questions for Horn. And then you can go ask him personally…"

It probably wasn't a good idea, Jasmine knew, but she found it hard to care.

CHAPTER THIRTY-SIX

> There were also other limits. Although each member state was required to make a contribution towards the central government's funds, the central government was not allowed to actually collect those funds – or, for that matter, have more than a minimal oversight role in other matters. In effect, we set out to create a government that was both strong and hobbled. Time would tell how well we had succeeded.
>
> -Professor Leo Caesius, *Authority, Power and the Post-Imperial Era*

Rani was no stranger to bloodshed. Every time a starship had died at her hand, it had taken lives…even if they had just been the helpless captives on a pirate ship. Later, after she had taken power, hundreds of thousands of people had been killed on her command. She'd long since lost any inhibitions she might have had about killing people who got in her way.

But this was different. The framework of the Internal Security building was still intact – it was constructed from hullmetal, almost impossible for planet-side weapons to do more than scorch – but the interior had been completely destroyed. Dead bodies, some half-burned, lay everywhere. The stench was appalling, very different to the clean aseptic space warfare she'd learned and practiced in the Imperial Navy. There was something about the violent end of the building – and so many lives – that chilled her to the bone.

She stood, surrounded by bodyguards, and watched as disaster recovery teams probed the remains. The basements that had once housed the prisoners and hostages alike were gone. And the flames had been so intense that there was little point in looking for DNA traces. The only way she had to know that some people were dead was because they hadn't been recorded escaping the chaos before it was too late. And...

...Horn was dead. Rani considered the thought and found it not altogether unpleasing. There would have come a time, she knew, when his usefulness would have been at an end – and at that moment, she would have ended his life. He was a monster – a useful monster, to be sure, but a monster. And yet, the timing was suspicious as hell. He had been mounting a power play to expand his power base. Why would he *die* at such a time? Rani knew better than to believe in coincidence. The odds were vastly against his death being unrelated to the insurgency in the countryside.

And yet, with Horn dead, who should take over Internal Security?

"Take me back to the Governor's Mansion," she ordered. "And bring the highest ranking survivor of the fire to me."

It was nearly an hour – and she was safely back in her office – before her bodyguards brought Johan Patterson to her. Rani vaguely remembered meeting him and discovering, much to her private amusement, that Patterson was considered a weird man for not enjoying torture and the other perversions Horn had used as rewards for his men. Patterson was simply too calm and focused on his work to engage his emotions, which wasn't really a bad thing. Not everyone had the stomach for Internal Security, after all. Those who were honest about it were simply transferred to a less unpleasant department.

Patterson looked understandably nervous to be facing her. His suit was mussed, stained with sweat and dust from the fire. Rani studied him and he cringed under her gaze, suggesting that he feared that she was going to blame *him* for the fire. That wasn't too likely, Rani knew. The reports were contradictory, but it seemed that insurgents from outside the city had blown up a car as a diversion, then neatly attacked the Internal Security building when the guardsmen were running towards the scene of the first explosion. It had been an admirable operation in many ways. If only the planner was on her side!

"Be seated," Rani said, brusquely. One of her bodyguards pushed Patterson into his seat. "What happened to your superior?"

"I don't know," Patterson said, after a moment of wild staring. "I was...I was assigned to work on some of the security files, to see who might be aiding and abetting the insurgents. When the shooting began, I climbed out of the window and escaped..."

"Which leaves you as the senior surviving officer with more than one or two brain cells," Rani interrupted. She had no idea what had happened to any of Horn's *other* senior officers, but apart from one who had been sent into the countryside to 'support' External Security there had been no other survivors. Horn had kept his department at daggers drawn, believing that it would secure his position...and it had, until his death. Right now, there were few people who could step up into the higher positions without extensive retraining.

Patterson swallowed. "Yes, Admiral."

Rani considered him, grimly. It had been *useful* to have Horn so... deeply involved in his own perversions. He would never truly be able to leave – or betray her, not when it meant cutting off the source of his pleasures. Patterson wasn't so inclined to indulge himself, which meant that he was what she needed right now – but might be less useful in the future.

And perhaps he will be less interested in rounding up preteens for sadistic fun, she thought, sourly. Maybe she'd let Horn go too far after all.

"You will assume command of the remains of Internal Security," she ordered. Patterson's mouth dropped open. "No, don't argue. None of the other survivors are anything like as qualified as you to rebuild and reorganise the department. Forget the requirement to provide support to External Security; concentrate on repairing the damage Internal Security took. And I want to know just what Horn was doing before he died."

Patterson nodded, although he was still very pale. "Yes, Admiral," he whispered. The promotion had to have surprised him – and, also, painted a target on his back. If Horn could be targeted, so could he. "I'll do my best."

"Make sure you do," Rani said. She briefly considered insisting that he surrendered his wife and child as hostages, then dismissed the thought. Patterson was already on the edge. "Once you have reorganised the security forces, I want you to make a series of sweeps through the edge of the city. If there are unwanted immigrants from the countryside, that's where they will be hiding. While you're at it" – her lips twisted into a smile – "if you should happen to round up any escaped conscripts, I'd be very pleased."

"Yes, Admiral," Patterson said. He frowned, thoughtfully. "Do you intend to bring forward the next cycle of conscription?"

"I believe so," Rani said. She was still annoyed at losing so many conscripts in the countryside, even though evidence suggested that a number of them had deserted – or had been kidnapped by the insurgents. "But I want to improve Imperial Security first."

She smiled as Patterson left her office, clearly caught between elation at his promotion and fear of the consequences of failure, then stood up and walked over to the governor's window, looking down at the city. The insurgent attacks – and the destruction of the Internal Security building – was alarming, but mere pinpricks compared to her full force. If the enemy ever showed themselves so clearly, she would crush them like bugs. They knew it too, of course.

Shaking her head, she reviewed the latest data from the scoutships probing the edge of the Commonwealth. Given a few months, she would be ready for war – and then the Commonwealth would be in for a nasty surprise.

And even if they knew she existed, they wouldn't be able to produce enough hardware to stand up to her in time.

It was funny, Jasmine allowed herself to reflect, how imprisonment worked differently on different people. She had kept her integrity even under heavy torture, while Horn had screamed and bellowed and eventually collapsed after a few hours of merely being bound to the wall. Maybe the boredom had broken into his mind, Jasmine considered; she would have bet half of her salary that *he* would never have thought of using boredom as a torture instrument.

Under the light, Horn just wasn't very impressive. But then, he didn't need to be, not when he'd had conditioned bodyguards, thousands of sadistic subordinates and – at base – Admiral Singh's backing. Had he ever actually taken part in a torture session? Sid had poked and prodded her – and threatened much worse – but Horn had never laid a hand on Jasmine, at least until he'd thought he could rape her right at the end. But then, he'd been looking at the collapse of everything he'd worked for.

Perhaps he just intended to throw caution to the winds, Jasmine thought, ruefully. He might have been considered dead, but if he had survived Admiral Singh would have blamed him for the disaster. Both disasters; Marines sneaking through Landing City and Internal Security's complete failure to identify them before it was too late.

She leaned down, wrinkling her nose as she smelled urine and shit, and pulled off her mask. Horn's eyes went very wide, then he tried to scramble backwards, a completely impossible feat in the cuffs. Jasmine pasted a sadistic smile of her own on her face, which grew wider as Horn started to gibber in fear. No doubt he'd never considered that one of his victims would come back for a little revenge.

The smell of urine grew stronger as she produced the neural whip off her belt and held it out in front of her. Horn stammered, trying to speak… but his lips refused to cooperate. He was scared out of his mind. Jasmine pulled back the whip, stood upright and nodded to Blake, who was standing just outside the door. A moment later, a bucketful of cold water was thrown into the room and over Horn. Drenched, the pervert started to cough and sputter as water ran down his body.

"Listen carefully," Jasmine said, pushing as much of her hatred and rage into her voice as she could. "You have two choices. You can cooperate, freely, or you will be *made* to cooperate. Do you understand me?"

Horn spluttered for a long moment, spitting out water. "You need me," he said, finally. He gave her an odd little smirk. "You…"

Jasmine produced the whip and pointed it at his groin. "I'll cooperate," Horn said, quickly. He'd seen people interrogated by having their sexual parts abused, Jasmine knew; he wouldn't be able to face it himself. "What do you want to know?"

"Everything," Jasmine said. She produced the datapad and clicked on the recording function, then held it up in front of him. "You are aware, no doubt, that torture has its limits? But you must be, given how you treated me."

She smiled at him, showing her teeth. "The problem is that the victim will eventually tell the interrogator whatever he thinks the interrogator wants to hear, just to make the pain stop," she said. "Which can be quite a problem...unless, of course, one uses lie detectors. The vocal analysis software built into this datapad will tell us if you try to lie. If you do" – she brandished the neural whip – "you will be whipped. And whipped again every time you try to tell us a lie. I know the concept of being truthful is alien to you, but..."

"I'll tell the truth," Horn said. "I swear I'll tell the truth."

"It seems to think you're lying," Jasmine said, studying the display. She jabbed the whip at his face and he recoiled. "Will you tell the truth now?"

Horn nodded, desperately.

"Good," Jasmine said. "First question..."

"The little bastard inserted a CYA code?" Sergeant Hampton asked. "Perhaps we should just give him back to Admiral Singh."

Jasmine shrugged. It had taken five hours to complete the first round of Horn's debrief, five hours during which she'd had to zap him twice to convince him to stick to the facts. It was worrying for her to discover that part of her mind was sadistic, no matter how much Horn deserved to suffer before he died. She would never, she suspected, be allowed to serve as a Drill Instructor, ever. Drill Instructors were meant to act like sadists, but they couldn't *be* sadists.

But it *had* yielded a wealth of information. Horn – or, more likely, someone *working* for Horn – had stuck a CYA code in the main computer network. A CYA – Cover Your Ass – code granted the user permission to make changes to files, even ROM data, without alerting anyone in authority. From what Jasmine had heard, CYA codes allowed officers to cover themselves against charges by internal investigators – if something happened to go missing while on deployment, they could use the code to imply that it had never been there at all.

The Empire had banned the practice. Too many datanets were intimately involved with making the Empire work; senior officers were told that they were *not* allowed to devise such codes, even for their own units. It hadn't prevented them, even for a moment; the search for scapegoats was so prevalent through the military that officers were prepared to do almost anything to put internal investigators off the scent. If Admiral Singh found out, Horn would be assured a long and unpleasant death.

On the other hand, she used one of her own to take control of Trafalgar, Jasmine thought, wryly. It had taken time to draw the full story out of Horn – completing the interrogation could take months – but they now knew what had happened on Trafalgar. Officers and men who might have stayed loyal had been targeted for elimination – or rounded up and dumped on Penance, where they would have to work for themselves. Either way, they were out of her hair.

It still astonished her to see just how *much* could be done by controlling logistics. No doubt Admiral Singh's political enemies had thought that assigning her to System Command would torpedo her career, sending it down in flames. According to Horn, she'd refused to sleep with a senior officer and had been punished for it. Jasmine would have found that admirable if Admiral Singh hadn't created a nightmarish state of her own. Somehow, with time and patience and a cold-blooded dedication that her enemies lacked, Admiral Singh had parlayed her position into a formidable power base. She had to be stopped.

Horn had told her much about the other officers working for Admiral Singh, officers who Jasmine had only known from organisational charts. Vice Admiral Sampson was an unimaginative fellow, which was partly why he commanded half the fleet; he wasn't considered imaginative enough to rebel. It hadn't stopped half of his family from being lodged in a luxury resort on the other side of the mountains, just in case he decided to become more ambitious. In fact, almost everyone in high positions had at least one hostage in the luxury resort. Anyone would have thought that Admiral Singh didn't trust their relatives.

And why not? Jasmine asked herself. *If Admiral Singh could conspire to commit mutiny – and then commit mutiny – who else would do the same thing?*

They'd heard almost nothing from the Empire since they had been exiled to Avalon, but there had been rumours – strange rumours. Some had hinted that military officers had declared independence, taking their fleets with them; others had warned that the Grand Senate was sending out loyalty officers to make sure that the Admirals and Generals didn't develop ambitions of their own. No one really knew anything for sure... and she hadn't thought to ask Horn what he might have heard. Not yet.

"Yes, he did," she said. "It gives us a chance to insert data into their network."

"Unless whoever created it took the code out after his death," Sergeant Hampton pointed out. "They would need to cover their tracks if their protector was no longer around to protect them."

"We'll have to test it, carefully," Jasmine said. But between the code – and the rest of the information she'd learned from Horn – she had a feeling that she knew *exactly* how to topple the Admiral. And once she was down, she was out. "But if it works, we can start inserting our own people in some *really* important positions."

"If," Sergeant Hampton said. "It strikes me that we don't really have a plan yet."

"Of course we do," Blake insisted. "We *always* have plans."

"Yeah, and then we have to *improvise* when the plans go wrong," Carl added.

"Quiet, the pair of you," Jasmine said, lifting one arm. She pushed the datapad towards Sergeant Hampton, nodding for the other two to copy the data to their own terminals. "Review the data I pulled out of him, then start thinking about other possibilities. Where is Danielle right now?"

"In a safe house, we hope," Blake said. "You want us to bring her here?"

"I'll go there," Jasmine said. She needed *out* of the house; after her imprisonment, being confined felt thoroughly suffocating, whatever the motives behind it. "And then I think we can start moving onwards."

There was a knock on the door. Hands reached for weapons, then relaxed as Canada entered the room.

"I just had a message passed to me from Wolf," he said. "Patterson has been appointed to take Horn's place."

Jasmine felt her mouth fall open. They couldn't be *that* lucky, could they? It had to be another trap.

But if it was, Patterson was sacrificing his wife and child...

"I need to ask Horn a few more questions," she said, standing up. She hadn't bothered to ask him how he'd set the trap to capture her, it hadn't seemed important at the time. But now…could it be that Patterson hadn't *intended* to betray them? They would have to find out. "And then we will have to decide how to proceed."

CHAPTER THIRTY-SEVEN

> However, funding a fleet could only be a Commonwealth-wide endeavour. The alternative created problems; if each planet contributed its own fleet units, some would very rapidly become stronger than others. Eventually, we ensured that fleet crewmen and officers were sworn to the Commonwealth, rather than to its separate member states. It was a far from perfect solution, but the alternative was chaos – and, eventually, war between the member states.
> -Professor Leo Caesius, *Authority, Power and the Post-Imperial Era*

"This strikes me as a very bad idea," Blake said.

Jasmine glanced at him in surprise. After she'd been captured, Blake had taken command...and it seemed that the experience had matured him. On the other hand, he was also being very protective – which was exactly what she didn't need after her captivity, even if her body still didn't feel quite right. She'd gone to a lot of trouble to earn her Rifleman's Tab and she was damned if she was going to allow a brief session of pain to destroy it.

"I don't think we dare let it pass," she said, reluctantly. Part of her – the part that remembered being tortured – was reluctant to return to Patterson's house. It seemed impossible that Admiral Singh didn't know what was going on – and yet she'd promoted Patterson to high office. And Horn had admitted that he hadn't reported her capture to his superior. "Besides, we still have his family."

Patterson, according to Horn, hadn't reported his family's capture to his superiors. He'd been lucky, Jasmine knew; his family being held hostage would have made him a security risk even to a less paranoid security organisation. If someone hadn't realised that something was wrong, Jasmine would never have been taken prisoner. She shook her head as she approached the rear of the property and looked around, checking for signs that another trap had been laid. There was nothing.

"Keep me under observation," she ordered, as they returned to the front gate. According to the observers, Patterson had returned home barely an hour ago, as night was falling over the city. "If something happens, don't hesitate to jump in."

She nodded to him and walked towards the gate, then opened it with a quick touch of her multitool. Inside, the house seemed dark and cold, save for a single light burning from an upstairs window. Patterson had to be tired, Jasmine knew; he'd taken on a challenging position, even without the additional strain of losing his family. She wouldn't have blamed him for going to bed almost as soon as he reached his house. Or, for that matter, finding someone who could help him relax after a long day at work.

The door clicked open and she stepped inside, picking her way through the darkened corridor until she reached the living room. Patterson seemed to have pulled half of the books off the shelves and scattered them on the floor, although she couldn't see why – unless he'd been angry and terrified and lashing out at the first thing he could. A moment later, she heard someone walking down the stairs and concealed herself in the shadows, peering through the darkness as Patterson walked into view. He looked dreadful.

"I know you're here," he said, his voice echoing through the darkness. "I want to talk."

Jasmine hesitated – her stealth clearly wasn't what it had been – and then stepped out of the shadows. "Good evening, Mr. Patterson," she said, calmly. "I trust that this visit will be less…exciting?"

Patterson's face twisted into a bitter sneer. "They didn't tell me about the trap," he said. "I wasn't even aware that you had been captured until it was too late."

"And now your boss is gone and you're the head of Internal Security," Jasmine said, softly. She allowed her voice to harden. "Funny how things change, isn't it?"

She smiled inwardly at the expression on his face. No one would believe that it had been sheer luck that he'd been promoted, after losing his family and pledging to do whatever it took to get them back safely. It was far more likely that Admiral Singh would believe that Horn had been deliberately set up for assassination, along with most of the other potential candidates for his job. And that would make Patterson far more than some poor bastard whose family had been kidnapped. It would make him an active collaborator with her enemies.

Patterson blanched. No doubt the same thoughts had occurred to him. Whatever persona he showed to the world, he couldn't be naive enough to ignore the realities of his job. It was bad enough that his new subordinates would be plotting his death, but if Admiral Singh ever found out the truth, his life would certainly be forfeit. And the fact that he *hadn't* planned to gain promotion wouldn't help when the Admiral had him killed.

"Yes, it is," he said, tightly. He turned and walked into the living room, clicking on the light as he stepped inside. "What can I do for you?"

Jasmine stepped inside, picking her way over the books that had been scattered on the floor. "We need you to help us get some people inside the system," she said calmly, trying not to show her inner fear. If Patterson decided that his family wasn't important after all, telling him so much would allow him to set up another betrayal, one that would prove completely fatal. "You will ensure that they get permission to go wherever they need to go."

Patterson's eyes narrowed. "That's it?"

"For the moment," Jasmine said, as if it wasn't particularly important. "We will have other tasks for you to do, later."

"Right," Patterson said. There was a hint of desperation in his voice. "And my family?"

"Oh," Jasmine lied, smoothly. "I almost forgot."

She reached into her pocket and produced a folded sheet of paper. "Your wife has written to you," she said, as she passed it to him. "Sirius was reluctant to actually *write*, but he condescended to sign it after we asked very nicely. I trust it will serve as enough proof."

Patterson scowled at her. He knew, better than most, just how easy it was to fake evidence; someone with access to copies of his wife's handwriting could easily have forged a letter claiming to be from her, then disposed of his wife's body somewhere where it wouldn't be found easily. On the other hand, coming up with irrefutable proof that she was still alive would be tricky, even for the best-prepared kidnappers. After all, *anyone* could have written the line where Patterson's wife congratulated him on his new job.

Jasmine watched as he unfolded the sheet of paper and read it quickly. Even asking his wife to write a note had been a risk; it was quite possible that they'd agreed on a code beforehand for such situations, allowing her to slip her husband some information. Jasmine was fairly sure that the woman didn't know where she and her son were being held, but she knew better than to take anything for granted. And yet there was no choice. If Patterson came to believe, no matter how incorrectly, that his family were dead, he would betray them. How could she blame him?

"You could have forged the note," Patterson said, when he'd finished reading it. "Or…"

"Of course we could," Jasmine agreed, tartly. "But you have the choice between assuming that your family are already dead or doing whatever it takes to keep them alive."

Paterson scowled at her. "And how long will it be before I see them again?"

Jasmine shivered inwardly at his expression. Kidnap victims – like blackmail – were only useful as long as the kidnapper kept the victims under his control. Once they were sent back, they were completely useless to him, even when slow poison or suicide implants were inserted into the mix. Patterson knew that Jasmine would be in no hurry to return his wife and child, if only because she would lose her hold on him the moment they were home. And yet, the more he did for her, the less likely that Admiral Singh would forgive him when it came out.

Not that is really a concern, Jasmine thought. *She won't forgive him in any case.*

"When we have finished our operations," Jasmine assured him, "they will be released, as they will no longer be any use to us."

She hesitated, then pressed onwards. "And you will be granted safety as well," she added. "We will protect you from the mob."

Patterson seemed to frown, a complex series of thoughts passing across his face. Did he know who she was and what she represented? There was no way to know; Horn had guessed the truth, but he'd been captured before he'd had a chance to tell anyone else. Jasmine had no idea what sort of bureaucratic infighting had discouraged him from telling Admiral Singh about the infiltration party, yet it might just have saved their lives.

"Thank you," Patterson said, finally. Perversely, he sounded almost grateful. "What else would you like me to do?"

Jasmine smiled. "What progress have you made in hunting down the people responsible for the destruction of Internal Security's prized headquarters?"

Patterson shot her a sharp look. Internal Security, according to the observers, had been forced to relocate to another secure building, a skyscraper that had belonged to one of the oligarchs before Internal Security had pushed him and his people out. They, in turn, had moved into a smaller skyscraper, setting off an entire series of office relocations all across the city. Jasmine honestly hadn't realised how much chaos a simple relocation could cause, but it shouldn't have surprised her. She'd studied logistics, after all.

"Very little," he said, finally. "We certainly don't know who you are."

"I hope so," Jasmine said, dryly. She reached into her pocket again and unfolded a map. "I want you to concentrate your efforts on searching this part of town."

Patterson blinked in surprise. "That's not a very...important part of the city," he pointed out. "And there will be...political complications."

Jasmine smiled. Her first thought had been to try to frame Horn, claiming that the bastard had been behind the insurgents all along, but it had just been too unlikely to convince Admiral Singh. Horn was a corrupt depraved pervert, yet he wasn't stupid enough to weaken the person who he depended upon for his own survival, not when almost every other senior officer wanted him dead. Instead, she'd pointed the security forces towards the red light district, where the crime lords made most of their money and the population tried to gamble away its woes.

"They managed to wipe out a large number of security officers," she said, dryly. "I'm sure that if you muster the right kind of evidence, the Admiral will not be amused."

Patterson stared at her. "And if she refuses to grant permission for us to ransack the area?"

"Do your best," Jasmine ordered, dryly. "We *do* have other ways to keep an eye on you."

She wondered, absently, where the spark of amusement at his flinch had come from. Was she becoming a sadist herself? After all, if she hadn't told him, he might just have asked the Admiral without trying to convince her – and then turned around and told Jasmine that he'd done his best. It would be unfortunate if he believed that he wasn't being monitored.

But we don't have good sources inside the new security office, she thought, grimly. *He will be outside our view from time to time.*

"I will be in touch," she said, as she stepped backwards. "I suggest that you ensure that your forces start looking for the insurgents."

Patterson nodded. "I have a question for my wife," he said, before Jasmine could vanish. "Ask her what was happening when we first met. Please."

"Very well," Jasmine said. It was a good trick; if she hadn't been able to bring him the answer, he would have known that his wife and child were dead. "Do you have a question for Sirius too?"

"Just tell him I love him," Patterson said.

Jasmine shuddered at the despair in his eyes. Whatever else happened, Patterson knew that he was likely to end up dead – and that his family's lives would depend upon their kidnappers, who would have no further use for them once Patterson was gone. Jasmine had assured him that they would be safe, but he would be a fool to take that for granted. He worked with people who would think nothing of murdering a woman and her child after they became useless.

"I will," she promised, cursing herself under her breath. What sort of monster was she becoming? "Here."

Patterson took the datachip she passed him and looked down at it quizzically. "And this is?"

"The people we wish you to clear," Jasmine said. "Make sure that they all have excellent security clearances and completely clean records. I'll see you again in a few days. By then, make sure that it is done."

She nodded to him and stepped out of the door, walking back along the corridor and out into the darkness. No one leapt out at her as she made her way down the garden path; Blake, she realised with some irritation, was lurking right by the gate. He would have been almost completely invisible to anyone else, but it was still annoying. Didn't he trust her on her own?

You're a cripple, part of her mind pointed out. *No matter how much you might wish to deny it, you're a cripple.*

"Mission accomplished," she muttered, as they started to walk down the street. "Was there any trouble?"

"Almost none," Blake said. "A security patrol passed, forcing me to stay in the shadows, but they never even came near me."

Jasmine smiled. Most of the security forces had been withdrawn to guard the heart of the city, leaving the outskirts almost completely undefended. The crime lords had not been slow to take advantage of it, which was going to ensure that they received a nasty shock once Patterson started security sweeps through the red light district. Their anger would help destabilise the regime still further...and hopefully keep the Admiral from noticing the true threat before it was too late.

Unless it's all just an elaborate trap for us, she thought, grimly. She'd decided that she *hated* cloak-and-dagger operations. If Admiral Singh knew more than she'd told Horn, or anyone else, she could just be waiting for Jasmine and her people to expose themselves before she struck. Or she could be preparing the final stages of an offensive against the Commonwealth by now. *There's no way to know until it is too late.*

If Patterson did his work well, they'd have a few hundred cell members on the orbital platforms – and on some of the ships. Not all of them, she knew, and not enough to run the ships afterwards...which meant that they'd be gambling everything on a single roll of the dice. It was frustrating to know that most of Admiral Singh's conscripts would be happy to switch sides, particularly those who had been dragged away from other planets to serve the Admiral, but they didn't dare approach more than a handful of them. An insurgent cell being uncovered among the conscripts would be far too revealing.

She'd studied the textbooks carefully and they'd placed a great deal of focus on subverting the enemy's counter-intelligence service. But then, the books had been written for someone who was already involved with the process, not someone coming in from the outside. At least they had a mine of information in Horn, thankfully. Without him, Jasmine knew, it would be much harder. But once the operation was over, Horn was going to die.

And if he knows it, he might try to screw us, she thought. Her read of Horn suggested that he was a coward, someone who would give up everything he knew just to escape pain. But what if she was wrong? Some people had hidden depths…and Horn, of course, had been in command of one of the most vital parts of Admiral Singh's regime. What if there was more to him than anyone realised?

Jasmine shook her head. They'd just have to make damn sure they didn't allow him to trick them at the worst possible time.

They reached the base without incident and slipped inside, encountering the doctor on the stairwell. "I thought I told you to stay in bed," the doctor said, eying Jasmine crossly. "You do realise that you could have damaged yourself further?"

"I couldn't stay in bed," Jasmine said. Laziness wasn't a qualification for being a Marine. "And I feel fine."

"Right," the doctor said, sardonically. There was absolutely no give in her voice at all. "Go upstairs, get some rest and let me have another look at you in the morning. You are *not* recovered from your experience yet."

"Better go," Blake advised. His dark eyes were filled with concern. "We'll take care of the rest down here."

Jasmine scowled at him. "You too, Brutus?"

"You need to rest," Blake said, firmly. He hit her with a series of reasons before she could object. "Lieutenant, you need to be in perfect health for when we go active – and you need time to heal. You are not in a good state."

"Fine," Jasmine said. Maybe he was right. The surge of anger and resentment she felt would have been alien to her pre-torture personality. Had she ever resented a senior officer for giving her instructions? Or was it just a side-effect of the torture? Had there been real damage to her mind? "Tomorrow morning, wake me up bright and early. I have some work to do."

She walked up the stairs, stumbled into the bedroom and lay down on the bed without bothering to undress. And yet it seemed hours before sleep overcame her.

CHAPTER
THIRTY-EIGHT

But why, you might ask, was all of this necessary? Does it not seem that we went to too much trouble? The problem was that we needed to fill the void left behind by the Empire – and the Empire had been viewed as legitimate. In order to obtain that legitimacy, we had to obtain the consent of the governed.
-Professor Leo Caesius, *Authority, Power and the Post-Imperial Era*

"She wants *what*?"

"Weapons," the communications officer said. "Almost our entire stock of weapons."

Layla scowled down at the message. It had been transmitted from the surface to *Lightfoot* and then relayed outwards to *Harrington* – along with a brief and heavily-encoded outline of what Lieutenant Yamane had in mind for the coup. Smuggling weapons from the surface, it seemed, was nearly impossible, no matter what sort of access one had. But getting them from deep space to orbit seemed much easier.

And if Mandy gets caught, the operation might be blown, Layla thought. But they couldn't allow fear to paralyse them or they'd never get anything done.

"Have them transferred into pallets," she ordered. They'd keep their personal weapons, naturally, but there was little point in stockpiling assault rifles on a starship. "Then transfer any other supplies from *Butcher* that they might find useful."

"Aye, Captain," the logistics officer said. "They'll probably want communications gear as well as weapons. If the enemy reacts quickly enough to take down the datanet..."

"The plan will likely fail," Layla concluded. "See to it."

She looked over at the display as her officers scurried to carry out her orders. A civilian might well have missed it, but Admiral Singh was very definitely assembling a task force, spearheaded by at least four battleships. Enough firepower, Layla knew, to break through Avalon's defences and take control of the high orbitals. The last time someone had broken through, the Marines had boarded the ship before it could make good its threats of planetary bombardment. Admiral Singh wouldn't make the same mistake.

"And then prepare the drones," she added. "We don't want any mistakes when the time comes to tip our hands."

Shanna sat in the small room, trying to make the cup of coffee last as long as she could. The madam was strict with her girls, but she understood that they needed to take breaks from time to time – even if they were rarely allowed to do anything else. After all, they effectively belonged to the brothel; if they fled, the madam's contacts in the government or the criminal underground would suffice to hunt them down and return them to servitude.

She looked up at the mirror, fighting – once again – the urge to smash it and wipe her reflection out of existence. Was this the life she'd hoped for when she'd left the farm, three years ago, and moved to Landing City? She'd been told that there were job opportunities for young men and women willing to work for a living – and promised that she'd have her own apartment in no time. Instead, Admiral Singh had taken control, the economy had suffered, her debts had been called in…and she'd wound up working in a brothel. It wouldn't be long, she feared, before she died. She was already painfully thin after several months of malnutrition.

"Shanna," a voice bellowed. "Get into your room, you wretched girl!"

Shanna shuddered as the madam poked her head into the restroom. Once, being naked – and all of the madam's workers were expected to be naked at all times – would have bothered her dreadfully. Now, it was just one more humiliation – and a minor one at that, compared to being forced to entertain over a dozen men a day. She gritted her teeth as she drank the last of her coffee and pulled herself to her feet, wondering if this would be the day when she'd just give up. Maybe if she sat down and closed her eyes the end would come swiftly.

Perhaps I should just inject myself with drugs, she thought, grimly. The madam handed them out to girls who had the habit, but Shanna had never picked it up. *An overdose would end me...*

There was a loud series of knocks at the door. Before the madam or anyone else could open it, there was a much louder crash and the door fell inwards, revealing a handful of guardsmen wearing green and blue uniforms. Shanna gulped, wondering if they had come for her – she wasn't a legal resident in Landing City – before realising that the security forces would hardly send an entire army out to capture her. It was much more likely that...that what? The madam had paid off the security forces, hadn't she?

"I gave your superior his payment," the madam snapped, in her strident tone. "I..."

A hand caught her and shoved her into the wall. Shanna felt her heart jump as the guardsman grabbed the madam's hands, yanked them behind her back and wrapped a plastic tie around them, then pushed her into a sitting position facing the wall. The sight of her tormentor being tormented gave Shanna hope, even as the guardsman moved on to her and secured her hands too. She glanced at the madam, who was clearly fuming in rage, and concealed her inward amusement. It might do the bitch good to be someone else's plaything for a while.

But what was going on?

She considered it as the rest of the girls and their customers were brought downstairs and separated, the customers led outside and marched to armoured vans. Maybe the madam hadn't paid off the right person – but it seemed an odd mistake to make, after two years of living under Admiral Singh. Or perhaps something else had changed. Maybe the madam was in trouble for something else...she was still mulling it over when the guardsmen returned, having searched the whole building, and started to drag the girls to their feet.

"Get outside and into the van," one of them growled.

The madam started to protest, listing all of her powerful friends...

"Shut up," the guardsman ordered, slapping her across the face with a gloved hand. "You are under arrest."

Shanna couldn't hide her amusement any longer, nor could most of the other girls. They might have been naked, their hands tied behind their backs, but they couldn't stop giggling as they were marched into the van and the door was firmly closed behind them. If nothing else, at least they'd watched their mistress being humiliated...

But what was going on?

Guard Sergeant Ron Tomlinson had listened to his orders in some considerable puzzlement – and then taken the risk of actually *questioning* them. Everyone in the security forces knew that the red light district was effectively off-limits. The crime lords kept the insurgents from using it as a base and, in exchange, the security forces left it alone. Everyone needed some room to blow off steam, Ron had been told, and besides most of his superiors loved to drink, gamble and enjoy themselves with whores.

But the orders were clear. He was to lead his men to a series of addresses and arrest everyone inside the building, no matter who they were. Arresting prostitutes and lower-ranking gangsters was one thing – everyone knew that they would only be held for a day or so before being released – but senior gangsters were quite another. Those men had *connections*! Ron's career could come to an end if he messed with them...but his orders left him no choice.

He watched as the last of the prostitutes stepped inside the van – the driver had strict orders to drive directly to the holding pens – and then climbed back inside his own vehicle, heading down the street to the next address. It had started life as an office block before the economic crash, he realised as the vans braked to a halt; the crime lord had simply taken it over and turned it into a very different kind of office. He cursed inwardly – no matter what decision he took, his career was doomed – and started to bellow orders to his men. They sprang out of the vans and rushed to secure the entrances to the office block. No one would be allowed in or out without being arrested.

"Squad one, follow me," he ordered, briskly. "Squads two and three, hold the perimeter."

Ron led the way into the building, stunner in hand. Standard procedure when entering a hostile building was to stun everyone first and ask questions later, once the victims had been taken out of the building and identified. It was quite possible that some of the people inside were innocent, although *that* seemed unlikely given who owned the property. He pushed the thought out of his head as he came face-to-face with armed guards. They were already raising their weapons when the guardsmen stunned them.

"Keep moving," he ordered, wishing that they knew more about the internal layout of the building. He was sure that the plans were on file somewhere, but they'd been given no time to look them up, let alone take the plans with them. "Take them all down."

The small pile of stunned captives grew larger as the guardsmen made their way through the building. Most of them were small fry – gangland enforcers or secretaries, doing the menial work of running a criminal empire – but a handful were actually quite important. Ron allowed himself a smirk at some of their expressions before they'd been stunned, as if they hadn't expected the forces of law and order to come arrest them. But then, *he* hadn't expected to be tasked with arresting them either.

Finally, they pulled all of the captives into the lobby, secured them and checked for anyone on the list of principal targets. The office block belonged to Crab, a known crime lord, but there was no sign of him among the arrestees. Ron guessed that someone in the office had hastily called the bastard as soon as the guardsmen had been given their orders, prompting him to escape. And plot trouble, Ron was sure.

His radio buzzed. "Sergeant," the dispatcher said, "we have reports of crowds gathering throughout the red light district."

Ron grimaced. "Secure the prisoners in the vans," he ordered, tightly. The red light district had never been gripped by fear, certainly not like the rest of the city. "And hurry!"

He saw the crowds forming at both ends of the street as the prisoners were hastily bundled into the vans and prepared for transport. Crab must have orchestrated it, he realised, or perhaps one of the other crime lords – or *all* of them. They were hardly likely to take this official intrusion into their territory lying down. He clambered into the front of the van and barked orders to the driver, telling him to drive right at the crowds. They scattered, as he expected, allowing the vehicles to pass through…

…And then a hail of debris rained down on the van from high overhead, followed by a handful of burning bottles and faeces. Ron gritted his teeth, reminding himself that the vehicles were armoured and it would take more than a bottle full of burning fuel to hurt them, before the front tires seemed to explode. They'd been shot out by a sniper…he reached for the radio, cursing under his breath, as the crowds started to close in again.

"Move faster," he snarled. Whatever concerns he'd had about hurting the crowd had faded away as he realised that they were in very real danger. "Run the bastards down if you have to."

The driver gunned the engine…which suddenly spluttered to a halt. Ron stared in absolute disbelief; how had *that* happened? And then the locks clicked open and hands started to pull open the doors, yanking them wide open. Ron found himself staring into a sea of angry faces, baying for his blood. He pulled the stunner off his belt and started to point it at the nearest face, but it was yanked out of his hand before he could pull the trigger. A moment later, strong hands grasped his trousers and pulled him right out of the cab.

"No," Ron cried out. He'd seen people torn to death by mobs before. It was never pretty. "I…"

His head hit the hard pavement and he knew no more.

———

Lukas heard the crowd baying its approval as the guardsmen were torn apart and shivered, inwardly. The crowd seemed a living thing in its own right, hundreds of minds – perhaps thousands – bound together into a single entity that wanted pain and blood and suffering. All of the guardsmen were dead...

He found his way to the edge of the crowd and slipped off into the side streets. No one was quite sure why the guardsmen had decided to raid the red light district, but the crime lords had come out in force against them; Lukas had planned to make demonstration raids of his own, as his orders had specified, but in the end they hadn't been necessary. Instead... he looked back at the burning vans, after the prisoners had been extracted from them, and smiled to himself. Maybe Admiral Singh would respond in force, but for the moment he had the satisfaction of hitting back at his tormentors.

A dozen helicopters flew overhead as he walked away from the crowd, their pilots staring down at the chaos below. God alone knew what they had in mind, but unless they intended to open fire on the crowd Lukas couldn't see what they could do to stop the riot. The crime lords and their lieutenants were already trying to direct it out of the red light district, funnelling the hatred and pent-up rage towards the people who worked directly for Admiral Singh. It was a challenge to her authority, he'd been told, that she couldn't ignore.

And it would win the resistance time to think and plan for the next round...

Rani glared down at the displays, each one showing scenes from riots that seemed to be spreading out of the red light district. Evidently the crime lords had seen fit to play both sides by working with the insurgents as well as her loyalists, as if they didn't believe that she controlled enough firepower to destroy a hundred worlds. She'd authorised a set of raids to show them her power – and they were trying to show her theirs in response.

"Have the reserves moved up and block their passage out of the red light district," she ordered, crossly. Ground combat wasn't her forte, but luckily this was a fairly simple tactical exercise. "And if the reserves are incapable of holding the crowds, the helicopters are authorised to use knock-out gas."

She scowled over at Patterson. "I thought you told me that this could be controlled," she snapped. "What went wrong?"

Patterson paled – as well he might. "Someone in the office contacted the crime lords," he said, finally. "They had enough advance warning to escape."

"Find that person," Rani growled. "And once you find them, make sure they *suffer*."

She thought, rapidly. If she simply destroyed the red light district, it would teach them a lesson – but she needed it as a safety valve, a place for the discontented and dispossessed to fade away into nothingness. It was why she had tolerated it – and its masters – for so long, rather than exterminating them when they had first shown themselves. Besides, the crime lords had profited from her rule. Why would they want to turn against her?

But if they thought that the insurgents might actually *win*, they would want to be on the winning side…and the only way to do that was to assist the insurgents.

"Then flood the area with additional troops and find the bastards," she added, angrily. If they had ties to the insurgents, they would be found out – and then they would be used to destroy the insurgency. "I want absolutely *no* mistakes – or escapes."

"Yes, Admiral," Patterson said. "If I may make a suggestion…?"

Rani lifted a single eyebrow, icily.

"We need to reconsider all of our security arrangements in the city," Patterson said. "With all due respect to my predecessor, the security procedures should have been re-examined every year or so – and were not. The crime lords have gotten so far by taking advantage of structural weaknesses within our system, weaknesses that should have been closed by a yearly examination. If we'd just picked up everything and looked at it every so often…"

He sounded hesitant, but Rani took the point. Perhaps they had become too comfortable while securing the rest of her empire.

"Start looking at ways to reconfigure after we have dealt with the crime lords," Rani ordered, simply. "Very well said, Mr. Patterson."

He flushed, as if he wasn't used to praise.

Rani watched him leave her office, then turned back to the attack plans for the Commonwealth. The scouts had brought in enough data for her to draw up the first set of plans, although she wasn't convinced that the Commonwealth was truly dependent on Avalon. *She* might have been dependent on Corinthian, but then she'd wanted to keep everything under her control. The Commonwealth didn't seem to have a single dictator in command.

But that would change, she told herself. And soon.

"The CYA code works," Canada said. "We got right into the network!"

Jasmine snorted in grim amusement. Horn had *definitely* bent security regulations until they snapped in two. Using a CYA code alone was bad enough, but setting it so that all evidence that the code was used was automatically erased...Admiral Singh would definitely have had him killed.

"Good," she said. Hopefully, between the crime lords and the planned reorganisation, Admiral Singh would have too much else to worry about to notice the jaws of a trap forming around her. "Now, all we have to do is wait. And see."

CHAPTER THIRTY-NINE

This may seem contradictory. The Empire never seemed to enjoy the consent of the governed, did it? But the truth was that the vast majority of citizens found life in the Empire to be tolerable, even if it was far from perfect. Those who rebelled were always in the minority until the Empire reached the last few decades of its life. Even an entire sector falling into revolt could not destroy the entire edifice.
-Professor Leo Caesius, *Authority, Power and the Post-Imperial Era*

"I missed you," Danielle confessed.

"I hope so," Trevor said, as he snuggled up to his wife. He still hadn't quite forgiven her for convincing him that she and their daughters were dead. "I missed you all the time on the platforms."

"I know," Danielle admitted. She shook her head tiredly. "And I don't blame you for being mad at me."

"You should have told me," Trevor said, as he stood up. "Those moments when I thought they were dead were the worst of my life."

He walked into the shower and washed the weak spray of water over his body, then dried himself quickly with a half-damp towel. The flophouse's owners hadn't bothered to install anything more than the basics, believing that the visitors wanted anonymity more than luxury or anything else. They were probably right, Trevor had concluded after his first night. God knew that he'd just wanted to crawl into a bottle and forget everything else.

Danielle was weeping silently when he emerged from the shower, worn down by her role in the Democratic Underground and the lie she'd allowed her husband to believe. Trevor felt a brief pang of guilt, then tried to push it aside. It refused to fade; Danielle had concealed her past to protect him and their children, and then she'd helped fake her death to provide additional protection. She might have mishandled events, but she hadn't meant ill.

"I'm sorry," he said, as he wrapped his arms around her. "I know you meant well."

His wife sobbed into his shoulder for a long moment, then let go of him. "You'd better get dressed," she said, shortly. "You have a briefing to attend. One *I'm* not allowed to attend."

Trevor almost pointed out that she'd kept a secret from him for over two years, but stopped himself just in time. Instead, he pulled on the uniform he'd been given along with his promotion and headed towards the door. Danielle blew him a weepy kiss and then stepped into the shower, leaving him alone. Trevor hesitated, then walked out of the door and down towards the second apartment. There was no time for his wife any longer.

Something *big* was happening, he was sure. Ever since he'd been brought into the conspiracy, ever since he had started work on building his own cell, it had been with the vague promise that something would happen in the future. He'd been told that, whatever else happened, he was to keep his head down and not make waves, apart from recruiting new cell members. Now, however, something was different. The fighting in the countryside, the riots in the red light district…and the summons to the flophouse. Something was definitely happening.

He knocked on the door and stepped inside, suddenly very aware of unseen eyes. The woman he'd met before was seated at a table, facing him, her dark eyes fixed on his face. There was something about her that worried him, a kind of edged *hardness* that was so very different from his wife's personality. What *was* she? And she'd changed somehow, since their last meeting…

"Be seated," the woman ordered. "I trust that your last report was accurate?"

Trevor flushed. "They don't train us to make mistakes in the field," he said, sharply. "The report was as accurate as it could be without sacrificing security."

The woman's eyes glinted with humour. "That rhymes," she pointed out. She looked down at the datapad on the desk, then back up at him. "This room is completely secure. You should have asked first, by the way."

She held up a hand before Trevor could muster a retort. "In two weeks, perhaps sooner, you will be called upon to take command of your new duty station," she said. "You will..."

Trevor blinked. "My *new* duty station?"

"Indeed," the woman informed him. "You and several of your cellmates will be transferred to Defence Station II. Admiral Singh has been building up the planet's fixed defences to ensure that she can hold the world if her planned war goes wrong. Your task will be to secure control of the station. Ideally, you will take it while the station is still operational; failing that, you will knock out the systems and weapons so it will take several days to repair the damage."

"Oh," Trevor said. He hastily remembered what he'd learned about defence stations. Most of the Empire's technology was standardised, to make it easier to build and maintain, but he'd never served on a defence station. "I don't know how..."

"You will receive instructions on precisely how to take control of the station or sabotage it," the woman said, briskly. There was no doubt at all in her tone. "You and your men will have the highest level of security clearance available – barely underneath Admiral Singh's picked cadre of officers. Taking the vital locations on the station from the inside should be simple enough – and should you succeed, you will have automatic control of the weapons platforms surrounding the station."

Trevor shivered with a mixture of anticipation and fear. Anticipation because all of the planning and recruitment was finally going to find a focus; fear, because the whole operation could easily go wrong. He wasn't a violent man and knew too many who were. If Admiral Singh's security forces caught up with him, they wouldn't have to work hard to get him to talk.

"I understand," he said, swallowing hard. "And what if I get caught."

"Danielle will be out of the city by the time the shit hits the fan," the woman informed him. "We will do what we can to get you out of their cells, should they find you, but it may take some time."

Trevor nodded. After the upset the security forces had suffered – the complete blackout on information had only encouraged rumours, each one crazier than the last, to spread through the system – they'd be desperate for a victory. If they caught up with him…they'd use him to break open his cell. It was funny, he realised, how such a victory really wouldn't lead them very far. He knew no one outside his cell apart from Danielle and the woman facing him.

"I understand," he said, flatly. "I won't let you down."

"Good," the woman said. She pulled a datachip out of her pocket and passed it to him. "You'll find most of the information you need on this chip, buried in the memory layers. The password is your wife's maiden name, but we suggest you change it as soon as possible. In theory, the chip should pass scrutiny as yet another instruction manual…"

Trevor nodded, feeling cold ice congealing around his heart as he took the chip. Hiding data in a chip's memory layers was hard to detect without specialised equipment or knowledge – but he had a feeling that the security officers would test out any chip that fell into their hands, no matter how legitimate it seemed. And then he would be dead.

"Meet your team tomorrow, before you get shuttled back to orbit, and go over the plan then," the woman added. "Remember, the interior of the orbital stations are heavily monitored. One careless word and you'll be in deep shit. *Do not* forget that."

"I won't," Trevor promised. He hesitated, then asked a different question. "What will happen after…you know."

"I hope that everything will return to normal," the woman said. "But whatever else happens, you and your family will be safe."

She smiled, although it didn't quite touch her eyes. "Go say goodbye to your wife," she ordered. "You won't see her again until after the coup."

Jasmine watched Trevor Chambers go, feeling an odd pang of envy at how he obviously cared for his wife. He was mad at Danielle – it didn't take much perception to realise that – and yet he still loved her. Danielle was a lucky woman, luckier than she deserved; Jasmine wasn't sure what *she* would have done to anyone who convinced her that her children were dead, but it wouldn't have been pretty.

She looked down at the datapad on the table, then stood up, stuffing it into one of her pockets. Trevor Chambers held the most important task in the planned operation, more important than even the one Jasmine had assigned to herself and the rest of the team. It galled her to rely so much on a civilian – she would have been happier dealing with a Civil Guardsman – but there was no choice. It would be tricky to have the Marines moved up into orbit, even if she hadn't had other tasks for them on the ground. They still had to trap Admiral Singh, after all.

And complete the rest of the illusion, Jasmine thought, sourly. She'd been taught to avoid elaborate plans when she'd been studying at the Slaughterhouse; the more that could go wrong, the more that was *likely* to go wrong. But Admiral Singh was just too powerful to take on in a straight fight, even if the planet itself wasn't at risk. She needed to knock the Admiral off balance and then checkmate her before she recovered.

She walked towards the second door and stepped through, smiling as she saw Blake standing there. His constant presence was still a little irritating, but as she'd recovered she'd felt better for having him there. The doctor had insisted that she take plenty of rest – and Blake had threatened to sit on her, just to make sure she did – in-between plotting the Admiral's defeat. It was irritating too, but what could she do?

Blake leaned forward, as if he hadn't been listening to the conversation. "Mission accomplished?"

"I think so," Jasmine said. "He should do as he was told."

It had taken liberal use of the CYA code as well as Patterson's servitude to get most of the cell members primed to go to orbit. The plan was going well and Jasmine distrusted it; every time a plan was going perfectly, she'd been told, it was about to go spectacularly wrong. Horn had told her that the various security forces had been badly disrupted – and Jasmine had worked hard to make that disruption worse – but what if Admiral Singh was quietly preparing her retaliation?

"I hope you're right," Blake said. "What about the rest of the cells?"

"They can get their advanced training in the next two weeks," Jasmine said. Luckily, the CYA code could make people disappear from the records – or appear to be part of the security forces. As long as they didn't attract the attention of the Admiral's senior officers, they should be fine. "And they should be ready by then."

She scowled. Most of the Marines outside the city had been brought inside to help plan the final offensive, but she'd left Sergeant Harris outside, tasked with finding the hostage camp. Once located, the camp could be taken – and then the hostages could be used as bargaining chips. If everything went well, most of Admiral Singh's followers would sit on their hands and wait to see who came out on top.

And if it doesn't, she thought, grimly, *we will just have to improvise.*

Her lips quirked into a smile as she stepped outside. If nothing else, Admiral Singh's self-confidence was about to take a nasty blow.

Lukas stepped inside the lobby and, out of habit, took one of the masks from the basket and donned it before walking further into the building. A masked man nodded in approval and motioned for him to enter a large room, big enough to hold nearly a hundred young men. There were at least fifty people standing inside, he realised as he walked through the door, all wearing masks. Their faces were hidden, naturally, but he was sure that they all seemed both excited and nervous. Just how many of them, he asked himself, had been involved in the riots that had consumed the red light district.

"Welcome," a voice said, after the rest of the group had assembled. Another masked man stood at the front of the room, standing on a small stool that lifted him head and shoulders above the crowd. "You should all be aware that you are now officially trainees for the security division, a subset of Internal Security. Your ID cards will be passed out as you leave – just show them to any recruiting officer and they should leave you alone."

Lukas smiled. He had no idea how the plotters had managed to obtain the cards – although the crime lords might have helped, as they couldn't be pleased with how they'd been attacked over the last few days – but they'd be very helpful. If they seemed to have an official excuse for not being conscripts, it was unlikely that they would be hassled too much. Or so he hoped.

"The purpose of this meeting is to teach you how to use the SI-56 and prepare you for action," the man continued. "You will probably not have received any formal weapons training in your lives prior to Admiral Singh's arrival. The SI-56, thankfully, is a very simple weapon and with a few days of training you should be able to use it with reasonable competence. *Do not* attempt to take any of the weapons out of this building. They will be prepared for you when the time comes for action."

Lukas groaned – and heard several others making the same sound. They *wanted* the weapons, they *wanted* to feel powerful – as powerful as the guardsmen, when they were pushing the civilians around. But the tutor was right; if they happened to be caught with the weapons, they would be arrested and interrogated savagely. He'd heard enough since he'd joined the rebel cells to doubt his ability to remain silent indefinitely.

The tutor knelt down and picked up a simple cloth bag, opening it up to reveal the assault rifle. "This is the Standard Issue Assault Rifle, designed originally for soldiers who could only be given a few weeks of training before being thrown into battle," he explained. "You will notice that the rounds – the bullets – are supplied in sealed clips. This was intended to allow magazines to be interchangeable and – more importantly – to prevent idiots trying to mess around with the propellant. The Civil Guard was full of idiots who thought that trying to dissemble a loaded clip was a good idea."

There were some faint chuckles, but most of the crowd were just staring at the weapon.

"You take the weapon apart, like so" – the man demonstrated – "and then clean every last component using the oil that we will supply. Thousands of years of workmanship has gone into designing and building this weapon, which will all be wasted unless the user remembers to clean it every so often. Whenever you have a free moment, strip down your weapon, clean it and then put it back together again. Later, once you have the hang of it, I will personally whip anyone who fails to keep their weapons clean."

He put the weapon back together and held it up. "You insert the magazine clip here, through the handle," he said. There was a sharp *click* as it slotted into place. "The weapon is now loaded. If you see the lever here, you'll notice that it has three settings; safe, single-shot and rapid-fire. Keep your weapon on safe unless you are about to use it. Anyone stupid enough to ignore that instruction will be beaten half to death and then thrown out. And I am *not* joking.

"When using single-shot, you fire one bullet at a time," the tutor continued. "When switching to rapid-fire, you can burn through your entire clip in seconds. You should be aware that accurate aiming is almost impossible under such circumstances…"

Lukas listened as the explanation wore on, trying to commit everything to memory. They said that it was a simple weapon – and yet there was so much to learn, backed up by threats of grievous bodily harm if they made a single mistake. By the time they were allowed to finally hold a weapon for themselves, he was too keyed up to enjoy it.

"The green-coloured magazine clips contain training ammunition," the tutor explained, once they'd practiced taking the weapon apart and then putting it back together. "It provides all of the experience, without actually firing bullets. The Civil Guard used to believe that was sufficient for actual training and only issued live ammunition when the guardsmen were sent into actual combat. We're not that foolish, but it will allow you a chance to get used to pulling the trigger without actually firing off real bullets."

One of the boys hesitated. "Sir," he asked, "what if someone *hears* us?"

The tutor chuckled. "It took you long enough to ask," he said, dryly. "This building is soundproofed, fortunately. Later, when you're outside, firing off weapons will probably attract attention."

Lukas felt himself flushing. It had honestly never occurred to him to question their security – and it should have done. What if they'd been caught because they didn't check for sound-proofing? Or what if the ammunition produced a smell that could be easily detected – and recognised? Or what if...?

He looked over at the tutor, but the man didn't see his look.

"Now, load up the training ammunition," the tutor ordered, instead. He seemed disinclined to discuss the issue of security further. "And then we can try out some *real* bullets."

CHAPTER FORTY

> Only when the governed feel that they have a stake in how their society is governed can society survive, no matter how much 'legitimacy' it claims. It took centuries for the lack of that stake to eventually destroy the Empire. How long would it take for the far smaller Commonwealth to be destroyed if that stake didn't exist?
> -Professor Leo Caesius, *Authority, Power and the Post-Imperial Era*

"Is the weather this bad on Avalon?"

Sergeant Chester Harris looked over at Kate as she crawled forward, the endless downpour soaking its way through chinks in her waterproof garments. Like him, she looked like a drowned rat, rather than one half of a happy couple enjoying a romantic walk in the countryside.

"It can be worse at times," Harris shouted back to her, as they slipped and stumbled onwards. "You should see the Badlands."

Lightning flashed, followed rapidly by a wave of thunder that blotted out her reply. Harris gritted his teeth and pressed onwards, reminding himself of the origin of the term 'Marine.' It had been a very long time since the Marines had been a wet-navy service; indeed, outside of intensive swimming and water operations courses on the Slaughterhouse, he'd never used a boat. But hadn't there been Terran Marines who had?

The pathway grew treacherous as they inched their way between the two mountains, heading into the hidden valley. Water ran down from both sides of the valley, washing past them and threatening to send them falling helplessly towards the lake at the bottom of the valley. Chester was only dimly aware of small furry animals running past them, a handful squeaking in dismay as they sensed the two humans. From what he'd been told, the animals made good eating, if they could be caught. Seven hundred years of settlement had taught the animals that it was a good idea to stay well away from humans who might want to kill and eat them.

Kate found brief shelter under an overhanging rock and, after a moment, Chester joined her, taking advantage of the pause to wring as much water as possible out of his sodden clothes. They had planned to tell anyone who caught them that they were on a romantic walk, but somehow Chester found it impossible to believe that *anyone* would believe that story, not when they were completely drenched in water. Smart couples would probably have holed up somewhere and waited for the rain to stop. It wasn't an option for them.

He looked over at her and saw her manage a smile. "I think we can go onwards now," she said, reluctantly. "The rain will cover us, won't it?"

Chester nodded. If the camp they were approaching was anything like as important as Lieutenant Yamane had suggested, the enemy would have it constantly patrolled and monitored by distributed sensors. Even the best of them, however, would be disrupted by the rain, making it harder for the enemy guards to sense their approach. And in this weather, drones would be even more unreliable. He re-donned his plastic hat, smiled at her, and stepped back out into the rain. In the few seconds they had used to rest, it seemed that the path had managed to become even worse.

A final volley of thunder echoed across the sky and then the rain slowly began to come to an end. Chester grinned at Kate and led her onwards, finally reaching a vantage point they could use to peer down into the valley – and see the camp that Admiral Singh had hidden from prying eyes. Chester lay down on the ground, motioned for her to do the same and pulled his binoculars out of the bag. Thankfully, the bag had lived up to its promise and protected his tools from the water.

"All right," he muttered to himself, as he put the binoculars to his eyes. "Let's see what we have here."

For a moment, the sight of the camp confused him. Marines knew how to establish POW camps; they really needed little more than some wire, a few tents and a handful of guardposts. Even the Civil Guard would have had little difficulty in establishing a basic prison camp. But this was weird. The wire surrounded a handful of small houses, several with their own private swimming pools. If it hadn't been for the guard towers, with the guards clearly staring inwards, into the camp, he would have wondered if he'd made a mistake.

"That's a very odd prison camp," Kate said, in disbelief. "Do you think that the prisoners even *want* to leave?"

Chester snorted, rudely. No doubt Admiral Singh had plenty of unpleasant penal camps for people she wanted to keep prisoner, but the men, women and children in the hostage camp were people she needed to keep reasonably sweet. The camp – it had probably been a luxury resort before Admiral Singh had arrived – would keep everyone in decent shape; hell, given enough food, drink and entertainment, they could probably forget that they were hostage, held prisoner to ensure the good behaviour of their relatives.

He scowled as he tried to contemplate how many people might live in the camp. It was easily large enough to accommodate over a thousand hostages, but that wouldn't have been very comfortable, let alone luxurious. Each of the houses, he calculated, could probably hold around twenty to thirty hostages; it would be cramped, but survivable. No doubt the younger children saw it as an endless vacation rather than a deadly serious prison camp. He panned his binoculars over the lakeside, studying the small barracks that presumably held the staff. If they were being used to hold prisoners too…it would add another hundred or so to the overall figure. It seemed surprisingly low, somehow.

"Kids," Kate said, softly. "They have *kids* held hostage."

"Best sort of hostage," Chester grunted. Man's inhumanity to man no longer surprised him. "And Admiral Singh wouldn't miss such a simple trick."

He scowled as he saw the children running down towards the lake. Children were less experienced than adults, less capable of thinking up workable escape plans…and it was harder for anyone short of an outright sociopath to purposely put their lives in danger. All of Admiral Singh's unwilling allies would be very reliable indeed as long as they thought that their children were under threat.

The younger kids looked happy, as if they were unaware of the true nature of their accommodations. He looked at the older kids, including a number of teenagers, and scowled again as he realised that they knew the truth. There was something in the way they moved that suggested that they knew their lives hung by a thread, no matter how much they enjoyed being surrounded by luxury and playing on the lake. Absently, he wondered if the local doctors were prescribing rebalancing treatments for the children. It might have helped keep them under control.

"Poor bastards," he muttered. "Trapped in a luxury prison camp."

He studied the rest of the camp, paying careful attention to the guards. There were eight towers, spaced out around the perimeter; their weapons were pointed inwards, towards the prisoners. The camp itself was surrounded by two layers of wire, each one designed more to keep people in than out. Typically, there was only one entrance, guarded by a blocky guardhouse and several emplaced machine guns. It just didn't look very secure to him.

"Three men in combat suits could take it out in moments," he said, wishing that they *had* combat suits. Unfortunately, their raids on armouries hadn't yielded anything more dangerous than grenades and mortars. Admiral Singh seemed to believe that her garrisons in the field didn't need anything more to hold their positions and keep the countryside under control. "Failing that..."

A thought struck him and he panned the binoculars across the camp again. "Where do the guards live?"

"They could live in the guardhouse," Kate said. She shook her head a moment later. "It's too small, isn't it?"

"Yeah," Chester said. "Even if they're doubling up, it's still too small to house them all."

He studied the camp, trying to solve the mystery. No matter how he looked at it, the camp just didn't seem to have enough living space, not enough to keep both the guards and the hostages sheltered from the rain. Maybe there was a smaller camp, a place for the guards, not too far away. That would make a certain amount of sense; the guards could be rotated in and out of the region every so often, as well as keeping reinforcements within shouting distance.

"We'll have to find out," he said. "Or it will explode in our faces at the worst possible moment."

It wasn't hard to devise an attack plan for the camp, he realised; the wire just wasn't designed to keep out a serious attack. They'd have to check for landmines and other unpleasant surprises, but judging from what he could see, there weren't any scattered between the two fences sealing the camp off from the outside world. Not that mines were *meant* to be visible, of course; they'd have to shake the ground before they risked transporting the hostages out and into the countryside. But the mystery of where most of the guards actually slept kept bothering him until they inched away, further down the valley.

"There," Kate said, with heavy satisfaction. "*That's* where they sleep."

Chester nodded as he studied the second camp. It was much more like a proper prison camp, making him wonder if the enemy commanders were ever tempted to move the hostages into their camp and use the luxury camp for themselves. If they were anything like some of the Imperial Army commanders he'd met, they'd probably been tempted to move *themselves* into the luxury camp…the thought made him smile as he surveyed the camp, considering possible angles of attack. Overrunning the camp would be costly, but it would be simple enough to keep the guardsmen pinned down until it was too late for them to intervene.

"Tell me," Kate said, "have your Marines ever had to guard a camp of hostages?"

"No," Chester said, stiffly. "Marines are just too damn capable to be wasted on guarding prisoners. Once we take them prisoner, we send them to the Civil Guard."

The thought made him scowl. Abusing prisoners was against regulations – which hadn't always stopped the Civil Guard abusing prisoners in their custody. A number of prisoners who had been handed over to the Civil Guard on Han had vanished, suggesting that they had been murdered by the guardsmen; eventually, the Marines and Imperial Army officers had taken to demanding receipts for the prisoners, ensuring that prisoners who had been killed in custody didn't vanish without trace.

"And that doesn't always work out for us," he added, remembering some of the teenage girls in the hostage camp. "I wonder what the Admiral does to keep them in line."

"Perhaps she takes their families hostage too," Kate suggested.

Chester considered it as they slipped away from the camps and back towards the mountains, keeping a careful eye out for roving patrols. It was easy to imagine that the guardsmen wouldn't bother to mount patrols around the camps, but he knew better than to rely on it, not when all of the tactical manuals insisted that roving patrols sent out at random intervals were the best way to prevent the enemy from amassing an attack force near the place you were meant to be guarding, let alone carrying out surveillance on a potential target. He kept one eye on the sky as they crawled further away from the camp, looking for watching drones, but saw nothing. The enemy seemed to be playing dumb and he didn't like it.

He stopped a moment later, holding up a hand as he heard *something* moving through the underbrush. There were feet tramping towards him; quickly, he motioned for Kate to get off the half-ruined path and into hiding behind a bush. He followed her a moment later, just before a line of guardsmen appeared and walked past where they were hiding. They looked just as drowned as Chester felt, water dripping off their sodden uniforms as they marched past, heading down towards the camp. It didn't seem that they were very alert.

Not that it would be easy to stay on alert in a rainstorm, he thought, sourly. *I wonder where they found shelter…*

They encountered two more patrols as they moved around the mountain and back down into the forest, the second almost coming close enough to surprise them before they managed to hide. None of the patrolling guardsmen looked very enthusiastic, unsurprisingly. They knew how vulnerable a single patrol was to the insurgents, even if there hadn't been any attacks on the garrisons near the mountains. Chester, who had been helping plan the attacks, hadn't known that there was anything worth attacking nearby until the Lieutenant had discovered the existence of the hostage camp.

Once they were inside the forest, they moved down into the hidden pathways and made their way towards the camp. Chester had been astonished to discover just how many men were hidden from enemy view under the trees, even though his previous experience should have suggested that a small army could hide in the forest. But then, the bandits on Avalon and the insurgents on Corinthian both had good reasons to want to hide. At least Admiral Singh's forces weren't trying to sweep through the forests yet, although Chester doubted that it would be long before they started trying. They just needed to boost their manpower first.

The camp itself was carefully hidden, its few power sources shielded to prevent detection and its occupants scattered around under camouflage netting. Chester allowed himself a smile as the insurgents came up to greet him, looking around at their beaming faces. Most of them had *known* that they didn't stand a chance until the Marines had arrived, even though they had been almost impossible for Admiral Singh to eradicate completely. Now, they felt that they could fight back and win.

"It's good to be back," Chester assured them. "Were there any changes to our orders from Landing City?"

"None," Lori said. The farmer's daughter had effectively taken over communications, although it mainly consisted of picking up messages passed from courier to courier and transporting them back to the camp. They didn't dare use radios or even microburst transmitters anywhere near their camp, not when it might attract attention and call in a KEW strike from orbit. Several early insurgent camps had been destroyed through not observing strict communications security. "Your boss just sent a brief update."

Chester took the datapad and skimmed through it, noting the various code phases that stated that Lieutenant Yamane and the others were still alive and not operating under any form of duress. That was a relief; the countryside insurgents hadn't shared the location of their bases with anyone from the city, but he'd still been worried when he'd heard that the Lieutenant had been captured. Who knew *what* piece of useful information would point the enemy towards their camps?

"So we move ahead as scheduled," he said. "I see."

He scowled. *That* was going to be tricky; assuming the enemy kept maintaining the same patrol patterns, it would be hard to slip an entire force into attack range without being noticed. And, after all the attacks they'd launched in the past month, they would have real problems taking out a patrol without sounding alarms all over the continent. They couldn't gamble on another rainstorm coming at just the right moment. Marines could have done it, he was sure, but most of the insurgents had no real training at all, just raw talent.

"We'll have to move additional weapons into place," he said, concealing his thoughts. It would take several days to move the supply dumps closer to the camp, then they'd have to crawl through the mountains at the dead of night. "And then we will have to risk taking out the patrols."

Lori led him back to the heart of the camp and pulled out the maps. Thankfully, the maps the insurgents possessed were actually up-to-date, which made a nice change from some of the maps they'd had to use for tactical planning in the past. There was nothing marked on the maps, of course, but he knew where some of the bases were located. Tapping each point, he talked them through the first version of the plan and then listened as they offered suggestions and improvements. They might not have had the training, but they did have far more experience with the local terrain than any of the Marines. Their insights were often helpful.

"We need to get the hostages out alive," he said. "And we have to make sure that everyone knows what's happened."

Lieutenant Yamane's orders had been very clear. The hostages had to be liberated – and then their freedom had to be announced on the radio and over the planetary datanet. Doing that *would* attract attention; it was quite possible that Admiral Singh would call in a KEW strike, just out of spite. Her empire would be on the verge of falling apart.

"Should be doable," Lori said, finally. "Do you think we can get anyone into the enemy camp?"

Chester shook his head. The guards watching the hostages, according to the Lieutenant, were a special force, reporting directly to Admiral Singh. No matter what papers any new guardsmen had, they could expect to be heavily questioned when they arrived – and if there was no confirmation from their ultimate superior, they would be captured or executed on the spot. It was just too dangerous to risk.

"No," he said, tiredly. "We'll just have to do it the old-fashioned way."

He smiled. "It should be fun," he added, more to reassure them rather than himself. "One way or another, Admiral Singh's regime will *not* survive."

CHAPTER
FORTY-ONE

> In essence, to look at a different example, Admiral Singh's government lacked even the checks and balances possessed by the Empire. It was, in effect, a pyramid structure, with the Admiral on top and her senior officers just below, each one wielding vast power that came directly from her. However, it had no protections against either incompetence or arbitrary decision-making at the top; even the Empire, in its mixture of patron-client relationships, had more checks and balances. And, maintained as it was by force, it would eventually either be destroyed by greater force or rot away from within.
> -Professor Leo Caesius, *Authority, Power and the Post-Imperial Era*

"This is a new contract," Tam said, as the crewmen started to load the sealed pallets into *Lightfoot's* hold. "It is vitally important that nothing goes wrong."

Mandy nodded, staring down at the datapad. The contract seemed to be a waste of HE3; why would *anyone* hire an interstellar freighter to ship supplies to a handful of defence stations in orbit around their homeworld? But most of the freighters Admiral Singh had under her command had headed out of orbit four days ago, after taking on a vast amount of supplies for an undisclosed mission. Reading between the lines, Mandy suspected that she was looking at a fleet train being formed.

"It won't," she assured him, feeling a tiny stab of guilt at manipulating him. After the pirates, manipulating Tam was easy, although she was careful not to say anything without thinking first. A single word out of place could blow her cover. "We're being paid too much to allow something to go wrong."

Tam smiled at her weak joke. "Definitely," he said, firmly. "Next time, *you* can take me to dinner."

Mandy smiled back, then went back to supervising the loading. She had wondered how she was meant to slip the pallets from *Harrington* onto the defence stations, but now she knew; Jasmine had somehow ensured that *Lightfoot* received a legitimate contract that allowed her to dock at the defence stations. And, with their new status, it was unlikely that they would be searched thoroughly, which was a relief. If the enemy had discovered the weapons, they'd know that something was badly wrong.

"Done," she said, finally. "Are you going to be coming with us?"

Tam shook his head. "I have a logistics exam in half an hour," he admitted. "If I pass, I may be promoted."

"You deserve to be promoted," Mandy told him, trying to think of how she could pry more information from the young man. A logistics exam suggested that Admiral Singh felt that she needed more logistics officers. And *that* suggested that she intended to expand her empire again. "Good luck."

"Thank you," Tam said.

He gave her a quick peck on the cheek and walked off, leaving her staring after him. She took one last glance at the datapad, ran her eyes down where the pallets had been stowed, and then headed towards the bridge. Once there, she could take her ship out of the loading station and head for their first destination. And then another piece of the plan would slip into place.

Tam's a nice boy, she thought she heard her mother say. *You might like him.*

Mandy shook her head, tiredly. Tam *was* nice – but her job was to help overthrow the regime that had put him in a position of trust. Maybe he'd still be nice afterwards or maybe he was a bully towards freighter crews that didn't happen to have pretty commanders. Quite a few of the unwilling volunteers who'd worked for the pirates had gone to work for the Commonwealth Navy, afterwards; maybe Tam could do the same. Or maybe he'd be killed when the shit hit the fan.

She stepped onto the bridge and nodded to the helmsman. "Bring up the drive," she ordered, "and then tell them that we're on our way to our first destination."

Trevor's first sight of the orbital defence station had left him with an impression of thunderous power that lingered in his mind, even after he and his crew had started to explore the interior of the station. Defence Station II had enough firepower to match a squadron of battleships and enough armour to stand off a savage attack, as well as projectors capable of generating three or four gravity shields at a time. Maybe the station wasn't invincible, but it did seem almost powerful enough to check an advance on the planet by itself.

It wasn't until they'd explored the innards of the station that he'd realised that the design had its weaknesses. As long as someone held the command centre, the power core and the armoury, they could hold the entire station, at least until someone on the outside could bring in enough firepower to melt through hullmetal and recapture the station. The heavy weapons the outsiders would need to break through the sealed airlocks were simply not stored on the station, something that had puzzled him until he'd asked the XO. She'd pointed out, rather sardonically, that Admiral Singh's men had used heavy weapons to take over Trafalgar's support stations and she didn't want someone else doing the same to her.

The other vulnerable point lay in the station's datanet. It was as secure as the Imperial Navy could make it, but given the right command codes *anyone* could make the station sit up and beg. The designers had been paranoid enough to insist that the codes could only be used in the command centre, yet if someone happened to *take* the command centre... the thought made him smile, despite the nerves that threatened to overcome him. As long as they followed the plan, they should be able to secure the station before the command crew realised that something had gone wrong.

He watched, as dispassionately as he could, as the freighter settled into the dock. His crew – almost all of them were part of his cell, while the three who weren't were carefully kept in the dark – scrambled forward to open the hatches and release the pallets of missiles. Admiral Singh's senior officers had been working hard to beef up the planet's defences in recent months, he'd heard while he'd been on the industrial platforms, but no one actually knew why, although rumours were spreading like wildfire. Judging by what his wife's contact had said, it seemed that Admiral Singh intended to go back to war. Perhaps she felt that it would distract the population from considering the weaknesses in her system.

The freighter's commander looked almost absurdly young for her role, although *that* wasn't uncommon under Admiral Singh. She was pretty enough to force Trevor to remind himself that he was a married man; her shipsuit was tight enough for him not to care. He took the datapad she held out to him, carefully noted the location of the extra pallet, and then signed for the official pallets. Once she took the datapad back, he started to bark orders to his crew, taking care to ensure that cell members took the additional pallet. Their weapons had arrived.

He gritted his teeth at the thought. Part of him had hoped that it would all be cancelled, that he wouldn't have to keep his word to his wife – and to her mystery contact. He'd feared that it was all a trick to expose disloyalty, or a power play within the regime rather than anything from outside the system, yet he hadn't dared do anything apart from follow orders. Now that their weapons had arrived, it was clear that they were committed…

But I was always committed, he thought, numbly. *The moment I saw Danielle again, I was committed.*

He glanced down at his wristcom, noting the date. Four days; four days until the shit hit the fan, four days until he would be expected to take command of Defence Station II or die trying. It just seemed impossible, even though cold logic told him that it would be relatively simple, assuming everything worked properly. And if it didn't…he'd tried to imagine contingency plans, but he just didn't have the background to be sure that he'd covered everything that could possibly go wrong. What if he'd missed something important?

Shaking his head, he returned to supervising his crew. The extra pallet was already on its way to his quarters, where it would be opened and the contents distributed when it was time to move. Until then, he could do nothing...but wait and pray.

"There have been no new security alerts, apart from the persistent shots in the red light zone," Patterson reported. "I've had additional soldiers moving up to provide cover for the patrols – hopefully, we can discourage the criminals from pushing back too hard."

Rani nodded, absently. The attack plans for the Commonwealth lay in front of her, followed by detailed reports from the tactical planners who had organised the fleet train. Compared to that, the persistent attacks on her people seemed unimportant. She was finally going to war against a genuine opponent!

"Good," she said, when it became clear that Patterson was waiting for a response. "Do you think that we can keep them in check indefinitely?"

"I'd prefer to sweep the entire district and arrest everyone inside," Patterson said, briskly. "If not, however, we can probably keep the area under control for a few more weeks."

"See to it," Rani said. The red light district was becoming a headache; the crime lords couldn't match her in a direct confrontation, so they were doing their best to launch a series of small attacks on her forces, just to remind her that she couldn't crush them completely. She was seriously tempted to forget that she needed the red light district and just send in the troops, but she didn't have time to worry about it now. The attack was about to begin. "Once the Commonwealth is crushed, we can move on and deal with the criminals from a position of strength."

"They have to be losing revenue," Patterson offered. "Just losing their customers will cost them plenty of money."

Rani nodded. Crime lords *needed* to maintain a constant flow of money to keep their positions; it had been why it had been so easy to subvert them, back when she'd taken their world. But now their defiance had brought them into open confrontation with her – and she wasn't going to lift the blockade on the red light district until they came crawling to her and begged for mercy. For a start, she had already decided, they could hand over their contacts with the insurgency for her interrogators. And after that…she hadn't decided, but they would have to *work* to regain her favour.

"It's possible that some of their subordinates will take over," Patterson added. "If we made a sweet enough offer…"

"Offer them a strong position in the post-war world," Rani ordered. She *needed* the red light district – and it didn't really matter who ran it, as long as it was run properly and the insurgents were kept out. "And make sure they understand that they will be expected to be loyal."

"They're loyal to their money," Patterson said. "Anything else would be unlikely."

Rani sighed and turned back to the attack plans. The Imperial Navy's planners had never had to worry about a fleet train, but then the Imperial Navy's battleships hadn't faced other battleships for thousands of years. No one was entirely sure just how much firepower the Commonwealth possessed – Trafalgar had been the closest base with any battleships on permanent station – but Rani dared not assume that they were *weak*. And if her battleships shot their magazines dry, they'd be nothing more than big expensive targets for enemy missiles.

Typically, the ammunition ships the Imperial Navy had designed had been intended for its lighter units, the workhorses of the fleet, rather than battleships. Rani had had to order fifty freighters converted into support ships, just to ensure that she had enough missiles on hand to meet any conceivable requirement, and then redesign several more to allow her to tranship missiles into the battleships. When the time came to design newer battleships, she promised herself, they would be constructed to make it easier to reload outside a shipyard. How had the Imperial Navy not realised that was a dangerous thing to overlook?

Because the battleships were never actually tested against a serious threat, she thought, answering her own question. *They weren't deployed against most rebels because that would have been smashing flies with sledgehammers.*

She looked up, realising that Patterson was still there. "Yes?"

"I have finalised plans for the security reformatting," Patterson said. "Do you wish to inspect them?"

"Later," Rani said. "For the moment, I have work to do here."

She watched Patterson go, then turned back to the attack plans. A little fiddling here and there, she told herself, and then they could go to work. And then she'd be back in space at the head of her fleet, where she belonged. She didn't dare trust any of her subordinates, even Sampson, with that much firepower. Besides, with the divided command structure on Corinthian, her subordinates would be too busy busting their balls to prove themselves loyal in her absence, rather than plotting against her.

So tell me, Bainbridge, she thought, coldly. *What would you think of me if you could see me now?*

Bainbridge had had to die; if there were any remaining loyalists on Trafalgar, he might have proved himself a rallying point for a counter-mutiny. It had been quick, which was more than he'd deserved. Rani had spent her first few months of exile devising ever more unpleasant ways for the corrupt and well-connected officer to die. But in the end, he'd taken a bullet through the head. There had been no time for indulging herself.

You'd hate me, she thought, feeling a flicker of grim amusement. *What have you done, in all of your life, that matches what I have done?*

Jasmine sat on the rooftop and peered upwards into the darkness, watching as lights moved rapidly across the sky. Corinthian had never lost the ability to reach space, unlike several worlds that had joined the Commonwealth after they'd been liberated from the pirates, and had been settled long enough for low orbit to be filled with industrial and habitat stations. It was hard to pick out the real stars against the orbital band of light...

She pushed the thought aside, rubbing her eyes. Everything was prepared now, or so she thought; the cells were active, weapons had been distributed and H-Hour was barely four hours away, when Sergeant Harris would lead the assault on the hostage camp. After that...Jasmine knew that her remaining cells were ready to start their attacks, both real and diversionary, but she had no idea how many of them would perform, when the shit hit the fan. Even the planners on Han had known more about their forces than she did about theirs.

Keep It Simple, Stupid, she reminded herself, although in truth she had avoided anything *simple* when she'd devised the plan. The more elements involved, the more that could go wrong…even timing might be a problem when they were operating over several different time zones. Thankfully, Corinthian – like the Commonwealth worlds – used Imperial Standard Time as well as local time. Everything should go off at the right time.

She scowled as she stood up, fishing through her pocket for a stimulant. Using drugs anywhere near combat was normally forbidden, but she didn't see any choice. She hadn't had much time to rest over the last few days, even though she'd insisted that Blake and the others get as much sleep as they could. Afterwards, when the mission was completed, she promised herself that she would sleep for a week. If they held the orbitals under their control, as well as the insurgent cells, the rest of the planet would be theirs too.

And then the locals would have to put their planet together again…

Jasmine chewed the stimulant slowly, shaking her head at the thought. It was quite likely that the operation would fail – or succeed imperfectly. There would be time enough to worry about the future after Corinthian was secure and Admiral Singh was dead. It was far too possible that the locals would fight a civil war afterwards, but…she shook her head again. There was no point in worrying until after the Admiral was dead. It would just distract her from fighting the coming battle.

Walking over to the hatch, she dropped down into the building, nearly landing on top of a pair of rebels. They'd been outfitted with guardsmen uniforms, complete with a yellow armband to identify them to other friendly forces, as well as enough weapons to fight a minor war. They both straightened when they saw her, coming to a parody of attention that probably owed its existence to bad war movies. Jasmine smiled, returned their makeshift salutes and headed onwards. The final state of the operation was about to begin.

Blake stuck his head out of the door, nodding to her. He was meant to be sleeping, Jasmine reminded herself, but it looked as though he couldn't sleep either.

"Get your body armour and weapons here," he carolled. "Hurry up before they're all gone."

Jasmine surprised herself by laughing. "Thank you," she said, as she stepped into the room. Carl was sitting at one of the desks, painstakingly counting out bullet magazines they'd stolen from the guardsmen. "Are we ready?"

"As ready as we'll ever be," Blake said. "And most of the enemy forces are surrounding the red light district."

Jasmine grinned. Hopefully, that would keep most of the Admiral's forces busy until it was far too late.

"Good," she said. She took a piece of body armour and buckled it on, silently cursing the guardsman who'd designed it under her breath. The bastard hadn't seen the wisdom of designing armour for people with breasts. She picked up a rifle and grinned at them. "Shall we go?"

CHAPTER FORTY-TWO

> But this should not have been surprising. Admiral Singh, denied the chance to rise to a position matching her abilities by the Empire, saw fit to create one where she would be the prime determinate of everything that happened. As such, the system was highly personalised – and lacked any provisions for the succession. But then, Admiral Singh had no interest in looking past her death.
> -Professor Leo Caesius, *Authority, Power and the Post-Imperial Era*

"Dawn," Chester said, grimly. "Is everyone in position?"

"I think so," Kate said. She'd become his *de facto* XO. "What happens if they're not?"

"We're in deep trouble," Chester said. He'd coordinated attacks without communication systems during exercises, but never during actual wartime. If someone was out of place, the fog of war would hide the fact until it was far too late. "On my mark, launch the flare."

He scowled as he peered down at the hostage camp. They'd done all the preparations they could, but common sense told him that Murphy was probably going to put in an appearance. His plan to use mortars to shell the space between the two fences had had to be abandoned, just out of fear that the shells would fall into the camp itself. He didn't dare risk harming any of the hostages.

And the guards won't be that constrained, he thought, looking at the guard towers. A single command and the heavy weapons they'd mounted on the towers would rip through the camp, killing or wounding most of the hostages. *We have to take them out before the command can be issued.*

He gritted his teeth, then looked over at Kate. "Launch the flare," he ordered.

Kate lifted the flare gun, pointed it into the sky and pulled the trigger. There was a green flash of light as the flare was launched into the sky, then ignited, casting an eerie green light over the hostage camp. A moment later, the RPG teams opened fire, lobbing missiles into the guard towers and blowing them apart. The snipers, meanwhile, went after every guard foolish enough to stand out in the open.

Harris flipped his radio on and barked a command. "Drop shells on the guardhouse," he snapped. They'd positioned the mortars close enough to fire, but nowhere near close enough for the gunners to actually see their targets. He'd calculated the firing angles as best as he could, yet it was still a risk. There just wasn't any other choice. "Now!"

A brilliant flash of light blasted up from where the guardhouse had been, followed rapidly by two more. The first had come down within bare meters of its target, he realised, but the other two had made direct hits, punching through the concrete and utterly destroying the guardhouse. A handful of shots were fired as guardsmen scrambled over from where they'd been visiting one of the hostage huts, only to be gunned down by the snipers. They'd clearly never expected a serious attack.

Maybe they were right, he thought, wryly. *They parcelled out the farmer hostages among the guardposts, not to a single camp. The camp was reserved for Admiral Singh's inmates.*

His radio buzzed. "We've got them pinned down in their camp," Jeff reported. He'd had some genuine military experience, enough that Chester had taken the risk of putting him in command of the detachment charged with keeping the rest of the guardsmen out of the fight. "But we can't go in after them!"

"Just keep them pinned down," Chester reminded him. The guard barracks were constructed from prefabricated blocks of cement, if he recalled correctly. Heavy weapons would rip them apart, but there was a distinct shortage of such weapons on Corinthian. "There's no point in killing the bastards."

He jumped down and led the charge towards the camp, pulling the cutting torch off his belt as he reached the fence. It would have been unbreakable to a person using only their bare hands, but the torch burned through the metal links as though they were made of paper. Quickly, he checked the space between the fences for mines, seeing no telltale signs of their presence. As soon as he was sure, he moved through the gap and cut open the next part of the fence.

"Get the recovery teams in now," he ordered, as he ran into the camp. "Hurry!"

He put his hands together and bellowed orders. "WE'RE HERE TO TAKE YOU OUT OF THIS CAMP," he shouted, in his best parade ground voice. "GET OUT NOW, HURRY!"

Several doors opened, revealing stunned faces who stared at him. "Get out," Chester snapped, angrily. The former hostages looked undecided. "The Admiral is going to have this place bombed soon."

That got their attention. The former hostages started to move out of their huts, really too slowly for Chester's liking. The insurgents grabbed them and pushed them towards the gap in the fence, leaving Chester to glance through the various houses and make sure that no one was left behind. Several of the hostages were hiding under their beds, as if they thought that it would give them some actual protection. Chester shouted at them to get moving, helping one middle-aged lady along with a kick, then moved on to the next place. Their beds would have provided about as much protection as armour made from paper.

He finished sweeping through the houses – it really was more like a resort than a prison camp – and then turned to follow the hostages out of the camp, just as a pair of aircraft flashed by overhead. Chester scowled – someone must have sent out an alert before they were killed – and then smiled as he saw a HVM climbing up to smash one of the aircraft out of the sky. The pilot didn't have time to eject before his aircraft exploded into a fireball, the debris spiralling down to crash somewhere on the other side of the mountains. He looked around for the second aircraft and saw nothing. The other pilot must have decided that discretion was the better part of valour.

Admiral Singh has to be looking down at us right now, he thought coldly, as he looked up into the early morning sky. The flames burning through parts of the camp would have been noticed even if there *hadn't* been a distress call. *I wonder what she's thinking.*

He considered it, running through the calculations yet again. If the nearest garrison was under attack, the troops pinned down, there wouldn't be any attack from *that* direction. That meant that Admiral Singh's next closest garrison was over forty minutes away, at least on the ground. In her place, he would have sent airborne infantry into the area, just to try to recover the hostages before it was too late. Or would she concluded that it was too late and that she might as well call in KEW strikes in the hopes of catching some of the insurgents?

But if she does that, she'll kill off her own hostages too, he thought. The very idea of human shields was enough to make him sick, but he had to admit that it was effective. If she fired on the wives and children of her personnel, she was likely to face a mutiny even without the rebels cells Lieutenant Yamane had been carefully fostering within enemy ranks. *All she can do is try to get reinforcements here as quickly as possible.*

They'd set up the recording studio in a small hut on the other side of the mountains, carefully hidden from enemy view. As soon as they arrived, Chester and the insurgents sorted out the most important hostages and pushed them in front of the cameras, ordering them to tell the world that they had been liberated. Once the messages were recorded, Chester uploaded them along a landline to a hidden transmitter, several miles away. There, they were automatically uploaded onto the datanet.

Ten minutes later, a streak of light fell down from the heavens and blasted the transmitter into atoms, but it was far too late. The damage had been done.

"Get the hostages back to the camp," he ordered, doing his best to ignore the shocked and screaming children. They were idiots, he realised; they hadn't even understood that they were captives. The adults had done them no favours trying to hide it from them, not when it left them ill-prepared for rescue. "Smack the kids if you have to, just get them well-hidden by the time the enemy comes for us."

He smiled, then sobered. They were throwing almost everything the insurgency had been able to muster at the enemy garrisons, fighting to keep them tied down. If Admiral Singh escaped death and regained control, she would come out ahead. The insurgency would have spent itself in one desperate day. He looked towards the west, seeing plumes of smoke rising up into the clear blue sky. The Admiral wouldn't be so strong after this day was concluded, he told himself. But if she won the battle, it might not matter.

Trevor's heart was beating so loudly that he was surprised that the others couldn't hear it as they reported to his cabin. He'd taken advantage of the days between the delivery of the weapons and H-Hour to ensure that they all knew what they were doing, but it had been very difficult without the ability to speak freely. Now, with time almost up, he passed out the weapons and tapped out orders on a sealed datapad.

"Good luck," he said, feeling so nervous that he could barely walk. Part of him thought that he was going to throw up. "Let's go."

He'd concealed the weapons in the toolboxes maintenance crewmen were expected to carry everywhere. Now, seven of his cellmates followed him, while the others headed down to the power core and the armoury. The command core wasn't actually *that* far from his quarters – he didn't rate a cabin in Officer Country – but it felt like thousands of miles as they walked towards their destination. He couldn't help feeling that he was being pushed along by events that were completely outside his control. His lips moved in silent prayer as they reached the airlock that separated the command core from the rest of the station. Once they were inside, they would be almost impossible to dig out before it was too late.

Here we go, he thought, as they stepped into the airlock. He reached into the toolbox and produced the stunner, just as the first airlock slammed shut behind them. A moment later, the second airlock hissed open, revealing the massive command core. Trevor sucked in a breath – the sight was hellishly impressive, no matter what else could be said about it – and lifted the stunner. They'd been warned, in no uncertain terms, to stun *everyone* and sort them out later. A single verbal command from the fortress's official command could blow the entire mission.

It was somehow difficult to press down on the trigger. The stunner seemed to be resisting him, almost as though it were a living thing in its own right, until someone turned to look at them. Her mouth dropped open; somehow, Trevor managed to fire the stunner at the same instant, sending her crumpling to the deck. A moment later, the rest of his cellmates followed suit, waving their stunners over the consoles, making sure that no one was missed. Twenty seconds after they entered the command core, it was theirs.

Trevor wanted to collapse, to sag with relief until he hit the deck himself, but there was no time. Instead, he reached into his toolbox, found a pre-prepared datachip and looked around for the slot on the command chair. According to the briefing, the command network's primary access point was right under the CO's ass. Trevor pulled back the cushion, wondering what sort of mindset had hidden the slot there, and slotted the datachip into the reader. There was a long moment when he worried that it might have failed – or that it had all been a test that had destroyed his career – and then the screen lit up with cool green letters.

ACCESS GRANTED, it read.

"Good work," one of his cellmates said. "What now?"

Trevor sat down at the main console. Like almost everything built by the Imperial Navy, it was standardised – although it was also more complex than anything else he'd seen in his career. If there had been more time to practice…but there hadn't been anything like enough time.

"We contact the ship," he said, activating the command network. So far, no one seemed to have noticed that the station had been taken over. "And then we trigger the internal security system."

The designers had expected a mutiny, it seemed. If triggered, the internal security system filled the station with knockout gas – apart from the most vital locations. A simple facemask could protect someone from the gas, if they thought to don them in time. He keyed the command sequence into the console, silently praying that it would work. A moment later, he looked through the security monitors and saw crewmen stumbling over and collapsing onto the deck. The station was theirs.

"No alert yet," another cellmate reported. "No one seems to have noticed that we've gone off the air."

"Good," Trevor said. He keyed another series of commands into the system. "And now we wait."

Mandy felt her blood running cold as *Lightfoot* powered its way towards the colossal defence station. They had the right codes and excuses to visit, but if someone noticed that something was wrong, they were in deep shit. One defence station might be under rebel control, yet the others weren't – yet – and there were still the automated weapons platforms. The freighter was a sitting duck so close to the planet.

But nothing happened as they docked, allowing her to stroll onto the station and start walking up towards the command core, followed by two of her crew. The corridors were littered with crewmen and women, all knocked out by the gas; Mandy checked a couple of them, just to be sure, before telling herself that there was no need to be paranoid. If Admiral Singh was still in command of the station, she wouldn't need to play silly games.

She stepped through the airlock and smiled as she saw the rebels. "Good work," she said, reassuring them. They weren't Marines – or even Civil Guard – and yet they'd taken control of the station without losses. "Make sure you tie up your former allies. Stunned people don't stay stunned indefinitely."

"Understood," the leader said. He sounded terrified his face was sweaty…and yet he'd led his people to take the entire station. Admiral Singh's security officers would be humiliated when they found out. "The station is under your control."

Mandy nodded and sat down in front of the main console, testing it out. The station was still linked into the command datanet, but the datanet itself was only in low-power mode, which was a relief. If the datanet had been running at full power, trying to coordinate the defence of the planet, it would be impossible to disguise the fact that something had gone badly wrong.

"I've removed the command overrides," she said, after a long moment. "Half of the Admiral's fleet is within weapons range; the rest is outside, gathering its strength."

The leader looked at her, worriedly. "Is that going to be a problem?"

"I hope not," Mandy said, grimly. It had been a great deal easier sabotaging *Sword*. "But the bastards may become a wild card."

She keyed the final set of commands into the system, then smiled at him. "We're ready," she said. "All we have to do now is wait."

Vice Admiral Sampson was sitting at his console, monitoring the preparations to launch the striking fleet towards the Commonwealth when a new message popped up on his display. He frowned, puzzled, at the header – there was a vitally important message being relayed over the datanet – and then clicked on the message. The screen changed, displaying a young woman with long red hair. She seemed oddly familiar.

"…Been held prisoner by Admiral Singh, but I have escaped," the woman said. "My children and I were held in a hellish chamber to ensure that my husband would remain loyal…"

Sampson stared in disbelief. The woman wasn't just familiar; she was the wife of Commodore Hicks, one of his senior officers! Hicks was a loyal man, but Admiral Singh had insisted on taking hostages from his family anyway, just in case. Since then, Hicks had comported himself well, although Sampson was sure he'd seen pain in the man's eyes when no one was looking. Who knew *what* was going through his mind after his superior had taken such pains to assure herself that he would remain loyal?

The picture changed, switching to show a young girl with long black hair. "They touched me," she said, in a bitter broken voice. The camera pulled back to reveal that she was pointing to her thighs. "They…"

There was a motion behind him. Sampson spun around, one hand reaching for his pistol, to see the Operations Officer drawing his. Of course, he remembered; the man's own son was a hostage too. But now… he unhooked the holster and started to draw his pistol, but it was too late. The Operations Officer fired once, shooting him right in the chest, before turning his attention to the rest of the staff. Sampson stared in horror, feeling blood flowing out of the bullet wound, realising what it meant.

Admiral Singh's forces were no longer under her control. Everyone who had a loved one held hostage would turn on her.

And then the Operations Officer walked over to him, put the barrel of his gun against Sampson's head...and pulled the trigger one final time.

CHAPTER
FORTY-THREE

> This should not have been surprising either. Admiral Singh's government was personalised, rather than a deliberate attempt to build a new system. She was largely incapable of looking past any goal other than power, hence her willingness to embrace Horn and others who largely preyed on the weak and powerless. Her house of cards depended on her survival.
> -Professor Leo Caesius, *Authority, Power and the Post-Imperial Era*

"Admiral!"

Rani sat upright in bed, one hand reaching for the pistol she kept under her pillow. She'd told her staff that they weren't to bother her in bed unless it was truly urgent.

"Report," she barked, as she clutched the pistol. "What's happening?"

Her aide tapped the main display. "It's on all channels," she said. "The hostages have been freed."

Rani stared in disbelief as Charity Yamamoto, the daughter of one of her senior officers, told the world about how she'd been held prisoner – and abused. *That* wasn't true; Rani had given strict orders that none of the very important hostages were to be abused in any way, beyond losing their freedom. But it wouldn't matter, she realised dully. All of the officers she'd refused to trust without holding one of their family hostage would turn on her.

She gritted her teeth, thinking hard. Where *were* those officers? There were some on the orbital weapons platforms, some on the industrial nodes...and a handful on the starships. If they all turned against her...had they planned it out from the start? Had Horn's death merely been another part of their plan to take back their families and destroy her? Or were they only just realising that her hold over them was gone?

But Horn hadn't had anything to do with the hostages. Rani hadn't wanted to put a card like that in anyone else's hands – and besides, she didn't really trust Horn not to allow his baser tendencies to run free. What was quite useful when it came to interrogating suspects would be disastrous if used on hostages with powerful relatives. No, someone else was behind it – almost certainly one of her officers...

"Get it off the datanet," she ordered, sharply. "Now!"

"We can't," the aide admitted, cringing as if she expected Rani to shoot her at once. "Whoever is uploading it has the clearance codes to send the message everywhere."

"Then destroy the source," Rani snapped. She pulled herself out of bed and grabbed for her uniform. "And then order my shuttle prepped for launch."

The aide blinked. "Admiral?"

"I will be safer in space than here," Rani said, crossly. The main strike fleet contained plenty of loyalists – and *their* loyalty wasn't secured by hostages. It was possible that some of them might have thought better of supporting her, after the other hostages had been freed, but if she allowed that fear to paralyse her she might as well surrender now and beg for mercy. "And I can regain control of the empire through the fleet."

The ground shuddered. Rani's attention was drawn towards the window, just as there was a blinding flash of light in the distance, followed by a colossal fireball rising up into the air. External Security's headquarters were in that direction, she recalled, as well as several other departments. The rebels might have problems deciding if they wanted to take out External Security or the Civil Service headquarters. Her bureaucrats were hated almost as much as Horn's Internal Security, a remarkable achievement.

Her aide was listening to a message coming through her implants. "Admiral, there are reports of shootings and bomb attacks throughout the city," she added. "The insurgency is in league with the rebels!"

Patterson, Rani thought, angrily. The bastard had been *promoted* because of his superior's death. She saw it now; Horn had been deliberately assassinated, just to ensure that a rebel sympathiser was promoted into the top job. No doubt his plans to restructure their security had served as cover for moving insurgents into the city. She should never have trusted a man who wasn't driven by lusts and perversions beyond normal men. Horn had had plenty of incentive to stay loyal; he would have been torn apart if the rebels ever managed to take him alive.

"Get the shuttle ready," she ordered. How long would it be before the rebels had HVMs in place? If Patterson was on their side, they could have looted a weapons dump and obtained thousands of the damned things. And that would be enough to shut down aerospace traffic all over the continent. "And then order the soldiers to move away from the red light district to secure the centre of the city."

It isn't over yet, she told herself, as her aide scurried off to obey. *I can get into orbit and then I can regain control.*

The Governor's Mansion was an impressive building, Jasmine had to admit; the designer had modelled it on the classical period of early Imperial history, creating a blocky building that seemed to be almost completely indestructible. Built out of hullmetal as it was, nothing short of a nuke or bomb-pumped laser would do more than scratch it, although it was nowhere near as heavily armoured as a battleship. The windows alone weakened the design.

She allowed Blake to take the lead as they approached the guardhouse. Admiral Singh's ground forces, not unlike the Civil Guard, had almost no female soldiers or officers, in stark contrast to her space forces. Jasmine had puzzled over that before deciding that it didn't matter. If Admiral Singh had taken most of the Civil Guard into her service, they'd probably just stuck with the previous arrangement.

"Halt," the guard snapped. They were clearly nervous; the entire city seemed to be going up in flames. Jasmine had ordered hundreds of attacks to be launched almost simultaneously; it wasn't a real surprise that some had begun ahead of schedule. "Who goes there?"

Jasmine hid her smile as Blake stepped forward. "We have orders to serve as reinforcements" he said, holding out a datapad. The main datanet had already been updated to verify their credentials. "Where do you want us to go?"

The guard CO looked hesitant. Jasmine felt a moment of sympathy; the city was breaking down into chaos and new guards would be very helpful, but he didn't know them personally and they might have other motives for visiting the mansion. False uniforms was an old trick; for all he knew, he was looking at rebels in stolen uniforms. And if he allowed raiders into Admiral Singh's mansion, his career would be utterly destroyed.

Come on, Jasmine thought, silently willing him to do what she needed him to do. *Take the bait.*

"Get into the building and reinforce the inner defence line," the CO ordered, finally. "Right now, no one gets past us unless they're on the Admiral's list."

The Marines slipped inside, then – at a signal from Jasmine – turned on the guards. None of them were ready for unarmed combat; Jasmine knocked the closest one down with a fist to the face, then saw Blake and Carl dealing with two more. Seconds later, the entrance to the Governor's Mansion was secure.

"There's a private security network inside the palace," Canada explained. The young man looked terrified, holding his weapon as if he expected to need it at any second. "We can't break into it."

"We don't have to," Jasmine said. With one of the entrances under their control, they could bring in a large army. "Call the others. It's time to trap the Admiral. And remember – we need her alive!"

She smiled grimly as the insurgents slipped into the building. No alarm had been raised, but it would only be a matter of time – and then the Admiral would know what was happening, if she didn't already know. She'd used Patterson ruthlessly to try to suppress all communications between the hostage camp and Admiral Singh, but she doubted that she'd covered them all. Admiral Singh might well have established a private link between the camp and her office. And then there were the broadcasts the hostages were making…

She knows we're here, she told herself, firmly. *The only question is what, precisely, is she going to do about it?*

New alarms howled as Rani finished pulling on her uniform. "Alert," a robotic voice bellowed, "the mansion has been compromised. I say again, the mansion has been compromised!"

Rani felt ice running down her back as she checked the security monitors. A small army of insurgents seemed to have invaded her building, somehow having managed to get close enough to slip inside without being spotted. But if they'd had Patterson under their control, that wouldn't have been a problem. The bastard could have given them papers that would allow them to waltz right into the centre of her empire.

"Seal the building," she ordered, although she knew that it was already too late. The mansion was huge and it would take them time to search it all, but they'd find her eventually. She had to leave the mansion as soon as possible. "And then get the guards up here."

Lukas couldn't stop feeling awe at the sheer luxury of the Governor's Mansion, even as he crept down a wide corridor, weapon in hand. The walls were decorated with solid gold leaf, while there were hundreds of statues and paintings – some of them frankly pornographic – scattered everywhere. Lukas didn't know much about art, or why some paintings were worth millions of Imperial Credits while others were worth almost nothing, but it seemed to him that the Governor had squirreled away half of the planet's wealth in his mansion. No *wonder* he hadn't been able to run when Admiral Singh arrived.

He stopped in front of a pedestal, looking down at a tiny wooden box studded with jewels. There was nothing to indicate what it was, or why it held pride of place in the governor's display; absently, he opened the box and looked inside, only to discover that it was empty. Closing it, he gave in to temptation and slipped it into his pocket, before heading further along the corridor. He wasn't the only one taking advantage of the opportunity to loot.

The corridor came to an end, revealing a large ballroom that was just as ornate as the corridors, with a large golden throne at the far end. Lukas recalled from civics class that the throne was a direct representation of the Imperial Throne on Earth and that no one, not even the Governor, was allowed to sit on it. He couldn't help wondering, as the assault force stepped onto the dance floor, if the Governor had ever bothered to follow that law. The old man had certainly acted like a king before he'd been disposed.

He realised his mistake a second too late. Out on the ballroom floor, there was no cover – and the enemy were lying in wait. Shooting broke out an instant later, sending several insurgents to the ground; Lukas threw himself down, silently praying that the enemy wouldn't hit him. It took him a moment to recall that he was carrying a weapon and that he could return fire. Switching to rapid-fire, he blew through a whole magazine while aiming towards the enemy position, then rapidly switched the old magazine for a new one.

"Get back," someone snapped. "Now, damn you!"

Lukas crawled backwards as others provided cover, forcing the enemy to keep their heads down. He couldn't help noticing that seven of his comrades, boys he'd brought into the cells personally, were down, lying on the ground with blood staining the wooden floor. Bile rose in his throat as he saw that one of them seemed to have been cut open, his innards spilling out onto the floor. He couldn't help hoping that man was dead. How could anyone live like that?

There was an explosion ahead of them, where the enemy were hiding. Someone had thrown a grenade. Lukas had been taught how to use them, but his superiors hadn't handed any out before they'd slipped into the Governor's Mansion. He stayed down as others ran past, throwing the enemy backwards before they could withdraw. The training hadn't taught him how damn *terrifying* fighting could be.

"Get up," a voice ordered. Lukas felt a hand grabbing at his belt, pulling him up right. "Not long to go now, lad."

Rani could *hear* the sound of gunfire as she was hurried along by her bodyguards, heading for the stairs that led upwards to the Governor's private landing pad. He'd kept a luxury yacht for his personal use – Rani had given it as a reward to one of her officers – and he'd used an equally luxurious shuttle for transport between the ground and the orbiting ship. Rani had appreciated the precaution – there had been riots on the planet before her fleet had arrived, as rumours of the Fall of Earth spread through the population – but she'd replaced the luxury craft with a heavily-armed assault shuttle. It would provide much more protection for her escape.

"They're breaking through the barrier at level seven," one of the bodyguards said. He was conditioned – or Rani would never have trusted him, not now. Her senior officers had to be considering their own futures in a universe without her, even the ones she'd trusted without resorting to hostage-taking. One of them might even aim for supreme power. "They'll be up here within ten minutes."

Rani nodded, gritting her teeth. Most of her guards were fighting – and dying – to hold the line long enough to allow her to escape. Once she was safe, she promised herself, she would see to it that they were rewarded for their devotion. And if they didn't survive, she would reward their friends and relatives.

The building shook, violently. "Explosion in sector seven," another bodyguard said. "Cause unknown."

"Rebel attack," Rani said, bitterly. They'd pay. Oh, how they would pay! "Is the city secure?"

"Unknown," her aide said. "The soldiers are under heavy attack."

And their superiors were among those who had their families held hostage, Rani thought, bitterly. Maybe they no longer feared her. And why should they when she no longer had a weapon to hold over their heads? They'd pay for their betrayal in time.

They ran up the stairs as the sound of gunfire drew closer, finally reaching the landing pad. The shuttle was already powered up, ready to go. Rani allowed herself a tight smile as she was rushed onboard, the airlocks closing behind her, cutting her off from the Governor's Mansion.

Even if her attackers reached the landing pad, it was far too late to stop her from escaping.

Jasmine threw a grenade into the next room, waited for it to detonate, then ran forward into the blast. Several guards were dead or badly injured; the remainder trying desperately to organise a resistance before she shot them down. Blake and Carl moved past her, weapons at the ready, then jumped into the next room. The floor shook again as their grenades cleared out another nest of guards. And suddenly the gunfire died away.

"Upwards," Jasmine snapped, knowing that they had to keep moving. It hadn't been difficult to deduce Admiral Singh's escape plan, not when an Imperial Navy officer would be happier in space than on the ground. She had a shuttle and a way to reach it; the Marines had to cut her off before she made it out into space. "Hurry!"

The stairwell wasn't booby-trapped, an odd oversight. If Jasmine had been commanding the Admiral's bodyguard, she would have made sure to leave some booby-traps behind, just to slow up the pursuit. But then, all the signs were that the Admiral had been taken by surprise and there hadn't been time to organise a proper resistance. The Marines moved up the stairs as fast as they dared, keeping a careful eye out for unpleasant surprises. Admiral Singh's bodyguards might just have decided to lay traps at the end of their flight.

She heard the sound of the shuttle powering up in the distance and threw caution to the winds, running up the stairs as fast as she could. Blake and Carl followed her, frantically waving to the others to stay back. If there was a trap, there was no point in sending the entire platoon into it. She kept running until she ran right into the shuttlebay…and swore out loud as she saw the shuttle lifting off the ground and heading upwards.

"Hellfire," Blake said. "We need an HVM…"

Jasmine lifted her rifle, switched to rapid-fire and sprayed the shuttle with bullets. It was a gamble; it was unlikely that an assault shuttle would even be slowed by such an attack. She cursed as she realised that the attack had failed; Admiral Singh, not even bothering to avenge herself by firing on the Governor's Mansion, was heading up into orbit. And once she was there...

"Call the HVM teams," Blake snapped. "There has to be someone in position!"

"There isn't," Jasmine said, grimly. They should have carried the weapons – they would have, if they'd had the luxury of proper tools – but they'd only had a few of them. She'd issued the ones they did have to the teams attacking the Admiral's air bases. "Call Mandy – tell her...tell her that she has to shoot the Admiral down."

But she already knew that it would be futile. Defence Station II was not in a position to hit the shuttle, unless Admiral Singh altered course radically. And she wouldn't, not if she realised that the Defence Station was under enemy control. She'd just head out towards her fleet and join up with the battleships. And then...

Jasmine glared up after the shuttle, knowing that they'd failed. Admiral Singh had escaped.

And the only card they had left to play was a single desperate gamble.

CHAPTER FORTY-FOUR

Lacking any kind of legitimacy, she was forced to resort to darker means to keep control. Her senior officers were forced to surrender hostages to ensure their loyalty; her junior officers and civilians were kept in line through fear. It was the rule of the Strong in its purest form.
-Professor Leo Caesius, *Authority, Power and the Post-Imperial Era*

"Log into the orbital datanet," Rani ordered. "Show me who's in command."

She scowled as the display updated. Two of the Defence Stations seemed to have fallen out of the datanet, which meant...what? Were they disloyal or had their COs realised that the datanet was compromised? There were brief reports of fighting on the orbital industrial nodes, enough for her to realise that she was facing a very determined opponent. They'd taken the planet, at least one of the defence stations and most of the industrial nodes. The ones they hadn't taken would be under the guns of the automated weapons platforms, once they were secured. They would have no choice, but to surrender.

Other reports kept coming in, each one speaking of disaster. The five battleships she'd left in orbit were consumed with mutiny as her officers turned on each other, while some of the smaller ships were already fleeing – as if they expected there to be safety in deep space. Her main strike fleet was still loyal, but confused, uncertain of what to do. They needed leadership. Rani would provide.

"Tell them to isolate themselves from the datanet," she ordered. "And then shape our course towards their position."

She hesitated, then smiled darkly. "And *then* crash the network completely," she added. "They will no longer be able to coordinate themselves against me."

———

Mandy cursed under her breath as the invisible electronic war for control of the defences raged on. One Defence Station under her control, one seemingly split in two...and one still loyal to Admiral Singh. Each station controlled its own satellite network of automated weapons platforms, but there were – in theory – overrides that would allow one of the stations to take over platforms belonging to the others. Unfortunately, the loyalist station had realised the danger and was fighting back. So far, the fight hadn't turned physical, but Mandy suspected that it would soon.

She watched the shuttle carrying Admiral Singh, cursing the Admiral's luck – or skill. The shuttle wouldn't have lasted a second if she'd turned an automated platform on it, but there was no platform within range to hit the shuttle. One of the warships could have done it, if she'd trusted them enough to let them try. As it was, she'd broadcast warnings to the remaining ships in orbit that they would be fired upon if they brought up their drives. It had been enough to stop others joining the flight to deep space.

The display showing the datanet flickered and died.

"What happened?" Trevor Chambers demanded. "We've lost the datanet!"

"They crashed it," Mandy said, bluntly. She wasn't too surprised. Admiral Singh knew that some of her stations were disloyal, so she'd made it much harder for the rebels to coordinate their operations. They'd have to use radios rather than the datanet. "Bring up the laser communicators and use them to reassure the warship crews that we're still in command."

She glowered at the orbital display, which was rapidly reformatting itself. When the datanet was active, the display showed the live feed from every sensor linked into the datanet, putting together a composite picture that was far greater than the sum of its parts. Now, they had to rely on the station's sensors alone – and radio communications for signals from elsewhere. The defenders of the planet might not be able to hold against Admiral Singh's loyalist fleet.

It was a powerful force, she had to admit. Four battleships, thirty smaller ships...and nearly a hundred freighters, serving as part of a fleet train. Mandy had been intimately involved with building the Commonwealth Navy and she still found Admiral Singh's formation intimidating as hell. The Commonwealth might have made a few breakthroughs that had improved both weapons and starship designs, but they would still be dangerously outgunned. It was quite likely that Admiral Singh would blow through the navy and then range in on Avalon...

But was it enough to regain control of Corinthian?

If all three Defence Stations had been active, linked into a single datanet, Mandy knew that they would have given the Admiral a fight. The stations possessed more firepower and armour than the battleships, even though they were effectively sitting ducks compared to the more mobile fleet units. Now, however, with one station still loyal and the other two forced out of the datanet, it would be tricky. Admiral Singh could just sit at the edge of missile range and keep firing until the stations were taken out, then advance on the planet itself.

And then the threat of orbital bombardment would bring the rebels back into line.

"Send the signal to Captain Delacroix," she ordered, grimly. "It's time for Sleight-of-Hand."

Despite her show of confidence, Rani hadn't been entirely sure what sort of greeting awaited her on the battleship *Matterhorn*. Captain Lustrum was a true supporter of her – like Rani herself, his advancement in the Imperial Navy had been blocked by his superiors – but with chaos and anarchy breaking out on the planet's surface, he might have thought better of supporting her any further. He might even have considered replacing her. As it was, he greeted her with a salute and escorted her to the CIC personally.

"The fleet's datanet is still up and running," he assured her, as Rani sat down in the command chair. "We're ready to advance on the planet as soon as you issue the command."

Rani nodded. The remaining warships in planetary orbit wouldn't be able to put up much of a fight, certainly not if they believed that she was about to return and rip her foes to shreds. She wouldn't be able to talk the orbital battlestations into surrendering – their crews would know what she had in mind for them – but the warships should remain on the sidelines. And even if they didn't, she had enough firepower to cow them into submission.

"Good," she said, studying the display. The analysts had done their best to deduce which stations and ships remained loyal – and which were under mutineer control – but it was difficult to be sure. She'd broadcast orders for loyalists to stand down after she began her advance. That should separate the sheep from the goats. "Begin the advance."

She settled back in her command chair as the warships turned and started advancing towards the planet, slipping into the formation the Imperial Navy had dubbed the Hammer of God. There was nothing subtle about it, not even slightly. The formation was intended to give the impression of a ponderous mass advancing towards a truly fragile target that wouldn't stand up to the hammer blow that was about to come down on its head.

And if the rebels put up a fight, she promised herself, they would suffer in a way that would make Horn blanch.

"It's confirmed," Blake reported, grimly. "Admiral Singh's fleet is heading towards the planet."

Jasmine cursed. They'd swept the Governor's Mansion and broadcast faked surrender instructions that claimed to be from the Admiral herself, but with the Admiral herself still on the loose anything could happen. Most of the city was under their control, yet that wouldn't last. A handful of KEWs from orbit and Landing City would suddenly remember how loyal it was to Admiral Singh.

"Order the forces in the countryside to disperse," she ordered. Admiral Singh wouldn't hesitate to hammer the farmers back into submission, even if it *did* mean that there would be food shortages. Hell, she could just start growing algae and processing it into ration bars. It wasn't as if it was technically difficult. People would protest, of course, but after the insurgency had run its course they'd have little energy left to complain. "And then..."

She shook her head. Everything depended on Captain Delacroix now.

"We're in position, Captain," Jones reported. "The drones are ready to move."

Layla nodded. This was easily the most dangerous part of the operation. If Admiral Singh called their bluff, the entire mission was doomed. Lieutenant Yamane's contingency plan included destroying the Admiral's industrial base, crippling her ability to supply her forces, but it wouldn't be enough to save the Commonwealth. Admiral Singh would still have a major advantage over the Commonwealth Navy.

"Very good," she said, concealing her doubts. "Power up the drones on my mark..."

She looked at the display, timing it as carefully as she could. Only a fool – or an Imperial Navy senior officer – would try to coordinate an operation across light years. Admiral Singh would have to *believe* that was what they were trying to do – and if realised what was actually going on, they were dead.

"Mark," she ordered. "And then play the message"

"Admiral," the sensor officer said, alarm in her voice. "There are three whole squadrons of battleships on Corinthian approach vector!"

Rani whirled around in her command chair as new red icons sparkled into life on the display. Those ships weren't real, they couldn't be real. And yet they were there, advancing towards the planet as if they *knew* there was nothing the planet's defences could do to stop them. She gritted her teeth as the display updated again, revealing nearly a hundred smaller ships escorting twenty-seven battleships.

"We're picking up a message," the communications officer said. "It's broadcast on all channels."

"Put it on," Rani snarled.

A new face appeared in the display. "This is Admiral Hawking, Imperial Navy," a stiff voice said. The accent was certainly right for Imperial City, on Earth. "You are ordered to stand down and prepare to be boarded. The Corinthian System will be returned to Imperial jurisdiction; the rebel, Rani Singh, and her men will be taken into custody. Those who stand down and surrender to our forces on the planet will be treated leniently."

Rani stared. That *couldn't* be right. She'd surveyed all of the star systems for a hundred light years past her borders and there had been no trace of the Empire, let alone of a sizable fleet deployment. And yet…sending in a stealth mission to sabotage the defence grid was exactly what the Empire preferred to do, rather than see its battleships scratched by duelling with the orbital defence stations. What if…what if she'd been wrong?

Cold ice congealed in her chest. She'd been so *certain* that the Empire was gone, that there would be no retribution for her power grab. There had certainly been no sign of the Empire ever since she had taken power. But then, the Empire had always been patient. If it had taken two years to gather the force necessary to smash Rani's empire and return it to Imperial control, they would have taken the time – and sent in agents to ensure that Corinthian fell like a rotten apple into their hands.

The enemy battleships altered course, heading right towards her ships.

"Enemy ships will enter weapons range in thirty minutes," the sensor officer reported.

Rani barely heard him. The timing wasn't quite right – but then, it never was when one was trying to coordinate an operation across several light years. And *trying* was exactly what she would have expected from an Imperial Navy officer. This time, it seemed to have succeeded.

Briefly, she considered surrender – and then dismissed the thought. The Imperial Navy would show her no mercy, nor would the inhabitants of Corinthian. Perhaps she could make a deal…no, she would sooner fight and die than make a deal with the loyalists, even if she trusted them to keep their side of the bargain. And she didn't...

"Bring us around," she ordered, savagely. "I want a least-time course to the phase limit, now!"

Captain Lustrum blinked in surprise. "We're running away?"

"Tactical withdrawal," Rani said. There were a handful of hidden supply dumps scattered through her territory – and, of course, she had the fleet train. That would be enough to keep her fleet going while she gathered intelligence and plotted her return to power. "We will be back."

She leaned back in the command chair and watched the enemy battleships make a brief attempt at pursuit, before falling back to secure the planet. Corinthian was the true prize, she thought bitterly, not a handful of starships. Given time, they no doubt expected her to run out of supplies and either turn pirate or just give up. Or maybe they assumed that her senior officers would assassinate her in the hopes that the Empire would reward them.

Rani smiled, although there was no humour in the expression. She *would* be back.

"They bought it!"

"Quiet," Mandy snapped. "You'll jinx it."

The battleships weren't real, she knew – and if Admiral Singh had kept her nerve, she would soon have realised the truth. They were nothing more than a handful of ECM drones, launched from *Harrington* – and Admiral Hawking was nothing more than a computer composite. But Admiral Singh had seen Corinthian fall to a coordinated insurgency, witnessed the loss of two of her orbital defence stations...and fallen for the bluff. By the time she realised the truth, it would be far too late.

"Get the shuttles up and running," Mandy ordered, as the remaining warships and the loyalist station began to signal their surrender. "I want at least one team, armed with a nuke, on each of the ships and the station. Any backsliding once they realised that they've been fooled and we'll take the entire ship out."

She shook her head tiredly. Now that the orbital defence network was largely under their control, even without the datanet, the remaining garrisons on the planet could surrender – or die, when she dropped KEWs on their heads. She hoped they'd surrender; there would be a desperate need for manpower as Corinthian slowly recovered from the nightmare. And the provisional government might need the troops too. It was too much to hope that the planet would simply return to normal. One way or another, the old reality – the Empire ruling the sector – would no longer hold.

"And get some additional shuttles down to the planet," she added. "I want more troops up here, ASAP!"

Four hours later, just as the final warships were being secured, Admiral Singh's fleet crossed the phase limit and vanished.

***

"I think we won," Blake said. He slapped Jasmine hard on the back. "Congratulations, Lieutenant!"

Jasmine shook her head. Admiral Singh might have fled rather than face the ghost fleet, but there was far too much else to do. "Get our datanet up and running," she ordered, grimly. "And then broadcast a message to the population. Everyone – and I mean everyone, apart from our soldiers and medical crews – has to go back to their homes and stay there."

"That might be difficult to enforce," Blake pointed out. "There are a dozen parties going on…and rioters are searching for the Admiral's loyalists."

"Tell the loyalists to surrender to us," Jasmine ordered. "We can protect them."

Carl looked up from where he was peering out over the city. "Lieutenant, the population will want revenge," he said. "The loyalists won't be safe anywhere."

"They need trials," Jasmine said. She recalled the final days on Han, after the main body of fighting had been over, with a shudder. Rebels had been murdered out of hand…as had a number of people who had been accused, with little real evidence, of being rebels. Later investigation had revealed that they'd been fingered by their enemies, people who had intended to take advantage of their deaths. No one knew if those people had faced justice for their own crimes. "Otherwise the planet won't be safe at all."

"It isn't safe now," Blake said. "But we'll do our best."

We won, Lukas thought, as he led his team down the middle of the road, just as Admiral Singh's guardsmen had done. *The Admiral is gone! We won!*

He smiled as he saw the people, cheering and waving as the insurgents walked past. Some of them were very pretty girls; it occurred to him, in a moment of insight, that being part of the force that had raided Admiral Singh's mansion would have perks beyond the obvious. He was going to be *famous*.

His thoughts came to an end as he saw a handful of people being hauled outside by their hair and dumped in the street, right in front of the patrol. The man looked to have been beaten half to death, while his wife and kids had clearly been slapped around by the crowd. His daughter's top had been torn off, leaving one breast dangling free...he looked away, embarrassed.

"They're collaborators," someone shouted, as silence fell. "They deserve to die."

Lukas hesitated. He *hated* the collaborators, hated everyone who had prospered under Admiral Singh's rule...and the man certainly *looked* prosperous. But their orders had been clear. The collaborators were to be taken into custody, not harmed.

"They are under arrest," he said, feeling his voice trembling. Now he understood how the enemy guardsmen had felt, facing outraged crowds. They'd been terrified of the crowd. "We will take them to the penal camp..."

The crowd surged forward, pushing the patrol back. Lukas hesitated, then fired a shot into the air. There was a long moment when anything could have happened...and then the crowd fell back, revealing five dead bodies. Lukas stared in horror. The young girl's head had been crushed like an eggshell.

"Go home," he snarled, lifting his gun. The crowd, having tasted blood, fell back and retreated. "Now!"

He reached into his pocket, feeling for the box he'd taken from the Governor's Mansion.

It was broken.

CHAPTER FORTY-FIVE

The chaos that followed the defeat of Admiral Singh should have been predictable – stopping it, on the other hand, might have proved impossible. In order to govern, she had stoked hatreds and tensions among her people. As soon as her steel grip was removed, those tensions exploded into the light. It would be years before the planet reached a new balance.

But it serves as an illustration of our overall theme. Admiral Singh recognised no legitimacy, but force. When her power base was effectively destroyed, she could do nothing but run. We had to do better.
-Professor Leo Caesius, *Authority, Power and the Post-Imperial Era*

"Welcome to Corinthian, Colonel Stalker."

Edward returned Lieutenant Yamane's salute as he inspected the honour guard. Three of them were clearly Marines, but the remainder were locals, all somewhat more slapdash than the Marines. That wasn't always a bad thing; Edward had once been told that the Civil Guard had units that *looked* good and units that were good, but the two never seemed to mix. Most of his experience on Avalon certainly proved that claim.

"Thank you," he said. "You've done very well."

"The Provisional Government is eager to talk with the Commonwealth," Lieutenant Yamane added. "They're expecting to speak with you as soon as possible."

Edward frowned. There was something in her voice that was...*off*.

"I look forward to it," he lied, smoothly. He would have to speak with the Lieutenant alone, later. Whatever was bothering her had to be dealt with as soon as possible. "And I brought diplomats too."

The Lieutenant cleared her throat. "I think they would prefer to speak to you first," she said, diffidently. "And then I was hoping that you and I could have a word."

Edward nodded. "We will," he promised. "Take me to their leaders."

Danielle looked around the Provisional Government's chambers and scowled to herself. The previous council's chambers had been destroyed by Admiral Singh, forcing the Provisional Government to use the Governor's Mansion for a base. It had been badly looted before the rebel army had managed to seal the building off and clear out the remaining looters, leaving parts of the building looking oddly bare. And most of the stolen luxury items had been seen on the street markets in the days following the collapse of Admiral Singh's regime.

It hadn't been easy to get the streets under control. If it hadn't been for the arrival of another insurgent army from the farms, it might have been impossible; Admiral Singh's army had collapsed as soon as it had become clear that she'd fled. By the time the next dawn rose, Danielle had been seriously wondering if the rebels would win and then destroy themselves. It had taken several weeks to calm the streets enough for elections to take place and there were still some pockets outside government control. No one seemed to trust the Provisional Government any further than they had trusted Admiral Singh. The farmers, in particular, had inherited enough weapons to give them a power base that few others could match.

She looked over at Trevor and smiled. Her husband had been elected on the strength of his war record, just like herself. As a representative of the industrial workers, he had a strong power base of his own, a stronger one than Danielle's own. But was it strong enough to overawe the others who might tear the government apart? No one living outside Landing City trusted the Government any longer. And why, she asked herself bitterly, should they?

Their revenge had been terrible. Regime members, their supporters and collaborators had been ruthlessly hunted down and exterminated. Danielle had been half-inclined to let it go ahead before Lieutenant Yamane had pointed out that once the mob got a taste for blood, it would start hunting for new targets – such as the provisional government. Even so, it had been almost impossible to protect most of the collaborators, even the ones who would be needed to rebuild the planet's economy. In the end, they'd had to lift most of them into orbit and sort them out there.

It had been a relief when they'd discovered that the Empire *hadn't* returned to the sector – and that Admiral Singh's empire could join the Commonwealth instead. But even that was a gamble; too many people on the ground wanted complete independence, while the starship crews had largely declared for the Commonwealth as a body. Why not, when they'd seen the reports of even minor collaborators being torn apart? There were times when Danielle was sure that Corinthian would tear itself apart. The damage the planet was inflicting on itself was terrifying.

She smiled as Colonel Stalker was shown into the new Council Chamber. Perhaps there *were* people who wanted to keep Corinthian independent, but Admiral Singh was still out there somewhere – and there were other threats. And most of the off-planet facilities had *also* declared for the Commonwealth. Trevor had admitted that the industrial workers all felt the same way. How could they be blamed when they too were branded collaborators?

"Thank you for coming, Colonel," she said, pasting a smile on her face. "We are very glad to see you."

Horn looked up as the door to his cell cracked open, spilling in a beam of light. It had been…months, perhaps, since he had been taken prisoner. Or maybe it was years. Somehow, he had lost all track of time. He blinked, trying to cover his eyes against the light, as strong arms grabbed him and hauled him out of the cell. By the time he recovered himself, he was chained to a chair facing a judge and jury.

"Director Horn," a voice said. "You have been found guilty of many crimes, including murder, abuse of power, abuse of prisoners…"

When the list finished, Horn could say nothing. It had never truly crossed his mind that Admiral Singh could be defeated, not when his survival was so desperately reliant upon hers. Now, if the judge was telling the truth, she was gone…and Horn was alone. He knew better than to think that any of his former subordinates would come to the rescue, not even Patterson. Even his most trusted ally would disown him rather than do something that might get them in trouble too.

"You will be taken from this place and publically hung," the judge said. "And may God have mercy on your soul."

"Lieutenant," Colonel Stalker said.

Jasmine turned from the window where she'd been watching Horn's march to his execution. As she had suspected, his courage had deserted him and he'd had to be dragged by two masked men, wearing the same uniforms as his own subordinates had done, back when he'd been the master of all he surveyed. At least Patterson was safe – and, once his wife and son had been restored to him, he had played a vital role in uncovering all of Horn's crimes. There had been no hope of mercy, but at least there had been justice.

"Colonel," she said, saluting.

"Well done," Colonel Stalker said. "*Very* well done. I don't think that anyone has managed to capture an entire planet with just a handful of men."

"I had allies," Jasmine reminded him. She dug into her uniform pocket and removed a sheet of paper. "This is for you."

Colonel Stalker read it, slowly. "What is this?"

"My resignation," Jasmine said, flatly.

The Colonel lifted his eyebrows.

Jasmine felt a dam bursting inside her. "Colonel, during the course of my operations here," she said, "I took hostages, used torture and threats of torture and eventually sent hundreds of people to their deaths. I broke every regulation in the book."

"I rather doubt that," Colonel Stalker said, mildly.

Jasmine glared at him. "You should be putting me in front of a court martial, not complimenting me," she said, sharply. "I was responsible for war crimes."

Colonel Stalker gave her a long considering look. "We're not bound by the Empire's impractical rules any longer," he reminded her. "If your actions were necessary, you should not be charged or punished for them. I can convene a court if you like, but..."

"*I held a little boy hostage to force his father into compliance*," Jasmine snapped at him. "How can anyone justify *my* actions? I'm as murderous as the fuckers who burned down the oligarch mansions while keeping them barricaded inside."

"I do not see that you had much choice," Colonel Stalker said. He held up a hand, cutting her off before she could say a word. "You did what you had to do – and you were captured, tortured and managed to escape before you were broken. What you did was unfortunate, but necessary."

Jasmine looked at him. "I'm not fit to call myself a Marine..."

"Not fit for duty right now, I'd agree," Colonel Stalker said.

Jasmine flushed at the realisation that she'd been shouting at a superior officer. The Marine Corps might be informal, but it wasn't *that* informal.

"Take a leave of absence, regain your health and then decide if you truly want to resign," Colonel Stalker added. "If nothing else, the job isn't yet completed. Admiral Singh is still out there, somewhere."

Jasmine nodded, mutely. He was right.

She'd been tricked.

Rani stared down at the report in her hand, finally seeing just how badly she'd been tricked into believing the worst. The Commonwealth had tricked her, forced her to flee...and now she was cut off from her base. By now, they'd be ready for her if she went back.

So we go elsewhere, she promised herself, bitterly. *And then we rebuild and prepare to take revenge.*

She stood up and headed for the bridge. It was time to reassert her authority…and prepare a new home base.

And then she would be back.

And then all of her enemies would pay.

The End

AFTERWORD

Fifteen years ago, I was in Manchester during the run-up to the Iraq War. The rational seemed clear to me; forget WMDs, Saddam's very regime was a blight on the Earth and anything that helped to destroy it was a Good Thing.

It was not a view widely shared by the local student community, most of whom were anti-war and marched in protest against the invasion. I found their attitude repugnant; they had the freedoms of a democratic population and yet they chose to use them in support of one of the worst dictators in recent history. Even those who disliked Saddam were reluctant to support an outright invasion, pointing out that even in the best-case scenario the Iraqi people would bear the brunt of the war. Why, they asked, could Saddam not simply be removed?

I have heard that question on many occasions, both when discussing current politics and when exploring counter-factual versions of the past. Why not end the problems in Libya by killing Gaddafi? Why couldn't Adolf Hitler have been assassinated? Would the USSR have survived if some kindly soul had put a bullet in Stalin's head?

The problem is that the world doesn't work that way.

Humans have a tendency to personalise politics. American Presidents such as Obama or Bush are often seen as metaphorical figureheads; they bear the blame for their subordinates failings, even though they may not have been remotely involved in the affair. We speak of the Obama Administration rather than the *American* or even *Democratic* Administration. In the West, however, the elected leadership comes and goes, but the political party remains intact. The precedence of the party is upheld by the system.

This is not true, as a general rule, of unfree states.

There are basically two ways to rule in human society; the rule of law, such as the United States and much of the West, and the rule of the strong. For the former, as I said, the system supports the elected leadership and provides a procedure for their replacement by the next elected official. The latter, however...does not.

The successful Dictator – Saddam, Gaddafi, Hitler – succeeds by creating a social structure that supports his position and crushes all opposition. An alternate centre of power is a deadly threat to a dictator; in order to maintain control, the dictator must either bring it under his control or destroy it. A dictatorship might, therefore, look rather like a pyramid, with the dictator on top and lines of control running down to the very lowest levels. The upper levels will be filled with the dictator's cronies (family is a favourite choice) who will often have as much blood on their hands as the dictator himself, forcing them to support him – or risk being torn apart by outraged fellow countrymen.

If we look at Iraq as an example (I acknowledge in advance that I have simplified considerably) we see that Saddam promoted the interests of the Sunni Iraqis over the Shia and Kurdish Iraqis. This gave him a constituency that had a very strong motive to support him. By promoting their interests, he ensured that the Sunni knew that a lapse in his power would unleash civil war and ethnic cleansing when the Shia looked for revenge. (And he was right, as post-invasion events proved.) In effect, by ensuring that terror and oppression were *not* distributed equally, Saddam ensured that his position was fairly secure.

However, the process didn't stop there. Saddam created multiple military and security forces, each one charged with keeping a watchful eye on the other forces as well as preparing for its primary mission. Spies were spread through every military unit, ensuring that no senior commander dared risk showing even the slightest hint of disloyalty. Failing to ensure that all of the spies attended planning meetings, as one senior officer noted in the aftermath of the war, would almost certainly lead to arrest and detention; the spy, once excluded, would start reporting the 'secret' meeting to his superiors. And as those spies were meant to be unknown to the officers they were meant to watch, it shouldn't surprise anyone that Iraqi officers began to become neurotic.

Even ordinary citizens were not immune. Saddam's spies were everywhere. Failing to show the proper respect would have been disastrous. (The next time you see one of those great anti-American protests in a third-world country, ask yourself how many people were forced to attend, given flags to burn, etc.) Iraq became a republic of fear, governed by a man many hated, but none dared oppose openly. Western observers talked of the inevitability of revolt. The man on the street knew better.

For Iraq, the results were disastrous. Taking a decision – any decision – could prove fatal, forcing the officials to push more and more decisions up the chain to Saddam's more trusted officials and Saddam himself. Even if Saddam had been ultra-competent and experienced, it would still have been difficult to run a modern state. As Saddam was neither (his only competence was in securing his own power base) the results were pathetic. And, when war came, the reasoned judgements of senior officers in the military were pushed aside by Saddam, who insisted on imposing his own plan on the generals. It should have been possible for Iraq to slow the American invasion down, maybe even force a draw. Saddam ensured that wouldn't occur.

And when Saddam lost his grip, the Iraqi state imploded with a violence that surprised everyone.

This should not have been a surprise. Saddam had achieved a far greater level of control – his agents penetrated all parts of society – than many outside observers understood. Iraqi society crashed back to the tribal, racial, ethnic and religious divisions that Saddam had deliberately chosen to strengthen to help underline his power. In the absence of a strong power willing and able to say *no*, Sunni, Shia and Kurd found themselves fighting for survival, with Coalition troops caught in the middle.

It is a curious fact that distance lends enchantment. By any reasonable standard, Stalin's Russia, Mao's China, Saddam's Iraq and all of the other dictatorships on Earth (past and present) were truly awful places to live. They have been described, aptly, as prison camps above ground and mass graves below. And yet many truly decent people seem to believe that things are *not* as bad as they seem in the dictatorships...and rant and rail against the West's far smaller flaws. The protesters who marched through Manchester prior to the war would not have been allowed to hold their protests in a dictatorship. Those who doubt that might want to look at just what the Iranian Regime was prepared to do to those who marched against it. It was *not* a pleasant sight.

Why is that the case?

My personal theory is that it is simply a lack of experience. Those who have grown up in a democratic society find it hard to grasp the fear that pervades every level of a dictatorship, or just how heavily the media can be controlled overseas. A democracy allows a substantial level of press freedom, where the media can criticize to its heart's content; a dictatorship, by contrast, only allows news it considers acceptable to be printed and distributed. Someone unprepared for the *Pravda* approach to news will not recognise that it has been censored, if it wasn't blatant lies from the start. (Part of the reason Al Jazeera is even less popular among the governments of the Middle East than the West is because it was largely uncensored by their standards.)

The West is not perfect, but its flaws are far more noticeable to the average Western citizen. This tends to lead to a problem where people react to what they can *see*, rather than what *is*. For example, there is no moral equality between the limited torture, used in desperation, by the West after 9/11 and the torture routinely handed out to political prisoners in dictatorships. Yet many on the Left will choose to ignore the dictatorships and focus entirely on the West's flaws. Worse, perhaps, many on the Left chose to support the USSR, even though it was one of the worst regimes in human history. They saw the little flaws of the West (in comparison to the USSR) and failed to see the major flaws that would eventually bring down the Soviet Empire.

Many of them told themselves (and others) that they were being politically *neutral*. That is, quite frankly, nonsense. Neutrality implies nothing more than refusing to take a side. But tell me; if one person has £1000 and the other has £100, should I be 'neutral' and regard them as equals or acknowledge that the first person is richer than the other? Avoiding the question is a meaningless act; at the end, one is still richer than the other.

To call yourself neutral when contemplating the differences between the West and its enemies is an act of pointless moral cowardice. How can *anyone* look at the facts and remain 'neutral'?

Consider this; if you happen to be homosexual, there are places in the West where you cannot 'marry.' Terrible. But if you live quietly, you are generally allowed to live your life as it pleases you. What if you'd been born in the Middle East? You would be arrested, perhaps killed, just for loving your own sex.

Or…if you're a woman in the West, you are often faced with mass sexualisation; porn can be found everywhere. And there are businesses where there is a glass ceiling. Terrible, right? But what if you'd been born in Saudi Arabia or Taliban Afghanistan? You would be, to a very great extent, *property*. Your male relatives would rule your life, chose your husband and insist that you wore an all-enveloping garment when you went out of doors. Being born a woman would make you an automatic second-class citizen.

You want to be *neutral* when such evil exists? Please!

I shall close this essay with an observation. Every so often, there are political protests in the West, some of which get out of hand. The police move in, arrest a few dozen people and then…well, generally they get released. And yet there are people who admire the protesters, who say that they are *brave*. Maybe they are.

But it's easy to protest when your life isn't in real danger. Those who protest in a dictatorship, on the other hand, are very likely to end up dead. *They* are the ones who show true bravery.

And yet their sacrifice is often ignored.

Christopher G. Nuttall
Kuala Lumpur, 2013
PS. Turn the Page for a Free Sample from Book V - *The Outcast*.

THE OUTCAST

PROLOGUE

From: *The Rise of the Trader Queen.* Professor Leo Caesius. Avalon Publishing. 49PE (Post-Empire).

When did the Galactic Empire fall?

It seems an absurd question. A cursory glance at a history book will reveal the dates that Earth was destroyed, the Sirius Sector declared independence, the war between Hecate and Heartland began and a thousand other events that formed part of the final collapse of the Empire. But when did the Empire actually die? At what point did the fall become unavoidable?

I think it truly became unavoidable when the economy started to collapse.

The empire was held together by a combination of military force and economic ties. Together, they held thousands of worlds in a common union. But the former was wearing away and the latter was being destroyed by the Grand Senate. The economy was being strangled at precisely the moment it needed to breathe. In short, the Grand Senate was not only robbing Peter to pay Paul, it was also eating its own seed corn.

This was disastrous. As imperial taxes grew ever-higher, more and more freighters and interstellar shipping companies were forced out of business – or became smugglers. Entire planetary systems and even sectors started opting out of the Empire's economic network, forming their own units that existed in isolation. Indeed, as the big corporations started to lose their profits, they pulled out and abandoned hundreds of planets to their own devices.

Chaos spread across the Rim. Pirates went on the rampage, attacking trading starships and entire planets. HE3 supplies started to run out, forcing planets to revert to an earlier stage of technological development if they couldn't build their own cloudscoops. Isolated colonies fell completely off the trade routes, such as they were; entire planets died out because they could no longer maintain their life support systems…the end of history seemed at hand.

But this also offered opportunities for those who were prepared to think outside the stifling centralised control of the Empire.

One such person was Sameena Hussein.

Or, as she became known, the Trader Queen.

CHAPTER ONE

A very famous philosopher once referred to the study of economics as the 'Voodoo Sciences,' suggesting – in effect – that there was no true science behind economics. Human experience tends to agree. All attempts to devise a science for economics have failed.
- Professor Leo Caesius. *The Science That Isn't: Economics and the Decline and Fall of the Galactic Empire.*

"Good work, Sameena."

Sameena beamed with pride at her father's words. It was unusual for a girl to receive any formal education on Jannah, let alone be granted the chance to use it, but her father had recognised her talent from a very early age. The family business would be passed down to her brother Abdul – a girl running a business was unheard of – yet he'd already promised her that she could continue to work behind the scenes. Her brother had no talent for business and knew it.

"Thank you, father," she said, as she looked down at the figures. Honestly, they weren't very complicated at all. "I could do the next set right now."

Her father made a show of stroking his beard in contemplation, then shook his head. "Your mother will want help in the kitchen," he reminded her dryly. "Or we will have no food tonight."

Sameena rolled her eyes. "I burn water, father," she said, hoping that he would change his mind. "You should put Abdul in the kitchen."

Her father's eyes twinkled with amusement. The only male cooks on the planet were the ones who cooked in the mosques, feeding the men who travelled from town to town spreading the word of Islam. It was unlikely, to say the least, that Abdul would ever join them. He was simply too fond of games to take up a career in the mosque.

"Cheeky brat," he said. He reached out and patted her on the head. "Go help your mother while I check the figures. You can do more sums tonight."

Sameena stood up and bowed, then walked out of her father's study and down towards the kitchen, where the smell of cooked meat was already starting to waft through the house. Her mother was a wonderful cook, she knew, but Sameena herself had no talent for cooking. In her fanciful moments, she wondered if she had inherited the gene for trading from her father, rather than the gene for cooking she should have had. Most of her friends saw nothing wrong with spending most of their time in the kitchen.

She stopped in front of the kitchen door and hesitated, catching sight of her own reflection in the mirror her mother had hung on the door. A dark-skinned face looked back at her, surrounded by long dark hair that fell down over her shoulders. She looked almost mannish, her mother had said, apart from her hair. The doctor they'd taken her to had said that she was simply a late developer. Shaking her head, Sameena pulled her hair into a ponytail and pushed open the door to the kitchen. Her mother was standing in front of the stove, boiling a piece of beef in a large pan.

"There you are," her mother said, crossly. A strict traditionalist, her mother had little time for the work she did with her father. Only the tradition of female obedience had stopped her from making more of a fuss. "Go wash the pots and pans."

Sameena sighed. "Yes, mother," she said, as she walked over to the sink. As always, her mother seemed to have gone out of her way to use as many different pans and utensils as possible. "Why don't you get Abdul to do it?"

Her mother gave her a sharp look. "Because he is at study," she said, sharply. It was her latest scheme to make something of her son and she'd nagged her husband until he'd agreed to pay for it. "And because men don't work in the kitchen."

It hardly seemed fair to Sameena. She was better at maths than her brother, better at reading…why did she have to get married and spend her life in the kitchen? If her father had wanted to marry her off, he could have done so from the moment she'd become a woman. She'd been lucky. Some of her girlfriends had already been married, or had been practically chained to the kitchen inside their houses, permanently supervised by their mothers. But why was it that way?

She pushed the thought aside and started to work on the pots and pans. Her mother kept adding to the pile, or scooping up items she'd washed and using them again, forcing Sameena to wash them again and again. She just wanted to walk away, but there was no point in leaving. Her mother would be angry and her father would be disappointed in her. Where could she go if she left?

"Take this out to the dining room," her mother ordered. "And then come *straight* back."

Sameena took the dish of curry gratefully and carried it out of the kitchen, down towards the dining room. It was the largest room in the house; her father used it to entertain his business partners or the bureaucrats from Abdullah every few weeks. Sameena had been allowed to listen to some of the discussions – although she hadn't been allowed to speak – and she'd learned more about how the world worked than she'd learned from her mother, or the tutor her father had hired for her education. They hadn't bothered to conceal anything from her.

Her father was already sitting on the floor. "Put it down there," he ordered, tiredly. "And then you…"

There was a crash as someone opened the front door. Sameena looked up to see Abdul as he stepped into the room, grinning from ear to ear. Her brother was handsome, some of her girlfriends had said, but Sameena didn't see it herself. But then, he'd been two years old when she'd been born and they'd practically grown up together. She'd been very lucky in her brother as well.

"You're late," her father said, sternly.

"I had to talk to the teacher," Abdul said. He was still grinning. "Can you believe that he got something wrong?"

Their father stared at him. "…What?"

"The teacher, the one who came all the way from Abdullah," Abdul said. "He was basing his arguments on a discredited *hadith*, so I had to tell him…"

Sameena looked at her father and saw the blood draining from his face. "What did you tell him…?"

Abdul dropped into classical Arabic and started to explain. Sameena scowled at him – girls were not encouraged to learn classical Arabic and she could barely follow one word in ten – before looking at their father. He'd gone very pale.

"You utter *idiot*," he said, when Abdul had finished. "You…you've ruined us all!"

"But I was right," Abdul protested. "I…"

"Fool of a boy," their father thundered. "Do you really think that matters?"

He started to pace around the room. "He will have complained about you to the Guardians of Public Morality," he snapped. "You will come to their attention. And anyone who comes to their attention is lost forever."

Abruptly, he turned and headed towards the door. "Eat your dinner, then stay in your room," he ordered. "And *don't* talk about it with your mother."

His gaze moved to Sameena. "You too," he added. "Don't talk to your mother about *anything*."

Sameena watched him leave, unable to suppress the nervous feeling in her chest. She'd seen the Guardians of Public Morality – dark men in dark robes, carrying staffs – from a distance, but she'd never spoken to one. And yet she'd heard the rumours of what they did to people who stepped too far outside the lines drawn for Jannah's population. Those who came to their attention *always* regretted it.

She would have asked Abdul, but their mother bustled just after their father left and started putting the rice and bread down on the mat. Instead, she ate and worried.

THE OUTCAST

Two days passed before her father returned to the house. He must have said something to her mother, Sameena had decided, if only because she didn't seem worried by his absence. But then, he'd often had to make business trips, either to Abdullah or to the spaceport out in the desert. Having to leave at short notice wasn't uncommon. Even so, she couldn't help worrying about what was going on. Abdul hadn't been very talkative and had spent most of his time in his room.

Sameena was sitting in her room, reading a book, when her father opened the door and came inside. As master of the house, he could go anywhere without bothering to ask permission, but he normally respected her private space and knocked before entering her room. It was so out of character for him to barge inside that she almost panicked. Just what was going on?

"I have arranged for you to marry," her father said, without preamble. The look in his eyes chilled her to the bone. "You will marry Judge Al-Haran and…"

Sameena gaped at him. "Father," she protested. "He's married! He has *two* wives!"

"You will be his third," her father said. He put a small purse of gold coins on her bedside table. "He has agreed to take you. It is a very great honour."

Sameena felt her world crashing down around her. She had known that she would be married, sooner or later; it was very rare for a woman to remain unmarried past her late teens. Even those whose morals had been called into question were married off; they just had to become second or third wives. But *she*…

Her father had promised her – *promised* her – that she wouldn't be married off unless she approved of the groom. And her brother, who would become her guardian if her father died before she married, had made her the same promise. She'd *trusted* them – and yet now they were selling her off to the highest bidder. How could she be a third wife? She'd heard the older women chatting, when they thought their children couldn't hear, and she knew what it would be like. The third wife was a slave, in all but name. She would be bullied by the senior wives as well as her husband.

And she'd met the Judge, once. He hadn't impressed her.

"Father," she said, gathering herself as best as she could, "I will not marry the Judge. He's fifty years old, and smelly, and..."

Her father slapped her.

Sameena fell backwards, more shocked than hurt. Her father *never* hit her. She'd been slapped by her mother more than once when she'd been disobedient, but her father never hit her – or Abdul. Her cheek hurt...she lifted a hand to it and touched her skin, feeling it throbbing in pain. She'd never been *scared* of her father before.

But when she met his eyes, she realised that he was scared too.

"Your idiot of a brother has made powerful enemies," her father said, very quietly. "I have it on good authority that the Guardians of Public Morality have already been alerted and that they're just waiting for permission to act. No matter what bribes I offer, I cannot save my son, or my wife, or myself. You know how many enemies merchants have on this world."

Sameena nodded. Merchants kept the world going, yet the local governments often disapproved of them. She'd done the sums and knew how much money her father had to pay out in taxes – or bribes – just to keep going. A charge of disbelief, of unorthodoxy, might be impossible to bury underneath a mass of bribes. Even their friends might back away if they realised that the fallout might land on them as well.

And all it took to unleash the Guardians of Public Morality was a brief dispute in a mosque between a young man and a teacher...

"But I can save you," her father insisted. "You'll go to the Judge, you will become his wife and they won't be able to touch you. We can go to his house and he can perform the ceremony...don't you understand? There is *nothing* he can do to you that is worse than what the Guardians of Public Morality will do, if they get their hands on you."

Sameena remembered the worst of the rumours and went cold. How could their lives have turned upside down so quickly? But there was no point in crying over spilt milk, as her mother had said more than once. If her father was right, she had no other choice. There was no one else who would give her the same protection as the Judge...

A thought struck her. "But father, given what Uncle Muhammad has been doing for the government…"

"They won't take that into account," her father assured her, grimly. "He isn't your *real* Uncle, after all. If we're lucky, he won't be involved at all."

He tapped the purse of gold. "You won't be able to take much with you," he added. "But take that – in a few years, maybe you'll be able to seek an alternate arrangement. Legally, he has to leave that with you…"

Sameena shook her head in absolute despair. Maybe, just maybe, the Judge would grant her a divorce once the whole affair had died down in a year or two. But if he refused, there was no way that she could find a legal separation. The law wouldn't be on her side, whatever he did to her. And he could take her gold and no one would be able to stop him.

She looked out of the open window towards the darkening sky and shuddered.

"I can't do anything else," her father said. "All I can do is make the best arrangements I can for you. And pray."

He gave her a hug, then stood up. "I'll come back in an hour to take you to the Judge's house," he told her. He sounded almost as through her were pleading. "Please don't do anything stupid."

Sameena felt hot tears prickling at her eyes as he closed the door, leaving her alone. Her thoughts danced in crazy circles through her head. How *could* he do that to her? But what choice did he have? Abdul had ruined the whole family and her only hope of escaping the coming dragnet was to surrender to a lecherous old man. No doubt the Judge had struck a hard bargain. Everyone thought that merchants were rich, even when they weren't.

She picked up the purse and counted the coins silently. Nearly five thousand sultans – and, buried at the bottom of the purse, an Imperial Credit Coin. There were only a handful on the entire planet; whatever Imperial Law happened to say, Jannah rarely used any currencies apart from its own sultans. She doubted that she could find someone who would accept the coin, at least outside the spaceport. Mere possession of the coin would raise suspicions of spiritual contamination by off-worlders.

There was no formal law against women possessing such sums of money, but it was almost unheard of. Her dowry would go to the Judge; if he knew that she had the rest of the money with her, he would be within his rights to take it for himself. All that was hers would become his. She would have to hide it, somehow. And then...

And then what? She asked herself. Her life was utterly ruined.

She heard a dull crash from downstairs. Worried, she stood up and opened the door very quietly. A harsh male voice echoed upstairs, demanding that everyone in the house present themselves for arrest and formal interrogation. Sameena felt her blood run cold as she realised that her father had been too late, after all. The Guardians of Morality had arrived to take them all into custody.

Her mother started to scream. There was the unmistakable sound of a scuffle and the screaming cut off, abruptly. They'd knocked her mother down, she guessed; how long would it be before they searched the house? She'd heard too many rumours to go gently into their custody, but there was no point in fighting. Even if she'd known how to fight, there were just too many of them.

She turned and scooped up the purse of coins and stuffed them into her pocket. At least she'd worn loose trousers rather than a dress; it would have been far harder to escape in one of her dresses, even if her mother *did* like seeing her in them. She picked up her headscarf a moment later – she normally didn't wear them in the house – and then slipped over to the window. Was that footsteps she could hear coming up the stairs? She couldn't tell, but there was no longer any time to hesitate.

It had been five *years* since she'd last scrambled out of her window and climbed down to the garden below, but her hands and feet still remembered where to go. She was heavier now, she realised, as one of the footholds almost broke under her weight and she slipped, thankfully only a few inches above the ground. As soon as she touched the ground, she turned and fled into the woods behind her house. There were no guards outside to catch her before she could escape.

She and her brother had used to play in the woods and she knew them like the back of her hand. If the Guardians of Public Morality came after her, they'd have problems...she hoped. They'd played hide-and-seek before, but never with adults...catching her breath, she looked back towards the house. No one seemed to be coming after her.

But they would, she knew. Everyone knew that the Guardians of Public Morality never gave up. Give them a day or two and everyone in the town would know that they wanted Sameena, dead or alive. No one would shelter her, not even the Judge. And going to him would mean swapping one kind of captivity and torture for another.

And yet...where could she go?

A thought occurred to her. It wasn't something that she would ever have considered before, but what did she have to lose? And besides, the Guardians of Public Morality would never expect it, not of a girl.

And if it worked, she would be *far* outside their reach.

CHAPTER TWO

Humans being what they are, considerable attention is focused on the handful of people who have successfully predicted the future of the stock markets. Those winners have made vast sums of money. It is generally ignored, however, that thousands of people have lost money by predicting the future... unsuccessfully. The separation between winners and losers is as much a matter of luck as judgement. They, of course, would not agree.
- Professor Leo Caesius. *The Science That Isn't: Economics and the Decline and Fall of the Galactic Empire.*

The call to prayer was echoing through the air when she reached the other side of the woods and paused, staring at the house ahead of her. It belonged to a very religious family, one that had two daughters who had been her friends before their parents had decided that a merchant's daughter was an unsuitable companion for their children. They were so religious, Sameena knew, that everyone in the house would make their way to the local mosque for prayers, even the women and servants. The house would be left empty.

She waited in the woods until she heard the prayers begin, then slipped into their garden and walked over to where the clothes were hanging from the washing line. The family had a younger son who was about Sameena's height; she took his shirt and tunic from the line, then found a turban that would cover her hair. Theft bothered her, but there was no choice, not with the Guardians after her. They could only kill her once.

Back in the woods, she pulled the shirt and tunic on, then wrapped up her hair inside the turban. Wearing clothes belonging to the other sex was asking for a whipping, but most people wouldn't look past the male clothes to see the girl underneath – or so she hoped. She bundled up her former clothes, glanced down at herself to ensure that she didn't look very feminine, then walked down to the road and headed eastwards, down into the town.

She felt terrifyingly exposed as she walked down the street, catching sight of a handful of Guardians on the other side of the road. If they caught her…women were not supposed to go anywhere, anywhere at all, without a male escort. Sweat was trickling down her back as she walked past the Guardians and headed towards the bus station in town. Getting caught meant that there would be nowhere left to run. But no one tried to stop her as she entered the bus station and climbed onto a bus. Four stops later, she was near the spaceport – and near Uncle Muhammad's house.

Uncle Muhammad wasn't really her uncle, at least not in any biological sense. He had been her father's partner, once upon a time, before they had separated their businesses and gone their own ways. Sameena's father had told her enough for her to realise that he could not be trusted, but there was no other choice. Besides, it was quite likely that the Guardians would pick him up as well, unless he had enough warning to round up some political support from his allies. She hesitated, looking at his huge house, then walked forward towards the main entrance. There was no point in backing out now.

She pushed the bell and waited. Moments later, Muhammad's son appeared and peered at her suspiciously. He'd been mentioned as a potential candidate for Sameena's hand, she knew; it was quite possible that he would recognise her, despite the flimsy disguise. But there was no point in concealing herself any longer. She pulled off the turban, allowing her hair to spill down over her shoulders, and smiled at him. He looked utterly flabbergasted.

"I need to speak to your father," she said, before he could say a word. "Now."

He *must* have been shocked, she reflected, as he led her into the house. Normally, a man would grow stubborn at the mere thought of taking orders from a woman. She smirked inwardly as they walked down luxurious corridors and past artwork that would probably give the Guardians heart attacks, including several that were rather indecent. Uncle Muhammad seemed to believe that one should flaunt the wealth one had, despite the Guardians. So far, his services to the government had been enough to keep him safe. Sameena hoped that was still true.

"I should fetch my mother," Muhammad's son said, as they reached his father's office. "I…"

"No need," Sameena said. Her reputation was hardly a concern any longer. Oddly, the thought made her feel freer than she'd felt ever since she'd realised the difference between male and female. "I just need to talk to him in private."

She ignored his doubting look and strode into the office, leaving him outside. Uncle Muhammad was a tall man, considerably overweight, with a neatly-trimmed beard that tried to give him an air of distinction. Sameena, who had been raised by a trader, knew better than to take him for granted. He would keep the letter of any agreement, but would have to be watched carefully to prevent him using any loopholes to his own advantage. No wonder her father had preferred to separate himself from his former friend.

"Sameena," Uncle Muhammad said, carefully. "Why are you here?"

Sameena couldn't blame him for being surprised – and alarmed. It was almost unheard of for girls to travel on their own, certainly outside the towns…indeed, it was quite rare for girls to travel at all, no matter what their husbands did. The Guardians believed that women should remain at home and enforced their beliefs on everyone they could reach. Her presence here, without her father or brother, spelt trouble.

"The Guardians came for my family," she said, and outlined what had happened. "I need your help."

Uncle Muhammad narrowed his eyes. "And if they're prepared to arrest the Judge," he said, "what makes you think that *I* can protect you?"

Sameena stared at him. "They arrested Judge Al-Haran?"

"He was taken away a couple of hours ago," Uncle Muhammad informed her. "Your father was evidently unaware of how many enemies he had. Quite a few of the Guardians thought that he was too merciful to captured criminals."

His eyes bored into hers. "And I ask again," he said. "What makes you think that I can protect you?"

He was talking to her, Sameena realised numbly, as if she were a man rather than a woman. It would have pleased her under other circumstances, but right now…she couldn't help wondering if the religious tutor who'd lectured on a woman's place in the world had had a point after all. She would have liked to put the whole matter aside…angrily, she shook her head. Denying reality wouldn't make it any less *real*. And she could only rely on herself.

"You have connections to off-worlders," she said, remembering the credit coin her father had given her. "I want you to get me off the planet."

Uncle Muhammad's eyes went very wide. "You want to go off-world?"

"Yes," Sameena said. "Where else can I go?"

He considered it for a long moment. Sameena knew what he was thinking. The Guardians would not stop hunting her – and she couldn't live on her own, not as a young woman. She could hide in Uncle Muhammad's house, but that couldn't last forever – and besides, she wasn't sure that she would *want* to stay even if she could. She certainly couldn't get married without announcing her identity to the clerics, who would alert the Guardians.

"The alternative would be to…ah, *marry* someone without registering it," Uncle Muhammad said, finally. "You would be safe and…"

Sameena felt her blood run cold. She'd heard about such marriages – and about how they lacked the handful of legal protections offered to registered marriages. It was effectively prostitution, something she wasn't supposed to know about. But her brother had always talked too loudly and Sameena had listened carefully. Knowledge was power.

"No," she said, flatly. "I am *not* a whore."

Uncle Muhammad flinched, as if she'd struck him. "Getting you into space would be risky…"

Sameena threw caution to the winds. "So will trying to sell me to a brothel," she said, sharply. "I will go to the Guardians and tell them everything, all the details of your trade with the off-worlders, if you refuse to help me now."

He clenched his fists. She realised, suddenly, just how easy it would be for him to crush her neck. They could bury her in the garden and make sure that no one would talk. Perhaps the Guardians would realise that there was a connection between Uncle Muhammad and Sameena's father in time, but it would be far too late to help her.

"I also know a few details of my father's business that you need to know," she added, lowering her voice. "They will be yours."

Uncle Muhammad muttered a word she didn't recognise, then glowered at her. "What do you want?"

Sameena fought to keep her face expressionless. "Get me onto a ship leaving the system, with something I can use to support myself," she said. She didn't want to admit to having the Credit Coin, not if it could be avoided. "And then I will be out of your hair for good."

"And you will tell me what I need to know," Uncle Muhammad said. He paused. "I should warn you that the Guardians patrol the spaceport quite heavily. You'll need to be smuggled onboard and that could be risky."

Sameena surprised herself by smiling. "I have made it here," she said. Few women on her homeworld could have done that, even if it was a bare fifty kilometres from her hometown to the spaceport. "I understand the risk."

"I will take you to the library," Uncle Muhammad said, standing up. "I'll give you pen and paper; you will write down everything you know that I might need to know. In the meantime, I will make the arrangements to get you onto a freighter. After that, you're on your own."

He could still betray her, Sameena knew, as he led her down the corridor and into the library. Or simply kill her outright. But there was no other choice. She had to trust that he would do as he had promised.

"Here," Uncle Muhammad said, shoving a piece of paper at her. "I'll be back as soon as possible."

Sameena watched him go, then looked around the library. It was crammed with books, ranging from the standard textbooks on Islamic thought to a number of volumes that would thoroughly displease the Guardians, if they found them. Several of them, she realised, were on off-world science and cultures, a number clearly imported rather than produced on her homeworld. But that wasn't surprising, she knew. Her father had told her, more than once, just how many restrictions there were on printing new books. It could be very hard to gain permission to publish a book.

She took the piece of paper and wracked her brains, writing down almost everything she could remember that she thought Uncle Muhammad would like. Her father would be angry, she knew, if he knew…but he would never be released. Nor would anyone else in her family…they'd want to make a horrible example of her brother, just to ensure that no one else dared to question the religious tutors. Sameena felt tears welling up in her eyes, now that she was somewhere relatively safe. She wanted to weep for her family.

Uncle Muhammad took almost an hour to return to the library. When he did, he was accompanied by his third wife, a thin-lipped woman who gave Sameena a stern look that would have promised trouble, if she'd just made a normal visit. Sameena ignored her and looked directly at Uncle Muhammad, no longer caring to remain demure and downcast. It wasn't as if she could get in more trouble.

"I have made some preparations," he said, shortly. "You will be transported into a cargo pod that will be shipped into orbit and loaded onto a freighter. After that, you will be on your own. I trust that you speak Imperial Standard?"

Sameena nodded, wordlessly. Her father had insisted that she learn along with her brother, although Imperial Standard wasn't something that women – or men, for that matter – were encouraged to learn. Talking to off-worlders risked contamination, the Guardians insisted – and besides, there were few opportunities to practice. But she knew how to speak to the off-worlders if necessary.

"Good," Uncle Muhammad said. He gave his wife a sharp look when she began to splutter in disbelief. "Now, you need to take a careful look at these."

He pulled a set of sealed plastic bags out of his pocket and dropped them on the table. "Most of our trade goods are impossible for me to obtain on such short notice," he said. "These, on the other hand, will be worth a considerable sum of money off-world. I suggest that you treat them with considerable care – and *don't* let anyone know what they are, at least until you're sure that you can trust them. I've attached a set of instructions for using the berries and producing more."

Sameena picked up one of the bags and frowned. Inside, there were a dozen berries and seeds, just waiting for soil and water. What *were* they?

"Sunflower Berries," Uncle Muhammad said, seeing her puzzlement. "They're almost worthless on this world, but off-worlders are very fond of them." He tapped the set of instructions. "I think you would be able to grow new ones, if you tried. Is gardening one of your skills?"

Sameena shook her head.

"Don't worry about it," Uncle Muhammad said. He nodded to his wife, who scowled at Sameena. "My wife has taken the liberty of preparing some additional clothes for you, as well as food and drink. However, I honestly don't know *what* will happen once you're in orbit. You may end up staying in the cargo pod for days before the ship reaches its destination."

He looked back at Sameena. "You *could* stay here," he added. "I would hide you."

Sameena saw the look on his wife's face and knew that wouldn't be safe. Uncle Muhammad wasn't her *real* uncle, after all; there would be no legal objections if he wanted to marry her, particularly if he didn't register the marriage. And she had no strong male protector to help her escape. The Guardians would probably thank her for betraying her new husband right before they killed her for daring to try to escape them.

But she knew next to nothing about life off-world. There were stories and rumours, but nothing concrete, nothing she could trust. She might starve to death in the cargo pod, or be caught and killed by the freighter crew, or...the only thing she could trust, really, was that there would be no Guardians. She would be well away from them.

"I'm going off-world," she said, firmly. She passed him the sheet of paper. "This is everything I can remember. I hope you can use it."

Uncle Muhammad nodded. "My wife will help you dress," he said, as he turned to walk out of the library. "And then we'll be on our way."

Away from her husband, Uncle Muhammad's wife seemed to warm up slightly as she helped Sameena to wash and then dress in a new set of male clothes. Sameena glanced at herself in the mirror, wondering if she shouldn't hack her hair off while she had the chance. Her hairless chin was far too revealing, but if someone pulled off her turban they'd see long hair and know that she was female. Then again, if someone came that close to her she was in deep trouble anyway.

"The cargo pods are unloaded outside the spaceport," Uncle Muhammad explained, as she joined him in the car. "One of them is being sealed in an hour or so; I want to get you inside before then, along with your supplies. After that, you're on your own."

He passed her a small vial. "This is a sleeping drug," he added. The car roared to life and bounced out of the driveway, heading towards the spaceport. "Once you're inside, I suggest you take it. You don't want to make any sound before you reach orbit, or they'll hand you over to the Guardians."

Sameena took the vial and studied it, thoughtfully. It was utterly unmarked. She scowled, realising that it could easily be poison; Uncle Muhammad was unlikely to forgive her for her blackmail threat, no matter her reasons for threatening him. Her dead body wouldn't be discovered until she was hundreds of light years from the Guardians or anyone else who might care to identify her. Maybe she shouldn't take it…

…But he was right. There was no choice.

She sat back and forced herself to relax as the car entered the loading compound and braked to a halt. Uncle Muhammad climbed out of the car and beckoned for her to follow him into the warehouse, where a large metal crate sat in the centre of the room. It was open…and completely empty. The men surrounding it were sealing it up, piece by piece."

"I'm going to call the men away," Uncle Muhammad said, very quietly. "When they go, you get inside and hide in the shadows. And good luck."

Sameena gave him a surprised look, then watched as he walked away to speak to his men. As soon as they followed him out of the warehouse, she ran forward and slipped into the cargo pod. Inside, it was as dark and silent as the grave. She held her breath, not daring to make a sound, as she heard the men returning and slamming the final seals closed. Darkness surrounded her like a living thing.

Bracing herself, she opened the vial through touch and swallowed its contents. It tasted foul.

Moments later, she fell asleep.

Purchase The Complete Novel Now!

Printed in Great Britain
by Amazon